HISTORICAL

Your romantic escape to the past.

A Wedding To Stop A Scandal
Virginia Heath

Least Likely To Win A Duke
Emily E K Murdoch

MILLS & BOON

A WEDDING TO STOP A SCANDAL
© 2023 by Susan Merritt
Philippine Copyright 2023
Australian Copyright 2023
New Zealand Copyright 2023

First Published 2023
First Australian Paperback Edition 2023
ISBN 978 1 867 29824 3

LEAST LIKELY TO WIN A DUKE
© 2023 by Emily E K Murdoch
Philippine Copyright 2023
Australian Copyright 2023
New Zealand Copyright 2023

First Published 2023
First Australian Paperback Edition 2023
ISBN 978 1 867 29824 3

MIX
Paper | Supporting
responsible forestry
FSC® C001695
www.fsc.org

Published by
Harlequin Mills & Boon
An imprint of Harlequin Enterprises (Australia) Pty Limited
(ABN 47 001 180 918), a subsidiary of HarperCollins
Publishers Australia Pty Limited
(ABN 36 009 913 517)
Level 19, 201 Elizabeth Street
SYDNEY NSW 2000 AUSTRALIA

Cover art used by arrangement with Harlequin Books S.A.. All rights reserved.

Printed and bound in Australia by McPherson's Printing Group

A Wedding To Stop A Scandal
Virginia Heath

MILLS & BOON

When **Virginia Heath** was a little girl, it took her ages to fall asleep, so she made up stories in her head to help pass the time while she was staring at the ceiling. As she got older, the stories became more complicated, sometimes taking weeks to get to the happy ending. Then one day, she decided to embrace the insomnia and start writing them down. Over twenty books and three Romantic Novel of the Year Award nominations later, and it still takes her forever to fall asleep.

Visit the Author Profile page
at millsandboon.com.au for more titles.

Author Note

I am going to let you in on a secret. Whittleston-on-the-Water, the location of my Very Village Scandal series, isn't entirely fictitious. It is basically what I imagine my little corner of Essex would have been like back in the 1800s. Like my hometown, Whittleston is within spitting distance of the River Thames estuary and just twenty-one miles from London. The long lane that leads into the fictional village is where I actually walk my dog, Trevor. It's twisty and narrow and covered in places in a dense canopy of trees. Picture-perfect and relatively busy during the day but quiet and slightly scary at night, so I've often thought about casting it in a story somewhere. Preferably involving someone getting stranded and obviously in bad weather. Fortunately, Dr. Sam Able, Miss Rose Healy, an unusual emergency and a rogue blizzard close to Christmas gave me the perfect opportunity...

DEDICATION

For Judy Johnsen

Who started out as one of my readers
and is now a trusted friend.

Chapter One

November 1818

'Aunt—I really must go!' Rose shouted that up the stairs in the vain hope that it would chivvy her relative into coming down them. 'The poor coachman is freezing up on his perch thanks to all the snow!'

'One moment, dear!' Some crashing and banging came from above. 'It has to be in this last box.'

Although why her Aunt Agatha suddenly needed to send her brother and Rose's father an old book about farming was beyond her when her papa would certainly have no interest in it. Here was a progressive farmer keen to experiment with new ideas and Papa wasn't one for reading at the best of times unless it was about one of those new ideas. All it would do in their house in Suffolk was languish on a shelf there, unloved and gathering dust, just as it was here. Which, she supposed, so would she when she returned. A depressing prospect she wanted to be at peace with but wasn't.

Yet.

There was some more crashing and banging and then a whoop of triumph. 'I've found it!'

'Hallelujah,' muttered Rose under her breath as she signalled to the clearly irritated coachman that she would be with him in one minute. 'Finally.'

Not that she was particularly keen to leave Whittleston-on-the-Water either, but she had rather run out of excuses to linger longer. She had only come to stay with her aunt to escape watching her former fiancé become a parent with the woman he had jilted her for and originally only planned to stay for the summer. But then she had extended things so that she could be still here when her new friend Sophie had her baby—as well as to put off facing heading back to her own village for a bit longer. Now Sophie's little girl had not only been born, little Lillibet had been christened so she could not even use the excuse of that to dally any longer, despite wishing she could.

Aside from the inescapable fact that she was still too wounded by her former fiancé's very public betrayal to want to be confronted by him again, especially when he had left her for another woman almost a year to the day, she rather liked Whittleston-on-the-Water. Nobody pitied her here. That was likely because very few people here knew she had been jilted back in Suffolk, and those that did didn't judge her for it nor did they ever bring it up, which suited Rose just fine. She was able to function so much better in blissful denial that she had loved and lost while never being loved reciprocally in return. It was the latter that hurt the most now because she should have seen it coming sooner. Especially when it came to light that most of the village knew of her fiancé's affair long before she did. That was the undeniable downside of life in a close-knit community. Everybody knew everybody else's business and that was all well and good until it was your business that fuelled all the local gossip!

And her feckless former fiancé's betrayal had, for the longest while, been a gift to the inhabitants of her little corner of Suffolk, where little occurred and scandal was thin on the ground. Because not only had he absconded to Gretna Green at Christmas, without making any mention of it to her, he had shamelessly returned in the New Year with his new wife, who within a few more months was already so pregnant it showed. Not that the pair tried to hide it at all. Or disguise their delight at the impending birth nor hide how besotted they were with each other. In fact, to further rub salt into Rose's humiliated, gaping wound, they became the most tactile couple her village had ever seen! Always holding hands and gazing at one another with soppy, lovesick expressions on their duplicitous faces while she just had to grin and bear it until her bludgeoned heart bled and her teeth hurt!

Why on earth would any sane person be in a hurry to return to that?

But not wanting to face them again wasn't the only reason Rose would rather stay here. Nor was avoiding returning to all the brutal gossip she had been subjected to for months after her jilting. She had made some wonderful friends here too, all of whom she would miss. Sophie and Rafe, Ned and Isobel. Archie and the irrepressible Mrs Fitzherbert. She would probably miss her twice-weekly teas at that old lady's house almost as much as she would miss her aunt. Yes, Agatha Outhwaite was a judgmental, slightly pompous busybody with affectations of grandeur—but her heart was in the right place. At least as far as her family were concerned.

She was a bit of a harridan towards everyone else! But for all her flaws, she had treated Rose as if she were her own daughter these last six months and she owed her a huge debt of gratitude for taking her in and giving her a safe place to lick her wounds in private. Even if she had sent her half mad with her constant meddling and moaning in the process.

And then there was the enigmatic Dr Able, who she would be sorrier to leave than perhaps was wise, given recent events. But as birds of a feather flocked together, she and the handsome doctor had hit it off straight away and had, almost immediately too, formed a pact to fend off all the rampant matchmakers who were rife here in Whittleston. As two single people both actively avoiding any romantic attachments whatsoever, they had spent the last six months chatting together at every social occasion to ensure neither of them had to chat to anyone eligible foisted upon them. She had no clue why he was so against potentially romantic liaisons—because they were, by tacit agreement, more convenient friends than confidantes—but thanks to her feckless fiancé's treachery, she had sworn off men for life.

Rose's heart had mended—after a fashion and albeit with deep and indelible scars that had left her jaded, untrusting and cynical—and her father and mother missed her dreadfully. And her brother Daniel was coming home on leave from the army at Christmas and he too would expect to see her—so it was time to go. It was also time to face her past, put all the hurt and all the cruel gossip behind her and try to formulate her future. Whittleston-on-the-Water had been a marvellous distraction when she had needed one, but it was still limbo.

A transient and convenient sanctuary rather than a permanent home. More was the pity.

'I knew I had kept it!' Her aunt appeared at the top of the stairs heaving a giant, thick volume that was bigger than the altar Bible at St Hildreth's and which must have been at least fifty years old. 'My father, God rest him, swore by this book and I dread to think how my brother has coped all this time without—' She stumbled a third of the way down the staircase.

'Let me help you, Aunt.'

As she waved her niece away she tottered momentarily, fighting for balance. Before Rose could get to her, the heavy book flew out of her aunt's hands, missing her by a whisker before her flailing relative fell forward.

Rose tried to stop her and take the bulk of the impact, but when that failed they rolled head over heels until they hit the hard hall floor together with a thud.

Pain shot up Rose's knee and she yelped.

Despite withstanding a similar impact, her aunt, however, was ominously silent.

Even as she untangled their entwined limbs and sat up to shake her the older woman was motionless. 'Aunt Agatha…?' No response. 'Are you all right?' She gently prodded her and still heard nothing.

The commotion had brought both the maid and the waiting coachman scurrying in. Unlike the young and startled maid, the coachman rushed forward to assist as Rose tried to arrange her aunt into a less awkward position on the floorboards so she could check to see if she was still breathing.

She was, thankfully, but there was a deep cut on her forehead that was oozing blood and her eyes had rolled back into her head. Enough to make the wide-eyed maid whimper in fear.

'Go and fetch the physician!' Rose barked out that order and all the panicked maid did was blink. 'Mary!' She snapped her fingers. 'Get Dr Able! Now!'

The final command galvanised the girl into action and she ran out through the door while Rose prayed that the good doctor was home. He might only live a few yards across the market square, but he was a busy man who served all the villages hereabouts.

Unsure whether attempting to move her aunt would cause more harm than good, she instead shuffled her bottom to sit closer to the older woman's head and did her best to soothe her as she stroked her hair. 'It's all right Aunt.' She sincerely hoped it was, although all the blood said different. Her aunt's usually ruddy face was ashen and slack. 'Help is on its way.'

'Urgh…' The mumbled groan simultaneously flooded Rose with relief and fear. 'Hurts…'

'Where does it hurt, Aunt?'

'Back…head…' She tried to lift her head and collapsed again. 'Dizzy.'

'Shh. Rest. The doctor will be here soon.'

Above her, the coachman held out a handkerchief, and in the absence of anything else practical to do, Rose used it to stem the flow of blood still leaking from the deep cut on her aunt's head.

'Want me to go and check on him?'

She nodded. 'Please. If he's out on his rounds take the carriage to find him. And send someone to fetch my uncle from the newspaper office.' Uncle William would want to be here. He and Aunt Agatha weren't only devoted to one another, they were all that each other had. Especially if this was serious and…

Rose swallowed past that negative and unhelpful thought, annoyed that her mind had lapsed back into cynicism rather than the practical here and now where it was most needed. 'Can you move your fingers, Aunt?' With some concerted effort, it turned out that she could. 'And your toes?' Two feet wiggled slightly, giving her some hope that her poor aunt wasn't paralysed.

'What happened?'

She did sag in relief when Dr Able rushed in, glad to be able to hand over all medical duties to the supremely competent physician who had been trained in such things. Thanks to years of being her father's right hand on the farm, Rose knew how to alleviate a horse's sprain or how to treat milk feather in a cow, but her knowledge of human anatomy and remedies left a lot to be desired.

'She fell down most of the stairs. Knocked herself out but she's conscious again now.' A pointless thing to say when her aunt was staring directly at him and the wide-eyed Archie Peel, who was clutching the physician's medical bag.

'That's a nasty cut you have on your head, Mrs Outhwaite.' He knelt beside them to examine it. 'One which I fear will need a stitch or two to close it.' He turned to his self-appointed assistant, who worshiped him like a hero. 'Prepare me a suture, Archie, and ready the iodine.'

The lord of the manor's young brother immediately complied, and did so with surprising competency. Surprising on two counts. Firstly, because despite his one and twenty years, Archie had been born with a condition which rendered him childlike for ever—a boy trapped inside a man's body—so having the ability to prepare a suture was impressive. And secondly, because the kind-hearted physician had clearly spent hours training Archie to do the task for no other reason than to make the lad feel useful whenever he decided to follow him around like he had today. Knowledge that did odd things to Rose's insides.

Satisfied that the head wound wasn't life-threatening, Dr Able moved to Aunt Agatha's torso. 'Tell me if you feel any pain.' With a competent and calm briskness that was reassuring, the doctor began to run his big hands gently down her limbs while he searched for broken bones. He flexed her arm at the left elbow first and then rotated her shoulder. That made her aunt wince. 'Do you have pain in your shoulder?'

'No.' Her aunt's voice was small, her face ashen. 'My back.'

'Let me just check your legs.'

As he examined them, Rose tried to be helpful. 'She can move her hands and feet.'

'That is a good sign.' He smiled at her and then at his patient. 'There are no signs of breakages so far, but where backs are involved its always best to err on the side of caution so I need you to lie here until I can find enough stretcher bearers to get you upstairs.' He gestured to the Archie to go and find some burly villagers who could assist. 'Miss Healy, if I could ask you to fetch a cushion or pillow while we await them?'

'Of course.' She winced herself as she stood, and of course he noticed that.

'My apologies, Miss Healy, I did not realise that you had been hurt too.' He went to stand to assist her and she waved him away.

'It's nothing. Just a sprain.' To prove it was just a sprain, she gritted her teeth and tried to ignore the pain in her knee and walk to the parlour as normally as she could. A task that became almost impossible as she carried the cushion back and caught him glaring at her.

'Go and sit before you do more damage to yourself,' he barked, pointing to the narrow settle in the hall, 'and I'll see to you once I have finished with your aunt.'

'There really is no need.'

He responded with a scowl that could curdle milk. 'If you don't mind, I shall be the judge of that on this particular occasion, Miss Healy. I am the trained medical professional after all.'

She did mind, but she decided not to argue until he had dealt with her aunt.

She minded because something about Dr Able had always unsettled her, and it wasn't just the thought of his competent hands exploring under her skirts that suddenly made her feel…all peculiar. It was because she had always considered herself excellent at reading people—her cheating former fiancé aside—and despite liking him a great deal, she couldn't quite work him out, no matter how hard she tried. Often he was affable, occasionally he was charming and worryingly disarming. Then sometimes, like now, he could be brusque and no-nonsense. He was, however, no matter which of those versions of himself he chose to be, depending on his whim during a particular day or situation, always inscrutable.

Sophie and Isobel had mentioned that was because he preferred to keep himself to himself, although neither knew quite why when she had asked. He had been married once, though, and his wife had died. Information Ned had managed to prise out of him one night after they had both partaken of one too many ales. All they knew beyond that was that he had arrived in the village three years ago after he had left the army and taken over the previous aged physician's practice when he retired. Since then, apart from all the extensive doctoring he did here, he kept his private life very private and himself politely aloof. An important, central part of this close-knit community but not quite part of it at the same time.

In other words, a complete and quite frustrating conundrum—but one she could not help liking. Or empathising with. How he had lost his wife was nobody else's business, so she did not blame him for keeping that secret—unless he had murdered her, of course, which seemed highly improbable, given both his profession and character. If he had chosen to keep that part of his life hidden it suggested he had come here to escape all those constant reminders of a love lost.

She knew from bitter experience how awful it was for an entire community to publicly witness an intensely private heartbreak. All the well-intentioned pitying looks and expressions of sympathy alongside the hurtful speculation as to the real cause of her cheating fiancé's rapid abandonment ensured you never got a chance to forget things or move past things. The constant, optimistic advice was even worse. Always unprompted and never welcomed, it only served as a constant reminder of what you had lost and wouldn't get back.

'Agatha!' Uncle William dashed in in a blind panic. 'What have you done to yourself?'

Hot on his heels came Archie, with the butcher and the baker, and all were briskly pressed into service by Dr

Able. Within moments, they were using a thick blanket as a stretcher and with the minimum of disruption to their patient's comfort, her aunt was transported up the stairs.

As Uncle William insisted on being by his wife's side, Rose could do nothing beyond wait outside their bedchamber with Archie, who had helped her limp up the stairs, then insisted on holding her hand for support, while the doctor finished his examination. He was so thorough he took over half an hour before he emerged.

'She has a minor concussion, a bruised coccyx and likely has ruptured a disc in her back. She will need constant observation until the morning for the first problem and several weeks of bedrest for the second until all the swelling has gone down, but she should make a full and complete recovery.'

'I told you not to worry,' said Archie with a devoted smile at the doctor. 'Dr Able is the best physician in the world.'

'I wouldn't go that far, Archie.' Amusement danced in the doctor's hazel eyes. 'But I will concede that I am definitely the most *able* physician in Whittleston-on-the-Water.'

'That's because you are the only physician in Whit-tleston-on-the-Water!' Archie laughed. then promptly stopped. 'What's a coccyx and ruptured disc, Sam?'

'I'll explain it later.' Dr Able gently pushed him away. 'In the meantime, make yourself useful and fetch Mrs Outhwaite a nice cup of tea to help calm her nerves after her nasty fall.'

'What *is* a ruptured disc?' Only once Archie was gone did Rose repeat his question.

As if he was expecting it, he explained in uncomplicated layman's terms. 'Between each vertebra in the spine is a small, disc-shaped cushion of cartilage that prevents the bones from scraping together. Sometimes, and usually as a result of an injury, one dislodges slightly so the cushion is no longer there.'

'Hence the pain, because her vertebrae are rubbing together?'

He nodded, not even slightly patronising, his whole demeanour so calm and matter-of-fact it was reassuring. 'It could just as feasibly be the bruising as it is a popped disc, of course, because she'd got an impressive one at the base of her spine already, but the treatment is still the same. Bedrest until either the disc finds its way back to whence it came or the swelling goes down. Often those two things are linked anyway, and she has full feeling in all her limbs so there is no sign the damage is permanent.'

'That is good news.' For the first time since the accident had happened, the knot in Rose's throat loosened. 'What can be done to aid her recovery?'

'In the short term, I've given her the tiniest bit of laudanum to help with the pain for now and we'll be able to increase that once she stops seeing stars. I shall give her some more if I am happy with her progress in the morning.' He smiled. 'But after that, the dosage will need to be carefully monitored as laudanum often does more harm than good in the long run and a patient can easily become addicted. I would heartily recommend that that medicine be kept under lock and key rather than be left on Mrs Outhwaite's nightstand for her to administer to herself. People in pain will do whatever it takes to stop it and laudanum is infamous for causing confusion—and for killing those who take too much.'

'I've read about that so I will ensure that it is safely stored downstairs where she cannot get at it.'

'Other than that, there really isn't much you can do apart from see to her needs, give her plenty of willow bark tea, a twice-daily cold poultice to ease the swelling and let nature takes its course.' He held out his hand and she took it without thinking, allowing him to help her up. 'Now, which of these bedchambers is yours, Miss Healy?'

'I beg your pardon?'

He slanted her a withering glance. 'I've not forgotten that you were injured too and now I need to examine you.'

'Trust me, Dr Able, it is nothing. Just a twang. A slight sprain. Nothing worth making a fuss over.'

Her uncle chose that exact moment to poke his head around the door. 'Thank you for all your help, Dr Able. And thank you especially for your supreme patience with my wife just now. Agatha has never been a particularly good patient and always thinks that she knows best.'

'That is a trait that clearly runs in the family, Mr Outhwaite, as her niece has also been injured and is trying to avoid being treated too.' He flicked her an irritated glance. 'Because clearly she knows best and that overrides all my years of medical practice.'

'Oh, for goodness' sake, Rose! Not you too!' Her uncle shook his head. 'Go with the good doctor immediately and let him do his job!'

As he disappeared back to tend to his wife, Dr Able offered Rose a smug smile. 'You heard what your uncle said, and if that isn't encouragement enough to do the right thing, know that I am not leaving your side until I am satisfied that it *is* just a sprain. Know, too, that you are not the most stubborn person currently standing on this landing, Miss Healy.' He gestured with his medical bag. 'So which one of these rooms is yours?'

Chapter Two

Sam regretted his insistence on examining Miss Healy in her bedchamber the second he escorted her into it. At the time it had seemed like the most sensible option, because she had been visibly limping while trying to pretend not to be in any pain and he didn't want to cause her more pain by dragging her back downstairs. He had tried not to give passing thought to the fact that his patient was Miss Healy.

Miss *Rose* Healy, with the beguiling green eyes and mischievous conversation. The woman who had, for some inexplicable reason, become his regular partner during the weekly post-church whist tournament up at Hockley Hall. The woman he cheerfully spent hours conversing with at the monthly assemblies while they both avoided having to have dancing partners thrust upon them by all the local matchmakers. The Miss Rose Healy he might have had three or four very errant, very vivid and highly improper dreams about in the last few months. Dreams that he had rolled his eyes at and put down to the annoying remnants of his manly urges, which had refused to die when the love of his life had, and then hastily dismissed because he had no place in his life for such dangerous attachments any more.

Not one of those things had rung glaring alarm bells when she had needed medical attention because why would they? He was not only a physician to his core but healing his patients here in the environs around Whittleston was his only reason for being nowadays. Besides, it wasn't as though he didn't examine women all the time in their bedchambers and was always proudly professional and dispassionate while he did so, so he had no reason to expect examining her to be any different.

Except now that they were all alone in her bedchamber and she was lying atop the mattress, blinking up at him as warily as he suspected he was blinking down at her, it did not feel quite as dispassionate as it should have. It felt…awkward…and oddly intimate in both a physical and cerebral sense. Which was terrifying when intimacy in all its forms was something he actively avoided nowadays. You couldn't keep a person at arm's length if they were in your head!

Why the hell was she suddenly in his when he hadn't thought of any woman like that in years?

Not since the love of his life had died in his arms and he had as good as ceased living himself.

As the walls of the tiny room contracted, cocooning them in loaded discomfort, he tried to focus on her as his patient and not as the only woman who had piqued his masculine interest in four comfortably numb years. 'Where does it hurt?'

'Just my knee.' Her smile was apologetic. 'I am sure it is nothing.'

'Do you mind if I…?'

Oh, good grief, he was going to have to feel her leg!

Lift up her skirts, peel off her stocking and touch actual skin! Soft, sensual, feminine skin!

'Not at all.'

Rather than groan aloud at the prospect, he faked an unbothered brusqueness he did not feel as he balanced his backside on the mattress beside her. He took half a second to give himself a stern talking-to, reminded himself that he was dead inside, then grasped the hem of her very fetching green dress. He slid it upward, almost groaning aloud again because, of course, she had a splendid pair of legs, being taller than the average woman. They were long and as shapely as her fine pert and feminine figure. To torture him further, her ivory stockings were made of the finest gauge of wool imaginable. Slightly thicker than silk but only by a whisker. The garters, however, were silk, and the couple of inches of creamy skin above them was divine.

Heaven help him.

'If you could just…um…undo those and expose your knee?' Sam used the urgent need to rummage in his medical bag as an excuse not to undress her. Then panicked when he realised there really wasn't a damn thing in his bag which was necessary for a physical examination. In desperation, he grabbed a bandage and some iodine while he prayed her injury was indeed a sprain so he could use the liquid on the bruises before binding them.

He turned and almost choked on his own tongue as he caught the erotic sight of her rolling the stocking down and entirely exposing the whole of her left leg to his gaze. The flesh on her calf was smooth alabaster, married by just one freckle the size of a ladybird which sat like an old-fashioned beauty spot above her ankle. He wrenched his suddenly hungry gaze from it to stare at her knee and only then, as he forcibly pushed the un-welcome and wholly unexpected surge of lust from his mind, did he remember that he was a doctor.

'It's very swollen.'

Willing his mind to focus on his job, he sucked in a calming breath and probed the area with his finger-tips. Except his fingertips refused to react in the way a dispassionate doctor's should and heated as they examined, and while they categorically did not touch her inappropriately, they flatly refused not to want to. That was a new and worrying development after so many years of blissfully feeling nothing.

'Unfortunately, that knee bore the brunt of my fall.'

Her eyes focussed on the wall rather him and that suited Sam just fine. The last thing he needed was to accidentally show how off-kilter he was by his body's sudden reawakening. It was bad enough watching her chew her bottom lip, drawing the plump flesh through her teeth as he tried and failed to focus on her injury.

'But I can still move it, so it is probably something muscular rather than any actual damage to the joint.'

'Remind me again where it was that you did your medical training?' He wasn't entirely sure why his sarcasm came out sounding a tad too flirtatious for his liking. Or why he was smiling, but it made her giggle and that went some way towards breaking the ice.

'I've dealt with many a horse's sprained muscles on my father's farm and we Healys have famously strong bones. I cannot think of a single family member who has ever broken one so… I am presuming, Dr Able.'

'A decent physician works on facts and not presumptions, so if you don't mind…'

'Pray continue, Doctor.' She laughed again. 'And I shall try not to be presumptuous.'

Every nerve-ending seemed to fizz with unprofessional awareness as he touched her again, his fingers fumbling during the brisk and supremely self-conscious examination while she tortured him by chewing her bottom lip some more. Before he groaned aloud, he sat back and huffed as he reached for the iodine.

'Much to my chagrin, it appears that you are right and it is just a sprain.'

He dabbed the chemical on the bruise, then managed to wrap the bandage around her knee in record time. A small miracle when something about her leg in his hands made his heart race.

'I prescribe plenty of ice, tea and a couple of days of sitting in a chair with your foot elevated and you'll be back to avoiding waltzing with all the undesirables in time for the next dreary Whittleston assembly.'

He shot her a grin, glad that that was safer and more familiar ground for them both, because avoiding well-intentioned but ill-considered matchmaking was what they usually did together. However, Sam also experienced a simultaneous flash of regret alongside the relief as he returned her skirts to an appropriately modest level. When a part of him, the part that was supposed to be dead and buried and devoid of all human emotions, wanted to lift them higher.

'I am afraid you are going to have to find another conspirator to help you to evade all the matchmaking in future as I shan't be there, Dr Able.' When he frowned, baffled, she chuckled. 'Clearly you have forgotten that I am finally returning to my home in Suffolk?' She gestured to her attire. 'Hence the travelling dress and the waiting coachman.'

'You are leaving *today*?'

That news really unsettled him although he couldn't put his finger on why. Obviously, he had noticed the travelling dress. The green wool caressed her enticing curves like a lover, and he might well be dead inside, but he wasn't blind! He had also known she was going at some point. It was one of the main reasons why he had lowered some of his guard and allowed himself to enjoy her company at all the social events the local physician was obligated to attend. He preferred transience to permanence. Transience required little emotional investment and a very little was all he was prepared to risk nowadays. Losing everyone who mattered to you did that to a person.

'That came around fast.'

He had been so blasted busy of late he had clearly missed that her departure was more imminent than he realised. Or he had realised but had avoided thinking about it because he had been making a concerted effort this last month not to think of her at all, thanks to all the erotic dreams she had featured in of late. He probably should be glad she was going—especially now that his errant eyes, as well as his nocturnal thoughts, regarded her as an attractive woman rather than a patient—but he wasn't.

And that was beyond worrying!

'Actually, it came around much slower than originally planned.' She rolled her eyes at his continued bafflement. 'I know that you're a busy man, Dr Able, but surely even you noticed that I was meant to leave at the end of August and in two weeks it will be December?'

He shrugged, sheepish. 'I truly *am* a busy man.' Which he was, by design. His work was his everything now that his everything was gone.

It was the only reason he got out of bed each morning. He made sure to fill every waking hour with medical purpose, because if he didn't misery swamped him and he was nought but an embittered and broken husk again, in constant pain. With genuine purpose he was able to lock all the heartbreak and hopelessness in a box in his mind which he rarely reopened as that was safest. That was why he never turned down a patient. The more he had, the merrier he was. And by merrier, he actually meant sane. Functioning.

However, he had also developed a habit of pushing certain other, uncomfortable things to the back of his mind too, rather than think about them, and Miss Healy was one of those things. Had he purposely avoided thinking about her because she called to him? Not on a heart and soul level—he did not have it in him to do that again, nor any heart left to do it with—but he liked her. And liking a woman in *that way* was a danger to his hard-won equilibrium that he wasn't prepared to risk.

As if she read his mind, she huffed. 'I would say try not to miss me, but I can see that you won't.'

She nudged him playfully and, still not quite over the visceral impact of her shapely leg, his stupid body felt it everywhere.

'Some friend you have turned out to be!'

In an equally teasing tone, he parried, despite the strange panic going on internally, 'I've always thought of us as more acquaintances than friends.'

Which was also true. Acquaintances were safe, because they could be kept at arm's length and friends couldn't. He avoided the emotional attachment of friends too nowadays as it was simpler.

He'd had plenty back in his early army days, before he'd watched too many of them die to feel any incentive to replace them. Witnessing death was an integral part of a doctor's life and he had felt too many too keenly—and one in particular—not to be conscious of the enormous toll it took on you.

Now he supposed he had a few trusted acquaintances who did not try to get too close. They were people he respected and could count on in crisis but who knew how to mind their own business and give him his space. People like the gruff local farmer Ned Parker, who Sam was more than happy to drink a pint of ale alongside at the pub, or Rafe, the new lord of the manor here in Whittleston, who had fought Napoleon too and really didn't want to talk about it either. Or even Archie, Rafe's younger brother, who was a man trapped in a child's body, who followed him around asking constant questions and didn't mind being put to work if the need arose. Those were his almost friends now—almost but not.

'Acquaintances!' She pushed him from her mattress in faux disgust. 'I take back what I just said about you needing to find a new conspirator to help you fend off all the husband-hunters as you clearly do not need my help to get rid of them. All you need to do is use that unique charm you just used so effectively on me, and they'll all avoid you like the plague.'

She went to stand and he gently pushed her back.

'Might I remind you, madam, that you need to keep your weight off your knee and your foot elevated?'

'Which I shall do for the entire, arduous six-and-a-half-hour carriage ride back to my father's house in Suffolk. But before I do, I need to check on my Aunt and then say my goodbyes to her.' She stood again and sailed past him like a limping but regal duchess. 'Goodbye to you too, Dr Able. I would like to say that it has been a pleasure being your acquaintance…' she shot him a saucy smile that was as devastating to his equilibrium as her damn legs were '…but I'd be lying as I daresay I'll fail to remember you five miles down the road. Such is my lack of interest in you.'

Chapter Three

'I couldn't, in all good conscience, leave her dependent on the servants for the next few weeks. Not after everything that she has done for me.'

Like all news in a small English village, gossip of her aunt's accident yesterday had spread like wildfire around Whittleston. That was why it was barely nine in the morning and Mrs Fitzherbert, Sophie and Isobel were all currently sipping tea with Rose in Aunt Agatha's much too ostentatious parlour.

'Besides it is only for a few more weeks, so it is hardly a hardship as I will still be back in Suffolk for Christmas.'

'Of course you had to stay,' said Sophie, in complete sympathy for that partial truth. 'There is nothing worse than being tended to by anyone other than your nearest and dearest when you are at your most vulnerable. It was very decent of you to put off your trip to nurse her.'

'Never mind that Agatha's clumsiness gave you the perfect excuse not to leave, young lady.' Never one to mince her words, Mrs Fitzherbert eyed Rose dubiously over the rim of her teacup. 'You've been looking for a good enough reason to avoid that scoundrel in Suffolk for weeks.'

She was about to argue when the old lady's cane came down on the floor with a thud.

'Or are you going to barefaced lie to us all—your three closest and most loyal confidantes here? Claim that you are perfectly at ease returning to a village where your former fiancée is raising a family with the woman he impregnated and then left you for? Because I do not believe for one second that you could be at ease with it. I certainly wouldn't be and I have thrice the bravado of all of you combined.'

'If my poor aunt hadn't fallen down the stairs, I would be in Suffolk now! My trunks were loaded and my gloves were on!'

'I did not say that you weren't intending to go, Rose.' Mrs Fitzherbert sniffed. 'Only that you were relieved by the reprieve—because we both know that it was a reprieve, young lady. One that I should imagine felt like a king's pardon as soon as you realised Agatha was conveniently invalided enough to require your help.'

'It would be uncharitable to find any joy in my poor aunt's recent misfortune and I resent the implication.'

She tried to summon all her bravado to maintain some pious indignation at that accusation as, to her great shame, she had quickly not only seen the benefits that came from her poor aunt's injury, she had seized them with both hands. No sooner had her uncle declared that he would close his newspaper for the duration of Aunt Agatha's convalescence so he could nurse her through it himself Rose was reminding him of his civic duty to ensure the *South Essex Gazette* continued to be the twice-weekly honest beacon of news all its legions of readers deserved. When the truth was they could just as easily read the daily copies of *The London Times* which arrived only a day late on the mail coach.

But no! Just as Mrs Fitzherbert had accused, she had finally found an excuse to stay for at least another month. She'd immediately had her baggage unloaded and the coachman despatched back to Suffolk with a hastily written letter to her parents. A letter that, to her further shame, over-embellished the extent of her aunt's incapacity. She had promised that she would be home in Suffolk for Christmas come hell or high water, though, to appease her parents, so it was still more of a reprieve than a pardon.

'Besides, I am not entirely sure how effective you will be as a nurse,' continued Mrs Fitzherbert, unrepentant, 'when you are injured too.' She used her cane to prod Rose's raised foot.

'My injury will be healed in mere days—hers will take weeks.'

Was it wrong to pray for months to avoid having to face all her scandal and her treacherous fiancé in Suffolk just a little bit longer? Of course it was. She was a dreadful niece. A dreadful person *and* a coward.

'My uncle has stepped into the breach for the first few days but he cannot do so indefinitely when he still has a business to run. Who better to relieve him of one of those tasks than me?'

'If you say so.' That came from the highly amused Isobel, who had so far remained quiet but who was also as blatantly unconvinced as Mrs Fitzherbert. 'Let's dress your latest avoidance up as benevolence.'

'It is benevolent,' said Sophie coming to her defence, 'and staying to look after Mrs Outhwaite an admirable thing to do. That it also saves poor Rose the awfulness of facing the wretch who broke her heart for a little longer is simply a bonus. As is the fact that we all get to enjoy the company of our friend for a little while longer, so you can both stop trying to rile her when not three days ago you were both plotting to find an excuse to keep her here longer.' She glared at Mrs Fitzherbert.

Mrs Fitzherbert went to argue, but instead pressed her lips together because they suddenly, and much too stealthily, had a visitor.

One who had lifted Rose's skirts and touched her naked legs without stockings! And one who had given her body all manner of improper yearnings as a result!

Oh, good heavens above, she wasn't anywhere near ready to face him yet!

Not when he must have heard her sharp intake of breath when he had first touched her! And perhaps even felt her pulse quicken beneath his much too talented and intoxicating fingertips.

'I thought you had left for Suffolk?'

Rose's cheeks began to heat. Partly because she didn't want to be challenged again by Mrs Fitzherbert in front of someone who knew nothing about her unfortunate jilting but more because her flesh tingled from the memory of his unsettling caresses.

'I had a last-minute change of plan.'

'She's staying to take care of her aunt,' said Sophie loyally, with a veiled warning towards Whittleston's most incorrigible and only nonagenarian in case she threw any doubt on that. 'Once she is back on her own feet, of course.'

'I'm glad to see that you are actually following doctor's orders, Miss Healy, because when I left you yesterday there was a little too much rebellion against them for my liking.'

And just like that Dr Able was coming towards her smiling.

'How is the knee this morning?'

'Much better.' It was actually worse now that the swelling had taken hold, but she wasn't going to admit that in case he insisted on investigating. 'It's clearly the mildest of sprains. Milder than mildest in fact.'

Please don't say I'll be the judge of that!

'I'll be the judge of that.'

Fiddlesticks!

'And I might as well take a look at it now before I see your aunt.'

Double fiddlesticks!

To her horror, he gently lifted her foot from the footrest so that he could perch on it, then rested her foot in his lap.

'How is your aunt this morning?'

Rather than hoist up her skirts while in polite company, his hands delved under them to feel the injury above her stockings and that was somehow worse. It seemed clandestine. Felt naughty.

Naughty but, to her body and to her utter mortification, oh, so nice.

The sublime warmth of his hands burned through her thin stockings and awakened the tender flesh beneath again. Instantly her pulse ratcheted and for a moment emptied her mind of everything else—including his question. It was only when his fingers paused that she remembered he had asked it and that it still hung in the ether.

'She had a fractious night.'

Because Rose had never been one of those women who blushed prettily, she willed the ugly blotches from blooming on her face but they refused to listen. Heat suffused her neck as the dratted things multiplied.

'And struggled to get comfortable.'

Which was the politest way she could think of of saying that her Aunt Agatha had run her poor husband and the maid ragged with her constant demands.

'The first night is always the worst.'

Dr Able's hands made one devastating final sweep over her leg that left her breathless before he withdrew them.

'Just as the first day after a sprain is always the worst.'

Thankfully, he took her shoeless foot from his lap and removed himself from her footstool so that she could breathe again.

'Your knee is very swollen today. Try to wrap it in a cold compress every couple of hours until it subsides.'

'I will, Doctor.'

'Splendid. Then I shall leave you to your tea, ladies, and attend to Mrs Outhwaite.' He grabbed his bag and inclined his head.

He had barely climbed half the staircase when Isobel's teacup clattered into her saucer and she grinned. 'Well, if that wasn't conclusive proof, I do not know what is!'

As both the smugly smiling Sophie and Mrs Fitzherbert were also clearly convinced of something too, Rose felt left out. 'Conclusive proof of what?'

'The palpable attraction you have for Whittleston's inscrutable local physician is deliciously mutual.'

'I'm sorry?' Rose blinked while her entire face exploded in a blush so ferocious it scorched her ears.

'Didn't I tell you that she had a *tendre* for him?'

Ignoring Rose's outrage completely, Isobel leaned closer to the others and they all began to discuss her as if she wasn't there.

'They always find a way to have a private little moment at every social event, and they both have that same look in their eyes whenever they look at one another.' Her friend smouldered at Mrs Fitzherbert to illustrate, and the old woman smouldered back. 'We all might have been invisible just now as Dr Able only had eyes for Rose too.'

'That frisson between them was indeed *palpable*. Especially when his hands disappeared beneath her petticoats.' Sophie fanned herself with her hand. 'For a moment I didn't quite know where to look.'

'I know.' Isobel again. 'I felt like a voyeur, watching them.'

'Well, I didn't,' said Mrs Fitzherbert. 'At my age, I have to live vicariously through you young girls and that display really was everything a good bit of unfulfilled lust and longing should be. I thought Rose, especially, did an outrageously poor job of disguising her desires.'

'I have no desires for Dr Able!'

'You went as red as beetroot when he examined you.'

'That, Isobel, is because I am not accustomed to allowing a man to touch my legs!'

'You also bit your lip as he touched them,' added Sophie, drawing her own lips seductively through her teeth in a manner that, if Rose had been guilty of it, basically would have made her a shameless wanton. 'And your bosoms heaved as you breathed.'

'They did not!'

'There was some definite heaving.' Isobel stared at

her chest pointedly. 'I would also be prepared to wager that there was some fizzing and tingling going on beneath your ribs too, because your voice came out all breathy and strained when you finally managed to answer to him.' Then, to rub salt into the wound, she mimicked and exaggerated Rose's strangulated sentence. '"My aunt h-had a f-f-fractious night, Doctor…and so did I. I couldn't stop thinking about your manly hands exploring my needy flesh."'

While Mrs Fitzherbert threw her head back and laughed, Sophie fanned herself again and that was the final straw.

'Have you all gone mad?' Rose's face was on fire. Her heart was hammering and yet she knew she had to nip this much-to-close-to-the-bone teasing in the bud now or her three incorrigible friends would never stop. 'Do you all seriously think that a woman who has only just had her heart publicly broken would seriously be on the market for another man?'

'We aren't suggesting that you want to marry him, Rose,' said Isobel with a suggestive wiggle of her eyebrows, 'more that you wouldn't mind having your wicked way with him.'

'I would if I were you.' Mrs Fitzherbert's brows also began to wiggle. 'Nothing makes you forget a disappointing man faster than one who doesn't disappoint in the slightest, and what better way to regain your shattered confidence with the opposite sex than a passionate affair with a handsome gentleman like him? Who is a doctor, to boot, so one would hope he has an extensive and thorough knowledge of a woman's *particular* anatomy and an innate eagerness to want to make it *feel better*.'

Rose's jaw gaped in shock and remained hanging for several seconds until she regained control of it to hiss her outrage. 'That is even worse!' If her dratted knee had been up to it, now would have been the precise time that she'd have stormed out. 'As if I would ever behave so…so…scandalously.'

'It would only be a scandal if it were public, and I can attest that even here in Whittleston it is possible to take a discreet lover without causing any gossip. None of us would tell anyone outside of this room.'

That came from Sophie. Sophie—who was supposed to be the most rational and sensible of her three friends. Not to mention, as the new lady of the manor, supposedly the most respectable!

'Indeed it is! I've enjoyed many over the years and at least half have been a complete secret.' Miss Fitzherbert sighed at the memories. 'There is something quite invigorating about a covert liaison. I highly recommend it, Rose. It is exactly what you need right now to raise your spirits. Then you can leave here feeling like a beautiful temptress and not one idiot's leavings.'

'But you had been widowed! Such behaviour is politely ignored if one is a widow!' Rose couldn't believe what she was hearing. 'And I haven't yet been married!' As that irrefutable logic did not seem to permeate their thick skulls she added to it. In panic. 'I am all done with men and still not over being jilted—but if I did change my mind in the future, how would I explain my lack of chasteness to my husband on our wedding night if I did take the doctor as a secret lover?' Even as she said it, she knew it was the wrong thing to say as all three faces lit up. 'Not that I will ever want Dr Able as my lover! You are all wrong on that score. So wrong I cannot even begin to tell you.' She attempted a laugh which she feared only dug a deeper hole for herself.

'I blamed all the horse riding I did in my youth for the lack of my maidenhead.' Mrs Fitzherbert cackled with delight at that admission. 'Only on my first wedding night, of course. It was rather a moot point for all the others. Although, to be fair to all three of my husbands, I don't think they cared overmuch about who I had been with before them—they were more interested in me *being with them* in the moment! I've always been very adventurous in the bedchamber.'

'You could do worse than have a fling with our intriguing local physician, Rose.'

Isobel was like a dog with a bone. They all were. And she was a sitting target thanks to her knee.

'You never know, what starts as a fling could well become more. Isn't that right, Sophie?'

'It is indeed. Rafe started out as just a fling and look at us now.' She wiggled her wedding ring finger. 'From little acorns…'

'You see…' Isobel ignored her horrified expression to continue. 'Something wonderful might come of it and, for what it is worth, I think you and he would make a *wonderful* couple. The attraction is already there…'

'Oh, for pity's sake!' Rose surged to her feet, swallowing the pain. Bad knee or no bad knee, she wasn't going to entertain this a second longer. 'I wish I had returned to Suffolk yesterday as I think I would much prefer having to face him than listen to your nonsense!' She limped to the door, but before she stormed through it she turned to wag a warning finger at all of them.

'Kindly get it into your meddling heads that I do not currently need a lover to raise my spirits!'

She spun and marched straight into a warm and solid wall.

She scrunched her eyes closed rather than look up. The unwelcome fizzing and tingling beneath her ribs confirmed it was the doctor before he spoke.

'You do, however, need to raise your foot to keep your weight off that knee, Miss Healy, so kindly sit back down.'

Chapter Four

Sam had avoided visiting Mrs Outhwaite for a few days. He had blamed medical business, which was easy to do when he was the only physician in a five-mile radius and everyone seemed to be suffering from the same persistent winter cough that was doing the rounds. But it wasn't only business that had made him reluctant to darken the Outhwaites' door—it was Miss Healy.

For reasons best known to his usually level and dispassionate head, she had laid siege on it and given it all manner of inappropriate ideas that a doctor really shouldn't have for one of his patients. Especially a doctor who was dead inside and no longer had the inclination or the capacity for that sort of yearning.

He wanted to blame her legs, because they were a particularly striking pair, but it wasn't just those that had haunted his dreams these past three nights, it was apparently all of her. Her eyes. Her skin. Her voice. Her effervescent and mischievous character. Her humour. All those things suddenly called to him on a visceral and worrying level and he couldn't silence that call no matter how much he tried.

And he had tried!

Tried everything from keeping himself extra busy to a chilly sluicing at the pump before bed and none of them made a blind bit of difference. Something unwelcome within had risen from the dead and it was unsettling beyond measure.

Of course, it did not help that he was convinced he had inadvertently walked in on her friends trying to matchmake the pair of them, any more than it helped that Miss Healy clearly hadn't been impressed by the prospect.

When Isobel and Mrs Fitzherbert got their teeth into a notion, nothing short of a miracle was going to stop it. Isobel had certainly cornered him when he had made the grave mistake of going into her shop to buy some boot polish yesterday, and then found himself stuck in a never-ending circular conversation about how marvellous it was that Rose was staying longer, albeit under the most unfortunate of circumstances and wasn't she looking lovely lately.

Thankfully, he hadn't seen Mrs Fitzherbert since, but was dreading the collision as she was unlikely to be as subtle as Isobel and, knowing her, had likely already opened a book on them. Because here in Whittleston-on-the-Water, wagering on gossip was almost as rife as the gossip itself. He had certainly put a few shillings on Rafe and Sophie getting together when that book had opened, and he had almost won the pot on Ned and Isobel.

Almost.

Until Mrs Fitzherbert had practically cheated to get the pair married at record speed. He had no desire, however, to give the gossips any fodder concerning him or to encourage the interminable meddling which went hand in hand with all the speculation. By its very nature, speculation involved prying and prying involved inter-action, and he preferred to keep an impersonal distance between himself and other people nowadays. It might be a lonely way to live, and frankly he likely deserved no less after he had failed his wife so catastrophically, but it was less messy. Less complicated. Now that he had been hollowed out by grief and rendered a blissfully empty emotional shell, he didn't have the care about anyone beyond the superficial or the professional—and vice versa. That way, when they eventually succumbed to whatever malaise destiny inevitably chose for them, he wouldn't have to feel it. At least in any way more than any physician should feel the inevitable demise of a pa-tient he couldn't save.

He could like them before that happened, of course, just not too much. Enjoy a little of their company, but not too much in case he formed an attachment. And he certainly did not want the added complication of at-traction in that mix. Yet he was undeniably attracted to her, enjoyed her company immensely and liked her more than he had allowed himself to like anyone since his wife. Therefore, avoiding Miss Healy was not only prudent in his current unsettled state, it was necessary. At least until his emotions settled and he was back to being fully dead inside, as he preferred.

But there was no avoiding her now. Mr Outhwaite's urgent note this morning about his wife's continued pain and the need to increase her laudanum meant he had no option but to make the call he had been putting off.

He brushed the snow from his shoulders before he steeled them and knocked the door.

The maid answered and immediately showed him

upstairs to her mistress's bedchamber. Mr Outhwaite, who had summoned him, was nowhere to be seen.

'Thank you for coming, Doctor.' Miss Healy rose, all smiles until Mrs Outhwaite started to speak.

'It's about time too, as I could have died in the time it has taken you to return!'

Sam dealt with that politely, too used to Mrs Outhwaite's acid tongue and theatrical tendencies to take any issue with her pithy tone. 'My apologies, but I have many sick people under my care, most much sicker than you, and I must prioritise them according to need. Especially in November, when the deadliest chills and influenza are rife. Little Ramstead has been hit particularly hard and at least half of that village is presently unwell.'

An answer his grouchy patient did not like. 'Why are you wasting your time in Little Ramstead when your practice is here? It is not good enough, Dr Able!'

'Now, Aunt,' said Miss Healy, shooting him a pointed but exasperated look, 'that is unfair...'

'Of course it is fair! Little Ramstead should employ their own doctor rather than stealing ours, and priority should be given to the patients who live closest!'

'It is the pain talking.' Miss Healy was clearly mortified by her crochety relative's outburst. 'My aunt does not mean to offend you.'

He waved that away with a wry smile at his patient, who was propped up in bed rather than lying flat as instructed. 'She does mean to offend me, and yet she still hasn't.' He reached for Mrs Outhwaite's wrist to take her pulse. 'That is because I am very aware that your aunt's bark is worse than her bite and that she has always been a foul-tempered and ungracious patient who would try the patience of a saint.' The older woman went to argue, but he cut her off. 'Anger is not good for healing, Mrs Outhwaite, and you know better than to try to browbeat me into submission. Have you been taking your medicines?' Sam stared blandly at the cold cup of willow bark tea on the nightstand. 'Or are you doing your usual and refusing them like a petulant child because they don't taste nice?'

'Well… I…er…'

'I shall take that as a no.' He shook his head. 'I don't suppose you have even bothered with the poultice.'

'It's cold and slimy and smells—'

Sam sighed. 'In summation, you haven't taken any of the medications, you refuse to do anything that might lessen the swelling and insist on sitting upright on an unsupportive mattress rather than a chair, when you know full well that that puts undue pressure on the injured disc because I explained that to you.'

That was met with pursed lips and folded arms. 'I am bored stiff lying flat, have no time for your quack cures, and I *do* take my laudanum as that is the only thing that works on the pain and allows me any sleep!'

'She wants more of it, Doctor,' said Miss Healy wringing her hands, 'and refuses to heed all your warnings about its prolonged use. In fact…' She gave her aunt a chiding look. 'She has browbeaten my uncle into going to the apothecary to fetch more—which is why I insisted that he also summon you. In view of your dire warnings, I didn't want my aunt taking more without your approval if it will harm her, and already I think that she has been taking too much.'

So it had been Miss Healy who had sent for him?

Good for her! Mr Outhwaite had never been able to stand up to his wife.

'Thank goodness someone in this family has some common sense as you are quite right, Miss Healy. Laudanum is dangerous. It is highly addictive and turns the brains of addicts to mush. To be honest, if I had any sway over the government, I would ban its sale in apothecaries tomorrow and make it a medicine that could only be administered under the strict supervision of a physician. However, seeing as Mrs Outhwaite's flatly refuses to heed any of my advice, if she has decreed that only laudanum will aid her recovery then I suggest we both leave her to it.'

'What?' exclaimed both women in unison.

'Indeed. Let us wash our hands of her. You can head back to Suffolk safe in the knowledge that you tried your best, and I have too many patients on my books as it is. Mrs Outhwaite has always been one of my most troublesome, so I'll be glad to be shot of her. I am also certain the village will enjoy gossiping about her rapid decline into a drooling, incoherent, opium-fuelled stupor. They do so love a scandal here in Whittleston. Especially when I inform them that she brought it all on herself because she knew best. There is nothing like hubris to turn an upstanding member of the community into a pitiable laughing stock.'

He couldn't resist tapping his chin, as if pondering her decline, to rile his current most ornery patient.

'I can only imagine how vicious all the gossip will get then as, in my experience, people have little sympathy for opium eaters.' Sam reached for his bag, snapped it closed, then stood. 'However, kindly take note that when the hallucinations render her nonsensical, incontinence sets in and her poor, nagged husband begs me to do something to save her from a slow, painful and drooling death, I won't. There will be nothing I *could* do for her by that point.' He shrugged, enjoying himself. 'Except put her out of her misery by smothering her with a pillow, and I'm afraid the Hippocratic Oath prevents me from doing that.'

As Mrs Outhwaite stared, open-mouthed, her mischievous niece stifled a smile and decided to play along. 'Will it really turn her brain to mush, Doctor?'

'I am afraid it will. Rapidly and irretrievably so. Brains do not heal like a cut or a graze. When a part of it is damaged, it dies. Withers like a grape on the vine. Of course, the decline usually begins with impaired reasoning and erratic behaviour. I've known patients dance naked in public after increasing their dose.'

Mrs Outhwaite's face blanched.

'There was one poor chap in the army who not only stripped himself naked, he became convinced he was a chicken and wandered around the camp flapping his imaginary wings and pecking in the dirt looking for corn. We had to lock him up for his own safety, but even after we gradually weaned him from the drug he still pecked at his food and tried to lay eggs.'

Maybe he was over-egging things now, but his lie was making Miss Healy's fine brown eyes twinkle with amusement, so he didn't care.

'The poor man. What became of him?'

'There are only so many times you can fail to lay an egg, Miss Healy, before the spirit shatters for good.' How he said that with a straight face he had no clue, but it seemed to be doing the trick because Mrs Outhwaite was scared. Scared enough to grab his arm.

'But if a patient has only taken one or two doses more of it than was prescribed, surely that isn't catastrophic?'

'In the short term, no. But prolonged use at such high levels over more than three days or four days...' he pretended to pluck that number from his extensive medical knowledge rather than his imagination '...and the rot sets in. That's when the laudanum starts to control the taker, so I would always advise alternative treatments in the long term that are equally as effective but nowhere near as dangerous...' He allowed his voice to tail off as heard Mr Outhwaite's arrival in the hall below, doubtless with enough blasted laudanum to knock out a horse. 'But obviously you do not have to listen to my advice now that you are no longer my patient.'

'But of course I am still your patient!' Outrage mixed with the fear. 'At least as far as I am concerned. You are the one who made idle threats, Dr Able. And to a defenceless sick woman too.'

That last bit was said for her husband's benefit as he had just climbed the stairs—clutching a much too large bottle of the drug.

'Oh, they weren't idle, madam. If you continue refuse to follow my precise instructions, persist in your stubborn insistence that only laudanum will work and try to bully your husband or your niece into giving you more of the stuff, I *will* wash my hands of you.'

That brought her up short and she bristled. 'Physicians are supposed to have a kind and sympathetic bedside manner and you, Dr Able, are nothing but mean.'

'My job is to heal the sick, Mrs Outhwaite, not pander to them.' He took the offending bottle from Mr Outhwaite's hand. 'Now, if you will excuse me, I have some very sick people to attend to in Little Ramstead. I shall return to check on your progress in a few days, when I shall expect to see that you have followed my treatment plan to the letter. This is no longer on it.' He pocketed the bottle. 'Henceforth, it is willow bark only for the pain, and I will send over a sleeping draught to help with your insomnia. And if you must sit, then do so sparingly in a proper chair for no more than a half an hour at a time. Do I make myself clear?'

'Crystal, Doctor.' It was Miss Healy who answered. 'I shall show you out.' As soon as they were alone, she grinned. 'Thank you for that. My uncle struggles to say no to her and she needed...'

'A swift kick up the backside?' Sam smiled back before he could stop it. 'You were right to send for me, but I fear it will not be the only intervention you will need to make to get her to see reason. Your aunt truly is one of the most infuriating patients I have ever come across. When she broke her wrist two summers ago, she was so outrageously demanding I honestly came close to telling Hippocrates and the Royal College of Physicians that they could go to hell and smothering her with a pillow to put myself out of *my* misery.'

She laughed as she started down the stairs and instantly he felt taller and lighter. Which was another worry when he was content to remain dead inside.

'Aunt Agatha can be a difficult character, to be sure, but her heart is mostly in the right place.'

'She needs standing up to.'

'I can do that. Perhaps not quite as assertively or as entertainingly as you just did, but I have my own methods. Getting rid of Uncle William will help, and I fully intend to march him back to his newspaper tomorrow as he is honestly more hindrance than any use in the sickroom. He will do whatever it takes to have a quiet life, whereas I am not so easily—'

'Trampled over by Mrs Outhwaite's iron will?'

'I was going to say rankled, but I suppose your version is more apt. I suspect the next few weeks are going to be much harder work than I anticipated.'

With perfect timing, Mrs Outhwaite began to wail from above in exaggerated agony as her henpecked husband tried to assist her.

'No good deed goes unpunished, Miss Healy, and your first mistake was not getting on that carriage bound for Suffolk once you learned her wounds weren't fatal.'

'In my defence, she has allowed me to hide here these past six months so it felt like the right thing to do.'

'Hide?' Ned had mentioned to him a while back that she had had her heart broken, but Sam did not know the details. Nor had he wanted to, because probing too deep into a person's private life wasn't the most prudent way to keep them at arm's length. Yet all of a sudden he wanted to know all about her. 'From what?'

She pulled a face, clearly regretting her choice of words, then shrugged. 'If you think the gossip and meddling here in Whittleston is vicious, it is double that in my village. Much like your chicken man, there are only so many times a woman can be pitied for remaining unmarried before it shatters the spirit.' She lingered on the bottom step, her chin defiant and proud. 'And in case you are now terrified that that was an unsubtle hint that I am in the market for a husband, Dr Able, as I am sure that you must be after you overheard my friends' unsubtle attempts to matchmake the other day, please don't be. Without going into unseemly details, I have recently had quite enough of men to last a lifetime, and irrespective of how convinced my friends are of our suitability, I am quite content to remain without the disappointment of one for the foreseeable future.' She shot him a wry grin filled with sarcasm as she marched to the door. 'Try not to be offended by that bitter blow.'

He was, oddly, but didn't want to analyse why because he knew he wouldn't like the answer. Instead, he decided to focus on the fact that he respected her for tackling the great unsaid head-on when the easiest thing would have been to leave it hanging. Yet in one fell, direct and courageous swoop, she had demolished any need for further awkwardness between them.

'I shall do my best to get over it quickly. Although I daresay the village won't. If Mrs Fitzherbert is involved, then there will be a book on us half filled with bets already as to when we will succumb.'

'Isn't there always?' She chuckled, unperturbed. 'It is their money to waste.'

'I suppose it is.'

It would be easier being the subject of unwelcome matchmaking gossip now that he knew there was no substance to it. Miss Healy wasn't the slightest bit interested in him in that way, thank goodness, so he could put all that to the back of his mind again where it belonged.

Thank goodness!

He gestured to her leg with his bag to change the subject. 'You're walking better.' Only the barest limp remained.

'I am indeed now that the swelling has subsided. The enormous, purple bruise it has left in its wake, however, is quite something to behold.'

He wanted to behold it. However, as his reasons for wanting to see it were probably more to do with her splendid legs than any legitimate medical reason, he decided to let sleeping dogs lie and opened the door to leave.

'Bruising is a good sign. It means the body is doing its best to fix the problem. But still, you should take things easy on it for at least the rest of the week. If, that is, your demanding aunt allows you to.'

'Are we still on for whist on Sunday afternoon or would you feel more comfortable with a different partner now that you know Sophie, Isobel and Mrs Fitzherbert fancy the pair of us for Whittleston's next bride and groom?'

She really was one for grabbing the bull by the horns and looked him square in the eye as if daring him to be the one with less mettle.

'Forewarned is always forearmed, and you are too competent a whist player to lose on the back of a silly piece of idle gossip.' He inclined his head politely, for some reason smiling again. 'While we continue to trounce them all and steal their money, we can watch all their machinations safe in the superior knowledge that we are immune to them.'

'I do so love to feel superior.' The glint of mischief was back in her eyes. 'Perhaps we should find a way to put a sly, anonymous bet on the outcome too? If we are going to be subjected to no end of machinations between now and my departure, then we should at least benefit from it. I'd be in for half a guinea that I leave here before Christmas Eve without a ring on my finger.'

It was another dare, but one he happily took as it cemented their new accord.

'I'll match that stake and, if you are truly game, I'll find someone to place the bet anonymously for us.'

'You could do that?'

'I am the most *able* physician in Whittleston-on-the-Water and I am owed quite a few favours hereabouts.'

'Then I insist that you call one in and look forward to counting our joint winnings.'

He inclined his head, suddenly glad that they had cleared the air. 'Until Friday, Miss Healy.'

Chapter Five

They'd cleared up at the whist tournament on Sunday afternoon. At Dr Able's insistence, the usual stakes had been doubled, and after a spirited final game they'd won the pot, which Rose had found most satisfying.

It was almost as satisfying as all the amusement they had mutually found in the subtle but shameless match-making they'd been subjected to that night. Made all the sweeter by the fact that he had been true to his word and had placed a bet through the local constable on them *not* getting married, when nobody else had. Which meant the odds they'd got were phenomenal. She didn't need the money, any more than she suspected he did, but she was determined to win it and enjoy it regardless.

Therefore, as it made financial sense to make the villagers think there was a frisson between her and the handsome doctor, she had playfully flirted with him over the card table. With some cajoling he had almost flirted back, and that had had a profound effect on everyone watching. Eyebrows had arched and eyes had slanted sideways and the amount of people whispering, obviously about them, had been very satisfying to see.

Then they had laughed about their evil plan as they had split their winnings after Mrs Fitzherbert insisted that he had to escort her home in his curricle—seeing as they were both going the same way and it was broad daylight.

That short trip had sent the local gossip into a frenzy, because everyone had seen them sitting side by side in the close confines of his curricle, laughing away, which in turn, meant more people bet on their union and the prize pot they weren't supposed to know about, let alone be part of, became increasingly more worth winning.

For her own amusement Rose had stirred the pot a bit more by acting all distracted and dreamy at the Friday Sewing Circle, even pretending to blush when she was accused again of fancying the doctor around that crowded table, where she'd issued a half-hearted denial.

After all, if they were all going to think it anyway, she and her new partner in crime might as well profit from it.

Tonight was the night of the local assembly, and for once Rose was looking forward to it. Not only would it give her a welcome few hours' respite from her demanding aunt, but it would fan the flames of gossip further if she and Dr Able played their cards right.

To that end, she had put on a wholly inappropriate gown. The deep crimson silk wasn't particularly revealing, but the colour was bold and it was the sort of gown a woman wore when she wanted to make a special effort for someone. She hoped that the village hall would be as stuffy as it usually was during this well-attended gathering, as silk and short sleeves were a ludicrous combination when it was freezing outside.

'You look very fetching this evening.' Uncle William beamed with approval over the newspaper he was reading as she poked her head around the bedchamber door. 'I sincerely hope that a certain learned gentleman appreciates all the effort you have gone to.' He flicked a knowing glance at his wife.

'Of course he will appreciate it.' Aunt Agatha smiled smugly. 'Our Rose is quite the catch. The rate things are progressing, I wouldn't be at all surprised if Dr Able makes a formal declaration of interest soon and then they can start officially courting. Perhaps we should insist he stays for tea the next time he visits to help expedite matters?'

The word expedite set alarm bells ringing, as did the mutually wiggling brows.

'Or should we invite him to dinner instead, seeing as we only have until Christmas?'

'I don't think that either is wise.'

Rose wasn't surprised that her own kith and kin had also put a bet on her and the local physician as her aunt had been dropping unsubtle hints for days. But she didn't want them to either build their hopes up or lose too much money on her. She also found herself not wanting to build her own hopes up either. For some reason, the idea of a bit of romance between her and her handsome co-conspirator was no longer being quite as unappealing as it should be. Was her heart mended? Mending? Or just plain hopeless?

'I am nowhere near ready to think about courting again.' The mere thought of courting again, trusting again and laying herself open to more humiliation again should surely make her panic?

Her aunt waved that away. 'Never say never, dear, and remember while he might not have a title, he is a *doctor.*' Her aunt had always been obsessed with status. 'A well-respected one at that.'

'Even so, I am still not interested.'

Maybe, sometime in the distant future, she might be tempted to dip her toe back into those murky waters again. If someone truly worthy and genuinely trustworthy came along. But her faith in mankind—with the emphasis on the *man*—needed to have been fully restored first. It still bled inside her chest from time to time and she still felt humiliated.

'I know the entire village is abuzz with rumours and speculations after the last card game, but you are two of the few people who know the fraught circumstances which brought me here to Whittleston and how deeply it all affected me.'

Hers had been such a brutal and public humiliation. Made unbearable by the pathetic fact that she had been utterly in love with her fiancé and completely blindsided by his callous betrayal. But there was no point attempting to deliver that pessimistic prediction when her entire family hoped that she would not only recover from the mighty blow she had been dealt but would move on. And the sooner the better too.

'Therefore, I feel that I can be completely honest with you and say that while I like Dr Able as an acquaintance, and maybe even as a friend, I really do not have any desire to know him on any other level.'

'Yes, but—'

'In short—' Rose gave them both a pointed look of her own '—what I am really saying is do not waste your hard-earned money wagering on me and Dr Able skipping off into the sunset together as it isn't going to happen.' While her aunt pouted at that disappointing news, Rose bent and kissed her on the forehead. 'I have to go.'

'Do you need your uncle to escort you to St Hildreth's?'

'No need. I shall be constantly under the watchful eyes of Mrs Fitzherbert, Sophie and Isobel.' Who would all be hoping to see some spark of confirmation that their futile quest was working. 'And I have an escort. He should be here any moment.'

'He?' Another knowing look passed between husband and wife. 'I don't suppose *he* would happen to be a besotted doctor, would he?'

'He wouldn't.' She rolled her eyes with a smile. 'Archie is my escort.'

'Archie!' Aunt Agatha flung her head back on the pillow in exasperation. 'Did Dr Able not even ask?'

'Have you taken your sleeping draught?'

'We both have.' That came from her uncle, who had clearly reached the end of his tether too and needed oblivion.

'Then goodnight.' Rose grinned as she exited the bedchamber. 'Don't wait up, Uncle. You both need your rest and I shan't be too late.'

She was tying the ribbons of her bonnet when her dashing escort arrived. Typically, the younger brother of the new lord of the manor was grinning from ear to ear as she opened the door.

'Look, Rose! It's snowing again.' He held out his gloved palm to display the smattering of flakes he had caught. 'I hope it settles so that I can go sledding again down the hill!'

Archie might well be knocking on the door of two and twenty in actual years but, thanks to his condition, he was half that inside and always would be. Bizarrely, it was part of his unique charm and she, like everyone else in Whittleston-on-the-Water, absolutely adored him. He was as exuberant as he was inquisitive, as kind as he was irrepressible, stubborn, frequently unreasonable, always insisted on an intricately tied cravat to go with whichever bold waistcoat he decided to wear and never failed to make you smile no matter how low your spirits.

'You can come with us again if you want to.'

'Not after last time, thank you.'

She still wasn't fully over that last time, a fortnight ago, when she had agreed to it, assuming that Archie actually possessed a proper sled. The sort she was used to with a seat and some sort of mechanism to steer it. Instead, he had produced an enormous metal tea tray which he had cajoled her onto and then almost killed her on it.

'I shall stick to throwing snowballs at you—if it settles.' She caught a few flakes of powder and watched it melt on her skin. 'Which I sincerely doubt it will when the roads are still so wet from the last flurry we had.'

Thank goodness. It had been nothing but alternating treacherous ice and filthy slush for weeks now.

'It's going to settle,' said Archie, with all the confidence of a terminal optimist. 'It will be six feet deep by the time we leave the assembly. Mark my words.'

He held out his arm like a proper gentleman, then kept up a constant stream of excited chatter for the entire five-minute stroll to the village hall behind St Hildreth's, then quickly abandoned her the second they walked through the door.

Rather than hunt about for company, Rose lingered in an alcove while she took in the familiar scene, grateful

that she had one more assembly in this quirky little village. Whittleston had been both her sanctuary and her
salvation. A reminder that life went on and bad times
faded. She was no longer a broken, defeated mess. She
was battle-scarred and battle-hardened, but she looked
forward to getting up in the mornings again and had
finally found her smile.

She was smiling at all the revelry when the hairs on
the nape of her neck danced with awareness.

'I have it on the highest authority that the book is
now worth a healthy seven guineas in total and only us
two have betted against ourselves falling into the par-
son's trap before the end of Advent.'

She turned to see the doctor holding two cups of
what the Reverend Spears insisted on calling punch.

He passed one to her and toasted her with his cup.
'Here's to our guaranteed win.'

She clinked her cup to his. 'Three and a half guineas
each isn't to be sniffed at, so well done us.' A woman
could buy a lot with that, and she was resolute that the
first thing she would treat herself to was the daring
off-the-shoulder evening gown she had found in the
fashion plates in Isobel's haberdasher's, and which her
talented seamstress friend had promised her that she
would make before she left. She would wear her outrageously bold new gown at the Suffolk assembly on
New Year's Eve. An assembly where she intended to
dance every dance, laugh in the face of adversity and
show her feckless former fiancé once and for all that
she was over him.

And perhaps she finally was? Rose certainly no longer felt as weighed down by his rejection as she had
been and that was progress. He also didn't cross her

mind as often as he had either—unlike her charming companion tonight, who had rather taken root in it.

'I reckon it will be closer to four by the time you leave.' Dr Able quirked one dark brow towards the onlookers. 'Just look at the way they are all pretending not to watch us. Can you believe that the odds currently stand at three to one for a Christmas Eve wedding? How trite and sentimental is that?' He pulled a face, then took a sip, then pulled a worse one. 'Good grief, this is more dreadful than usual!'

Rose took a tentative taste herself, then winced. 'I think the wine is off.'

'This isn't wine, Miss Healy, it's vinegar. Maybe even acid.'

'It's a travesty, that is what it is.' Mrs Fitzherbert made them both jump. 'Give those cups to me to dispose of while you two go and dance.' She winked at them. 'The first waltz is next.'

'I c-can't,' stuttered Rose as she panicked over how much the old lady had heard, and panicked more at how much the prospect of waltzing with him suddenly appealed. 'I have a bad knee.'

'Which she must still keep her weight off.'

Dr Able offered her his arm. It was solid and strong beneath her fingertips. The solid muscle would give the most vigorous farm labourer some competition. How on earth did a village physician develop such an athletic physique? And he was so lovely and warm. Enough that she, in her stupid short sleeves, wanted to burrow against him to absorb it.

'Let us find a chair.'

The sight of her holding his elbow caused everyone to stare. Only some did so surreptitiously; the rest did it with such glee it was shameful. Almost as shameful as her improper enjoyment of the feel of his bicep.

'Do you think she heard us talking about our bet?'

'If she had, she would have made her presence known sooner.'

He helped her into the chair even though she needed no help, but the solicitous way that he did it sent the gossiping villagers into a frenzy. Almost as much of a frenzy as the gentle weight of his palm on her back affected her bouncing nerves.

'But if she did, it will make no difference. Knowing the ladies of this parish, any resistance would be seen as a challenge. A giant gauntlet thrown down which will simply result in them all redoubling their efforts to push us together. Thankfully we know that it won't work.'

'It most definitely won't.'

'Because you are sworn off men for the foreseeable future and I am incapable of ever loving again.'

He meant that as a throwaway line, but it sparked Rose's interest exponentially—while simultaneously and inexplicably disappointing her. 'Incapable? Am I allowed to enquire why? Or does that break the unwritten rules of acquaintanceship.'

His lips flattened and for the longest moment she thought he would say no, but instead he sighed. 'That part of me died with Catherine. I could never…' He stopped himself, then huffed. 'Take it from me, hearts don't heal, Miss Healy.' He smiled without humour at his unintentional pun. 'They might pump blood effectively after being broken, but that is all they will do.'

Which did not bode well for hers stitching itself back together any time soon.

'How did she die?'

Again, he was silent for so long she did not think he would answer, but he did. After another huff. 'Typhus. I'd been posted to Lisbon and had been at the main camp there for over a year. But as there were no signs of the war ending and I was nowhere near the front at the time she wanted to be with me. I, as I am sure you can imagine, was adamant that she should stay home, where it was safe, not just from the war but from all the horrors that come with it.'

He swallowed and never had one instinctive swallow conveyed so much pain and regret.

'But because Catherine was stubborn to her core when she set her mind to something, and because other soldiers' wives followed the regiment from camp to camp as a matter of course, she thought I was being unreasonable. Behind my back, she managed to convince the Colonel of the Essex regiment to allow her to travel with the new recruits to Portugal and surprised me there in the middle of an epidemic. Before I could get her on the next boat home she caught it.' His eyes were suddenly haunted. 'And that was that.'

'I am so sorry.' And she was. It must have been awful for him—a doctor—not to be able to save her. 'I cannot imagine how painful that must have been for you.'

The haunted eyes shuttered. 'I daresay it was more painful for her. Typhus is a brutal disease.'

Something tragic and desolate skittered momentarily across his pinched features before he pushed them away. The supreme effort that took was visible for barely a moment before he changed the subject.

'Am I allowed to enquire how your heart got broken?'

'What makes you think it was broken?'

'It takes one to know one.'

'I was jilted, Dr Able, almost a year ago to the day.'

He clearly hadn't expected that and his expression widened with shock before the inevitable pity manifested.

'The irony is that I was supposed to have a "trite and sentimental" Christmas Eve wedding—but it never happened.'

He winced. 'My apologies for putting my big foot in it. When I said that a Christmas wedding was trite...' His words trailed off when he saw her wry smile. 'I'm sorry.'

'So am I, but what can you do?'

As always, tears of humiliation pricked her eyes but she refused to acknowledge them. She had cried enough for a wretch who, frankly, did not deserve her efforts, then for a bunch of malicious gossips who had made her life a misery afterwards. It was better to channel all her sadness and humiliation into anger. Perhaps not healthier but it hurt less.

'His absconding the month before wasn't the worst of it. Everyone back in my village saw it coming long before I did and yet none of them told me. They were so busy trying to spare my feelings that they inadvertently had a hand in crushing them to pulp.'

'How so?' His gaze was sympathetic.

'I suppose all the clues were there the first time he postponed our nuptials, six months after his proposal, because it was obvious then that he wasn't in a hurry to spend eternity with me. But, alas, love is blind and pathetically forgiving. I believed all his nonsense about wanting to prove himself worthy out of his father's shadow and even found it romantic that he wanted to stand on his own two feet when he walked me up the aisle. I even believed it the second time too, which

I suppose makes me as dim as a pauper's candle...'
The wry smile faltered a little. 'But as he was making
some half-hearted attempts with the stock market, I let
it slide. When his attempts failed and he seemed depressed about it all I didn't push for another wedding
date for at least six months.'

'How long were you engaged?'

She could see that even the frowning physician had
worked out that all those delays didn't bode well.

'Two and a half glorious years, Doctor. So long that
it—and by "it" I mean me—was becoming a bit of a
joke in Suffolk. But of course being a foolish optimist
back then, I gave him more of the benefit of the doubt
and blithely looked forward to my extra-special Christmas wedding. However, while I was busy organising
my wedding trousseau, and eagerly counting down the
hours till our nuptials, he was busy conducting a rather
torrid affair with a young widow whom I'd believed
to be my friend. Such a good friend that I even sipped
tea with her in her parlour the day before the pair of
them eloped to Gretna Green. Where she allowed me to
waffle on about how excited I was for my future. And
I brought her a cake which I had thoughtfully baked
myself.'

Her duplicitous friend had nibbled at it in near silence while Rose had made cringing enquiries about
what to expect on her wedding night, because her prudish mother had not been able to bring herself to have
that conversation. Entirely unaware that the woman
was more familiar with the intimate workings of her
philandering fiancé's body than she could have possibly imagined.

'That's awful.'

'Isn't it? She let me leave, still thinking she would be my bridesmaid, and he didn't even have the decency of informing me that the wedding was off until he remembered to post me a letter ten days later—from the Highlands, where he was on honeymoon. It was a curt missive too.'

Rose was purposely flippant. Ever hopeful that if she could pretend to the world that it didn't matter then it would stop mattering to her.

'Only six lines, but straight to the point. He wanted me to know that he had never intended falling in love with another woman, but now that he had he was relieved.'

'*Relieved?*'

Dr Able was shaking his head, outraged for her, while she inwardly cringed some more. Despite burning that letter within minutes of reading it, every cruel word had been engraved on her broken heart.

'Indeed. Without any attempt at apology, he stated that he realised he wouldn't have strayed in the first place if he truly had loved me, and that he should never have proposed to me when he knew, deep down, that marrying me would have been the biggest mistake of his life.' Rose always experienced a violent surge of anger whenever she recalled that part of his letter. 'Which was *lovely* to hear.'

'Ouch.'

Clearly unthinking, he reached for her hand and that somehow meant the world.

'I would say that you are undoubtedly better off without him and that there are plenty more fish in the sea, but I won't as that most definitely would be trite. I daresay you've had enough well-meaning people offer you those empty platitudes and, as previously discussed, it wouldn't help your poor heart any. For some of us, there was only ever meant to be one fish.'

'I thought I was the only one who had developed an aversion to fishing.'

'I surrendered my net and rod when I put Catherine in the ground.'

One of the busybodies from the sewing circle scuttled past, then stopped dead when she spied them holding hands. As he tried to pull his hand away, Rose tightened her grasp and winked as she stared deep into his eyes. Only when the woman had dashed off to spread that delicious new piece of gossip, did she let go. Shocked to her core because, thanks to the stormy depths of his gaze and the potency of his touch, something had shifted within her.

He was cautiously amused but definitely wary. Hardly a surprise when the way he had stiffened at her touch wasn't the slightest bit flattering. Especially when her entire body had done the exact opposite and had positively melted instead.

'And what, pray tell, was that about, Miss Healy?'

Off-kilter, she flapped her fan while she stared at the dancers rather than into his wit-scrambling eyes. 'I was merely adding a little more fuel to the fire. Gilding the lily to ensure that we both make a pretty penny once Whittleston's latest matchmaking debacle is over.'

That was her story and she was going to stick to it.

She forced her gaze to flick back to his, amused rather than unsettled. 'Now that we are partners in crime, you really need to make more of an effort to look enamoured of me too, if you want to be assured of four guineas apiece. You did agree to our ruse, after all.'

'I agreed to place a bet for us, Miss Healy, not fabricate a romance.'

'Spoilsport.' She nudged him with her elbow. 'With some acting and some judicious flirting, I think we might even be able to get that pot up to five apiece. Or have you always been no fun?'

'I used to be fun.' His smile was wistful. 'I also used to be a dreadful flirt too. Before...'

She knew exactly how he felt. 'It's funny, isn't it, how one tragedy can so fundamentally change you?' It was actually quite refreshing to be allowed to feel hopeless alongside someone who empathised. 'I used to be a sunny optimist, with effusively romantic notions, and now I am an embittered and distrusting cynic.'

Albeit one who was having some effusively romantic notions right now.

'You do not act like a cynic.'

'I am flirting with a man for no other reason than to win a bet—if that is not cynicism, Dr Able, I do not know what is. But when you have nothing but despair and more regret to look forward to, I see no reason why we irrevocably damaged souls cannot take whatever amusement we can if the opportunity presents itself.' She twirled a finger in her hair and batted her eyelashes like a coquette. 'I am twisted like that. Bitter and twisted—it is a classic combination. And, take it from me, the twisted part makes life the tiniest bit more bearable. It also helps that I am gifted with a warped sense of humour and find amusement at the most inappropriate times. For example, in full grip of my heartbreak, I had the most marvellous time pretending to be besotted with Ned last summer to make Isobel jealous. Only a tiny part of that was because I could see they were both in denial about being head over heels in love. The rest was all selfish self-amusement.'

'I suppose you do have an exemplary record of fooling people.'

'Which bodes exceedingly well for us winning our bet. People never imagine that lightning can strike twice, therefore the entire village will believe our faux flirting is real.' She took the tiniest sip of her foul drink to glance coquettishly over it. 'Just look at Mrs Fitzherbert and Isobel over there.' They were watching them like excited hawks while doing their utmost to pretend not to. 'They are completely fooled by my superb performance already.'

He was silent again for the longest time, staring aimlessly at all the dancers. When they stopped and a fresh crop began to regroup he nudged her. 'How is this for twisted, then? I bet we could push the pot to reward us with six guineas apiece if we dance both the first and the last waltz together tonight.'

Unaware that his suggestion had both thrilled her and unsettled her in equal measure, he slanted her a sinful glance that suited him too much.

'I am game if you are, Dr Able.'

She held out her hand in readiness, her foolish, misguided heart jumping for joy while her wayward body rejoiced at the opportunity to press itself against his.

'Welcome to the dark side.'

Chapter Six

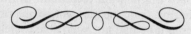

As always, the final waltz signalled the end of Whittleston-on-the-Water's monthly assembly. Normally, Sam would have escaped long before in case he got pressganged into that torture, but tonight he had not only stayed, he had also danced it. And at his own instigation too. A situation which would have been unthinkable only a few hours ago.

That he'd remembered the steps was a bloody miracle as he hadn't danced it since his honeymoon six years ago. There had never been much call for waltzing while Napoleon had been at large and even if there had, he had been too besotted with his pretty wife at home to want to. The waltz was the dance of love after all, and he had been so hopelessly in love with her that it would have felt wrong to perform it with another. A betrayal of his vows almost. But it was hardly a betrayal when those vows had died with Catherine.

He'd expected to be riddled with guilt because it was Miss Healy he was holding in his arms instead, but he hadn't been. Maybe that was because they were partners in crime on a joint quest to amuse themselves by winning a bet? Or maybe it was because he knew the dance meant nothing because they were both irrevocably damaged souls? Whatever the reason, twirling around the floor with the most beautiful woman in the room while the other single men looked on with envy had felt marvellous.

And there was no doubt that she was the most beautiful woman in the room.

While Sam might want to remain immune to her feminine charms, from the moment he had first set eyes upon her tonight he had not been able to help noticing that the deep red gown suited her. The cut displayed a womanly figure that drew male stares like bears to honey—including his. It contrasted perfectly with her chestnut hair, and the bold colour and the confident style matched her slightly irreverent, slightly mischievous character.

Thanks to her witty observations and tendency towards sarcasm, she was as entertaining on the dance floor as she was off it and they both found amusement in all the gawping spectators. Despite all the dangerous and distracting ideas holding her in his arms was giving his body, waltzing with her had been *fun*, exactly as she had promised. More astonishing was that, during it, he had even forgotten to feel dead inside and that had been...oddly liberating when he was usually grateful to be numb.

No doubt he would pay for it in guilt later, when he tried to sleep and the images of Catherine's last moments haunted his dreams to remind him of all his failings, but for now he was content to enjoy the feeling of lightness just a little while longer. Therefore, conscious that they were still being scrutinised, and enjoying the ruse immensely, he insisted with helping her on with her cloak before he handed her over to Archie, who was waiting impatiently to walk her home.

Why Archie was her designated escort when he lived at Hockley Hall, almost a mile away in the wrong direction, when Sam and Miss Healy were practically neighbours he did not know. Beyond that it simply wasn't done for a single gentleman to escort a single lady home on foot in the dark. Archie, although undeniably technically a single gentleman himself, was deemed safe because he was Archie, whereas Sam was obviously a potential despoiler. Which was laughable when he'd had to examine her in her bedchamber unchaperoned and nobody had even thought he might despoil her then despite his wanting to! But dark deeds were apparently only done in darkness, and even in this parochial little enclave of Essex where the strictures of society were mostly ignored some improprieties were unforgivable.

Therefore, despite them heading in exactly the same way, out of respect for that ludicrous propriety, he had to hang back on some pretence. Then leave a respectable five minutes later than the woman he had spent the entire evening with because that was the done thing.

Except the moment he stepped out onto the pavement, he saw Miss Healy and Archie were still there. As was the Hockley carriage, from which Archie's elder brother was frowning while pointing to the ground, where large, robust flakes of snow were now falling with a vengeance and settling fast.

'No, Archie.' From the set of his little brother's jaw, Rafe was arguing with him. 'You will get into this carriage now so that I can drive Rose home. I am not letting you wander all the way back to the hall alone in a blizzard!'

It was nowhere near a blizzard, but Sam understood why Rafe did not want his brother out alone in this. If Archie got confused and lost his way—a very real possibility when Whittleston was a blanket of fresh white and the younger Peel had the faculties of a boy prone to panic—it could be dangerous.

'He's right.' Miss Healy laid a hand on Archie's arm as she tried to be gentle. 'I would never forgive myself if you got lost, so you must get in the carriage with your family.' Then she smiled at Rafe. 'But as the snow is already deep enough to cause you issues too, I can honestly walk myself home faster than you can drive me, and I don't want to be the cause of you getting stuck.'

'But it isn't proper for you to walk home alone in the dark and I promised to protect you!' Archie stamped his foot. 'A gentleman's word is his bond.'

'You would still be escorting Rose home if we take her in the carriage!' Poor Rafe was clearly at his wits' end. 'Therefore, I would appreciate it if you would stop arguing and get in this blasted coach quick-sharp before all this snow makes the roads impassable.'

'Your big brother is right.'

Sam decided this was as good a time as any to announce his presence. Archie listened to him. Sometimes. He had always been in awe of the fact that Sam was a doctor, as if that alone meant his word was gospel.

'The lane up to Hockley Hall is steep and prone to snowdrifts that block it. The sooner your brother tackles it, the more chance you all have of getting home tonight. If you are worried about Miss Healy, you can appoint me as your second to fulfil your promise to protect her. Surely you trust me to get her home safely?'

He did his best impression of a man about to be wounded as he knew Archie hated to upset people.

'Well... I...' The lad blinked, wavering. 'Of course I trust you, Dr Able, but...'

'Then that is the perfect solution!' Before Archie's legendary stubborn streak came to the fore again, Miss Healy pushed her intractable escort towards the carriage. 'You go home with Rafe before the road becomes blocked and I'll walk home with Dr Able.' With surprising strength, she shoved him into the seat next to his sister-in-law. 'Goodnight, Archie.'

She slammed the door closed with a wink at Rafe, and the carriage lurched forward.

'I honestly thought we would be standing here all night arguing.' She grinned, making her fine eyes sparkle. 'Thank you for stepping into the breach.'

'It was hardly any trouble when we are practically neighbours. I would have risked the dreadful scandal and offered before, but Archie was adamant that you specifically asked him to do it.'

'Only because I did not want to inconvenience my uncle—who also would have insisted on escorting me the short five minutes home too if I didn't have a trustworthy alternative in place. Which is ridiculous when this is sleepy Whittleston-on-the-Water and I would be perfectly safe. But no. I must be wrapped in cotton wool for the sake of my fragile reputation! Being a woman is so irritating sometimes.'

Sam chuckled at her perfectly logical complaint. 'For what it's worth, in my professional experience women are always the stronger rather than the weaker sex as we are always told. They seem to work twice as hard and bear everything with more fortitude and grace than most men do.'

'That is very forward-thinking of you.'

'One can be bitter and twisted and forward-thinking, Miss Healy. They are not mutually exclusive.'

That comment made her laugh—until she skidded on the snow. She grabbed his arm to stay upright and when she let go wobbled some more, so he naturally offered it to keep her upright. Then regretted it when she took it, because her touch awoke something primal.

'It turns out that dancing slippers have absolutely no traction.' She scowled at her inappropriate footwear, then shivered. 'They are not particularly warm either. I knew I should have changed into my walking boots the second I saw the weather, but I didn't because they wouldn't have gone with my gown. That will teach me to put vanity over practicality.'

'At least it is only a short walk back.'

Something he was suddenly grateful for, because her arm in his felt nicer than he was comfortable with. Thanks to Archie's protracted altercation with his brother and the snow, all the other revellers had dissipated, so they had the path from St Hildreth's to the village square to themselves. The snow had muted all the usual sounds of the night and the lack of stars above made the world suddenly seem more intimate. As if they were the only two people in it. Something that made the shrivelled husk of his heart race.

'You will be back with your aunt and uncle well before frostbite sets in.'

'On the subject of my aunt and uncle, you should probably know that they might have also placed a bet on us getting together—despite all my protestations to the contrary—so there is a high chance you will get an impromptu invitation to take tea with us, or dinner, so have your excuse ready. It is unlikely tonight, as they both decided to partake of your sleeping draught, but forewarned is always forearmed. My aunt, especially, has been desperate to find me a replacement fiancé since the scoundrel I was engaged to replaced me.'

Despite the flippant tone, hurt shimmered briefly in her eyes and he experienced the overwhelming urge to throttle that scoundrel for his callous treatment. To his surprise, his fist had even clenched, so Sam flexed his fingers and tried to make light of it for her sake— because that was what she always did.

'I am surprised Mrs Outhwaite considers me good enough when she fancies herself a cut above all of us here.' He blurted that before he had the good sense to censor it and instantly regretted it. Mrs Outhwaite was still her aunt, and blood was always thicker than water. 'That was unkind and uncalled-for, and I apologise.'

She sighed, unoffended. 'I adore my aunt, as she has been nothing but kind to me at a time when I need to be reminded that not all in the world is bad, but I am not blind to her shortcomings. She and my uncle were never blessed with children, and I suppose, in the absence of a family of her own to love and respect her, my aunt overcompensates by trying to command the respect of everyone here in Whittleston instead. Unfortunately, she has gone about that entirely the wrong way. She puts too much stock in nonsense like status and doesn't possess the...*diplomacy*...necessary to correct that. Of course—' she tugged his arm playfully '—it doesn't help that she is prone to theatrics and has no understanding of the concept of tolerance. You should be flattered that she is prepared to tolerate you, Dr Able, as that is a rare accolade.'

'Then I suppose I should be honoured that she considers me tolerable enough for her beloved niece and will endeavour to keep my uncharitable opinions about her to myself going forward.'

'Do not flatter yourself too much, though, Dr Able, as in the same breath she did say that beggars could not be choosers.' There was that infectious glimmer of mischief in her eyes again as they turned onto the square. 'I sincerely doubt she would tolerate you at all if she didn't fear her scandalously jilted niece was doomed for a life gathering dust on the shelf. As being jilted does, ironically, render a woman rather unweddable. No man wants another man's cast-offs at the best of times, and they all will now wonder what it was about me that sent him running to the hills in the first place. Especially since he and his new wife and adorable baby have ingratiated themselves back into my village.'

'They didn't have the good grace to move away?' Her story just got worse and worse.

'His father is the wealthiest landowner and biggest landlord in my village, and nobody wants to upset the man they pay their rent to—even if they genuinely do think that his son is scoundrel. Forgiveness has been surprisingly forthcoming despite their despicable treachery —aided, no doubt, by some rather salacious rumours which have cast doubts upon my character and given some of the more stupid or most intimidated some sympathy for the wretch. Which is marvellous for my former fiancé, because he gets to go about his life unchallenged, but not so marvellous for me.'

'What sort of doubts?' He had the inexplicable urge to avenge them all.

'Fabricated nonsense that nobody sensible believed for a minute.' She waved it away with a sunny smile that did not quite touch her eyes. 'But it still was a blow to my self-esteem.'

She flicked him a wry glance intended to convey that she was over it, except her acting skills weren't quite good enough.

'Not much goes on in Suffolk, so it was all anyone talked about for far too long. Especially after the pair of Judases returned and his father got involved. The only viable solution to the awkward problem of our enforced proximity and the continued speculation, as far as my family are concerned, is for me to marry. And the sooner the better. Their desire to get the job done—alongside the impending birth of the adorable child those two back-stabbers created—was the reason I came here. Hoping to escape it all. Except, like my misguided and well-meaning parents, my usually picky aunt would rather I shackled myself to a nobody, like you, Dr Able, than remain a pitied and infamously discarded spinster for ever.'

He wanted to hug her, but instead continued in the same droll, sarcastic tone. 'A *nobody*? Thank you very much. Some friend you are.'

She could not resist another dig. 'Friends? I thought we were merely aquaintan—'

'Dr Able! Thank God!' Ted Dewhurst, the son of one of the tenant farmers from Little Ramstead suddenly appeared out of the snow. 'One of my father's mares has been foaling all day. The babe is still stuck fast and she's in such a bad way now he thinks we might lose them both!'

'I am not an animal doctor, Ted. I know absolutely nothing about mares and foals.'

'It's November—are you sure she is foaling?' That came from Miss Healy. 'She could have colic.'

'Positive,' came the lad's response. 'She's the size of a house and you can see the babe moving inside of her. Her season has always been odd because it's near constant. Her last foal came in January. That was a big one too.'

'Last January? So recent?'

'Aye, miss. It came as a surprise to us too that it had happened again so fast, but she had no problems then so we assumed it would be all right. But this time...' Ted turned to plead with Sam. 'You need to come, Doc! It's stuck and you're our last hope.'

'I'm really not sure what help I can be.' It wasn't in his nature to allow anything to suffer, but he didn't relish the prospect of shooting a horse to put it out of its misery. 'If it was a human baby—'

'Oh, for goodness' sake, Dr Able, surely the basic principles of a birth are the same? Go and fetch your equipment and curricle this instant!' Miss Healy pointed to his door like an exasperated schoolmistress. 'Humans and horses are both mammals, after all.'

'With very different anatomies! I barely know which end of a horse is which!'

'Then it is lucky for you that this farmer's daughter does, isn't it?' She turned to Ted, her suddenly snippy tone gone. 'You go home and we'll be with you as soon as we can. Tell your father to get plenty of straw and rope ready. If it's a large foal we might need it, and if it is large and also breach, as I suspect it is, we will definitely need it.'

Intrigued and slightly peeved by the way she had taken charge with such confidence and forced his hand, Sam made short work of readying his curricle, and by the time he had fetched his equipment, she was already seated in it, huddled inside her cloak like a monk to stave off the cold. Snow had settled on her hood.

'This weather is worsening, and this could take hours. You go home and I'll go alone.'

'Because you know so much about horses that you are confident you can save her?' Her jaw set stubbornly and she did not budge.

'Because of propriety, Miss Healy! Because it isn't the done thing for a single man and woman to walk home alone in the dark together after an evening of public waltzing and flirting, let alone ride off into the night in a curricle together!'

'Oh, stop being so silly. Little Ramstead is less than five miles away and we will likely be back before anyone misses us.'

'Being ruined isn't silly, Miss Healy, and despite the unfairness of it all a woman's reputation *is* fragile!'

'It will be a cold day in hell before I put my already tarnished reputation before what is right! I have the knowledge to save that foal and I am going to use it, even if I have to find another horse and ride by myself to Little Ramstead!'

'Please—be reasonable.' Sam spread his hands and tried to temper his tone. 'If your aunt or uncle are waiting up for you then this could be catastrophic for both of us.'

She pointed towards their house. 'Can you see a lamp burning anywhere but on the porch?'

She had him there as all the windows were dark. The

downstairs ones were devoid of curtains too, no doubt so the outrageous gossip Mrs Outhwaite could keep a close eye on the comings and goings in the square, so it was plain to see that nobody was awake.

'They both sleep like the dead so I can assure you that neither will notice me arriving home a little later than usual! My aunt is the lighter sleeper and thanks to your sleeping draught she has been practically unconscious between the hours of ten and ten.'

'Still, this isn't wise, nor proper, and—' Sam found himself talking to a raised palm.

'A horse is more than a conveyance to a farmer, Doctor. It is an intrinsic part of his livelihood and the loss of one can have dire repercussions. Especially if the farmer happens to live from hand to mouth as I suspect Ted's father does.'

He might have known this canny minx would spot the patches and holes in the lad's clothes.

'I will not see a family starve because you think that my helping them is improper and I sincerely doubt anyone in this village will think it the least bit improper if they ever find out the circumstances. This is prime farming country and when a crisis happens the people in these close-knit villages rally round and happily forgive the odd bit of impropriety if it is necessary. I've visited countless farmers in the middle of the night when a neighbour needed help and still retained my reputation.'

She folded her arms and glared at him from the perch.

'So stop being silly and let's go. You might be the one with the medical degree, but I'll wager I've brought more foals into this world than you have.'

'On your own head be it, then.'

He would have argued more fervently, but she was right, damn her. Sam had no clue how to birth a foal and he wasn't confident he could save the mare. Knowing his luck, he'd kill the mother and the child. Ted's father had been struggling to keep his head above water for years and he didn't want that on his conscience.

Conscious of her inappropriate evening gown and slippers, he made a quick about-turn to retrieve an additional blanket from inside and tossed it to her, then climbed up beside her. Thankfully, to prove her right, despite it being barely after ten, Whittleston-on-the-Water was as silent as the grave when they set off, as everyone else had had the great good sense to weather the storm in their beds. Not a single lamp burned in any window in the square, which was just as well. There was gossip and there was gossip, and two single people suddenly disappearing together at midnight, no matter how innocent or necessary, was bound to put the fox amongst the hens. Especially after the two waltzes they had foolishly engaged in to pique all the busybodies' interest.

'Seeing as you are the expert, and I am apparently your assistant in this endeavour, you should probably tell me what you need me to do when we get there.'

'Pull, Dr Able.' She smiled. 'Pull on the rope like your life depends on it. That is your role tonight.'

'And yours is?'

'To attach the rope to the foal's hooves.' She held up one gloved palm. 'My hands are smaller than a man's and therefore can manoeuvre themselves into tighter crevices. It won't be pretty but I daresay you've seen worse.'

Miss Healy took immediate charge when they arrived at the farm, insisting on more light, more straw, some cooking fat and a bucket of hot water. Then she examined the horse, whispering soothing words to the struggling beast as she massaged around her tummy.

'How long has she been lying down?'

'Three hours now,' said the farmer. 'She had a few spirited goes at pushing but all to no avail.'

'Let's see what's wrong.'

She cooed this to the mare, then stripped off her cloak. Her fine crimson silk gown was incongruous with her surroundings, but she was oblivious of that. Instead, she smeared her arms to the elbow in the fat, dropped to her knees and gently inserted one hand beneath the mare's tail.

When she next spoke, it was to no one in particular. 'It's not breech, thank goodness, but it's upside down.' For the benefit of those who barely knew one end of a horse from another, she elaborated. 'It's lying on its back in her uterus, which means every time she pushes its hooves are pushed into her intestines rather than the birth canal. I need to turn it.'

With that, she went to war within the mare, rolling about on the bloody straw as she wrestled with the foal.

After an eternity, which involved a great deal of grunting from the woman and the expectant mother, she finally gave them some hope. 'It's finally moving!'

There was more wrestling. More grunting. And then Miss Healy withdrew her arms and collapsed on the straw. 'The foal is in a better position but not ideal. It's also huge. Much bigger than average. And she's exhausted so I don't think she can push it out without assistance.'

Sam stripped out of his coat. 'Is it time for the rope?'

'I'm afraid it is.'

Miss Healy talked him through making a retractable loop while she caught her breath, and then visibly braced herself as he passed it to her.

'Once I get this around the hooves, plant your feet and give it all you've got. This will be a battle. Big foals have an annoying tendency to get sucked back inside if the line isn't taut, so whatever you do, don't stop pulling once you start. Once the feet are out, grab one.' She glanced at his cream evening waistcoat with a frown. 'I'm afraid this next part is going to get very messy.'

'I've seen worse.' He rolled up his sleeves. 'And I am ready when you are.'

Miss Healy managed to get the rope looped around the foal's feet with surprising speed but she was right about it being a battle. For the first few minutes all his pulling seemed to be for nought, until suddenly it wasn't. Sam staggered backwards and all at once, there were the hooves. Two slimy black beacons of hope still trapped inside the birthing sac. Miss Healy tore it open with her bare hands and shouted at him to pull harder, which he did with a growl. Quick as a flash, she wrapped her hands tight around one of the feet and heaved. Once he was certain she had a firm enough hold he did the same, and they tugged together until the legs were followed by a nose, then a head, and then, like a slippery bar of soap in the bath, the rest slithered out in one messy brown lump.

A lump that did not move.

The farmer and Ted set about clearing the foal's airway and rubbing it down with straw while Sam held his breath. Beside him, he could tell Miss Healy was doing the same. They both let it out in a whoosh when the foal finally came to life. It twitched its feet, wiggled its head and, as his exhausted mother used the last of her strength to lick him, wobbled precariously to his feet while still attached to the umbilical cord.

'Do we cut it?' For reasons best known to himself, Sam was grinning at the miracle of this birth. The relief and sense of achievement was so palpable he could almost taste it.

Miss Healy shook her head and then collapsed back onto the straw, the definition of a spent but elated force. 'Not yet. It should snap on its own once the placenta comes out and she tries to stand.'

Which, it turned out, was exactly what happened not ten minutes later, while they both gratefully sipped hot cups of tea after the coldest wash known to man.

Chapter Seven

Rose tossed her bundle of soiled clothes into the curricle. The stays and petticoats might still be salvageable, but the gown was so beyond hope she had left it with the farmer's wife to dispose of, supremely grateful for the warm dress the woman had lent her despite all its patches.

Dr Able helped her up, stowed the basket of eggs the farmer had insisted on giving them as payment because he couldn't afford otherwise, and then hauled himself in beside her.

'We did it.' She beamed at him, proud of them both, supremely thankful the mare and her foal would both live to fight another day.

'You did it. I just pulled.' He offered her a wry smile. 'I am impressed, Miss Healy. Not only at your superior knowledge of equine anatomy, but with your calm and level head in a crisis. You would make an excellent physician.'

High praise indeed, because he was an excellent physician.

'Aside from the outrageous fact that women aren't allowed to be doctors, I would be a terrible physician as the sheer responsibility would weigh me down and I would take every failure all too personally.'

Her gut told her, now that she had been allowed a small window into his soul, that he did too, and that perhaps the tragedy which had befallen his wife and left him devastated explained why he kept the world at a distance.

'I'd be distraught if we'd failed. An inconsolable, weeping mess.'

For a moment she thought that she had touched a nerve, until he pulled a face. 'Thank the Lord we succeeded, then, as I do not have the requisite bedside manner to deal with a weeping mess. I'd simply hand you the reins and jump from the curricle. No matter what speed it was travelling at.'

'Would you really?' It was difficult to imagine a man so capable being felled by a few tears. 'Even in this atrocious weather?'

'If you're asking if would I choose hypothermia over hysteria? Of course I would! I'm a man of science and science is always logical, even when our limitations in understanding it defeats us. There are books I could read on hypothermia. Effective tried and tested treatments I could administer that might work. There is no rhyme or reason to a woman's tears, no medical books on the subject, and certainly no logic. Worse, the only treatment is a handkerchief, and that's not guaranteed to be effective, or platitudes, which I am atrocious at.' He shuddered for effect as they turned back onto the lane. 'I think I'd actually dive headfirst into a raging flood to avoid floods of tears.'

'Have you always been a man of science?'

'I think so. I cannot recall a time when it did not intrigue me. But then my father was a physician, so I suppose it's in my blood.'

'Was he? Where?' Seeing as the tight-lipped doctor was finally in the mood to open up, Rose decided to take advantage of that.

'Here—in Essex. About forty miles north-east, to be exact. I grew up in Witham. Do you know it?'

'I know it well. It's on the road to Long Melford, where I grew up. Do you still have family there?'

He shook his head, frowning more at the worsening weather and deep snowdrifts on the road ahead than at the question. 'My father passed several years ago and I sadly have no memories of my mother, who died when I was still in leading strings. I was their only child and left the town to join the army a decade ago, so I have no ties to Witham now.'

'You weren't tempted to return there when you took up private practice?'

'No.' His expression shuttered again, so abruptly it shocked her. She had definitely unwittingly hit a very raw nerve this time. Had his wife come from Witham too?

Should she ask?

While she deliberated the wind whipped up and sent the falling snow swirling. Within moments the visibility went from passable to non-existent, and the need for further conversation became redundant as he struggled to see the road ahead.

The wheel clipped something, then slid sideways, and the horse began to panic, bucking his head and dancing on the spot, not keen to venture blindly into the abyss. Rose didn't blame him. The snow was so violent now each flake bit into her skin and burned her eyes, and she was bundled up in a protective cloak. All the poor horse had was blinkers, and they wouldn't protect him.

She didn't need to tell Dr Able to stop the curricle. He had already decided attempting to continue was suicide until the blizzard subsided, and was carefully manoeuvring off the lane and into a gap beneath a canopy of trees. The bare tangle of branches above didn't give them much protection, but afforded enough to calm the horse at least.

'I fear we are going to have to wait it out.'

She nodded.

'Hopefully, seeing as this wind has whipped up quickly, it will pass quickly.'

As if it had heard him mention it, a frigid gust blasted their way with such force it rendered the canopy above useless. Hard pinpricks of ice stung Rose's cheeks while the gale stole her hood and sent it billowing backwards.

'If you can turn the curricle to face away from the wind and push it closer to the trees, I'll find somewhere less exposed nearby to tie up your horse.'

Rose grabbed the blanket from her legs and gingerly slid off her seat. The snow came to her knees and the relentless south-westerly found every hole in the tatty borrowed dress to chill her skin, apparently now determined to get worse before it got better. Together they battled the elements to unhitch the animal, and while he attempted to use the other blanket to fashion a makeshift cover to shield the open front of his curricle, she led the horse several yards into the calmer woods.

Fortunately, it did not take long to find a spot so filled with trees that the whistling wind carried hardly any snow. It was still bitter, though, so she draped him from ears to tail in the blanket, and in the absence of anything else to secure it to the horse's body used several hairpins like wire laces under his belly and at his neck. Only when she was convinced his new woolly coat was secure did she tie him to a low-hanging branch, then retrace her steps.

Dr Able, in a misplaced display of gentlemanliness, was waiting for her outside the curricle, stamping his feet, shivering. His greatcoat was so covered in snow it was white. Somehow he'd secured the blanket to the canopy tightly enough that it flexed around the perch but refused to budge, no matter how hard the wind slapped it. He insisted on helping her into their emergency camp, then quickly followed.

Impenetrable darkness engulfed them as he knotted the only gap in the blanket shut.

Even in their cocoon it was bitterly cold. So cold that there really was no choice but to snuggle together to share each other's warmth—which did nothing for her equilibrium at all. Her bosoms, especially, were misbehaving wildly against the solid wall of him. She had never been so aware of her wretched nipples in her life, thanks to all the cold and the need puckering them!

While her body was busy conjuring all manner of improper scenarios that wound her tighter than a spring, his was undeniably tense. Unflatteringly so—as if he couldn't imagine a worse possible scenario—which only served to make Rose feel more self-conscious. Awkwardness hung in the confined space like a shroud. So intense it almost overtook her scandalous awareness of her own bosoms.

She tried to ignore it for as long as she could, but when her toes began to curl inside her cramped slip-

pers, from cringing more than from the cold, she had
to break the uncomfortable tension. Maybe some conversation would help take her mind off *things*?

'Perhaps, with hindsight, you were right and I should
have gone straight home after the assembly.'

'I did warn you on your own head be it.'

She didn't need to see his droll expression to picture
it. He was the king of the I-told-you-so glare.

'You could be curled up in bed right now, a fire roaring in the grate, safe in the arms of Morpheus. But instead you are stranded for goodness knows how long
in the middle of nowhere. Both of us stinking of the
stable and with no supplies beyond some foul-tasting
medicines and a dozen raw eggs.'

'But at least I am not still draped in inappropriate
silk, Dr Able, so every cloud…' She couldn't help finding that tiny consolation funny. Hilarious, in fact. Although she had no earthly idea why when there was a
very real possibility of them both freezing to death here
in the middle of nowhere in the middle of the night.

'You really do have a warped sense of humour, don't
you, Miss Healy?'

But because laughter was infectious, he was now
chuckling too.

'Laugh and the world laughs with you, Dr Able. Cry
and you cry alone.'

It was an ethereal grey inside the curricle when Rose
awoke with a start. At some point after their breath had
banished most of the chill from inside their cocoon
they both must have nodded off. Then clearly she had
snuggled closer to keep warm, as her head was resting
on his chest and his arm was draped around her shoul-

ders, the gentle heat of his big palm resting on the flare of her hip. Her own hand had burrowed into his greatcoat and had settled on his heart. The steady, slow beat beneath her fingers suggested he was still fast asleep.

She stealthily tried to extricate herself from his embrace, but he stirred with her first movement, muttering nonsense. His arm then tightened around her as he buried his nose in her hair. He sighed contentedly— then stiffened to granite when he realised with whom he was so intimately entwined.

Rather than have that awkward conversation, Rose briskly sat up to open the blanket. As her eyes adjusted to the change she was alarmed to see it was neither dark nor light outside, but at least the wind had gone. Dawn hovered dangerously close, which meant they must have slept for hours, but was still a little while away, thank goodness! The last thing either of them needed was returning to the village in daylight. It was one thing to be irrevocably tarnished by a jilting, another entirely to be compromised into complete ruination.

'The good news is that the blizzard has stopped.' She stretched some of the aches out of her body rather than look at him. 'It's still snowing, but not enough to prevent us getting home. The bad news is that it's almost dawn.'

'Oh, good grief! It's blasted market day!'

It was obvious from his tone and the haste with which he ripped the blanket from the canopy that he had also realised their situation was precarious. The square was a flurry of activity on market days.

It seemed to take for ever to get the curricle back onto the lane, and thanks to hours and hours of snow which had settled thick the short journey back to Whittleston was hard yards. Both in effort and atmosphere.

The easy-going man she had laughed with only hours before had disappeared and was now replaced with one who was implacable and worried. His dark brows were furrowed as he steered them ever closer to the village.

'What time is it?'

The orange-purple hue on the edge of the horizon warned the night was near its end, but the soaring spire of St Hildreth's against it reassured her that their journey was almost over.

He fumbled beneath his greatcoat for his pocket watch, then squinted at the dial in the stingy light. 'A quarter to six.'

'Then all is not lost.' She reached over to touch his sleeve and retracted it immediately when his arm stiffened. 'We have at least half an hour before the first market traders start arriving. We should both be safely home by then.'

'Unless your aunt and uncle have raised the alarm and sent out a search party!'

'Don't be silly!' Such was her confidence in that, she laughed. 'Neither are early risers. They sleep like the dead, remember, and both took your sleeping draught.' A fact that she hoped she could rely on. 'But to be on the safe side, once we reach the outskirts I shall get out and use the back alley. I can sneak in through the kitchen door without setting a single foot in the square where anyone might see us together, whereas nobody will bat an eyelid and think that you have been out on a call.'

'And if your aunt and uncle hear you returning and demand an explanation?'

'Then I shall tell them the truth.' Panicking for no reason now was pointless.

'Telling them we spent the night together is bound to end well!'

'We helped a farmer with his horse, got caught in a blizzard and had to wait for it to pass! We did nothing wrong, Dr Able, beyond helping a family in need, and they would not dream of telling anyone if I asked them not to. My aunt might live for other people's gossip, but she would do anything to avoid being tainted by a scandal herself.'

He didn't look convinced. Instead, he stared straight ahead with a surly, tight expression as he snapped the reins. Maybe it was his anxiousness rather than a premonition, but the nearer they got to the village, the more uneasy she became too. No matter how much Rose tried to reassure herself that they were unlikely to see a soul this early, last night's blizzard complicated things. People would have to get up sooner to inspect the damage and shovel paths from their front doors or would set off early to go about their business to ensure they did not arrive late.

Before they turned onto the main road into Whittleston she was so unsettled she had to listen to her gut. 'Drop me here and I'll take the longer way home through the fields on foot.'

The fact that he immediately steered his curricle to the side of the lane told her he was panicking too. 'If you're sure.'

'It's the safest option. Nobody will raise an eyebrow if you return to the square at dawn. They will raise merry hell if I am beside you.'

She was several yards through the drifts before he called her back. 'You forgot your things!'

As they were her most intimate things, she was grateful for the reminder. The last thing she wanted was him finding the parcel in the footwell later and inadvertently seeing her unmentionables. She held out her arms and he tossed the loosely tied bundle. To humiliate her, a frigid gust of wind came from out of the blue, unravelling the bundle in mid-air and sending her unmentionables everywhere.

She waved him away, wanting him long gone for two reasons now, and not just her ruination, but he was up and out of the curricle before she could stop him, in hot pursuit of her stays which were now splayed across the spiky bare twigs of a dead piece of hedge. He clearly had no clue what he'd been chasing until he retrieved it, then quickly bundled it into his fist once he did.

Mortified, she grabbed one limp stocking from the snow as she watched him bend for the other. She'd gone to grab the intimate garments from his outstretched hand when her foot found a hole and she fell forward. He lunged to catch her and must have found the same void beneath the snow, because they slammed together. Being bigger, and heavier, gravity was on his side, sending her backwards before he landed atop her.

The collision winded them both. Enough that neither could move for several seconds after the impact. When they did, it was in a tangle of arms, legs and her evening cloak, until they both froze as they were suddenly bathed in light.

A light which was quickly extinguished by its wide-eyed bearer—Ned Parker. But not quickly enough for the group behind him not to have witnessed the pair of them rolling around in the snow together as they all raised their own lamps, illuminating them again.

'I told you they were probably off having a tryst!'

The accusation which came out of the dark was from Whittleston's postmaster.

'Now, George...' Ned spoke, his arms outstretched to hold everyone back, while Rose and the doctor scrambled to their feet and she righted her skirts. 'I am sure there is a perfectly reasonable explanation...thanks to the blizzard and all.'

'There is!' Dr Able was in a panic. 'The Dewhursts had trouble with a horse and Miss Healy accompanied me to help birth a foal who was stuck. She's a farmer's daughter and—'

It was her Uncle William who pushed passed Ned and stayed him with a growl. In the lantern's dim light Rose could see he was quaking with anger.

'You left the Dewhursts' at midnight!' He prodded the doctor in the chest. 'I know that for a fact because I've just came from the Dewhursts myself! What the blazes have you been doing with my niece in the hours since? And while you are about it, you opportunistic scoundrel, explain to me why you didn't bring her home directly after the assembly, as you were apparently tasked to do?'

'We got caught in the storm as soon as we left and had to shelter from it!'

'The blizzard had stopped by two.' By the look of Reverend Spears as he approached, he was already concerned for their immortal souls. 'We know because we've been searching high and low for Rose since Mr Outhwaite raised the alarm that she was missing at midnight. That leaves a lot of unaccounted-for hours, young man. A lot of unaccounted-for and unchaperoned hours.'

'Where did you seek shelter?' Uncle William's eyes

had narrowed to slits. 'And, for the love of God, pray tell with whom?'

'In Dr Able's curricle, Uncle.' Rose tried to pour oil on troubled waters by reaching for her relative, who had slumped at that news. 'On the edge of the lane between the two villages.'

'If that is the case, why did Lord Hockley and I not see you? Nor did anyone else who's been searching for you for the last several hours! Because there's not a single person between here and Hornchurch who has seen hide nor hair of you, and between us all we've knocked on every door and checked every outbuilding. Nobody except for the Dewhursts—who have also been out searching for you since we woke them up at half-past two!'

'The snow must have camouflaged us.'

'Did it render the pair of you deaf too? You must have heard us approach and pass. Twice! Heard us calling for you? And you didn't think to flag us down? Or were the pair of you too occupied with *other things* after all your waltzing to notice?'

'Now, Mr Outhwaite…' Rafe stepped into the fray, all reasonableness. 'You know snow dampens sound, and if the curricle was covered in it it's unlikely we would have seen them.'

'That doesn't explain why they didn't head back to the village the moment the blizzard stopped!' Her uncle prodded the doctor again. 'What the bloody hell were you doing with my niece for all those hours?'

'Nothing untoward, if that is your implication! We waited for a good hour to no avail before we fell asleep and—'

'A likely story.' Uncle William held the lamp directly

in front of Dr Able's face so he could look him in the eyes. 'When we all saw the way you were fawning over her at the assembly!'

'He's definitely had his beady eyes on your Rose for a while now,' said the postmaster unhelpfully. 'Enough that we've all put a bet on them courting.'

'Courting involves doing things above-board and respectfully!' Uncle William invaded the doctor's space again, snarling. 'Not sneaking off to do dark deeds!'

'I trusted you, Dr Able!' Poor Archie was distraught and close to tears. 'I trusted you to get Rose home safe and you let me down!'

'I didn't, Archie. I promise. Miss Healy was practically home when Ted found us, and then…'

'I insisted on accompanying him to save the foal.' Rose addressed the whole crowd, seeing as they were all so whipped up they were baying for blood. 'Dr Able's knowledge of horses is limited and as a farmer's daughter I know more. Everything he has said is the truth. I swear it. He has been nothing but the perfect gentleman. The blizzard forced us off the road, and we both nodded off while we waited, but headed home as soon as we awoke.'

'Home is that way.' Uncle William jerked his lamp back towards the lane. 'So what were you doing in this field?'

'Well…' She could hardly say they'd been trying to avoid a scandal by sneaking home through the back fields as that would make it sound as if they weren't innocent. 'Um…'

Uncle William lifted the light to glare at the doctor again, and as he dropped it, it illuminated her stays, which were hanging from one of the buttons of his greatcoat.

'And why the blazes aren't those attached to your person?'

As all the onlookers gasped, her uncle's eyes widened like saucers.

'I can explain!'

But it was too late. Her uncle's fist was already flying towards Dr Able's chin. 'You filthy libertine!'

Chapter Eight

The lord of the manor placed a stiff brandy at his elbow and sighed. 'Whichever way you view it, it doesn't look good.'

Before Sam could be hung from the nearest tree by the angry mob, Rafe had bundled him and Rose into his carriage and driven them at speed to Hockley Hall while Ned did his best to calm everybody down. Which, of course, hadn't worked at all. Hence Ned was now at Hockley Hall too, braced for round two, and Sam was sitting with his head in his hands, his nose intermittently still bleeding.

'In the grand scheme of things, it doesn't really matter how innocently you came by Rose's stays. You still spent the entire night alone with her in your curricle while she wasn't wearing them. She's been comprised figuratively if not literally.'

'So now, despite being innocent of any wrongdoing whatsoever, I am expected to marry her? When I repeatedly cautioned her against coming with me for precisely that reason and she flatly refused to listen.'

Why had he allowed her to convince him?

Because he'd idiotically enjoyed her company and now he was paying the price!

'No,' said Ned with his typical gruffness. 'You could refuse to do the decent thing and she'll just have to suffer being ruined for life for, ironically, doing the decent thing by the Dewhursts. You'll have to move your entire practice elsewhere, of course, as no decent person within a fifty-mile radius will want anything to do with a libertine physician with no scruples nor morals. Especially if they have womenfolk to protect.'

'There was a bloody blizzard, for pity's sake, and I never laid a finger on her!' Although his fingers had itched to touch her when they had been all alone out there, snuggled together, and that scared the hell out him.

'Yet everyone saw her flat on her back, skirts around her waist, while you were fumbling on top of her.' Ned was matter-of-fact.

'Not to mention the stays swinging from your coat.' Rafe winced in sympathy. 'Or the silk stocking dangling from your fingers. People don't always believe what they see, Sam, but they always *see* what they believe, and apart from me and Ned here, they all *saw* a night of unbridled passion and seduction.'

'Never mind that any attempted seduction in all that snow would have likely left all my seduction equipment frostbitten and in real danger of dropping off!' Sam gestured to his groin, which had been annoyingly less dead than the rest of him of late because of her. Another reason why he had to get out of this. Miss Healy somehow called to a part of him that he had forgotten existed. 'It would make no sense for me to do the deed out in the elements in a field next to the village when I

could have done that more effectively and less dangerously within the curricle, hidden on the side of the lane!'

'Oh, they think you did that too,' said Rafe with another wince, 'which doubtless makes you an *insatiable*
libertine too, and is somehow worse.'

'Besides, everyone knows that when the passion is
mutual, the mood strikes and an opportunity presents itself...' Ned pulled a guilty face. 'Well, a bit of snow isn't
going to stop it, now, is it? It certainly wouldn't stop me.'

'Me neither,' said Rafe. 'And Whittleston-on-the-Water is blessed with a glut of similarly happily married
couples who will think much the same. After all, nothing gets the blood pumping and warms you up quicker
than a bit of—'

'Stop!' At this rate he'd be standing at the altar by
lunchtime! 'I do not want to marry Miss Healy.'

He couldn't marry. Not again.

Never again!

The very thought of the responsibility of another
wife—another life—was making him nauseous. He
was sweating like a pig, so dizzy he could barely lift
his head, and his shrivelled heart was racing so much
he genuinely feared an imminent heart attack! Or perhaps he was about to have a stroke? Certainly the loud,
ominous throb in his head wasn't normal.

'I can honestly think of nothing more abhorrent than
marrying Miss Healy.'

'That feeling is entirely mutual, I can assure you, Dr
Able! And rest assured I would not marry you if I had
a gun to my head and you were the last man on earth!
That is how abhorrent I find you!'

He managed to haul his spinning head up in time to

see her spin on her heel and march off while his two companions visibly cringed.

Sam glared at them, despite his roiling stomach. 'You might have mentioned she was behind me!'

'In our defence, we didn't realise she was until she spoke.' Rafe dropped his own head into his hands. 'Did you have to say abhorrent? Abhorrent is so... Good grief, poor Rose.'

'When I said abhorrent...'

How to explain why this was all so visceral and unthinkable to him without opening the Pandora's box of hideous emotions he kept locked away to stay sane? If he didn't, then he risked the volcano erupting again, and if it did, who knew how many months it would take to cap it and end the madness?

'It was more about the situation than the woman.'

A lie—because it had a great deal to do with the woman too. Because she was leaving he had let his ironclad guard down enough that he had allowed himself to like Miss Healy. Worse, he had allowed himself to enjoy their time together. He enjoyed their chats. He enjoyed her humour. Her irreverent take on things. He really enjoyed her mischievous side, perhaps because it felt so familiar and...appealing. He also, undeniably, found her physically appealing, so all in all she was a dangerous combination. Especially if she did not leave as he had been banking on her doing!

'I cannot marry again! Under any circumstances. It would...'

As the long-forgotten remnants of his dinner threatened to make an immediate reappearance, so too did Miss Healy's three friends. Sophie and Isobel looked ready to flail the skin from his bones, while Mrs Fitzherbert wielded her cane as if she fully intended to skewer his carcass on it once they were done with it.

'Excuse my language, Dr Able, but you are a cad!' Rafe's wife was quivering with indignation.

'He's worse than a cad.' Isobel's finger was wagging so fast it blurred. 'He's a scoundrel. An unconscionable, unfeeling, inhuman...'

'You are a callous bastard, Dr Able!' The tip of Mrs Fitzherbert's cane jabbed him hard in the ribs. 'Do you have no care at all for Rose's feelings?'

'When I said abhorrent...' Good Lord, but that really was an awful choice of word! 'I was referring to—'

'You didn't find her abhorrent when you waltzed with her last night!' The old lady's cane jabbed him again. 'Then you looked at her like a mouthwatering tart in the baker's window! What sort of despicable rogue makes a big show of fawning all over a woman, publicly beds her, and then refuses to do the right thing by her?'

'The sort who was only flirting with her to win the village pot, that's who!' As they all gaped in shock, he elaborated. 'It was Miss Healy's idea. We have an anonymised but substantial bet laid upon us *not* getting married and she thought we'd win more money if we were able to convince you all that we might.'

A devious plan that had been all hers and he now wished he'd had the good sense to have nothing to do with. He had allowed himself to be talked into her machinations, seduced by the thought of fun, and now he was expected to pay the ultimate price. For something that wasn't his fault! For something he had cautioned her against! Tried to stop her from doing! But she had blithely ignored his feelings, and now he was also supposed to ignore all his feelings to think of hers!

Like a wild animal caught in a trap, he was sorely tempted to gnaw his own foot off to escape it. 'Aside from waltzing with her, I've not laid a finger on her. We went to the Dewhursts to attend a horse, got caught in a blizzard, waited it out and then returned here as soon as we could. All facts which I am sure she will gladly corroborate if you ask her.'

'But you waited that blizzard out for several hours longer than you needed too, Sam, and it is those missing hours which are the crux of the matter.' Rafe was pacing now. 'What possessed you to take a last-minute detour into that field we found you on rather than brazenly driving into the village like two completely innocent people would have after such an ordeal?'

'I appreciate the field debacle looks bad, but...'

He was about to blame Miss Healy for that gross error of judgement too, but stopped himself because that wasn't fair. He'd been all for it at the time and, in her defence, if they hadn't got caught and she'd made it home through the back alley as she had intended, they wouldn't all be sitting here now.

'We knew people were likely to think the worst, and tried to mitigate against any gossip by splitting up so she could get home unseen.'

'Except you didn't split up and you were seen.' Ned punctuated the air with his finger. 'Seen doing things which would encourage anyone to think the worst.'

'I was helping her up after we both fell!'

'I'm sure you were.' Finally, Ned offered him one small concession. 'But it didn't look like that. In truth, I flung my lamp into the hedge because I was convinced we'd caught the pair of you at it. Her skirts were around her waist and you were between her legs.'

'For mere seconds.'

'For some exceptionally disappointing men seconds is all it needs.' Mrs Fitzherbert's disgusted shake of her head shocked them all, but she shrugged, unrepentant. 'It's not the length of time you were between Rose's legs that is the issue here, Doctor, it is the suspected length you slipped between them!'

'How many times do I have to tell you all the truth before you'll believe it?'

'I do believe it.' That also came from Mrs Fitzherbert. 'For truth is always stranger than fiction and your story matches Rose's completely.'

'Then, for the sake of reason and fairness, surely there has to be a compromise here?'

'The compromising has already been done!' Mrs Fitzherbert's cane thudded against the parquet. 'And what is done cannot be undone. It can only be atoned for!'

'Twenty people saw you atop her in the snow. Even if you can convince three-quarters of them that it was an accident, one quarter will always label you a shameless libertine and Rose a fallen woman.' Rafe stopped pacing and slumped into a chair with a huff. 'Mud sticks. The only way to unstick it and prevent your mutual ruination is to make yourselves respectable again by marrying. Like Ned did after he'd publicly ruined Isobel.'

'But Ned had actually ruined Isobel, in the literal as well as figurative sense, whereas I've not laid a finger on Miss Healy!'

'In view of last night's events, I think you should address her by her Christian name.' Sophie sat deflated beside her husband. 'You have been intimately entwined, after all. Albeit by accident.'

Despite his nausea, it was Sam's turn to pace. Waving his arms in the air in utter frustration to stop the walls from closing in. 'Surely the truth has to stand for something? Surely this village is capable of reason if the facts are laid out for all to scrutinise? Even a criminal is afforded a trial before a guilty verdict, and there is a glut of evidence that proves I am telling the truth. Or would they really rather watch two innocent people forced into the most miserable marriage imaginable purely for appearances' sake?'

'My lord…' Walpole, Hockley Hall's butler, made his presence known with a polite cough and a pained look towards Rafe. 'Mr Outhwaite is in the hallway and is demanding an immediate audience with Dr Able, while Miss Healy is donning her coat and demanding he take her home forthwith.'

'Then stop her and let him in.' Rafe didn't hesitate, despite Sam's groan. 'We need a definitive plan of action before anyone leaves.'

'Probably best to check he's not brought his pistols with him before you let him in, though,' added Ned unhelpfully. 'And maybe put a generous tot of brandy in Mr Outhwaite's tea to make him more amenable too, as the poor fellow isn't going to like what he is apparently going to hear from the doctor, who finds his niece abhorrent.'

It was said as a jibe, because Ned and Rose were good friends, and Sam took it as such.

'I am not going to be bullied down the aisle, Ned! Because I can assure that would be a massive mistake. One that would ruin her life!'

His was ruined anyway, and it had taken years to scrape enough of him together to function as well as he did. But he no longer functioned as he had. To keep going, to move forward, he'd had to close off all the vulnerable parts of himself. Banish all threat of the complicated and deep emotions which had ripped him apart. Husks didn't need to feel, they just needed to do until the doing was done. Sam was no longer capable of being a good husband. Or even of being a mediocre one. Wasn't capable of caring—not even slightly. He also wasn't willing to take on the responsibility of another person in his life. Couldn't! Wouldn't! His stomach churned again at the thought.

'In case it's escaped your notice, hers is already ruined, you selfish bastard!' Ned loomed, fists clenched. 'And she doesn't deserve that! If you are half the man we all hope you are, you'll step up and fix that!'

'She certainly doesn't deserve a future with me!' Sam's own fists clenched as his temper bubbled ominously. 'I wouldn't wish that living hell on anyone!'

Walpole reappeared again, looking anxious. 'I have put Miss Healy and her uncle in the morning room, where there is already shouting, my lord.'

Rafe stood to deal with that but Sam shook his head, forcing the anger back inside before years of pent-up fury and frustration escaped and consumed him again. 'This is my problem to sort. Mine and...hers.'

Although how they were going to sort it was a mystery when even the most reasonable residents of Whittleston clearly demanded a wedding. *Habeas corpus* certainly didn't seem to exist, because they had already been tried in the court of public opinion.

On leaden feet he left, and took a deep breath before knocking.

'Who is it?'

She sounded livid and he couldn't blame her.

'Me.'

He entered the room and closed the door behind him.

Mr Outhwaite was seated with a face like thunder. Miss Healy was standing, her hands clenched by her sides, her jaw set and her eyes red-rimmed. A sure sign that despite her defiant pride she had shed tears over their predicament—and perhaps his splendid misuse of the word abhorrent—but had wiped them away for this confrontation.

'My niece has informed me that a wedding is out of the question!'

'We did nothing wrong, sir.' Some deference seemed appropriate, despite the aggression in the older man's voice. 'Beyond attend to a distressed horse in the next village.'

'I beg to differ, sir!' Mr Outhwaite's eyes bulged. 'You were gone all night! Unchaperoned! Found intimately entwined!'

'And all those things have a perfectly reasonable explanation.'

There was no point shouting about it. Now that his anger was locked firmly back in its prison, where it belonged, Sam had enough of his wits left to know that oil needed to be poured on these troubled waters—fast— if they stood any chance of repairing the damage. Mr Outhwaite was one of the most important residents of the village, who needed to be convinced, so Sam sat.

'However, I do appreciate that we did, rather short-sightedly, behave recklessly when we went to attend the horse without a proper chaperon, and with hindsight we should have stayed with the Dewhursts until morning for exactly the same reason. As a result, we have now created an incorrect perception which we would beg you to help us change.'

He was being rather fast and lose with the 'we', but Rose didn't contradict him. Instead, without glancing his way she reiterated his point.

'I do not want to marry Dr Able, Uncle. Especially when all we are guilty of is being good Samaritans. As ill-considered as our unchaperoned trip to Little Ramstead was, it was done with the best intentions. I knew that I had the knowledge and skills necessary to birth the foal, so I argued with the doctor to take me there. I also threatened to go alone if he didn't, and then I panicked on the way home, insisting on leaving his conveyance in order to sneak around the back of the house. I was the one who fell and took him with me, and I convinced him to pretend to have some interest in me to win the bet, as I have just explained, so none of this is really his fault at all.'

'That's as maybe, but—'

She cut Mr Outhwaite off by kneeling before him and gripping his hand. 'Please try to help us get out of this! I cannot go from being jilted by one man who did not love me to being forced down the aisle with another who also doesn't. Have I not already suffered enough?'

'Well… I…'

'Dr Able and I are little more than acquaintances and totally incompatible. Expecting us to marry when my heart is still broken and he is still deeply in love with his dead wife is a recipe for disaster. Such a marriage is doomed from the outset to be miserable, and the only feelings that will flourish between us will be resentment and hatred. I know this is a dreadful scandal, Uncle, but scandals pass. This one will pass swiftly enough if we all hold our nerve and stick to the truth for the next few weeks, until Aunt Agatha is recovered enough for me to return to Suffolk.'

'And if the scandal follows you to Suffolk or, worse, beats you there? Then what, Rose?'

'Then we shall cross that bridge when we come to it. But I sincerely believe it will be little more than a ripple than a wave by the time it reaches there. Nothing more than a storm in a teacup.' Her forced smile was brave, if not reassuring. 'In less than three weeks I'll be gone anyway, so this will die a natural death here when I am out of sight and out of mind. We can all weather three weeks, surely?'

'Do you seriously think we can convince the entire village that what a significant number of reliable witnesses saw was completely innocent when it looked nothing of the sort?' Mr Outhwaite had gone from being angry to incredulous.

'Why not? Everyone under this roof believes us. You believe us. There's a newborn foal in the Dewhursts' stable that confirms at least half of the truth already. The constable will corroborate that we put a substantial bet on ourselves not marrying because he placed it for us, and it makes no sense that we would do that unless we meant it. Therefore, if Dr Able and I carry on as if nothing happened and we have nothing to be ashamed of beyond our lamentable disregard for society's rules, everyone will see that there is no attraction or romantic feelings between us. Isn't that right, Doctor?'

'It is certainly worth a try.'

While Sam was no longer capable of romantic feelings, it felt wrong to deny there was any attraction when he did feel that, regardless of how dead inside he wanted to be.

'It probably won't be easy to change minds—but it certainly isn't impossible. Especially if you lead the charge, sir.'

Like his wife, Mr Outhwaite was convinced he was widely respected. To be fair to him, as the proprietor of the *South Essex Gazette*, he was. He published a respectable paper filled with actual news and not salacious gossip, like the majority of the local rags did, and everybody hereabouts read it because of that.

'He's right, Uncle. If you appear wholly convinced of our innocence and swat away any criticism with good grace and humour, people might soon realise that Dr Able and I are as innocent as we claim.'

'We could try...' The older man wavered under his niece's pleading gaze, but his own gaze turned steely when it latched onto Sam's. 'But if it doesn't work I will expect you to step up, Doctor, and rectify this travesty in front of everyone in the church.'

'And I will.'

An affirmation that chilled Sam's blood and shocked Miss Healy enough that her mouth gaped.

'I am a man of honour and will not see your niece disgraced. However, I hope for her sake that this plan works as she deserves far better than I could ever give her.'

Before she left here, she also deserved to know why any union between them had to be a last resort. If the unthinkable happened and he had to walk her down the aisle, she had a right to know upfront what she was letting herself in for.

'I would be grateful, sir, if you would grant me a few minutes alone with your niece to apologise properly for what has happened?'

Chapter Nine

No sooner had her uncle left the room than the doctor's hazel eyes seemed to bore into her soul. There was a myriad of complex emotions swirling within them—all of them so sad she forgot to be angry at him for his cruel 'abhorrent' comment.

'I know this is all my fault, so if anyone should apologise for what has happened it is I.'

Rose was kicking herself at her own stupidity. Dr Able had tried to resist everything—from the bet to the fake flirting to the unchaperoned dash to save a horse— and she had trampled over his reluctance to do what she wanted instead.

'You did warn me on my own head be it, and you were right. You shouldn't have to pay for a mistake that was of all my making, so if the villagers here refuse to believe the truth I shall leave. Even if news of my stupidity reaches Suffolk, it will be less of a scandal there. It will all be hearsay, and such nonsense fades. Please do not worry that you will be stuck with me for all eternity, Dr Able, as I shall fix this.'

He didn't seem to find any reassurance in her words, and his expression became bleaker as he sat and gestured to her to do the same. Which she did, with a peculiar sense of unease.

'When I couldn't save Catherine I didn't want to live. There seemed no point in carrying on when she was my world. That same afternoon I drank two bottles of laudanum, lay down on the bed beside her and prayed that I wouldn't wake up.' He swallowed, his expression sad. 'Unfortunately, thanks to a much too good physician whom I have never forgiven, I did, and the army kept me under constant watch for two months to ensure that I couldn't find another way to join her in heaven. To thwart them, I applied for a transfer to the front, where I assured them that I would cope with my grief better if I could be kept busy. I was sent to follow Wellington, and immediately, rather than use them exclusively in the field hospital, I took my skills onto the battlefield. Preferring to treat the injured in the midst of the fray ostensibly to save more lives, but in reality simply to bring an end to mine.'

It was said so matter-of-factly, she realised he still regretted his end hadn't come.

'Each time I rushed in I prayed for a stray bullet or bayonet to find me and did nothing to save myself from any that came close. The sweet release of potential annihilation became the thing that kept me going, the only balm to the anger and pain which consumed me, and perversely I looked forward to every battle hoping that it would be my last. Sadly, fate continued to be cruel and kept me safe. For all my determined recklessness, I do not think that I even incurred a single scratch.'

His broad shoulders slumped, as if he still considered that a travesty, and Rose's heart bled for him.

She bit her tongue rather than tell him all the trite

things people said about grief. About time healing all wounds and life going on, or that he clearly hadn't been taken because fate knew he made a difference in the world and clearly had other, hopefully less cruel plans for him. Or even to take some comfort that his beloved Catherine had gone to a better place. Better it allegedly might be, but she was sure that if Catherine had loved Dr Able as much as he clearly loved her, then she would consider no place better than being by his side. How wonderful and empowering it must be to be so adored...

Sadly, it was not something to which she could relate as, while she had loved with her whole heart, and deeply, she understood now that it had not been reciprocated.

Rose also knew that while time probably—eventually —did heal most things, there were some things a person just couldn't get over in mere months or years. Like watching the centre of your universe die and not being able to do a thing to stop it. There was no denying that his wounds were so deep they made hers seem trifling. It was almost inconceivable to contemplate what he'd had to suffer.

Rather than resort to meaningless platitudes, she reached across to stroke his hand, but he was so lost in his own misery he did not appear to notice.

'When Waterloo failed to reward me with my last chance to meet my maker, I briefly turned to drink to numb my pain—except it didn't. Therefore I had to do something more drastic. I had to kill that part of me that feels. At least the part that feels anything beyond the superficial. Being dead inside is the only way for me to remain sane and...to continue.'

He twisted his palm up to hold her hand, sending

a jolt of awareness through her arm the moment their fingertips touched, then frowned down at it as if he had felt it too.

Although how could he if he were dead inside?

Perhaps the frown, like the devastation in his gaze, was merely further confirmation of his state of being. Perhaps he felt nothing, exactly as he claimed. And that felt like the saddest thing she had ever heard.

His attempt at a smile was more a tortured grimace, and even that seemed to take too much effort. It was then she realised that he was affording her a great privilege. He was allowing her to witness the real him, behind the façade of capable, no-nonsense, all-business doctor. It wasn't only his shoulders that had slumped…it was his entire being. The light in his eyes had dimmed. Deep lines of grief and guilt were etched upon his handsome face. Utter despondency and hopelessness manifested in physical form. So more intense and real than hers it made her ashamed for ever indulging in a moment of self-pity at the piffling inconvenience of being jilted.

She squeezed his hand tight, to give him some of her strength, because he appeared to need it in this tragic moment so much more than she did. 'There are many of us who are eternally grateful that you decided to continue. This village would be lost without you.'

'And I would be lost without this village. It gives me purpose—and that is all I have left nowadays.' His sigh was long and laboured. 'That is why I said that I can honestly think of nothing more abhorrent than marrying you. Because I am gratefully dead inside, Rose, and am not prepared to risk a resurrection under any circumstances. Catherine's death shattered me and scattered me into a million bloody pieces. I spent years in the most wretched, raging purgatory imaginable, trying to piece together enough of that mess to continue, and I do not have it in me to face anything like that again. You do not deserve being shackled to a man who cannot—nay, *will* not—care for you in any way beyond the superficial. I have no heart left to give you and no desire to imagine any sort of future, let alone one involving another. I live from day to day. Exist in the here and now. I left the best of me, the entire essence of me, in a sickroom in Lisbon, and all that is left now is genuinely what you see. A dry husk with a glut of medical skills that might save some and not save others, who uses them to pass the time and thus give himself some blessed relief from remembering.'

He stared into nothing for several, long seconds, then seemed to become self-conscious.

'Anyway… I wanted you to know why I would rather avoid ruining your life too. I am not, by nature, a cruel man, but fear I would be cruel with my determined indifference. There is nothing left inside me for more.'

He released her hand and moved to get up, but she touched his knee to stay him.

'Why couldn't you save her?'

It was a direct and intensely personal question, but one Rose needed to know the answer to. She suspected that he did too. It was obvious he was riddled with guilt and wanted to blame himself for her death. Maybe he deserved to? In his panic to heal her, maybe he had missed something? But she could not imagine that. He was too good at what he did not to have exhausted every possible avenue back in that sickroom in Lisbon, and his love was obviously so deep he would have moved heaven and earth to do so.

His nose wrinkled, and for a moment she thought he would seal up tighter than a drum. But he didn't. Instead, he took a deep, centring breath.

'Typhus is a contrary beast. It spreads with selective impunity and infects some more mildly than it does others. One hundred and fifty people were its victims back in Lisbon that summer. It did its worst, in varying degrees of severity, and spared a hundred and two. My darling wife was the final one of the forty-eight who perished. They kept telling me that there was no rhyme or reason to it and that we'd done all that we could— but how could it spare lesser individuals? Drunkards and layabouts lived to tell the tale and yet it took my Catherine. My effervescent and irrepressible girl. Who never did anything except spread sunshine and laughter and was never ill a day in her life before.'

His voice caught and that forced a huge change in him, because he surged to his feet. Stiff and jerky, as if every muscle and sinew was pulled taut.

Then he visibly went to war with himself, and Rose watched him fight all that raw emotion back inside. Within moments he was the no-nonsense physician again, completely in control.

'I trust that all I have shared with you will remain confidential, as I would prefer not to be the subject of gossip. At least more gossip than I fear we are both already about to be subjected to.'

'Of course.' She was touched and humbled that he had confided in her. 'Your past, like mine, is nobody else's business. But if you ever need to…talk… Sam…' They were so beyond mere acquaintances now that any formality seemed pathetic. 'Please know that you have a friend in me.'

He nodded, still awkward. 'Let us pray, for your sake, that your plan works, as I wouldn't wish what's left of me on anyone.'

Rose screwed up the note and tried not to feel upset by it. That was hard when it was the third such missive she had received in the last three days. Except this one had been poked into the thin gap under the front door by Mrs Spears, the Reverend's wife. A woman who was supposed to believe in the concept of forgiveness and of not casting the first stone! While that in itself was galling enough, and while the Reverend's wife had been the one to write it, it had actually come from the entire Friday Sewing Circle, who thought it best that she stayed away until the dust had settled.

Mrs Spears had penned the note in her small, neat handwriting.

> *Some of the ladies are worried about the message it sends to their own single daughters, to readily condone your regrettable lapse in judgement and decorum so soon without any apparent censure at all.*

As three-quarters of the sewing circle had made a point of crossing the road rather than speak to her since her 'regrettable lapse', she wasn't surprised her invitation had been rescinded, but it still stung.

Less than a week ago, and after six months of religiously attending the circle every single Friday since she had arrived in the village, she had counted most of those women as more than acquaintances. As such, she would have expected them to be on her side, or at the very least, as women, to have some sympathy for her unfortunate situation.

But no. She had been caught with a man between her legs, so obviously she was a harlot, just as it was somehow her fault that her former fiancé had replaced her. Women always held other women to a ridiculously higher standard than they did men. Probably because their reputations were so much more tenuous and easily destroyed. Women were also more spiteful than men, even if the initial censure had come from a man, which was why, every time one of those suddenly pious ladies crossed the road or cancelled her invitation to tea, they made an unsubtle point of muttering their abject disapproval to whoever they happened to pass. As if being a harlot were contagious, and any contact with her might label them fallen women too.

There were still those who were polite, but as those also scurried quickly by without meeting her eye they hardly counted as allies. Which left her with just Sophie, Isobel and Mrs Fitzherbert, who religiously took it in turns to call upon her and insisted on accompanying her into the square because they believed that her failure to hide would prove that she had nothing to hide.

Rose didn't hold out much hope that they were right, and feared that she would end up leaving here at Christmas as much a social pariah then as she was now.

She couldn't help wondering if Sam was suffering the same.

Or wondering about him in general and constantly since their *'incident'*.

People flung about the term 'a broken man', but it

was an apt description of him. Dr Samuel Able was a broken man, and she hated it that he seemed content to remain one. As if all his guilt and pain was his penance and that all he deserved to look forward to for the rest of his life was to work his fingers to the bone to heal the pain of others.

And work his fingers to the bone he did!

They might have been avoiding one another all week, while the dust apparently settled, but she had taken a keener interest in his punishing schedule now that she had had a window into his soul. It was easy to keep track of his comings and goings when his practice was a mere hundred yards across the square. Perfect for peeking at through the fussy lace curtains of her bed-chamber window. Sam certainly kept irregular hours. Even if he wasn't roused in the middle of the night for an emergency, he still visited his patients until late. Once his morning surgery finished at noon, he was off. Returning only to replenish his supplies once or twice over the course of the afternoon. He usually came home for an hour around six, where she presumed he ate what he needed to keep going, and then he was off again. As his practice covered not only Whittleston-on-the-Water but three of the much smaller outlying villages too, he did many miles in his curricle every day.

The mantel clock chimed noon and, without thinking, Rose edged towards the parlour window. Clearly his morning surgery had ended on time, because she didn't have to linger for more than a few minutes before he emerged from his door, bound for who knew where. Looking all handsome and capable on the outside but so achingly vulnerable on the inside that it—

'Can I have a word, Rose?'

She had been so engrossed in her contemplation of the troubled doctor she hadn't heard anyone approach, and jumped with a guilty squeak. 'Uncle William! Shouldn't you be at the newspaper?'

A creature of habit, he usually returned for luncheon every day at one, so it was unusual that he was here an hour early.

'I'm afraid...' his expression was grave '...our worst fears to have come to pass.' He produced a folded newspaper. 'This arrived on the morning post. It is from Suffolk. I can only assume that news of your...um... misfortune has travelled back via the same method and your former fiancé's influential father has twisted it ruthlessly to his duplicitous son's advantage.'

The second she opened the paper her heart sank.

The *Suffolk Sentinel* was a tawdry rag that thrived on local gossip and frequently printed scurrilous stories for the titillation of the entire county. They had gone to town when the news of her jilting had reached their ears, painting her—in the guise of 'the unfortunate Miss H'—as a nice but dim woman who hadn't had the good sense to realise what everyone else already knew until her man and his lover had fled for Gretna. While there had undoubtedly been more than a grain of truth in that depiction, because only she had been blindsided by that betrayal, they had printed all manner of falsehoods since. Falsehoods which had obviously then been enshrined as fact. Especially once her former fiancé's father, who leased the *Sentinel* their building, applied some pressure on them.

The newspaper had led the charge to *'gently'* assassinate her character. In the immediate aftermath of the jilting they had printed several hurtful pieces to try to sway public opinion her former fiancé's way. One story had claimed he'd got cold feet because he had suspected that she was a fortune-hunter and actually had no real regard for him. Another that there was something 'not quite right' about her, although it was unsurprisingly vague about what that was. Whatever it was, her former fiancé was apparently 'too much of a gentleman' to embarrass her by voicing it—which was laughable when he hadn't so much embarrassed her as utterly humiliated her without saying a word! But this unspoken flaw was concerning enough that it had sent her beau running for the hills. And who could blame a man with such glittering prospects for not wanting to be saddled with that? The most hurtful story had implied that she was barren and had been concealing that from him. That one had come out to coincide with the announcement that the cheating wretch and his two-faced spouse were expecting their first child. It had been too coincidental not to have been intentional, and too cruel not to have had a profound effect on her, when he knew that she had been eager to become a mother.

Like a trickle of water over rock, each of those stories had gradually begun to wear away at their readers, and she had become more and more pitiable in the eyes of her neighbours and that had been truly soul-destroying. Just like the members of the sewing circle, acquaintances began to talk to her differently—or not talk to her at all—and she had frequently been the object of all those side-whispered conversations that were had when people suspected more was going on than met the eye.

Therefore, in many ways, the *Suffolk Sentinel* was as

much to blame for Rose's escape to Whittleston as the prospect of the impending birth had been.

She had hoped they would have forgotten 'the unfortunate Miss H' after six and half months of absence, but three pages in it became clear that she was wrong. The news of her ruination, even seventy miles away, was just too good not to use to over-embellish and further the ludicrous lies that had justified her former fiancé's betrayal.

The sleepy Essex village of Whittleston-on-the-Water is abuzz with scandal, thanks to a certain Suffolk native who is no stranger to these pages. After scaring off one eminent and monied gentleman almost a year to the day, the jilted Miss was obviously keen to secure herself another potential benefactor as soon as possible. When all conventional means failed to attract one, we now hear that, like Delilah did Samson, this forsaken spinster used her charms to lure a respected physician into her lacklustre web of seduction.

The full details of that seduction are too scandalous for us to print here, however, we have it on the highest authority that she spent a whole evening flirting with her latest target at a dance and then managed to entice the gentleman away for the entire night afterwards!

But that is not all the desperate Suffolk resident did to secure a betrothal, for she shamelessly importuned him again and on purpose in a public place the following dawn, ensuring they were caught in the midst of a tryst!

However, despite her determined efforts, her

wanton machinations have rather backfired as
the gentleman concerned, while happy to sample
her wares as any man served them on a platter
would, has flatly refused to be honourable about
it. And why should he when she went out of her
way to entrap him? He has, rightly, called foul
and has declared that he will not wed the pitiable
wench for all the tea in China, no matter what the
consequences!

We await, with bated breath, her family's reac-
tion. Will there be pistols at dawn in Whittleston-
on-the-Water followed by a reluctant groom at the
altar? Or, as we suspect, will the unfortunate and
unweddable Miss H remain discarded and ring-
less for the second time in just twelve months?

'Oh, good grief!' Her head spinning and with bile
rising in her throat, Rose groped for a chair. 'My mother
and father will have read this!'

A quick glance at the newspaper's date confirmed
they would have seen it two days ago—before her own
letter of explanation had arrived in case word of her in-
discretion made its way down the Colchester Turnpike.
A letter she had foolishly dithered over writing because
it had been difficult to explain to them how she and
Sam had had their infamous dawn accident while still
ensuring the quite damning series of events sounded
completely innocent.

'I fear they have.'

'But how did all that rot reach Suffolk so fast?'

Her uncle laid a heavy hand on her shoulder. 'Nothing travels faster than bad news, and the post travels
through here daily. All it takes is one careless word—'

'Whoever gave them this awful story said more than one careless word! They eviscerated me!'

Furious at that faceless, spiteful gossip, she abandoned her chair to pace. 'If it wasn't bad enough that I am seen as a fallen woman here, I am now Delilah in Suffolk!' And as she was not currently in Suffolk, to accuse the *Sentinel* of the most outrageous libel, the story would fester and grow like a malignant tumour.

'What am I going to do?'

'I think, in the first instance, we need to urgently summon your parents, and in the second...' Uncle William had the good grace to blanch before he said it. 'We need, with all haste, to revisit the prospect of you and Dr Able tying the knot.'

Chapter Ten

'You are going to have to take my word for it that my daughter's cough is better, sir, as I cannot, in all good conscience, have a scoundrel like *you* examine her ever again!'

With that, the farmer's wife slammed the door in Sam's face.

It was undoubtedly the most insulting rejection he'd had in the last week, but it wasn't the only one. Sadly, he had been refused admittance to see at least twenty similarly young female patients since he had apparently ruined Rose, and his usually packed morning surgery had been whittled down to just two patients this morning. And both of them had come more in search of gossip than healing.

Thanks to one ill-considered midnight quest to save a foal, he had become *persona non grata*. More worryingly, instead of things getting better as time went on and they brazened it out, they were getting worse. Everywhere he went he felt the accusing eyes of every woman and every father, who all thought he should do the right thing and were thoroughly disgusted that he hadn't.

Meanwhile, the troublesome winter cough that was doing the rounds was clearly getting worse, because every other person who passed him by with downcast eyes was hacking into a handkerchief! It beggared belief that rather than see him they would prefer to suffer illness and, for some, risk it perilously corrupting their lungs simply because he hadn't done 'the done thing' and married the woman he had ruined despite not ruining her at all!

Whereas Ned, who still snarled at him whenever they collided, had flagrantly ruined Isobel mere months ago but was treated like a hero for saving her from her hideous father and any mention of her ruination was forbidden! All forgiven because right was on their side. Yet right was on his and Rose's side too, because they had saved two horses and a struggling farmer. But nobody mentioned that while they criticised.

The double standard was staggering. But also worrying. He sincerely hoped that Rose was right and this would all die down once she left. He had put down roots in Whittleston-on-the-Water and did not want to sell his practice and start from scratch again elsewhere. Not when it had taken three years to build it into enough that it kept him occupied from dawn to dusk.

Or at least it had until last week.

Dusk was a long way off and, seeing the door slam on this, the last of the calls he could make, he was at an uncharacteristic loose end.

He consulted his pocket watch and groaned before hauling himself back into his curricle. It was barely three in the afternoon and at least another seven empty hours now loomed ahead of him before bedtime. That was more than he was prepared to endure, because he knew that idle hands were the devil's workshop—or in his case idle minds.

He supposed he could always go and check on Mrs Outhwaite...

Under the circumstances that would be an unconventional move while all the gossip was still so rife, but it might go some way towards convincing people that as far as he and his innocence was concerned it was business as usual. One of his patients had had a nasty fall and he would be doing his duty as her physician to see to her ongoing care. It wasn't as if he wouldn't have visited her by now anyway, if the incident in the field hadn't happened, so he should brazenly head there now with his head held high. So high he'd even force a cheery hello on every villager he passed and slow his curricle to wait for them to say hello back.

No! That was a very bad idea! Primarily because all the gossips would start speculating on whether or not he had finally agreed to do the right thing and secondly, more worryingly, he knew, deep down, that it wasn't actually Mrs Outhwaite he wanted to check on. It was Rose. He had, much to his consternation, worried about her all week. Far more than he was comfortable with.

Ergo it was best left.

But Mr Outhwaite had done a very good job of putting the whole truth out there for scrutiny. He had put the entire story on the second page of his weekly paper and sent it out two days ago as news under the headline *Foal and Mare saved from Certain Death during Whittleston's Worst Blizzard.*

Everything from the fake flirting to the reason why her stays had been swinging from the buttons of his greatcoat had been peppered through the narrative.

Alongside were robust quotes from both the Dewhursts and the constable who had placed the bet for Sam, which corroborated their story. The piece had been finished with a comment from the oldest living resident of the village—Mrs Fitzherbert—who claimed the snowstorm had been worse than the Great Blizzard of 1736, in which three villagers had frozen to death. She was, she concluded, supremely grateful that, unlike then, nobody had perished. Not even the Dewhursts' foal.

All Sam had to do now was wait for those truths to permeate the thick skulls of the stubborn and judgemental locals and that would be that. No more empty surgeries and no more slammed doors in his face. For his own sake, Sam gave himself a decisive nod as the spire of St Hildreth's loomed. Rose was right. They had done nothing to be ashamed of and all they needed to do was hold their nerve.

In which case, why shouldn't he just check on Mrs Outhwaite now and be done with it? Show all those gossips that he felt no compunction to give Rose a wide berth because they had done nothing to be ashamed of? Checking on her was hardly crossing the line between caring and *caring*. Together they had been accused of a crime neither had committed and were both suffering as a result. Common decency demanded that he show his face to see if things were bearable for her, and what better way to do that than visiting her convalescing aunt? Two birds with one stone and one less troublesome thing to have to worry about. He would not be cowed or bullied by a bunch of contrary villagers with the worst double standards he had ever seen!

That decision made, he nudged his horse to a trot and went at some lick through the melted snow, enjoying the sunshine until it was time to turn into the village square. Like the innocent man he was, he slowed and tipped his hat to the gaggle of ladies gossiping at the corner.

'Good afternoon, all. How are we on this fine day?'

The reactions were every bit as awkward as he had expected, with several of the group acknowledging him with nothing but pursed lips. The rest still refused to look at him.

'Isn't it lovely, after so many weeks of gloom, to finally see the sun again?' He was going to squeeze some blood out of this stone if it killed him. 'It does wonders for the mood.'

To prove that, he smiled at them. It felt unfamiliar, because he had resurrected one of his old smiles. The sort he had deployed back when he'd used to be charming and fun and the sort, he had often been told, which always had a particularly pleasing effect on the opposite sex.

Except this time it was met with outraged eyes and turned heads. As if suddenly commenting upon the weather was one of the cardinal sins.

Only Mrs Spears, the Reverend's wife, dared to look at him and it was a look that could have curdled milk. 'Have you no heart at all, sir?'

He didn't, but that was by the by. He still did not appreciate her tone. 'How does being buoyed by the better weather make me heartless, madam?'

'Do not waste your breath on him.' Mrs Denby, the fishmonger's wife, dragged her friend away by the arm. 'If he has the gall to behave indifferently after today's developments, he is more of a cad than we suspected and clearly content to remain so.'

With that, the entire gaggle moved away as one, all

effectively giving him the cut directly in the middle of the street.

Sam sat on his perch for several moments affronted, sorely tempted to shout after them and call them all two-faced idiots, when a fragment of that insult permeated his outrage.

Today's developments?

What the blazes had happened between now and noon to suddenly make his perceived crimes worse?

With a sense of foreboding, he glanced towards the Outhwaites' house. There was a smart carriage outside it which he did not recognise, but something told him it had brought trouble.

He hastily parked his own conveyance behind it. Then, with all the traders and pedestrians in the square staring at him, he grabbed his medical bag in the vain hope that it might convince them that this was an official physician's visit before he rapped on the door.

A wide-eyed young maid immediately ushered him into the parlour, where a sombre crowd was gathered. Mrs Outhwaite was sitting in the sturdiest chair by the fire. Her husband was balanced on the arm next to her and there were two complete strangers he had never seen before. He presumed they were husband and wife, as they were both of similar middling years. The woman was on the sofa, cradling a teacup, looking as though the world had just ended. The man stood to attention at the mantel. The only one of the five of those present who did not appear relieved to see him was Rose.

'What's happened?'

Because something had. By the looks of her pale, stunned face, it was very bad indeed.

'Is this him?' The older gentleman with Rose's green eyes jabbed a finger in Sam's direction.

'Yes, Papa.'

Her voice was small and, as that was so unlike her it unsettled Sam more than anything else.

'This is Dr Samuel Able. Sam, this is my father, Mr Bernard Healy.' The older man offered him a curt nod rather than a hearty handshake, which boded well. 'And my mother, Mrs Anne Healy.'

'Mr Healy... Mrs Healy.' As solemnity seemed to be the order of the day, he kept his own expression suitably taut as he inclined his head to both. Then, because there was such a fraught atmosphere in the room, he spoke directly to Rose. 'What on earth has happened?'

'This.'

She passed him a crumpled newspaper and sighed as he quickly scanned it. When Sam's jaw hung slack in outraged panic, she used sarcasm to minimise it all, as was her way.

'It arrived on my uncle's desk with the morning post. Fearing Armageddon, Uncle William thought it prudent to urgently summon my parents, although that turned out to be quite unnecessary as my parents had already summoned themselves. And now we are all here, and in view of this latest scurrilous nonsense, while I would much prefer we all have a nice tea party, I suppose we must discuss our options instead.'

'There is only one option, daughter!' Mr Healy's head looked ready to explode. 'The pair of you must announce your immediate engagement!'

'Why?' Anger swirled hot in her lovely eyes. 'Because the *Suffolk Sentinel* has printed more lies about me? Let's face it—it isn't the first time and I sincerely doubt that it will be the last. I shudder to think what they'll print if Dr Able and I cave under their pressure and marry.' She swept her arm in an arc in the air. *'The unfortunate and unweddable Miss H has finally entrapped a more unfortunate man into marriage. He doesn't love her, of course, because frankly who would? But at least the pitiable halfwit now has a ring on her finger, so nothing else really matters. Most especially what she wants!'*

'Your father only wants our good family name protected.' That tone deaf comment came from Mrs Outhwaite. 'It is the right thing to do, Rose.'

'For who? You?' Rose pointed at her aunt. 'Or you? Or you?' Her finger jabbed at her father, then her mother. 'Because, if I might be selfish for a moment, it is certainly not what is best for me!'

Mr Healy's eyes bulged. 'Something you should have thought of before you spent the night unchaperoned with a man!'

'Nothing happened!' Rose shot out of her chair like a firework, obviously at her wits' end with her father.

'She's right, sir.' As tempers were clearly seriously frayed, Sam tried to pour oil on troubled waters. Hoping some calm diplomacy would show them a way forward. 'Nothing happened. Beyond Rose saving a valued working animal's life because I did not know how to.'

As all he knew about this man was that he was a farmer, he decided to appeal to his farmer's sensibilities.

A decision which immediately proved to be the wrong one.

'I beg to differ, *sir.*' Mr Healy's bulging eyes fixed on him. 'The moment you allowed my headstrong daughter to leave the village with you at midnight, you had already compromised her good reputation! At the very least, knowing my stubborn daughter's tendency to ride roughshod over others when she thinks she knows best, you should have insisted her uncle or a maid or some other respectable adult accompany you both. But you didn't, and that is on you!'

The finger of accusation pointed, unflinching, and Sam supposed the man made a valid point.

'Thanks to your initial lack of forethought, my daughter is not only ruined here in Essex, she is now thoroughly ruined in Suffolk too! How are we supposed to take her home unless she is made an honest woman?'

'Then this *dishonest* and *disgraced* woman shall move to Cheshire or Gloucestershire or Argyllshire! She will become a governess or join a troupe of travelling players.' Rose was ranting now, unhelpfully. 'And she will never darken Suffolk's judgemental door again.'

'Don't be ridiculous, Rose!'

'Which part do you find the most ridiculous, Papa? That I would consider moving or that I might actually be able to earn my own living?'

'And how, pray tell, daughter, do you hope to earn your living in a blasted troupe of travelling players!'

'In case it has escaped your notice, I have passed the age of majority, Papa, and can technically do as I please! And being forced down the aisle does not please me in the slightest! I would sooner walk a fiery tightrope while juggling plates!'

'You cannot juggle! In case it has escaped *your* notice, you can barely even catch!'

As they parried, and while Mrs Healy put her head in her hands and Sam felt the walls close in around him afresh, it occurred to him that Mr Healy and his daughter had identical tempers. An odd thought when your entire world was about to implode in the worst possible way—perhaps even a hysterical thought—but it was the only one he currently had.

Rose had only ever talked about her father fondly up until now, and by the looks of her mother, who had clearly witnessed many a similar altercation between her two equally headstrong kin, there was a chance that father and daughter were two peas in a pod. In which case, it boded well that, if nothing else, he would like his new father-in-law a great deal if he had no choice but to marry his daughter—once the man was done with the urge to wring his neck, of course.

'I'd learn to juggle swords if it saved Sam from having to pay for my stupid mistake!'

And there it was. The line that shouldn't be crossed. He couldn't and wouldn't allow her to wilfully ruin her own life simply to save his. Especially when his wasn't worth saving.

'Rose…' He exhaled slowly to quieten some of the roar of his blood in his ears. 'Could I have a private word?'

'If you've got something to say, young man, you'll say it out here—not skulk off and feed my daughter more excuses like a coward!'

Before Mr Healy boxed his ears with his meaty farmer's hands, Sam raised his own hands in surrender. 'Actually, sir, I want to propose, and fear that I will need several minutes of privacy to convince your daughter to accept.'

'Oh,' said Mr Healy, the wind knocked out of his sails.

'No!' exclaimed Rose, looking ready to punch Sam in his stead. 'This isn't right or fair!'

'Hear me out.'

He caught her by the elbow and, without breaking his stride, in case she dug in her stubborn heels, whisked her down the hall to the Outhwaites' small but typically ostentatious dining room.

'None of this is right or fair. I think we can both agree on that. However, it was a *mutual* stupid mistake that led us to this point, and we will pay for it together.'

As he closed the door she folded her arms. 'I do not wish to be trapped in a loveless marriage.'

'Neither do I. But in the short term I fear that we must both accept that that is what needs to happen.'

'And in the long term? Or are you about to propose that we might grow to love one another—given time?'

She was being direct, as usual and she was right to do so because there was no point in lying.

'I gave all my love to Catherine. I am incapable of doing that again.'

'I thought you were supposed to be convincing me to accept you, not reinforcing all my reasons for turning you down?'

'I might not be able to give you my love, but I can save you from a life of fiery tightrope plate-juggling.' He shrugged, resigned and oddly calm in view of what was about to happen. 'In giving you my name, I will restore your respectability and mine, and in a few months, when this scandal has run its course, I can give you your freedom.'

Sam was making this up as he went along. Trying to find a reasonably palatable compromise in this wholly unpalatable situation which suited them both.

'What? By granting me a divorce?'

'If that is what you want.'

'Thereby creating yet another enormous scandal? Because that will not delight the *Suffolk Sentinel* at all, will it?' She painted another scurrilous headline in the ether with her palm, making him wonder exactly what this newspaper had said about her in the past to make her so concerned about them. '*Jilted Delilah Discarded Again Via an Actual Act of Parliament Because She is So Unappealing.*' Her arms began to wave. 'And on what grounds, Sam? My barrenness? My supposed unfaithfulness? Or perhaps my declining mental state? Because we both know that since Henry VIII brought in divorce it is always the woman who is to bl—'

He placed his finger over her lips to silence her and regretted it instantly, because they were every bit as warm and soft as they looked.

'Couples separate all the time, Rose, and do not have to divorce. We wouldn't have to unless you wanted to, and I would only envisage you wanting to because you'd found someone worthier to marry than the dried-up, dead inside husk that has been foisted upon you. Nobody will judge you for leaving me once they see how unhappy being stuck with me has made you. You already know that I am doomed to be a distant and unaffectionate husband, so I would not correct you when you told everyone that. Tell everyone in Suffolk that I beat you, if you think it would help soften the blow. I will not deny it. Even though I obviously never would. And if you do not have any desire to return to Suffolk, I am not without means. Every penny I inherited from the sale of my father's house is still untouched in the bank, along with a tidy sum left to me by my grandfather.'

All the money he had squirrelled away, along with most of his army salary, to buy Catherine their dream house to raise a family in. It was doomed now to sit there for ever, so it might as well make someone happy.

'I will buy you a cottage in Cheshire or Gloucestershire or Argyllshire, if that pleases you more, and keep you comfortably for as long as you need me to provide for you. This doesn't have to be hard, Rose. If we stick together for a few months, my home is big enough for us to easily avoid one another within it and then you would be free by spring.'

Her outraged expression softened into one of confusion. 'You propose that I marry you, then immediately leave you?'

'I do.' And as that parody of a wedding vow felt fitting, he found himself chuckling at the unintentional irony of it. 'Let us do what needs to be done for only as long as it needs to be done, and then part exactly as we are now. Not quite friends, but not quite acquaintances either.'

She sank onto a dining chair. 'I'm not sure what to say.'

'Say yes, Rose. It's not as if either of us really has any other option at this stage.'

Chapter Eleven

Regardless of the noticeable subduedness of the bride and groom, the packed congregation of St Hildreth's were in a celebratory mood. Not only were they all attending a wedding, they were attending a Christmas Eve wedding, and those were rare and special beasts indeed. Whittleston had certainly not seen one in many years.

The irony of the atrocious timing was, however, not lost on Rose. It had been on this day precisely one year ago that she was first supposed to be a bride, and she had anticipated that day with such optimistic excitement.

Conversely, and for obvious reasons, she had dreaded walking up the aisle today. Her voice trembled as she made vows she did not mean, and beside her, her press-ganged groom did the same. Then they were spirited out onto a carpet of fresh snow and showered in dried rose petals, before she and Sam ate an equally subdued wedding breakfast at Hockley Hall with her family and their few closest friends.

But thanks to it being Christmas Eve the day improved, and she was swept up in the yuletide merry-making irrespective of her melancholy mood.

As it was it was Sophie's first Christmas as the mistress of Hockley Hall, and because all the village remembered the previous lord of the manor as an unapproachable, tight old skinflint, she and Rafe had thrown open their doors at sunset to welcome everyone from the village in for a feast. Therefore it was easy for Rose and Sam to avoid one another while they were coerced into party games and dances, and to her great surprise, after the interminable day, the evening passed swiftly.

As the festivities wound down in time for Midnight Mass she was dancing a jig with Archie while her new husband—how peculiar it was to call a man husband!— was reviving the baker's daughter. The poor girl had fainted because she had tied her stays too tight, to try and catch the eye of the innkeeper's son. A cocky lad, far too handsome for his good, who was blissfully unaware that the unconscious even girl existed as he flirted shamelessly with someone else.

'Could I borrow you for a minute?' Her mother touched her arm, her expression furtive and her body twitchy.

'Of course, Mama.' As soon as she had disentangled herself from Archie and caught up with her scurrying mother, she whispered, 'Are you all right?'

'Of course, dear.' That was said with little conviction. 'I simply wanted us to have a little chat before you go home with your husband for the first time.'

Her mother's cheeks blushed crimson and that sent alarm bells ringing, as it rather than suggested that the 'little chat' was doomed instead to be *the* chat. The one her mother had been so reluctant to have last year in the lead-up to her first wedding.

She found an empty room well away from the party

and gestured Rose inside with such pained awkwardness that she knew this was clearly going to be every bit the cringing experience they both feared.

'As this is your wedding night…' Her mama cleared her throat and tried to appear serene and matter-of-fact—and failed, because her entire head and neck were beetroot-red. 'You need to be prepared for what is to come.'

Oh, good heavens above, this was awful! For two reasons. The first being her mother's inability to meet her eye, and the second Rose's uncertainty that she was even going to have a wedding night.

It had not been discussed in any way, shape or form, which she supposed spoke volumes, when in the last three weeks, since the first of the banns had been read, on the few occasions when they had conversed, she and Sam had discussed a great many things about their marriage. Pretty much everything, in fact, had been laid out in stark black and white, like a map.

By mutual agreement, she knew already that it would technically end on the first of April. April Fools' Day—an irony that was not lost on either of them, but a date which made sense. That would give them three excruciating months to be seen to give the marriage a go before Rose went to Suffolk to visit her parents for Easter.

She would extend her stay into May, and then some time around Whitsun would write him a letter informing him that she had decided to stay for the entire summer too. By autumn, when she failed to return, gossip would be rife, and everyone in Whittleston would realise that she had left him for good. Whether or not she wanted to remain in Suffolk or find a new home elsewhere was, to Sam's mind, a decision for her. But, despite all her protestations to the contrary, about her father being a wealthy man so Sam did not need to feel obligated to support her, he'd refused to have that. He would see her right—on that he was adamant—and she would leave the marriage with enough to purchase a new home and a generous annual allowance to support her.

While she was grateful for his generosity, Rose still had to find a way to properly refuse it. She was to blame for their predicament, and she certainly did not expect him to pay any more for it! However, as they had reached an impasse on that particular discussion, she had put it to one side for now. She had three months, after all, to figure it out.

Until her departure.

They had also had plenty of discussion about all the other provisions he wanted to make for her. She had had to put her foot down and insist that the ridiculous amount of pin money he intended to give her would also be used as housekeeping money too, because to begin with everyone would expect them to at least try to settle into wedded bliss. She would, therefore, take charge of the running of his house for the three months she was 'stuck in purgatory' with him—his words, not hers.

It was hardly an onerous task, when he would hardly ever be at home and a maid came in three times a week to clean everything. If he *was* home, he had said, he would likely be in his surgery downstairs, so her evenings would be her own to do with as she pleased— which sounded dismal and lonely. Daytimes would be her own too, as he did not need any help with the running of his practice, nor with anything in his busy, ordered life, really, so goodness knew what she was supposed to do with so many empty hours in the day.

But she was at peace with it. She would find something she could do for him. Whether he liked it or not.

Obviously, for appearances' sake, they had decided it made sense to attend all social occasions as a couple, and they had mutually agreed that the only people who needed to know that their marriage was a temporary affair was them. Therefore, as much as she wanted to tell her mother it was all a sham, to spare them both the horror of *the chat* now, she couldn't. Especially as a part of her still hoped that the wedding night would happen.

Not because she harboured any silly romantic notions about the pair of them. He had been completely honest about that, and even if he hadn't been a blithering idiot could see that he wasn't ready to move on from his dead wife. But if she and Sam did end up shackled together for all eternity, albeit living in different counties, she at the very least wanted to appease the curiosity she had always had about such things.

Her fiancé had absconded before their wedding night, and she wasn't brave enough to consider taking a lover, like her friends had suggested, so this might well be her only chance to finally discover what that side of things between a man and a woman was all about. Especially since she had found out at the last Friday Sewing Circle, to which she had immediately been reinstated the moment she had become respectably engaged, that Sam had bought a new bed from Hornchurch.

Rose had, scandalously, once or twice—or perhaps nearer twenty times—indulged in picturing them both in that bed.

'A bed big enough for two,' one of the sewers had said, with suggestively wiggling eyebrows, 'with the best feather mattress money could buy.'

'Oak too,' Mrs Fitzherbert had added with a wink. 'So the pair of you are unlikely to break it.'

And with that several of the married ladies had given each other knowing looks as they had giggled—including Isobel and Sophie—as if beds broke all the time when passion was involved.

Rose would have much preferred having this awkward conversation with them, and had almost asked Sophie twice. But she had stopped herself because her friends' marriages were based on love and hers wasn't ever going to have that. As she assumed that making love involved *love* in some fundamental way, whatever happened or did not happen between her and Sam in the bedchamber tonight would be a very different experience. Probably more perfunctory than passionate—at least on his part.

She wasn't going to waste time trying to delude herself that she didn't feel desire for him, however. It had been growing and bubbling for weeks now, along with her futile affections for him. The only thing that hadn't been growing was any hope that he might miraculously feel the same. For him, there had only ever been one fish.

She had wanted to confide in Sophie and Isobel about that too, because it hurt. But, as her friends knew she was as reluctant a bride as Sam was a groom, she had shied away from discussing such personal things with them because she could not bear to witness any more pity in their eyes.

'The marital bed is not a place to be feared.'

Her poor mama was now staring at a spot on the carpet as if her life depended on it.

'And, contrary to what you may have heard from embittered wives, it doesn't have to be a chore.'

Suddenly Rose was staring at a separate spot on the floor, willing it to open up and swallow her.

'In fact…with a generous and tender man…it can be…um…quite pleasurable.'

Unwanted images of her parents intimately entwined swam before her eyes and her toes curled in revolt.

'After you are undressed, the man will…um…'

Dear Lord, please take me now!

'You do not need to explain any more, Mama. I am a farmer's daughter and know the mechanics.'

'In sheep, cows and horses, dear.' Her mother was squirming in her seat, clearly determined to carry on, despite looking ready to bolt. 'But it works differently in people.'

She made an odd gesture with her hands that made absolutely no sense to Rose.

'Of course you can do it in the same hasty manner as animals if the mood calls for it, but…um…usually people face one another…take their time and…er…kiss and…do *other* things.'

Her mother attempted a smile as she stressed the word 'other', then caught her daughter's eye and almost spontaneously combusted. In case she caught it again, she twisted in her seat and found another spot on the intricately woven Persian carpet to scrutinise.

'Like I said, those things aren't unpleasant. Although…um…it might smart a little the first time. But after that it will all be plain sailing.'

With that, her mother stood, signalling that this torture was finally over, and forced another smile. 'I hope that answers all your questions.'

It didn't, because Rose had no idea what the '*other* things' were, or what 'plain sailing' was supposed to resemble, but she nodded dutifully for the sake of them both.

Her mother's entire posture collapsed with relief. 'Splendid. That wasn't half as bad as I thought it was going to be.'

Which was hilarious, because it had been twice as bad as Rose's worst nightmare, but she smiled too, and thanked her mother, before they both gratefully fled the privacy of the room.

By the time they returned to the ballroom most of the revellers were gone to mass. Only a few strays who were keen to imbibe as much of Lord Hockley's free ale as possible hung around, alongside their hosts, her parents, her uncle and her aunt—whose back had healed enough to finally be relieved of bedrest…and Sam.

Her handsome new husband looked as uncomfortable as she felt. 'Are we ready to go to church?'

He asked that with an overbright smile which told her that he too would much rather stay here until the first of April rather than face what came next. But, as that wasn't viable, she nodded.

'Your curricle is waiting for you out front,' said Rafe, and gave them both a look. One that warned them that the horror of today wasn't fully over, as if he understood that this wasn't the cheery day of celebration almost everyone else was determined to pretend it was. Then in an aside he whispered, 'Gird your loins.'

Only because it was expected, Sam offered his arm and she took it. Then they both did their best to look both delighted and surprised when they saw the entire village was awaiting them outside. His curricle had been festooned in flowers and ribbons, and as he helped her into it they were again showered in rose petals and rice as the crowd cheered. Then it parted like the Red Sea, to allow Reverend Spears to pass, dressed in his most extravagant cassock and already clutching his prayer book, ready to perform the Christmas Eve service.

'My most hearty congratulations, Dr and Mrs Able.'

It was the first time she had heard her new name and it felt odd. Ill-fitting. But not completely wrong.

'You will be delighted to learn that, in honour of your nuptials, you are both excused church this evening.' That elicited a bawdy cheer from the crowd. 'Have a very *Merry* Christmas.'

At that unsubtle euphemism the crowd cheered again and they were forced to set off for home.

A good hour before Rose had steeled herself for it.

They rode in stiff silence up the lane. It was only when they were well out of sight of Hockley Hall that Sam broke it.

'Well, that was...'

'Mortifying? Interminable? Excruciating?'

He chuckled. 'All of the above. But at least the worst is over.'

'Is it? We've still got the awkward crossing the threshold nonsense to manoeuvre, and our first official night alone, then a horrendous day of unsubtle nudges and winks to endure tomorrow, followed by three long months of a sham marriage to navigate.'

He chuckled again. 'You do like to tackle things head-on, don't you, Rose? Get it all out in the open... upfront.'

'Being jilted and the last to know about it does that. It also prevents any nasty surprises and sets expectations.'

'I suppose it does.'

'Especially when we are, again, partners in crime. Trying to perpetrate another fraud upon this village and mine. That's going to be tricky enough without having to tiptoe around one another. Therefore, I think, between us, honesty has to be the best policy. No matter how uncomfortable the topic might be.'

'Agreed. It has certainly worked up to now.'

She waited for him to execute the tricky turn from the lane at Hockley Hall to the road, and then decided to properly practise what she preached. 'I hope you have no intentions of carrying me over the threshold.'

He stared straight ahead but his smile was wry. 'I was only intending to do it if anyone was watching. As we've left everybody back there...' He jerked his head backwards. 'I'll spare us both that chore.'

As the word 'chore' echoed a portion of her mother's painful *chat*, she took a deep breath. 'And our wedding night? How do you envisage that to look?'

He stiffened, but tried to hide it, and that said it all. He didn't want one.

'With you retiring to your room and me retiring to mine.' Then he attempted to smooth over the jagged shards of that damning statement with a smile. 'I've bought you a lovely new bed. New sheets and pillows. I've even bought you a very feminine washstand too, with a bowl made from a local pottery that I found on my travels. I hope you approve of it.'

'I am sure I will.'

Clearly, for all their frank and open discussions, and all the mutually agreed decisions they had made together since this debacle had begun, he had decided she had no say in his decision to deny her a wedding night. Which was just dandy for him, as he had already had one!

For a moment she resented him for that—until she remembered she had no right to resent that or him. Or even his dead wife, to whom he was clearly intent on remaining faithful, because he hadn't lied about any of those things. In fact, he had been nothing but honest, exactly as she had asked. Perhaps more so than she had been. Catherine had been his everything and still was, and Rose could accept that or send herself mad railing against it. Either way, it wouldn't change things.

'But you really didn't need to waste money on furniture that is only going to be used for three months.'

'It can follow you to wherever you end up. Save you the effort of buying two things for your new house.' He slanted her smile. 'Unless you secretly hate them, of course, in which case feel free to give them away or burn them on a bonfire. It's not as if I'll know their fate.'

In case she was in any doubt as to his feelings, that was another innocent but depressing window into his perception of their future.

Once she was gone, as far as he was concerned, she would be gone.

Done and dusted.

Out of sight and out of mind.

Was a wedding night ever as lacklustre and disappointing as this one?

He pulled into the silent market square and solicitously helped her down, briskly severing the contact as they walked together towards her new but temporary home.

'I'll give you a quick tour before you retire, and I see to the horse. I keep the key here.' He pointed to a hook hidden beneath the eaves of the small gabled porch. 'It saves me having to remember it if I have to rush out on a call. Not that I remember to lock the door most of the time, as Whittleston-on-the-Water is perfectly safe.' He pushed it open. 'But you might want to.'

She was already familiar with the hall, as his surgery was the first door on the left and she visited it with Mrs Fitzherbert whenever her gout flared up.

Mrs Fitzherbert had, on every single one of those occasions, joked to him that Rose was her chaperon, because she didn't trust him not to become overcome by the alluring sight of her wizened old legs, and he had always taken it in the same spirit. Replying, 'Very wise' or 'Quite right' or 'It's always better to be safe than sorry where men are concerned.'

He lit a candle and sailed straight past that first door to open the next door on the right. 'This is my office.'

It was, unsurprisingly for such an ordered and organised man, as neat as a pin, but the décor did not suit him at all. It was all dark upholstery, darker wood and old-fashioned furniture. Dour and staid—which he wasn't, despite his traumatic past.

'Did you inherit this from the previous incumbent?'

'Most of it.' He frowned at the room, as if seeing it with fresh eyes, then shrugged. 'I bought the entire practice lock, stock and barrel, and I did mean to change it, but time flies and the practice is busy. It's all service-able enough, so hasn't been a priority.'

He took her further down the hall to show her the kitchen. That, at least, looked less bleak, and would doubtless be quite light and bright when the sun shone through the large currently moonlit windows. There was a decent range, which radiated enough heat to ward off the December chill, and a door which led on to the yard beyond.

He noticed her looking at it. 'There's actually a little cottage garden out there. It's stuffed to the gills with flowers by May, which last all the way through to September.'

'It's too bad I shan't be here to see it as I've always loved a garden.'

'You'll see the early blossom and the buds, at least.'

He pivoted back the way they'd come and lit a lamp at the foot of the stairs. Just as they did in her aunt's house, a few yards away, the narrow stairs turned twice before they reached the upper floor. Then all similarities with her relative's home, disappeared because the bottom of this one was mostly used for business and the entire top was where living happened.

Except not much living seemed to occur in the parlour. It was a spartan space that smelled of beeswax. Neat and tidy, exactly like downstairs, but somehow even less like the man who owned it. All the requisite furniture for a parlour was there and, unlike downstairs, most of it was no more than a few years old. One wingback chair sat beside the fireplace, flanked by a small table. A short settee devoid of any scatter cushions seemed to have been purchased to fill the space, but it was too plump and rigid to have ever been sat on. There was an empty sideboard and an empty dresser, and a cold and empty grate which, judging by the frigid temperature which hit her in the face the second the door opened, clearly hadn't seen any sign of a fire in a long time.

She'd wager he didn't use this room and it showed, for there wasn't a single picture on the pale green walls nor a knick-knack in sight. It was an abandoned, forgotten, but telling space.

'Obviously I never have time to use this room,' he said, as if he could read her mind, 'so do not hesitate to make it yours for the duration.'

It was another window into his work-orientated existence and yet another unconscious reminder that their time together was finite, in case—what? She forgot he was only with her under duress and got ideas? That grated, but she bit back any comment and nodded. He was making her an honest woman after all, and that was her fault.

'The bedchambers are just along the landing.' Which was where he marched her next. 'There is a small attic room too, that is completely empty bar a table and a chair, which obviously you can use—or not use—whatever you wish, and this is your room.'

He paused between two opposite doors, the other clearly being his, and that brought her up short. She hadn't envisaged that they would be sleeping mere feet apart.

Would she hear him?

Sense him?

Probably. Every time he was within ten feet of her, her skin prickled with awareness, and it was always disconcerting.

He flung the door open and ushered her inside. The brand-new bed dominated the room and was indeed big enough for two. But it was the rest of the room which surprised her, because he had obviously gone to some effort for her in the last three weeks. Certainly more effort than he had put to his own comfort in the last three years. His considerations touched her and, oddly, felt significant.

The bedding was a crisp, plain white, lacy and feminine, although not in a fussy way. Four fat pillows stood to attention at the headboard. Each with a cluster of tiny red silk ribbon roses adorning one corner, while a thick, clearly expensive rose-printed eiderdown was folded across the foot. There was a small vase of fresh flowers on her nightstand—roses again, although heaven knew where he had found them this far from the city in wintertime—alongside a pretty beaded lamp.

The rose motif was echoed on the bowl of the pine washstand, which had been matched with the full-length pine looking glass, taking up one corner, and a wicker chair draped in a thick crimson blanket sat in another. It was the same crimson as the roses, and he had found a rug that matched. Beside a tall wardrobe were piled her two trunks. Atop them were all the books she had bought since she'd arrived at Whittleston.

'I arranged with your aunt to have everything delivered earlier. I thought you'd settle in easier with all your things close to hand.'

'That was very thoughtful of you.'

Rose had only packed a bag, and even that had been a last-minute thing this morning. Maybe because even until the absolute last minute she hadn't been entirely sure she could go through with this sham of a wedding. She had, of course, because there really hadn't been any alternative. Not only was it what everyone expected, her father had gone to great expense and trouble to engage a solicitor to force the dratted *Suffolk Sentinel* to print both a complete retraction and a correction. One which stuck closer to the real version of events, exactly like her uncle's article in the *South Essex Gazette*, but with the added embellishment that Dr Able had already proposed to her before they had inadvertently got trapped by the blizzard for the night in his curricle.

'Please tell me you didn't buy all this just for me?'

He waved the unnecessary and extravagant expense away as if it was nothing. 'I couldn't have you sleeping on bare boards, now, could I? Because that was all that was in here before.'

'You matched all the colours and the roses?'

'A rose for a *Rose* and I know you like red.'

He ran an idle hand over one of her pillows, smiling at his purchase, then froze as he realised what he had just said. He yanked his fingers away from her bedding as if he had been caught doing something wrong, and just like that the atmosphere in the room shifted. Became somehow more intimate.

Her flesh heated with awareness.

He swallowed.

Hard.

Perhaps because suddenly he, like her, was reminded that they were all alone in the candlelight with a bed big enough for two. On their wedding night! And everyone outside of this house—her own friends included—were currently in church and expecting them to be having one!

'Anyway...' He used his candle to light her lamp and strode to the door so fast it was a wonder he didn't break into a run. 'Buying all this gave me something to do while I was *persona non grata* and at a loose end, so I hardly went to too much trouble. Hardly any at all, really, as most of it came from the same shop and the shopkeeper suggested most of the choices.'

Was he blushing? He was definitely babbling. Shuffling from foot to foot, looking boyish, self-conscious and...and so appealing her pulse quickened.

'Obviously, if you hate it, you can replace everything.'

'I love it all.'

A rose for a Rose.

Heaven help her, but that had sounded so romantic. As romantic as this overtly feminine bedchamber was.

'Thank you.'

'Excellent...' He shuffled from foot to foot some more, winced, and then tried his best to pretend he hadn't. 'Then I'll leave you to get settled...um... Goodnight... Rose.'

'Goodnight, Sam.'

The door closed with a soft click, then she heard his boots hurry down the stairs. Leaving her staring at her pretty new surroundings, feeling off-kilter and wondering how a man who believed he had no heart left to give could be so utterly, charmingly, whimsically thoughtful.

Chapter Twelve

Bloody hell!

A rose for a blasted Rose!

What the blazes had he been thinking?

It was midnight on Christmas Day, snow was again coming down so thick and fast he could barely see the road ahead, and instead of concentrating on it as the weather demanded, Sam was still kicking himself for those wholly inappropriate and flowery words.

Who did he think he was?

Wordsworth?

Blasted Shakespeare?

Or, God help him, Romeo? Besotted and ready to woo!

And he had been so keen to show it all off too, and had basked in her approval. Patting himself on the back for getting things just right when in fact she was right! It was a ludicrous amount of effort for just three months. And, despite his hasty denial, sourcing all those things *had* been an effort.

He hadn't lied when he'd claimed to have been at a loose end, because he had been. During those first few days after their engagement, when the news of it hadn't spread the length and breadth of his practice and he had still been considered a libertine, a scoundrel and a cad, he had had too many empty hours to fill. He hadn't lied when he'd said that he had just been passing the pottery, because stopping to purchase the rose-covered washbowl and jug had been more by whim than design. But once he'd had it he had become a man on a mission to find the perfect things to go with it.

At the time, he had thought that he was being decent, because he genuinely did not want to make her short stay at his house any more awkward than it needed to be. However, with hindsight, he had been so obsessed with getting it right for her that he hadn't given much thought as to how that would look. He had lied about the shopkeeper choosing it all too, because not one of the dozen specialised merchants he had visited had suggested anything remotely suitable.

Everything had been too fussy, too frothy and too frilly for Rose's bold but understated elegance. So it had been he who had chosen the linens and the furniture. He who had matched the blanket and had the rug made to match the dark crimson of the lovely evening gown she had worn while they had waltzed on the infamous night of the blizzard, when he had been the envy of the room.

What the blazes had he been thinking, to treasure that memory enough that he'd instantly been able to pick the precise shade? He was supposed to be dead inside—had worked damn hard to be dead inside—and wasn't supposed to care about anyone like that. Yet he had cared then that she would like it, and to his horror he still cared now that she did.

He had tossed and turned all night, imagining her dark hair fanned out on those snow-white pillows, and she had invaded his dreams with a vengeance.

Worse than she ever had before.

He'd blamed the fact that she was sleeping directly across the hall, which was disconcerting enough for one used to being alone. He'd been convinced he could smell her perfume—blasted roses again—from his bed. The sultry, seductive scent had been a constant reminder that he was sharing his house with a woman, and his body hadn't enjoyed the touch of a woman in four long years. It hadn't helped that it was technically their wedding night, and wedding nights elicited certain carnal connotations that even a man who was dead inside could not fail to contemplate. Nor had it helped that their wedding wasn't a real wedding. Not when she had been mere feet away, lying warm and soft beneath the rose-covered eiderdown he had bought her, and each time his eyes had closed he'd wondered what it would be like to snuggle beneath it with her.

Then, as he'd slept, his imagination had run riot.

So much so he had awoken hot and hard. The hated nightshirt he had donned because he had a 'visitor' had been discarded in a fit of nocturnal pique, so he'd met the day naked, atop his tangled covers. His fist had conveniently already been wrapped around his painful, rigid cock so he could relieve himself. Which he'd figured he had to do to banish the hold the Rose of his dreams had over his body before he dared face her.

Then, to rattle him further, he'd had to face her almost immediately, because no sooner had he washed and dressed his less rampant body he'd opened his door the second she'd opened hers.

They had simultaneously muttered awkward greetings, with him hoping against hope that she hadn't heard the guttural grunt of his explosive release and her barely meeting his eye which rather suggested she might have. Then she had insisted on making his coffee while he finished getting ready for the obligatory Christmas Day church service, which they hadn't been excused from despite being newlyweds.

Newlyweds who hadn't spent the night honouring each other's bodies as their vows allowed—but only they knew that, and likely only he was suffering as a result.

The service at St Hildreth's had been every bit as cringeworthy as she had predicted, with everyone nudging and winking and slapping him on the back because they'd assumed he had had a good night. That had been followed by an interminable Christmas luncheon at the Outhwaites, with her visiting family, during which none of them had known quite what to say. Thankfully, a child with a fever in Ockendon had spared him the interminable evening of cold cuts and cards, and hot on the heels of that had come a youth who had broken his wrist after doing something idiotic with his friends in Great Ramstead.

Now Sam turned into the square, hopeful that his tempting new wife was already sleeping in her bed and he wouldn't have to relive that stupid, sentimental *a rose for a Rose* comment in front of her again until tomorrow.

The porch light glowed in an uncharacteristic welcome home. He'd certainly never had the forethought to light it before he dashed out to the next emergency in the dark, so she must have. Even so, he took his horse to its tiny stable first, rubbed him down, fed him, and put him to bed before he ventured inside. He wanted to prove to himself that he wasn't eager to return home, even though a part of him was.

That was a new and worrying development too, as this place was a means to an end more than a home. A place to conduct his business and rest his weary head. And it had been so until last night, when she had joined him here. But today he had thought of it as home for the first time, when that glowing porch light had felt like a beacon, beckoning him inside and away from it all.

She hadn't locked the door, and he toed off his snowy boots so as not to disturb her upstairs before he trudged towards the kitchen. Sam hadn't eaten since that fraught Christmas luncheon, and he was frozen stiff from the weather. In his mind there was a mountain of hot, thick buttered toast with his name on it, and by Jove he was going to devour it while he warmed his bones by the fire!

Rose had obviously tossed a fresh log on that fire before she had retired, because the kitchen was deliciously warm when he entered it. He retrieved a semi-stale loaf from the pantry, and was in the midst of sawing it to pieces when the hairs on his neck began to dance.

'You're home late.'

She was dressed for bed. Beneath her knotted robe the sensible high neck of her winter nightgown was visible. Her chestnut hair had been bound in a thick plait that hung over one shoulder and practically to her waist. Sam had no clue why the long length of her hair affected him so—but it did.

'What are you making?'

'Toast,' he said, his mouth suddenly dry. 'It's one of the few things in my culinary repertoire.'

'Toast isn't a proper supper, Sam, and I'm guessing you haven't had a proper supper.' She whooshed past him on a distracting floral wave to poke around the pantry. 'I'll make you something more substantial.'

'There's honestly no need.' He wasn't comfortable with her caring for him like this. It felt too wifely. Too personal. 'I am content with toast. I like toast. In fact, I practically live on the stuff.'

She emerged from the pantry empty-handed, with a furrowed brow. 'Well, that's just as well, as there is nothing in the pantry to make anything beyond toast. Please tell me that you don't really live off toast.'

'It's quick and easy for a man who keeps such odd hours. I do eat at the inn every so often, though, and the maid always makes a half-decent stew once a week, and that lasts a couple of days, so...'

She pushed past him to squeeze the bread and her dark brows kissed each other in consternation. 'Precisely how old is this loaf?'

'Er...no more than three days. The baker delivers it twice a week, along with a few pies and—' He stopped because her hands had gone to her hips and he knew he shouldn't be defending his poor diet when she was right. He was a physician, after all, and he'd have plenty to say if he discovered one of his patients ate like him. 'Stale bread always makes the best toast. Everybody knows that, and I'm quite capable of making it, so go back to bed.' He was too aware of her and it unsettled him. 'There is no point us both being up.'

She shot him a look of chastisement before she completely ignored him. 'Give that to me and go and dry your hair before you catch your death of cold.'

She snatched the knife from his hand and flapped him towards the table, tossing him a towel as he sat down. A towel which he was fairly certain hadn't lived in his kitchen before she had moved in, not twenty-four hours before.

With efficient economy of motion, several slices of bread were speared on a toasting fork and rested before the fire, before she returned to the pantry to fetch some milk, sniffing it gingerly and then pouring it into a pan once she had ascertained it wasn't on the turn.

'I see the snow has returned,' she said.

'It has, and I fear it's back for the foreseeable.'

'Well, I hope it pauses long enough for my parents to return home. I'd rather they left tomorrow as planned. My mother keeps trying to pull me aside to have chats about how to be a *good wife*.' She pulled a face full of distaste that said that Mrs Healy's advice strayed into areas that weren't quite as impersonal as making toast. 'And my father keeps interrogating me about your character and your prospects and asking if you are treating me as you should. My brother, obviously, still wants to kill you, but he won't—unless you give him due course.'

'And who can blame him?' Sam smiled at both her dry delivery and her uncanny knack of banishing awkwardness by tackling it head-on. Clearly she had come to the realisation much quicker than he that they were stuck with one another so they might as well find a way of existing that wasn't quite so painful as last night and this morning had been. 'Had I a sister, I'd probably want to murder the scoundrel who had compromised her.'

'I was so envious of you being able to escape today.' She slanted him an amused glance. 'Because the awkwardness didn't improve after you left. I almost stabbed myself in the forehead with a fork during supper, to end it all, it was such unmitigated torture. I do not blame you, either, for not coming back.'

'I couldn't come back.' He finished towelling his hair and found himself watching her as she made swift work of turning the toast. 'Lucas Midhurst, for reasons best known to himself, decided to ride his sled down the roof of his skinflint father's old barn. Suffice to say that the skinflint's roof hadn't been maintained, and the sled went halfway down before plummeting through it. Fortunately, he landed in the hay store, and that broke his fall, else I'd have had to set more than his wrist this evening.'

'Why on earth would he do a stupid thing like that?' She had found some forgotten chocolate, spices and sugar in his pantry, and was whisking it vigorously into the steaming milk. 'When sledding down a roof of any sort is never going to end well.'

'Because boys will be boys, I'm afraid, and do not have the sense of girls.' Much to his surprise Sam was enjoying this impromptu bit of domesticity. 'Honestly, of all the injured patients I have to attend as a result of stupid accidents that never should have happened, nine-tenths of them are males. The age of the male is no gauge of their stupidity either. Just last week the butcher, who must be at least fifty if he is a day, balanced a rickety three-legged milking stool on his countertop so that he could whitewash his ceiling, rather than fetch the ladder which was propped up against the wall of his yard not five steps away.'

'Is that how he lost both his front teeth?' She giggled, the sound so joyous it made him laugh too. 'He told my uncle that he was kicked in the face by a rampaging bullock at the slaughterhouse!'

'Yes, I heard that too.' Sam was transfixed as she slathered butter on the now perfectly golden toast, while simultaneously pouring two mugs of the frothiest hot chocolate he had ever seen. 'I always makes me laugh when I hear the outrageous stories men make up to cover for their stupidity. But sadly, if I'm involved, and it didn't happen in public, alongside other witnesses, I obviously cannot call them out on it, no matter how much I am tempted.'

'Why not?'

She deposited the toast and one of the steaming mugs on the table before sinking into the chair opposite, where she hugged her own mug in her hands. Clearly it wasn't enough that she had prepared his supper—she was going to keep him company while he ate it too. More peculiar was that he didn't actually mind. It was...*nice* to have some company for a change. To not come back to a cold, dark and empty house.

He decided not to worry about that. It was Christmas, after all, a time to make merry, and it was going to be impossible to keep her completely at arm's length when they were both living under the same roof—it wasn't a particularly big roof at that. They were doomed to bump into one another all the time, and the next three months didn't have to be awkward. Surely it wouldn't hurt if they were more friends than polite acquaintances for just twelve weeks?

'As a physician, I am bound by certain rules and regulations and one of those is the confidentiality of the patient. Their ailments are private unless they give me permission to say otherwise. Which means that I am privileged to know all manner of salacious things which I cannot technically tell another living soul, so kindly keep the truth about Jenkins' missing teeth under your hat.'

'My lips are sealed.'

She pretended to button them, drawing his eyes there.

Then those plump lips curved into a conspiratorial and very naughty smile.

'What sort of other salacious things can you technically not tell me?' She leaned her chin on her wrist and wiggled her dark brows, expectant.

'Nothing because I shouldn't have even told you that!'

'Of course you should have. I am your wife, after all. At least temporarily.' She batted her lashes. 'A good husband, even a transient one, should never keep secrets from his wife.'

'I really shouldn't...'

'But you are sorely tempted, aren't you?'

He was, because it would be fun to share some of the more ludicrous things he had squirreled away and, as she had so aptly said once, there really was no reason why two irrevocably damaged souls shouldn't take whatever amusement they could if the opportunity presented itself.

Chuckling, he took a sip of his chocolate and his eyes widened. 'This is delicious.' Ridiculously delicious. So delicious he would even go as far as saying it was the best cup of chocolate he had ever had in his life. 'How on earth did you make this with so few stale ingredients?'

She preened with mock arrogance. 'I have *the gift*. You have married an excellent cook, Dr Able. A truly *excellent* cook, if I do say so myself. And I'll be prepared to prove that every day for the duration of our temporary marriage, to spare you the next three months of toast, if I'm paid for my talents in scurrilous gossip that I swear I will never tell another living soul.' She batted her lashes again. 'You also have my solemn pledge that my stews aren't *half decent* like your maid's. They are legendary.' She kissed her fingers as she briefly closed her eyes. 'And the things I can do with pastry are *so* sublime they should be illegal.'

'All bold claims, madam...'

'Not claims, sir. The truth.' She leaned closer, elbows on the table and her pretty face resting in the cradle of both palms. 'So what do you say, transient husband? Bearing in mind that you did agree that for the duration of our sham marriage honesty was the best policy.'

He took a bite out of his toast and pretended to give it some thought, and when she huffed, he grinned. 'Do you remember, in August, Mrs Sheldon claimed to have been knocked out cold when she came home from evensong, after a gust of wind dislodged a roof tile which fell and hit her on the head?'

She leaned forward, her green eyes shimmering with mirth. 'Don't tell me she hadn't been hit by falling masonry, because I saw the huge bump on her forehead and it was so magnificent it could only have come from something very hard.'

'Of course it wasn't a roof tile. There wasn't a breath of wind all August, for goodness' sake... She carries a flask of gin everywhere, and had drunk so much that night that she tripped over her own doorstep and head-butted the doorknob.'

She threw her head back and laughed. It was an outrageously earthy and slightly dirty laugh. 'Mrs Fitzherbert has always said that mother's ruin will be the ruin of Mrs Sheldon...'

Before either of them knew it half an hour had passed and all of it filled with laughter. It was only when they both started yawning that it became apparent that it was time to call it a night. Yet it was Rose who was the one to bring their evening to an end, and not him, which was probably also something he should worry about.

'I have to wave my parents and brother off at six. If they aren't snowed in.' She rolled her eyes. 'Perish the thought.'

While she moved the crockery to the sink, he glanced outside to assess the weather. 'Well, it's stopped for now. Three inches of fresh snow aren't enough to stop a big carriage like your father's.'

'From your lips to God's ears, Sam.'

She led the way out of the kitchen and up the stairs, forcing him to behold the intriguing way her hips undulated as she did so. They didn't stop until she reached her bedchamber.

'Goodnight, transient husband.'

'Goodnight, temporary wife.'

His last image was her sleepy smile before she closed her door. It was an image that tortured his dreams for the rest of the night.

Chapter Thirteen

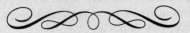

'I'm sorry, Mr Purdue, but it is still a no.' Rose pointed to the engraved plaque by the front door. 'Surgery hours are from eight o'clock to noon, Monday to Friday, and today is Saturday. Unless it's an emergency—and by emergency I mean that the threat of your departure from this earthly realm is imminent—you can come back then to collect your stomach powders on Monday.'

'But I have run out!' He was incensed at being thwarted. 'I get gaseous if I do not have them because I cannot digest my meat properly!'

'Then I suggest you eat only vegetables until then and, going forward, come to see my husband during surgery hours well before you run out again.'

'Dr Able has never once turned me away on a Saturday. Or a Sunday, for that matter, so—'

Rose stayed him with her palm. 'That was before he was married, Mr Purdue. Now that he is, he will be spending his Saturdays and his Sundays with me.' As the ruddy-faced merchant huffed, she offered him a cheery smile. 'Have a good Saturday yourself, Mr Purdue.'

Then she promptly closed the door and went back

to her pastry, hoping that the exchange hadn't awoken Sam upstairs.

Thanks to a difficult delivery of twins in Little Ramstead, and the worsening snowy roads, he hadn't got home till four in the morning and desperately needed some sleep. He wouldn't agree with her assessment, and would have roused himself to assist Mr Purdue without a moment's thought. But then he seemed to think that he could exist in perpetuity on three hours of sleep a night and only toast for supper. So, despite his medical degree, Rose had decided to take certain matters into her own hands. Like his diet, the number of hours he spent working needed to be balanced with a suitable amount of rest and relaxation or he would run himself into the ground. If that meant she had to run interference between him and the many patients who had no respect at all for boundaries, then so be it. Sam was their physician, not their servant.

She had barely rolled the next ball of dough out when the door was knocked upon again. This time it was Mr Bunion, the odious apprentice of the local solicitor, who had the most apt name in the world because, despite his dandified clothes and over-pomaded hair, he smelled like feet.

'Good morning.' He tipped his hat, grinning like an idiot and looking like one too, in the most intricately tied cascading cravat Rose had ever seen. 'I wonder if I could steal a moment of your husband's time.'

As he presumptuously stepped forward, she folded her arms and planted her feet. 'Why do you need to see him?'

'Well...obviously I have an ailment which I would like treated.' His smile this time was so oily it might have been made of lard. 'Surely you do not wish me to discuss the intimate details of it on your doorstep?'

'On Saturdays my husband only sees emergencies, Mr Bunion. If you do not mind me saying, you look much too hale and hearty today for me to believe that you are one.'

'If you must know, I have a boil.' He leaned closer to whisper this, and singed her face with his rancid breath. 'In a most unfortunate place. I am in discomfort, Mrs Able, so surely that is enough?'

'I am afraid discomfort can wait until Monday, Mr Bunion, because a boil, even a big one, can just as easily be treated at home. Apply a hot cloth to it for at least ten minutes, to draw it out, and then pop the poison out with a needle.'

He puffed up like an affronted peacock. 'I am a single gentleman, madam, and so do not have any reason to possess a needle!'

Affronted herself by the inanity she was hearing, she pointed across the square to Isobel's new haberdashery. 'Then I suggest you go, forthwith, to Mrs Parker's, to purchase yourself one, because it is my husband's well-earned day off and he won't be lancing it for you today!'

'This is outrageous!'

'Isn't it just? The general surgery will open Monday at eight o'clock sharp, should you still require it. Until then, good day to you, Mr Bunion.'

The door was halfway closed when he had the gall to start again. 'Oh, I shall be here at eight sharp, madam, be in no doubt! When I fully intend to apprise your affable husband of the fact that his wife is a rude shrew who has quite forgotten her place!'

'You do that, sir. And while you are about it inform

him that his rude shrew of a wife also suggested that you should go and buy some soap and some tooth powders because you smell, Mr Bunion! Very badly indeed!'

She slammed the door, so infuriated by him, and every other who had encroached upon her Saturday morning, that she marched into Sam's office rather than back to the kitchen.

She found a plain sheet of foolscap and on it, in big, capitalised letters, wrote a new sign for the door. Then she stomped to the kitchen to get some string, and used it to tie the terse message to the knocker, in case anyone else with precious little wrong with them thought it appropriate to ignore the general surgery hours etched on the brass plaque. Because she would genuinely strangle the next timewaster who interrupted her baking and Sam's well-earned day off.

Miraculously, it did the trick, and her second batch of pies was about to come out of the oven an hour and half later when a rather dishevelled and disorientated Sam finally made an appearance. He blinked at her, shocked, as if he had literally just fallen out of bed.

'Is everything all right?'

She glanced around, mimicking him exactly, minus the adorable tuft of hair that was standing up at a right angle to his head. 'Everything seems to be. What were you expecting?'

'Well, it's almost noon,' he said, as if she had lost track of time. 'Doesn't anyone need me?'

'I would have awoken you if they did.'

'I never sleep this late.'

'You must have needed it, then, don't you think?'

He pondered that briefly, then nodded. 'I suppose I must have.'

'Do you feel better for it?'

He gave that a moment's thought too, as if he rarely contemplated his own physical health. 'I suppose I do. I feel guilty, though. For not being here for my patients.'

Rose made a great show of looking around again. 'What patients? Clearly the whole of Whittleston is in fine fettle today. Including you, now that you are properly rested. For once.'

If he registered her dig, he chose to ignore it. 'Hmm... odd. Saturday mornings are usually fairly busy, as that's when all the people who forget to come in during the week come to see me.'

Which just said it all. He was condoning their lack of organisation without any censure at all and running himself ragged in the process.

'They shouldn't be.' She pushed him towards the table, trying not to notice the intriguing dusting of dark hair visible in the deep V of his open shirt, which he had obviously donned in a hurry. 'When, according to your sign outside, there isn't supposed to be a surgery at all on Saturdays.'

'I inherited that sign from the previous physician. I've never really abided by those hours, though.'

'Then perhaps you should make the most of today's reprieve, don't you think?'

There was no point getting into a fight about it as he would dig his heels in. They had only been married a week, and already she knew him well enough to know that he had no boundaries where work was concerned. He toiled from the moment he got up until he went to bed. The only respite he gave himself was mealtimes, and she put that concession wholly down to her superior skills in the kitchen, because he claimed to be too busy to stop working otherwise and, worse, she suspected he believed that lie too.

Yes, this was a large and busy practice, but on top of his daily surgeries, endless home visits—which couldn't all be necessary—and the steady stream of emergencies that he had no choice but to rush to, he also spent every other spare hour in his office, meticulously rewriting his patient notes, filing them away himself rather than paying someone to do it for him and reading medical journals. If he wasn't doing that he was mixing potions and powders in his surgery, labelling them and storing them on the shelves like soldiers on parade. Not once, in the seven days since they had taken their faux vows, had he set a single foot in the parlour, let alone sat down in it to relax.

Rather than nag him about that, it was better to distract him from his unnecessary labours with food.

'What would you like for breakfast?'

His nostrils twitched as he sniffed the sideboard. 'Those pies look and smell delicious. What are they—apple?'

'You cannot have apple pie for breakfast.'

'Spoilsport. Can I have it for luncheon, then? It's practically luncheon anyway, so...' He reached for one of the smaller ones and she slapped his hand away.

'I've got sausages, bacon, eggs...or some toast.'

'Yes, to all, please. I'm starving.'

'As you wish.' Rose smiled as she retrieved the loaded plate of all those things, already warming on the range, and placed it before him. Then slid a freshly fried egg onto it with a thick slice of toast. 'And before you ask, yes, I am a mind-reader.'

'I sincerely hope you are not.' He pretended to look worried and she shrugged.

'I heard you stirring through the floorboards. The ones beneath your bed creak and you are clearly a fidgeter while you wake.'

'I'm sorry,' he said, looking oddly guilty as he picked up his cutlery, as if his morning fidgeting was somehow something to be ashamed of. 'Thank you for this.'

Rose busied herself while he ate rather than sit with him, because she was enjoying these mealtime interactions a little too much since their wedding and didn't want him to know. She was no stranger to love, and knew the early warning signs too well not to realise that she was futilely suffering from them. Tiny butterflies had begun to flap in her tummy each time she heard his footsteps or his curricle. She smiled more. Laughed more. Made more of an effort each morning with her hair and her clothes. Today's choice of gown was no exception. This warm green wool ensemble was too warm for inside and was intended for outside pursuits, as it had been made with a matching pelisse with fur at the neck and cuffs. But this fitted dress did pleasing things to her figure, especially around the bust, and had always garnered compliments.

Did she want one from him?

Probably.

Hopelessly romantic masochist that she was!

She certainly basked in the glow of every compliment he gave her cooking, and against her better judgement Rose seemed to be on a mission to please him. This might well be a short, sham marriage, but she was settling into it rather well and was already protective and possessive of her transient husband's welfare. Even so, she had no intentions of getting her poor heart broken again, and she harboured no lofty belief that she could make him feel the same way. The strange stirring in her chest was all her problem. Sam was eternally bound to Catherine, would probably never let her go, and had been nothing but honest about that.

Therefore, some prudent distance and boundaries would not go amiss, and she would limit herself to one cosy meal with him a day. She would not overthink why she would prefer that meal to be dinner, when it was dark outside, they had more time and seemed to have the world all to themselves. Nor would she give much consideration to the desire she felt for him after those dinners, preferring to see that as part of her healing process and part of being a woman in her prime, and therefore not really anything to do with him.

No indeed. As all the signs were definitely there, prudent distance was the order of the day. Now that she had saved him from himself, and all the non-urgent patients who wanted to sabotage his day off, and had finally finished her batch baking, she would take herself out. Give her smart green frock and matching pelisse an airing by calling on some friends and putting the handsome but tortured man who was calling to her out of her mind until she fed him again tonight.

He savoured the last mouthful of his food, then washed it down with the hot coffee she had placed before him. 'Seeing as today is a quiet day, I might as well visit the big apothecary in Romford. I'm running low on a few staples, and the snow outside isn't too bad, by the looks of it today. A bracing run in the curricle is always good for blowing the cobwebs out of the mind.'

'It has melted quite a bit. Thank goodness.'

And a bracing run in his curricle did sound like the perfect activity for a lazier Saturday. It would also be the perfect airing for her smart green wool ensemble.

'If you fancy some company, I'd love to do some shopping in Romford myself.' That had popped out before she could stop it. So much for some prudent distance! 'Do not feel obliged to say yes, by the way, if you would prefer your own space.'

'I wouldn't mind some company.'

His answer came with no hesitation or pauses, and it came along with a devasting smile, so the dratted butterflies flapped some more.

'Give me ten minutes to look more presentable and we'll get going.'

Just shy of ten minutes later he bounded down the stairs with a fresh spring in his step. The lack of shadows under his hazel eyes reassured her that she had done exactly the right thing in letting him sleep.

'That's a pretty coat, Rose. Green suits you.'

She practically melted at the compliment, and the accompanying smile which he bestowed with it, but sincerely hoped she hid it well. In case her quickened pulse showed on her face, she turned slightly to pull on her gloves. 'Thank you. It's one of my favourites.'

He opened the door for her solicitously, and without touching she sailed through it. It was only when he closed it behind them that she remembered that she had forgotten to remove her sign.

Of course it was too big for him not to notice, and he paused to read it, his eyes scanning every word with increasing incredulity.

ONLY KNOCK ON THIS DOOR TODAY IF:

1. *You fear someone is about to die or*
2. *They have a severe fever or*
3. *Are delirious or*
4. *Are bleeding profusely or*
5. *Vomiting extensively or*
6. *They have a pox of some sort or*
7. *Are oozing noxious things that they shouldn't or*
8. *They are unconscious or*
9. *A bone is broken or*
10. *They are in labour or*
11. *You are delivering something or*
12. *You are a friend paying us a social call and require no medical assistance whatsoever or*
13. *The world is about to end*

In all other cases, please behave like a decent person and return during the surgery hours or the physician's new and furious wife will not be responsible for her actions that you interrupted his well-earned day off!

The words were etched in half-inch letters on the one-foot by two-foot plaque screwed to the wall.

'Well, I suppose that explains my unusually quiet morning.' His flicked her a glance that was more amused than annoyed. 'Dare I ask what prompted it?'

'Mr Bunion's boil was the final straw.' As Sam instantly pulled a face of disgust, at the mention of the man more than his ailment, she couldn't resist a grin. 'In the spirit of our brutally honest relationship, I should probably warn you that he took such umbrage at not being granted admittance he claimed he is going to give you a piece of his mind on Monday, over me and my poor attitude.'

'Well, that should be interesting,' he said, heading around the back to fetch his horse and leaving the sign in situ. 'I'll look forward to putting uppity Mr Bunion in his place.' And if his amused smile was any gauge, he really was.

As Saturday was market day in Whittleston, Rose passed the next few minutes chatting to some of the locals while he attached the horse to the conveyance.

Once he was done, he held out his hand to help her up, then snatched it back before she could take it. 'Do you know how to drive a curricle?'

'Of course I do! I'm a farmer's daughter, aren't I? Why?'

'Well, as it's apparently my day off, I figure I might as well enjoy the pleasure of being a passenger for once.' He gently led her by the elbow to the other side. 'Let's see if you have as deft a touch with the reins as you do with pastry.'

Chapter Fourteen

Rose liked to drive fast. Of course she did. Because she was a fearless minx who loved to milk the fun out of every situation. Not even the dark fazed her, and that didn't surprise him. There was an intrepid, devil-may-care streak in her that reminded him of Catherine. His first wife had been a force of nature too, and had never missed an opportunity to push a boundary or find the joy or the excitement in a situation.

She had crashed her father's phaeton once because of her love of speed. She had taken it out without his knowledge, taken a bend too fast and the whole thing had tipped over. Not before she'd flung herself into a haystack—thank goodness—and fortunately the horses had been unscathed too, so no living thing had been hurt in the incident. The damage to the poor phaeton, however, had been extensive, and had cost her father an arm and a leg to fix. As a punishment, Catherine had been consigned to barracks, or at least the civilian equivalent, and had been banned from leaving her father's house unchaperoned for three months. She had hated that.

'What are you grinning at?'

Rose's question interrupted his reverie and brought him up short—because he had been grinning. Over Catherine. Which was odd when normally all memories of her were tinged with such sadness it brought a lump to his throat and such bitterness that acid burned it afterwards. But that had been a fond recollection and, to his great surprise, not only had it not hurt but it had been a pleasant thought. One that did nothing to spoil his buoyant mood at all.

'Nothing. I am simply in a good humour.' And had been all day.

From the moment he had sat at the kitchen table to eat his breakfast, his impromptu day off had been a balm to his soul. The hour-long drive to Romford had been delightful. With Rose at the helm, and thanks to the freshly cleared roads, he had been able to watch the snow-covered winter scenery whip past. To take it all in and appreciate what a pretty part of the world he lived in.

While she had explored the busy market—the oldest and biggest in the South East of England—he'd then spent another hour browsing the apothecary's. Now he was confident that, stored safely in the back of his curricle, was all the stock he needed for the next month, because he had taken his time selecting it rather than rushing the job, like he usually did, and consequently missing something.

Once he had finished his shopping he had found her browsing a stall which sold carpets, where he'd discovered that she had purchased him one for the parlour, so it had become his task to heave the thing back to his conveyance, where some other purchases had also found their way. Some cushions and some tablecloths were wrapped in brown paper. There was a basket of eggs too, a wheel of cheese, a pile of second-hand novels and an enormous leg of lamb, which he was very much looking forward to eating.

Because Rose hadn't lied when she had said she was an excellent cook. She was better than excellent. She was sublime. He had never eaten so well in his life as he had this last week.

Despite knowing her food could not be topped, Sam hadn't taken much convincing to partake in a late lunch with her at the Golden Lion pub. Hence they were here now, the sun already set and the first flakes of fresh snow falling for the last mile of their ride home.

'If one day off puts you in such a good humour, Sam, maybe you should do it more often? Grant yourself maybe two or three of them a year?'

She had a particular expression when she wielded sarcasm. Her dark brows quirked, her plump lips pouted and her green eyes sparkled.

'Build yourself up gradually to perhaps even one each season?'

'Is that a subtle nag, temporary wife?'

'Oh, it wasn't subtle at all, transient husband. When one only has three months to try to make some meaningful improvements to a man in dire need of some improving, one cannot waste time on subtlety. You work too hard, do not look after yourself, and if you are not careful you will send yourself to an early grave.'

He almost said, *Perhaps that's what I want*, except, bizarrely, it wasn't any more.

When had that happened?

'Save your efforts, Rose, as I cannot be improved.' To further surprise him, he found he was in the mood to banter. 'How on earth does one improve on perfection?'

'Ha!' She never wasted an opportunity to skewer him. 'And you just inadvertently proved my point with that stupid response, as you are clearly so tired and addled you have become deranged and deluded. For there is a great deal of you that falls well shy of perfect.'

'Such as?' He folded his arms and pretended to be peeved. 'I am solvent and run my own business. I am well educated and well respected and certainly cure more than I kill. I have all my teeth and my hair, and even fancy myself not bad looking in certain lights. I'd wager any sensible woman would tell you that you have hooked yourself a catch, madam, so I have no idea what you are complaining about.'

'Stop!' She raised an imperious palm. 'That is almost too much humbleness to bear.' Then she snorted. 'Handsome you may be...'

The compliment heated his blood, because he liked the idea that she found him attractive. He shouldn't, but did.

'But you err too much on the side of seriousness and dourness to be considered a true catch. You are just four and thirty in years, but you seem to have forgotten that you are a youngish man in his prime and behave more like one three decades older sometimes. When was the last time you had some proper fun?'

Today—thanks to her. And yesterday and the day before. Mealtimes had become the highlight of his day—and not because she fed him like a king, but because she ate with him. Made him laugh. Made him feel lighter. Made him feel alive. At least in those moments they spent together at his kitchen table. He would miss all that when she was gone. Undoubtedly more than he'd intended and far more than was wise.

Rather than tell her that, which really wouldn't be wise, he rolled his eyes. 'That would be a month ago, when you enticed me into a foolish wager and, when it all backfired and we became social pariahs, I ended up shackled to you in a loveless, enforced sham marriage that neither of us wanted. *Such. Fun.*'

She threw back her head and laughed, and Sam experienced the most satisfying sense of achievement to have been the cause of it.

'You never resist an opportunity to remind me of my failings, do you, Dr Able? And with such pithy and precise sarcasm too!'

'You are not the only one fluent in it, you know.'

'What I do know already is that you will be *very* easy to leave and I sincerely doubt anyone will be surprised when I do.'

She twisted to look down her nose at him, but her smile spoiled the effect and that smile said it all. Said that she rather liked his company too, and that perhaps if fate had had them meet in a different life, where her heart not been irrevocably broken and his hadn't died and shrivelled to a husk, they might have gone together well. But...

As if she'd read his mind, she shrugged at the same time as he did, and the humour in her gaze morphed into bittersweet acceptance of their sad situations.

'Have you given any thought to what you might do and where you might go when this is over?' He didn't want to care what happened to her when she left, but he had a burning need to know she would be all right. 'Will it be Suffolk or the Outer Hebrides?'

She sighed and focussed on the road as she turned into the square. 'It will be Suffolk to begin with, but I think I should find myself a new place to live once the dust has settled. Close enough to my parents, so that I can easily visit them, but far enough away that I can spare myself all the inevitable gossip and start afresh. Reinvent myself somewhere I am not the unfortunate, unwanted and unweddable Miss Healy.'

Was that really what she thought of herself? Or was it what the local gossips and that rag of a newspaper had made her and others believe. Either way it was a ridiculous injustice. There was nothing unfortunate or unweddable about her, and as he swept his gaze down her jaunty green pelisse he couldn't imagine that any man with blood in his veins didn't want her. She was too alluring. Too attractive. Too effervescent not to want in all the improper and impertinent ways it was possible to want a woman. His heart might be cold but she certainly fired his blood.

'Norfolk is within a stone's throw, and there are some pretty villages in that neck of the woods.'

Her voice dragged him back from his lingering contemplation of her womanly figure.

'Or maybe I'll head to a town. Ipswich or Norwich, perhaps, where it's easier to live a life not scrutinised by all and sundry. Then I might set myself up in trade, like Isobel has. I quite fancy the idea of owning a shop and earning my own keep.' Before he could offer, she shot him a defiant stare. 'I do not need your money, Sam, and I do not want to spend the rest of my life doing nothing of any consequence. You, of all people, should understand how important having a purpose is. I'll go mad if I don't have one.'

He did understand. Only too well. If he hadn't been a doctor, with essential skills in constant demand, he dreaded to think where he would be now—or how he would be, for that matter. Drunk in a gutter somewhere, probably. Or still in uniform, chasing bullets. Or in the ground because one had finally found him and put him out of his misery.

A thought which suddenly left him cold rather than regretful. Which was…sobering. And…new.

'Then might I suggest you open a bakery, Rose? As the things you can do with pastry really should be illegal. You'd make an absolute fortune in a village or a town. Your cakes are pretty spectacular too.'

'Do you really think I could?' For moment she forgot to be bold and blasé, and he saw how much being jilted had knocked her confidence.

'Enough that I would happily invest in it.'

He wanted to reach for her hand. Squeeze it in reassurance. But of course he didn't, because that wouldn't be appropriate. Or wise. They might be temporary partners in crime, but he didn't need to muddy the waters by adding any unessential physical contact to their arrangement. Especially when he increasingly wanted to touch her, and most especially when he touched her with too much impertinence already, nightly in his dreams. Which reminded him… Now that he knew that the floorboards creaked beneath his bed, he would have to find a quieter place in his bedchamber to relieve himself of the torture of those dreams every morning.

His growing sexual attraction to her did bother him, but only in so much as it was dashed inconvenient to be so riddled with lust at the start of each day that he had to expel it immediately. He might not want to feel that way, but it was a normal bodily function. One that was universally acknowledged in academic circles to be intertwined with life. In all the creatures of the earth, the urge to mate was much like the urge to eat or breathe or sleep. It lived inside the blood. It was imprinted somehow into the muscles and the sinews in a way human science was still too primitive to understand. An intrinsic part of the laws of nature and not any sort of reliable sign that he wasn't still dead instead.

Ergo, his voracious morning lust for her meant nothing—just as Rose meant nothing and would remain meaning nothing to him beyond what they had now: a situational friendship borne out of unusual circumstances. Accepting that and enjoying it for what it was did not make him in any way disloyal to Catherine's memory. He hadn't broken any vows. He had simply said a second set, which he had no intentions of honouring. Enjoying a few months of Rose's company did not miraculously make him mended in any way. The status quo was unchanged.

Thank goodness.

'Will you stay here in Whittleston, Sam, or will you move somewhere your slate is clean too?'

It wasn't a question he had expected, or even considered until she had mentioned it, but seeing as she had, he shrugged. It made sense, he supposed, to seek a fresh start. Rose's aunt and uncle lived here, after all, so he would by default hear about her. It would be a darned sight easier forgetting about her if there wasn't that constant reminder—

'Dr Able! Thank God!'

Out of the snow, Bill Anderson the miller emerged, arms waving. By the looks of the twin icy quilted epaulets settled on his shoulders, and the amount of snowflakes covering his horse's mane and saddle, he had been waiting outside Sam's house for quite some time.

'My mother needs you! Her face has dropped.' He pulled down his cheek to illustrate. 'And she cannot move a muscle apart for the littlest finger of her right hand.'

'We'll meet you there!'

Rose didn't wait to be told to turn the curricle, and with a decisive crack of the reins they were flying back down out of the village within seconds.

Rose had never experienced death at close quarters before. Her only family members who had passed had been both sets of her grandparents and, while she had known many Suffolk acquaintances die, their connection had been distant enough that it hadn't touched her. Therefore, to be a quarter of a century old and first witness the exact moment of death was as unsettling as it was humbling.

One moment Mrs Anderson had been staring up at Sam, scared, petrified and frozen by the massive stroke she had suffered, her breathing so ragged and erratic it was haunting. The next the fear in her eyes had been replaced by an odd serenity and she'd sighed and that had been that. She was gone.

To a detached onlooker it seemed peaceful. It was also, strangely, a privilege to see, because something otherworldly had happened to the old lady in her final seconds. Whether that had been resignation or acceptance or, as Rose had decided to hope, the fact she had caught a glimpse of what lay beyond this realm and whatever it was it had given her enough comfort to stop fighting to stay in it.

Odder still was the shroud of death which fell over the room as Sam released Mrs Anderson's wrist, gently closed her eyes and confirmed that she was gone. By then, those gathered around her bedside had already begun to weep. Her son, her two grown grandsons and all their wives had felt her passing in the same visceral way Rose had, and had, within moments, passed from extreme worry to grief.

Mr Anderson Senior, however, was not ready to accept what everyone else had and still clung to his wife's hand, begging her to wake up.

In silent, tacit agreement, she and Sam both rose and left. Staying simply to watch his realisation dawn felt unnecessary and voyeuristic.

'I'm so sorry, Bill.' Sam rubbed the miller's shoulder as he followed them to the door. 'It's no consolation, but with a stroke that severe there was no chance of any recovery. Take comfort in the knowledge that she is free of any pain now.'

'Thank you for trying, though, Doctor.'

'Would you like me to notify the undertaker tonight?'

Bill shook his head. 'They'll be time enough for all that in the morning. Tonight we'd prefer to say our final goodbyes in private as a family.'

As there was nothing else to be said, they left on leaden feet, and a very ashen and subdued Sam was in the process of helping Rose up into the curricle when Mr Anderson Senior suddenly dashed out of the house, tears streaming down his wizened old face as he cried noisily, 'Dr Able, please!'

He grabbed Sam's sleeve and wouldn't let go, even when his son reappeared and tried to call him back.

'You need to give me something. Something strong that will take me to where my Eliza has gone.'

'I'm s-sorry, Mr Anderson.' Raw emotion choked her transient husband's throat. 'I cannot do that.'

'Yes, you can!' The old man dropped to his knees in the snow. 'Please! I don't want to be here if she isn't! I want to go with her! We've been together fifty-seven years! I'm no use to anyone anyway nowadays, and I don't want to spend another minute knowing she's dead and I'm not. You can fix that for me. Nobody needs to know...'

It was pitiable to watch.

'I'm sorry, Mr Anderson.' To his credit, Sam did not try to pull away from the man's iron grip, and left that to his son to do. 'My job is to save lives, not end them.'

'Even if mine just ended anyway?'

As Bill tried his best to gently extricate his aged father and drag him back inside, the old man lunged again and caught Sam's hand this time.

'You have to understand...she was my everything, Doctor. My everything!'

Words that made poor Sam's face blanch and rooted him to the spot.

Even when the bereaved father and son had disappeared indoors, he still stood on the same spot, shoulders slumped, as if reliving his own tragic past. Entirely lost in his own living hell.

Rose slid down from the curricle's perch and slipped her hand in his, tugging him gently. 'Come. Let's get you home.'

She practically had to push all six feet plus and goodness knew how many stones of him into the carriage, where he sat shocked and stunned while she hauled herself in beside him and then drove all the way home.

The snow was coming down thick and fast by the time they returned to his house and Sam's teeth were chattering. She suspected that had more to do with what had just happened than the cold, but despite her insistence of seeing to his horse, so that he could go inside and warm his chilled bones by the fire, he would have none of it. While she unpacked the curricle and took all their Romford purchases inside, so they didn't get ruined by the weather, he took the animal to the little shed it lived in around the back and spent so long rubbing it down and feeding it that the pot of tea she had made them both was cooling on the kitchen table.

He wasn't shivering when he returned, but he was still ashen and looked in dire need of some proper comfort.

'You did all you could have, Sam.' She reached for his hand but he snatched it away, as if angry all of a sudden at his own perceived incompetence.

'Did I? She'd been suffering there an hour before I got to her!' Guilt etched deep lines in his handsome face and his eyes were so stark they frightened her. 'Perhaps if I had got there sooner—'

She wasn't going to let him do that to himself and grabbed him by the shoulders and forced him to face her.

'She had a massive stroke, Sam. Massive. One that left her completely paralysed. That was your initial diagnosis. Before she died, you even told Bill on the quiet that you didn't expect her to survive the night. She was eighty. Very frail already. And hadn't been well for months. I heard you tell Bill that, too, just as I heard you explain to him that there are no effective treatments for stroke victims. That in time, if the patient is lucky, they might regain some of what it has stolen from them, but even if they survive they will not emerge from it unscathed. That in severe cases, such as his mother's, the immediate risk of a second stroke is very high and that would likely be fatal.'

As he tried to dismiss his own words, she shook his shoulders.

'Tell me, what else could you have done beyond giving her the pain relief that you did? You are a physician, Sam, not a miracle-worker.'

She thought she had snapped him out of it, because he blew out a calming breath and nodded.

'Sit down. Have some tea. It will not make you feel any better, I know, but the knowledge that a miracle from above was the only hope she had left should. People die, Sam. With the best will in the world, even you cannot save them all.'

She pulled out a chair for him and he eyed it with distaste before he spun on his heel.

'I'm going to bed.'

'To what? To stew? To second-guess yourself? To punish yourself with guilt?' But his long legs had already taken him to the foot of the stairs, so she caught his hand again. 'Sit with me. Talk to me. Rant at me. Let it all out and don't let this fester!'

He yanked his hand away and stomped up the stairs. 'I want to be alone, Rose!'

She raced up behind him. 'If you think I am leaving you alone like this, you have another think coming! You couldn't have done a thing more than you did!'

He stopped dead on the landing and she crashed into the solid wall of his back. 'Of course I could have! I could have done the decent thing and put that poor bastard out of his misery, like he begged me to!'

'You couldn't have done that!'

When he refused to turn around at her insistence, she pushed her way past him so that she could look into his eyes. They were lost in the hideous memories of Catherine's passing that tonight's parallels had clearly conjured and her heart bled for him.

She gripped his lapel with one hand and smoothed the other over his cheek tenderly. 'You knew that and he never should have asked—but he had just been plunged into the abyss of grief and didn't know what he was asking.'

'He knew what he was asking.' His voice was desolate. 'She was his everything.'

'And that will be reflected in the level of his grief. And, while unbearably tragic to witness, I know that if you asked him now if he would spare himself all of the pain he's in in return for not enjoying every single minute of their fifty-seven years together, he wouldn't. There is only one certainty in life, Sam.' She used both hands to cup his cheeks now, to ensure he listened to her every word. 'That is that each and every one of us must die. We walk blindly into love knowing that ultimately that must happen and accepting it as a fair price for all the joy it brings. The Andersons had fifty-seven years before one of them had to pay that price. He loved her so completely that if she hadn't died tonight he'd be willing her death by the morning, as watching her in pain would have broken him too. Don't make what happened about you and Catherine. No good can come of that.'

'I know… I know…' He nodded, swallowing. 'Usually I can keep it all locked within, but…'

'Tonight felt too akin to your own experience, and that's all right in the moment, but you are not being fair to yourself by torturing yourself with similarities when every death is a tragedy for someone and not every death needs to be a tragedy to you.'

He nodded again and allowed her to pull him into her embrace. 'I'm so tired of feeling broken, Rose...so tired of all the pain and hurt and bitterness that festers within me breaking free and overwhelming me.'

She stroked his hair, grateful that she could be his pillar of strength when he needed one. 'Perhaps it has to for you to finally let it go?'

He pulled away far enough to frown at her. 'I hate what it does to me. How helpless and hopeless it makes me feel.' He pressed his fist to his abdomen. 'How it overtakes all reason and renders me...useless.'

'All the more reason why you shouldn't be alone and why you need company. What can I do tonight to distract you?'

'Don't ask that.'

He huffed and shook his head, as if he had had an idea but quickly discarded it. Then his indecisive gaze locked with hers for the longest time, while he was clearly at war with himself, before it dropped to her mouth. She knew the moment he lost the battle, because he swiftly closed the distance between them and pressed his lips to hers.

Chapter Fifteen

It was a gentle but urgent kiss. Both an exploration and a surrender and potent as a result.

Rose melted against him, winding her arms around his neck in blatant invitation so that he was left in no doubt that she wanted this too. If this was the distraction he wanted then she was all for it. She deepened the kiss and Sam sighed against her mouth. Beneath her fingers, the knotted muscles in his shoulders and back softened as he let go of all the pain that had gripped him mere moments ago and lost himself in her.

He snaked an arm around her waist to tug her closer while his tongue tangled languidly with hers, pulling her hips flush with his so that she could feel the hard length of his desire. Had they not been married, it would have been an outrageous, improper gesture during a first kiss, but because they were—at least temporarily—it was oddly appropriate. Brutally honest from the outset.

He wanted more than a kiss, so she did something she had never done. Never dared to do. And pushed her hand between their bodies to stroke that impertinent bulge so that he knew he could have whatever he wanted.

He half moaned, half growled at her touch and walked her backwards, still kissing her, until her back touched a bedchamber door. She had no clue whose it was until he groped behind her to open it and they stumbled into his.

With no fire in the grate, and no moonlight or stars to illuminate the uncovered windows, it was pitch-black inside and somehow that was fitting. It suited the situation and it empowered her to be bolder than she would have ever thought possible, because she made short work of the buttons of her pelisse so that he could strip her out of it, then helped him untie the laces of her gown.

His hungry mouth never left hers as he smoothed the garment from her shoulders. Then the weight of the heavy green wool worked with gravity to puddle on the floor around her feet. It was immediately joined by his greatcoat, coat, and then his cravat. Her fingers fumbled with the small buttons on his waistcoat. It was impossible to concentrate on the task while he unlaced her stays and tossed them to one side.

They used each other for balance as boots were toed off. Rose tugged his shirt from his waistband, and he broke contact only long enough to strip it from his with one hand.

She was a wanton, breathless creature by the time it came to unbuttoning his falls, in a hurry to move on from kissing to more, and so was he. His breathing was ragged and erratic as he stepped out of his breeches. The meagre light was robbing her of the pleasure of seeing his nakedness in more than shadows—but, oh, my goodness, those shadows were filled with sinful promise. Broad, square shoulders that were almost twice the width of his hips. His erection standing rigid and proud and desperate for her.

Impatient, she ran her palms over his skin. The dusting of hair on his chest was an intriguing contrast to the satin-smooth skin stretched taut over the muscles in his arms and across his belly that she did not possess. Sam wrapped his arms around her waist loosely, nuzzling her neck as he manoeuvred them both to the bed, then lowered himself to sit on it so that he could peel her out of her chemise.

He removed that last barrier between them reverently, and with torturous slowness, trailing his lips over every inch of skin he revealed. The fabric caught on her breasts, which seemed fuller and heavier than usual, so he used his hands to free them, sliding his fingers beneath the tight neckline to cup one, then lifting it out so that he could kiss the upper swell of it, before repeating the task with the other.

Her puckered nipples tightened some more in the chilled air of the room, brazenly poking towards him and begging to be touched. As if he knew that was what her body craved, he kissed around them to torment her, smiling against her skin as she arched her breasts shamelessly towards his mouth.

His hands spanned her ribcage beneath them and fanned down over her fevered skin her to hips. The chemise whispered along her legs on its journey to the floor. He kissed her belly, her navel. Caressed her buttocks. Then, to her surprise, pressed a kiss at the exact spot where her womanhood met her thighs, his hot breath gently ruffling the soft curls between them.

He stood then, opened his arms, and without hesitation she stepped into his embrace, looping her arms around his neck as his tightened around her and their bodies touched everywhere. Her needy breasts found some satisfaction as they flattened against the hard plane of his chest and she marvelled at the insistent throb of his cock against her pelvis. Odd things happened between her legs as warmth and moisture seemed to pool there, but although they were both obviously now ready for more, they simply kissed instead. Thorough, lazy, but intensely intimate kisses that acknowledged there was so much more to come but they both wanted to squeeze every drop of pleasure from the experience by denying themselves the carnal release they craved.

Then, out of nowhere, they simultaneously concluded that the moment had arrived, because he edged her back towards the mattress as she pulled him down on her. They landed together, as they had on that fateful dawn in the snow, with his hips cradled between her legs, perfectly positioned to do what nature had intended those intensely personal and private parts of them to do. Even so, of their own accord her legs fell further apart and her hips tilted, to give him unfettered access, and his hardness dipped to sit in the crease—almost there but nowhere near enough.

She did not recognise the woman who gave the needy moan, begging for more, but as he denied her that his lips finally worshipped her nipples, and the pleasure was so intense, so unexpected, that she cried out into the silent night. Then she writhed beneath him, grinding her hips against his in utter desperation as he tortured each puckered tip with his lips, tongue and teeth. All the while his hardness seemed to grow and pulse against her sensitive flesh, and beneath her palms his body trembled from the force of his own need that he was now fighting to hold back.

'Please, Sam—have me.' She genuinely did not think she could last another second without feeling him inside her. 'I want you so much.'

'You cannot possibly want me more than I want you.'

He stared down into her eyes and she believed him. Because saw it all there. Lust. Desire. And once again surrender. And she rejoiced in all three.

'Every morning I wake up hard for you because you haunt my dreams. I crave you, Rose. Yearn for you. It's like a sickness and nothing cures it.'

'This will.' She tilted her hips enough that the hot tip of his manhood kissed her opening. Then, in case that wasn't a blatant enough invitation, she repeated herself. 'Have me...before I combust from wanting you.'

In one swift, fluid movement he pushed inside her, filling her completely but instinctively pausing at her maidenhead. That seemed to momentarily bother him, because clearly he did not want to hurt her, so Rose gripped his hips and jerked hers up to dispense with it herself, gasping at the slight discomfort while he held himself still above her.

He kissed her tenderly, waiting for her body to relax as it familiarised itself with the intrusion, before inching inside her a little more. He rolled his hips slightly, and that caressed the inner walls of her body so perfectly she sighed, and he smiled against her mouth as he did it some more. It did not take her long to learn the dance, and once she had she embraced it. Revelled in it. Her body blossomed and bloomed beneath his, every nerve-ending she possessed gloriously alive and tingling with each increasingly fervent but exquisite thrust.

She was almost there, although she had no clue where 'there' was, and knew that he was holding himself back, waiting for her to get there. Her hips bucked almost violently as she tried to find a way to get there for him and, as if sensing her frustration, he kissed her.

'It's all right, love.'

And suddenly it was as if the tenderness in his eyes made the universe tilt, and she realised that this—him— was exactly why fate had sabotaged her first wedding. Because she was destined for this. Heaven help her, but he was the one, and her damaged, foolish heart rejoiced at the realisation.

She smiled up and him, and he smiled back, and she decided not to fight it. Instead, she kissed him tenderly back. Infusing it with all of those wonderful, precious feelings that she hadn't intended to feel but that now swamped her.

He slipped his hand between their bodies to dip his thumb between her damp curls, where it found a knot of nerves she had not known existed and gently circled it. Once. Twice. The third was all she needed, and the intimate walls of her body began to pulse around his hardness as stars shimmered behind her eyes and her heart burst with joy inside her chest. And then she was falling. Falling mindless and boneless into an oasis of pure pleasure as she called his name until his release exploded on a cry and he joined her there. Holding her hand. Her name a benediction on his lips and his body pulsing within her in euphoric rhythm with the glorious fading ripples of her own.

Sam awoke feeling lighter and more at ease with himself than he had in years. Every muscle was loose. He was cosy and toasty, rather than hot and sweating as he was often prone to be when bad dreams plagued him or, as recently, when his dreams had been so vivid and carnal they left him wanting. This morning, however, his old chap wasn't standing painfully upright like a flagpole. At best, it was semi-erect, and as sleepy as he was, and that felt good. In fact, apart from the glaring daylight that permeated his eyelids, everything felt good.

He scrunched his eyes tighter and twisted his face further into his pillow to block out the sun—and then froze when hair tickled his nostrils. Because it wasn't his hair. His hair wasn't that luxuriant, and nor was it scented with a delicate hint of floral perfume. Just as the soft surface beneath his hand wasn't his mattress. It was skin. Silken, warm, caressible, feminine skin.

Rose's skin.

He cracked open one eye and indeed there she was. Lost in sleep. Her long lashes were sooty crescents against her alabaster cheeks. Her tousled chestnut hair fanned out over his pillow exactly as he had imagined in all his wild nocturnal fantasies—only better. One bare arm was thrown carelessly above her head, exposing the swell of a plump breast above the edge of his eiderdown.

She was utterly breathtaking in her beauty.

Enough that something unsettling and…scary stirred in his chest.

He retracted his hand gently, because he wasn't ready to face her or this right now, and it roused her. Not enough to wake her, but enough to make her stretch. The half-exposed breast instantly became a fully exposed breast, the dark nipple cresting and hardening in front of his eyes as the chill of the room hit it. Forcing him to watch, transfixed, as her hand appeared from under the blankets to unconsciously caress it until she sighed with sleepy contentment, as if it were a lover's fingers instead of her own.

It was the single most erotic thing he had ever seen.

Until the whole night before assaulted his memory with a whoosh and he was forced to recall that this wasn't the first time he had watched her caress her own nipple. Because sometime around dawn, he now remembered, he had witnessed it from another angle. From below. With her lovely long legs resting on his shoulders while he lapped at her core like a cat that had got the cream as she came to shuddering climax against his mouth.

That had undoubtedly been the single most erotic thing he had ever seen.

At least in this lifetime...post-Catherine.

His first wife had enjoyed that too, and he winced at the memory, feeling disloyal somehow for pleasuring another woman with such single-minded and selfish determination.

And everything he had done to Rose last night had been entirely selfish. In his addled, vulnerable state, after the sad events at the Andersons', he had forgotten to be dead inside and had been so desperate to stop the horrific pain and celebrate feeling alive he had used her outrageously. Taken her virginity without a second thought and then had her twice—no, thrice—over the course of the night, because after witnessing her shuddering climax at dawn he'd had to have her again.

Had to watch her come again while he was buried to the hilt inside her.

It had been, if he said so himself, quite a night, and one that in another life he might have been proud of, because he had always been a very attentive and thorough lover. But it had been the stupidest and most ill-considered thing in the world a man who was gratefully dead inside could have possibly done, when she had to leave and he had to let her, because he couldn't—wouldn't—allow himself to care for anyone like that again.

Bloody hell! What the blazes had he done!

He had just complicated the one thing he had needed to keep as uncomplicated as possible, and all because he hadn't been able to resist hauling the woman he needed to keep at arm's length into his arms!

They were hardly acquaintances now!

Not when his hands and lips had explored every single inch of her lush body and hers had done the same to his. Hardly friends either, seeing as she had kissed him down there too. Nor simply temporary, transient, situational partners in crime either.

They were lovers now!

Possibly even potential parents, as he had been so caught up in her he hadn't had the wherewithal to withdraw at the optimum moment.

Correction—optimum moments!

Because, heaven help him, there had been three of them!

Bloody, bloody hell! What had he been thinking?

Sam gazed at Rose again and his old chap instantly hardened, thanks to that one gorgeous and highly sensitive breast still on show. He groaned aloud. Then wished he could claw it back when she stirred and stretched again, rubbed her eyes with both hands, flung both arms above her head and, to torture him further, dislodged the other breast from beneath the covers. Then, after another undulating, wholly feminine stretch of her spine and wiggle of her hips, slowly her lids fluttered open.

She took one look at him and didn't balk or panic, like he was doing. There was not an ounce of regret on her stunning face as she smiled.

'Hello, you.' Her voice was deep and husky as she woke, so seductive he felt it everywhere. 'Did you sleep well?'

'Like a log,' he said, wondering how the hell he was going to fix this now that the cork was literally and figuratively out of the bottle and couldn't ever be put back in. How the blazes did you *un*make love to a woman?

It was a fairly momentous thing to make love to one, after all. Especially one who had never lain with another man before. He was always going to be her first. And the first time was significant. So significant, good manners dictated that he had to mention it.

'I hope I didn't…er…hurt you too much last night?'

She shook her head, shy all of a sudden at the mention of her 'downstairs', despite being apparently unashamedly bare-breasted upstairs. 'Some mild discomfort that didn't last long.'

'And now…?' *After I rutted inside you repeatedly like a randy, foaming bull in a field of cows in season!* 'Are you sore at all?'

The physician in him had to ask, but the guilt-ridden man dreaded the answer.

'I'm aware that you've visited, Sam, if that is what you are asking.' A bubble of embarrassed laughter popped out of her mouth and she blushed a little. 'But I rather like the feeling, so please don't offer me any poultices or potions, *Dr Able*. I am not in need of your medical services today.'

'All right, then...'

Was now the right time to bolt? To run screaming for the hills while he figured out what the hell to do next? Probably not, despite the internal chaotic whirling of every emotion he possessed. She didn't deserve that when she had bent over backwards to please him, both literally and figuratively. He suddenly recalled that the second time he'd joined with her, when she had briefly left the bed in the small hours to do...whatever she had needed to do...he'd met her in the middle of the bedchamber on her way back, moved her hair to kiss her shoulders and her back, and then had her hard and fast over the bedstead.

Bloody hell!

He glanced at her with remorse, and then, like the randy beast he had been, felt his eyes drift to her breasts. She noticed. But instead of covering them, like most former blushing virgins would have on the glaring dawn of their deflowering, Rose, of course, met him head-on. Fearless to the last and determined not to let him faze her. With the covers still bunched around her waist she rolled onto her side, propping herself up on her elbow while her hair cascaded over one shoulder in a riot of satin brown curls, and traced a seductive finger over his chest.

'But while I do not need your medical services, and we are already too late for the Sunday service at St Hildreth's, I am not so sore that I would say no to some of your other unique services, though.'

And just like that he was as hard as granite and desperate for her again.

Would it really matter if he had her for the fifth time?

The unholy mess was already made...

Her finger began to trail downwards, then disappeared beneath the covers, and her touch felt so good he was sorely tempted to ignore the screaming voice in his head to get the hell out of there. He would have too if he hadn't stared deep into her eyes, seen her smiling in anticipation of the mindless fulfilment to come, and that unsettling, scary thing stirred in his chest again. Jolted, actually. So dangerously close to his shrivelled husk of a heart that it had him sitting bolt upright.

'Sorry. Can't.'

Won't!

'I've got calls to make…' Which was a pathetic excuse for a Sunday, when everyone was likely currently sitting in St Hildreth's listening to the Sunday sermon. 'The Andersons…' He grappled for something—anything—vaguely plausible. 'I need to check on Mr Anderson Senior. I'm worried about him.'

'Oh…'

Her lovely face fell and he hated himself for hurting her, then hated himself more for making her feel ashamed of her desire as she gathered the blankets up to cover herself, as if she had somehow done something wrong.

'Of course…the poor man.'

She knew he was lying through his teeth. Knew he was trying to soften the blow of rejecting her—all of her—with nonsense, because he was too cowardly to tell her the truth.

'It's really not you, Rose…it's me.' Which was true. She was perfect and he was…nauseous. Suffocating.

Petrified.

'I need some time and space to think about…' He flapped his hand between them. 'This.'

'I understand.'

She nodded again, making him feel wretched, because he really didn't deserve her understanding after what he had done. Or what he was doing. How was this any better than jilting her? Rejection was rejection, and she was again bearing the brunt of one. But, typically, she was stoic about it.

Hiding her hurt behind an uncertain smile, she sat up in the bed and hugged her knees to her chest beneath the covers. 'I suppose this is…unexpected. But not so awful, I hope?'

'No,' he lied slipping gratefully off the mattress and groping around for his clothes. 'Not awful at all. Just… big.'

Huge. Monumental.

Unsurmountable!

'I need some time alone to square it in my mind, Rose.'

Had he broken his vows to Catherine? Were they even still valid now that she was gone? Did it matter when he wasn't capable of honouring them anyway? To love, honour and cherish involved caring, and he no longer had the capacity of will to care. Lust was lust, but Rose deserved so much more than that, and he…couldn't.

Wouldn't.

'Will you be back in time for the whist game later? Sophie and Rafe did invite us to luncheon too… But if you'd rather I cancelled and we talked about this instead…once you've squared it in your mind?'

And already *'this'* had become more complicated than he could bear, because he knew there was nothing really to square. The die had been cast, he had nothing tangible to offer, and he was going to have to hurt her some more however he tried to deliver that news.

'I'll be back in time for that, I promise.'

As he backed out of the room, clutching a bundle of clothes, he desperately wanted to kiss her goodbye and reassure her that he would try to work through the blind panic that had gripped him by the balls and made him sick to his stomach.

But he couldn't risk it and he couldn't lie to her. So instead he said the only thing that he could under the circumstances before he closed the door. 'This really isn't about you, because you are…perfect. But…'

'But Catherine was your everything and you cannot let her go.' She tackled the great unsaid head-on once again. 'I know that, Sam, so don't feel wretched about it.'

'Wretched' didn't even begin to cover what he was currently feeling. His insides were contorted with wretched guilt. Wretched pain. Wretched desire and wretched regret.

'I really am sorry, Rose.'

Chapter Sixteen

Rose had hated every minute of the weekly whist tournament so far. It might have been more bearable and less tortuous if Sam hadn't come, but he had kept his promise to be there, albeit arriving late with a profusion of fake apologies to their hosts, and somehow that made it all worse.

With some concerted effort, they both behaved as if nothing was wrong, still played as partners and still managed to win their first game, but to her it was obvious that the parameters of their relationship had shifted. And once again she hadn't seen it coming. Hadn't realised that she had stupidly opened her heart to a man incapable of loving her as she loved him.

And Lord help her, but she loved Sam. She wasn't sure how she had allowed that to happen, despite the manifestation of all the worrying signs beforehand, but she knew that it had as she'd floated back to earth after the first time they had made love. Knew it without a shadow of a doubt. Because she absolutely wouldn't have been able to have made love quite so freely and whole-heartedly, and with such blind trust otherwise.

Thankfully, she hadn't blurted out as much in the

throes of passion, so he was none the wiser. However, she did not fool herself that if she had his reaction this morning would have been any different. For him, it had been an unexpected and now regrettable night of passion, and not a celebration of overwhelming feelings that he did not possess. He had wanted her last night but did not want her now. He certainly did not want her for ever, and at some point today he was going to try to explain that to her as gently as he could. Because he wasn't a cruel man. Just another one whose heart belonged to another.

'What say you we swap the pairings up a bit for the second round?' Mrs Fitzherbert didn't like to lose, and was still smarting at the loss of her shilling in the last game. 'It might be fun if all the gentlemen move one seat to the left?'

Which would put Rose, who was considered by all present to be the best whist player, with Archie, who was undeniably the worst. It would also give her wily nonagenarian friend Sam, who was the second-best player, so nobody was fooled by the ploy.

Their host, Rafe, glanced at Isobel, who would become his de facto partner and shrugged. 'I'm game.'

Of course he was. Because Isobel could hold her own. But Sophie, who would be paired with Ned, was less keen, because Ned didn't really see the point of whist and only ever came for the food.

'Two chairs to the left,' said Sophie in challenge. 'Otherwise I say we keep things as they are. What do you say, Rose?' Her friend shot her a pointed look, searching for an ally, and it was then that Rose realised she couldn't bear it any longer. If an awkward conversation needed to be had, and she was going to get her heart broken again anyway, she might as well get it over with.

'I apologise—but I need to go home. I'm not feeling particularly well.'

Which wasn't a lie. She had been feeling wretched and humiliated—again—since Sam had bolted from the bed this morning. The look of complete abhorrence on his face was now carved into her bludgeoned heart, right beside the awful letter she had received from her former fiancé, in which he had said he was relieved to be shot of her. One look at Sam, however, confirmed that he wasn't anywhere near ready for the conversation, as all the colour had drained from his face.

'You can stay if you want to, Sam. I'm not that ill. I just need some fresh air and some quiet.'

And a private place to curl up into a ball, cry her eyes out and castigate herself for being such a bloody fool all over again.

He stood, looking concerned, and headed her way, every inch the concerned and caring husband despite his lack of any real care for her at all. 'Of course I am coming with you.'

'Indeed,' said Mrs Fitzherbert with a thud of her cane. 'What sort of a husband would he be if he didn't rush to your ailing side? We would all judge him—and very ill too. Of course, we shall all judge the pair of you once you leave, Rose, as we are not fooled in the slightest by your swift decline into a malaise that will doubtless necessitate, by doctor's orders, an entire afternoon in bed. But newlyweds will be newlyweds.'

She winked and everyone except Archie, who was oblivious to such blatant innuendo, sniggered.

Rose smiled tightly at her friend, wishing she was

brave enough to air the sham she was living so that she didn't have to pretend any more. 'You can think what you want, and doubtless will anyway, so I wish you all a pleasant afternoon. Please don't get up.' She gestured to Rafe and Sophie, who were now also standing. 'We can see ourselves out.'

Fortunately, that assurance was respected, and they were left alone to wait for Sam's curricle to be brought out front. He clearly sensed the real reason for their departure, as he stood beside her stiffly for all that time and didn't say a word. It was just as well, because Rose wasn't anywhere near ready to have a civil conversation with him. Not when she was so furious with the pair of them she wanted to lash out, with her fists as well as her tongue.

And she still had her pride.

He might not want her, and she might be both humiliated and devastated by that fact, but by Jove she still had her pride!

As their conveyance rattled into the courtyard of Hockley Hall she decided she would not be the wounded victim this time. At least not openly.

'Can I drive?' Being in control of the curricle would give her the upper hand and, if she needed it, the whip.

He nodded, his expression wary. 'If you want to.'

She did not wait for him to help her up, because the last thing she wanted to endure was his touch, and that left him severely on the wrong foot too as he had to traipse all the way around to the other side. By the time he climbed in next to her she was settled, and she purposely set off before he was ready, taking some small pleasure in the way he lurched and then had to grope for the seat to regain his balance.

'I take it you aren't actually ill?' he said, trying to take control of the situation—or at least the conversation. 'And that we need to talk.'

'You know me. I hate the great unsaid. And after you hot-footed it out of bed this morning, as if your absent breeches were on fire, there definitely need to be some words said. And, if you don't mind, I would like to start.'

She could tell he did mind, because his dark brows kissed each other in consternation and his eyes were troubled. He was bothered and scared that she was about to beg him to love her back, or at least give them a chance, the blithering idiot! When she would rather walk on hot coals barefoot than let him see how much he had hurt her.

'Go ahead.'

He stiffened his spine and physically braced himself against the sides of the curricle, and it took all of her strength not to scream at him.

'Say what you need to say.'

Rose focussed on the road, rather than the ache in her chest, and forced a wry smile. 'Well, firstly, I wanted you to know that while last night was…um…nice enough…' It wouldn't hurt to knock him down a peg or two with such an insipid endorsement of his exceptional skills as a lover. 'I am not sure it is wise to repeat the experience.' In her peripheral vision she could see that had surprised him. 'I need to leave in a few months, and I fear that any repetition of the passion which exploded between us last night might lead to inconvenient and uncomfortable feelings that neither of us need.'

'I see…'

But judging by his rapid blinking he didn't. He had intended to make this speech, had expected her tears and tantrums, and he wasn't able to dissemble quickly enough to accommodate the fact that there weren't any.

'With hindsight, we probably shouldn't have done it, because now everything has become horribly awkward.' She shuddered and then shrugged. 'But I'll confess I've decided not to regret it, because after being denied the first one I am actually relieved to have had a wedding night, as it makes everything more believable going forward. I mean, once we are separated it would seem very odd that I am still intact down below when the time comes for me to take another lover, wouldn't it?'

That made him frown some more. 'I suppose it would.'

'And what we did doesn't have to be more complicated than it is if we can both be adults about it. You and I have always been brutally honest with one another, after all, and it's not as if there is any love lost between us to make last night anything more than the slaking of some mutual lust. I like you and you like me. But your heart remains with Catherine and mine, much to my chagrin, still remains with Justin, no matter how much I also loathe the scoundrel.'

What was sauce for the goose was sauce for the gander, after all, even if she had just uttered a complete pack of lies. Apart from the loathing bit, of course, because she meant that. Just saying Justin's name made her boil with fury.

'Was that his name? *Justin?*' He said that final word with some distaste.

'It *is* his name. Sadly, the duplicitous wretch is still around to taunt me, but I feel that I can properly move on from him now, thanks to our sham marriage. Now when I return to Suffolk I can do so with my head held high, because I shall return a married woman. And thanks to that, and to you for making me an honest woman at last, once our separation becomes official I won't have to worry about nonsense like propriety any more. I can do what I like—and I will.'

She made sure her smile looked mischievous.

'Especially now that I've discovered that I don't dislike bed sport. So thank you for opening my eyes to all those delightful possibilities.'

His eyes widened with shock at that statement and so, purely for a little petty revenge, she decided to embellish it.

'I've also been giving some thought to where I will live, and in view of all the new freedoms I can look forward to I've decided to move to a big town rather than a village. More people but, conversely, less prying eyes.' She wiggled her brows like Mrs Fitzherbert, to let him think that she would be naked and on her back while she enjoyed most of those freedoms. 'And before you offer again, I shall do it without your money. My father is a wealthy man who will happily gift me the money to buy my own business, and once we separate I'd prefer a clean break, Sam. Not one muddied with unnecessary financial ties that bind us together. I hope you don't mind, but I want to be free and not feel obligated to you in any way.'

'Of course I don't mind.'

He was, she could tell, completely flabbergasted by all that he had just heard, and did not approve of most of it, so she patted herself on the back for a job well done. He had no right to tell her how to live her life. Not when he still had no intentions of being any part of it.

'Good. I'm glad we have had this talk and cleared

the air, transient husband. I'd hate to think that one ill-considered night of passion would ruin everything we have done so far to make our temporary marriage bearable.'

He was quiet for the longest time, clearly stewing in his own juices and still put out by her lacklustre endorsement of his *'nice'* performance in bed.

She was turning the curricle into the square when he broke the silence. 'Obviously we will have to rethink all that if we accidentally made a child last night.'

A sobering statement that brought her up short. 'I didn't think a woman could conceive during her first time?'

'That is a stupid old wives' tale—much like all the nonsense that you hear about breastfeeding being a barrier to conception too. Because a woman very much can get pregnant during both of those things. However, even if it wasn't an old wives' tale, we did it more than once—didn't we, temporary wife?'

'I suppose we did.' Off-kilter, she pulled up outside his house. 'But I sincerely doubt we have anything to worry about.'

Without waiting for him again, she alighted and sailed inside leaving him to see to his horse, supremely worried despite all her bravado. She hadn't considered the possibility of them making a child. Not once during their three splendid couplings and certainly not at all today.

To vex her, Sam didn't see to his horse and instead followed her inside and up the stairs. 'When were your last courses? And when do you expect the next?'

'That's really none of your business!'

She stalked into the parlour and slammed the door

behind her. She probably should have wedged a chair under the handle as it flew open again.

'Oh, I think it is, if I'm going to be a father, don't you?'

He didn't sound so much angry as horrified by the prospect, and that wounded. It must have showed because he spread his palms and tempered his tone.

'In some scientific circles it is believed that the middle of a woman's cycle affords her the best opportunity to conceive, and we can only rule out that worry if we know the usual duration of your cycle, the date of your last one and, more importantly, when you anticipate the next. I'm not trying to pry, Rose, more to be pragmatic. Just in case.'

'Two weeks,' she blurted, horrified herself now at the potential implications of having a child with a man who didn't even want a wife, let alone a family. To corroborate that fact, his brows flew skyward before he dragged them back down and tried to appear calm. 'They always coincide with the new moon.'

'All right…' He exhaled as he nodded, all the colour draining from his cheeks. 'Then we won't have to wait too long for the answer and we shall cross that bridge only *if* we come to it.' He attempted a reassuring smile, but it was anything but. 'Until then, we keep calm and try to make the best of things.'

Chapter Seventeen

With the frigid late February wind whistling through the dark village square Sam should have been grateful to finally be home, but he wasn't. It hadn't felt like home much since he and Rose had spent that fateful night of unbridled passion together almost six weeks ago. They were still civil, and on the surface did their best to behave as if nothing was amiss, but it clearly was. Their intimacy had changed things irrevocably, and no amount of pretending otherwise was going to alter that.

They had made a stab at their short-lived version of normality in the immediate aftermath, and he was certainly still making the effort to regain some of the easy friendliness they had enjoyed in that first week of their marriage. That pleasant initial seven days when they had been making the best of things while sharing their meals and laughing about their days felt like a short and much too sweet honeymoon now, compared to the stilted collisions they had nowadays. With each passing day, things seemed to get worse, too, and he didn't really understand why as usually some distance from an event lessened its significance as the world moved on.

In public at least they were their usual selves, and he found himself wishing away the days between all the obligatory social events that he'd used to dread. Probably because around others Rose and he still shared witty repartee, while being unbeatable at whist, and they had even danced together twice at the last assembly. All for show, of course, to maintain the façade, but he wished it wasn't.

When they were alone it was a very different story, because it was obvious that she was making a concerted effort to avoid him. She now ate at different times from him and went out more, so that they were little better than ships passing in the night. When they did collide, irrespective of the inanity of their safe but forced attempts at a chat, he could tell by the way she looked at him that she hadn't been able to get past the morning he had bolted from the bed. Whereas he, no matter how hard he tried not to be bothered by it, couldn't move on from her matter-of-fact dismissal of what had happened in it.

He veered between wanting to find evidence that it meant more to her than she had claimed and trying to feel relieved that she had let him off the hook as far as any uncomfortable emotional attachments were concerned.

He wanted to say that it all suited him just fine, but it didn't. He missed their conversations and he missed her sunny company. He didn't want to miss either, but there it was. He also didn't want to keep wanting her—but every time he saw her it took all his willpower not to haul her into his arms and kiss her until they were both mindless and breathless and beyond the realms of the common sense which paralysed them.

Or at least until he was breathless.

Since she had dismissed his efforts that night in his bed as uninspiring and 'nice enough', which still smarted, he wasn't entirely sure that he had ever truly made her breathless at all. Thanks to the disastrous attempt to hoodwink the village gamblers that had led them to this point, he already knew she could be a good actress, and now he worried incessantly that she had pretended to come apart in his arms that night simply to make him feel better.

At the time, he had been convinced that she had been overcome with pleasure from his efforts, and constantly placated himself with the fact that a virgin who had believed that a woman couldn't conceive during her first time wouldn't have any notion of faking an orgasm. Especially when she had been so surprised to have one in the first place it had been spectacular to watch.

But what did he really know?

For all his detailed medical knowledge of human anatomy, the simple truth was that a woman's body worked very differently from a man's. There had been tangible proof left behind on the sheets from his own orgasms that night, but all he had as confirmation of hers was what he had seen in the moment.

Or thought he had seen in his emotionally charged and irrational state.

Because, as Rafe had quite rightly said, way back before Christmas and before this mockery of a marriage had even started, people might not always believe what they saw, but they always saw what they believed. And that night, after he had made mad, passionate love to a woman for the first time in four long years, he had wanted see Rose enjoying it as much as he had. The fact that she had been quick to state that she wanted no repetition of that night, with him at least, all rather suggested that she hadn't, and he very definitely wasn't at peace with that.

Any more than he was at peace with the idea of her taking a lover in the future, after she left him a free woman, despite them both being free to live the lives they wanted always being the original plan.

Nor, if he was honest, was he happy about her leaving at all. But, as she made a point of reminding him— regularly—that she was eager to 'move on' once their transient sham was over, he kept that to himself. She seemed to be filled with gushing plans in which he didn't feature—and who could blame her when all he could offer was more of what they already had? Which was basically them muddling along stoically, thanks to the dried-up husk in his chest.

Perhaps things would have been different if they had made a child together. But, alas, that complication had quickly evaporated into nothing. On the morning of the new moon she had been visibly relieved to tell him that they had avoided the dreadful possibility of parenthood. Announcing it as she served him a particularly sumptuous breakfast with such a beaming smile of joy that had proclaimed, for her at least, that the arrival of her courses was a cause for celebration, and that had smarted too. Not because he'd wanted there to be a child, of course, as that was a complication he did not need. But...

As he closed the stall gate on his horse, he huffed at the stupid lies he was telling himself over and over again, when he knew, deep down, a part of him *had* wanted the complication. A baby would have been such an insurmountable problem that the pair of them would have had to change tack and at least try to make a go of things. But fate had either decided to be kind to him or to be cruel—he still wasn't sure which—and that had been the end of that.

In a month she would leave, and his life would return to its previous even and comfortable keel. Devoid of all temptations and all the messy, unpalatable emotions that he did not want to have to contemplate.

Just him, all alone again, undistracted from his work. With his toast.

The latter depressed him. The former... Well, what he felt about that was probably best pushed into the back of his mind with all the rest of the things he didn't want to think about, because each time he did he felt queasy. At least in a month he wouldn't have to think about it— her—at all. Except he suspected he would. He might not be capable of loving Rose, but he liked her a great deal more than he had thought himself capable of doing, and had, foolishly, become...used to her being around.

Sam stamped the slush from his boots in the porch, trying not to acknowledge how much the thought of seeing her buoyed him, and the rich aromas of one of her legendary stews wafting from the kitchen was already making his mouth water. However, when he pushed open the front door he could tell straight away that she wasn't there, because his flesh didn't tingle with awareness as it always did when she was near, and that, in one fell swoop, royally spoiled his appetite too.

Drat her.

Even so, he still trudged to the kitchen to eat what she had left for him. He needed the sustenance, and a lifetime of toast stretched before him, so it made sense to make the most of Rose's delicious cooking while it lasted.

He was halfway through his miserable, solitary but delicious repast when there was a hammering on the front door.

'Sam!' It was Rafe's voice and it was panicked. 'Sam! Are you home?'

'Yes.' He flung open the door, took one look at Archie's limp and profusely bleeding arm, clutched tight to his chest, and knew that something very bad indeed had happened.

'Bloody poachers!'

Rafe had to help his brother into the hall, because he wasn't in a good way. A great deal of that was probably down to blood loss but, knowing Archie as well as he did, Sam knew that the lad's panic and fear were also playing their part. He'd been crying so much his breath now sawed in and out in ragged gulps and all the blood had clearly frightened him.

'They've been laying deer traps again on my land.'

Sam rushed to support Archie's other side and together he and Rafe half walked him, half dragged him into the surgery.

'Archie tried to move one out of the way of his dog, and before I could stop him it snapped shut.'

'How long ago did it happen?'

'No more than fifteen, maybe twenty minutes ago. I figured it made more sense to bring him straight here than send a messenger and then wait for you to come to us.'

As a former soldier, Rafe knew only too well how dangerous blood-loss could be, and had used his cravat to tie a tourniquet around his brother's upper arm and kept it elevated, but it hadn't stemmed all of the blood, which dripped off Archie's fingers to the floor.

Aware of that, he dropped his voice. 'I didn't want him to lose too much, but—'

'You did the right thing.'

He didn't want Rafe to feel unnecessarily worse when he must be feeling wretched enough already. The truth was, had Sam been there, it was exactly what he would have done too, until he could work on the wounds.

He kicked open the door to his surgery and gestured to the table. 'Help me lift him up there and keep him as calm as you can while I work.'

A task that was easier said than done when the swooning, scared Archie lolled like a dead weight in their arms.

'I'm going to need to examine the wound, Archie, all right? Try to hold still and I'll do my best not to hurt you more than it hurst already.'

The lad nodded, clearly terrified, while Sam did his best to swallow the rush of nausea which always accompanied treating someone he knew well. Unfortunately, Archie wasn't the sort to allow you to keep him at arm's length, and Sam liked this man-child far more than was useful for either of them in this precise moment. The best medicine was always best administered dispassionately, and with a clear head, and Sam's was currently spinning with all the potential complications and implications.

He sucked in a few subtle, calming breaths, then gave himself a stern talking-to as he fetched some scissors to cut away Archie's bloody clothes, some water, and enough linen towels to clean the area enough when he had an idea of how to proceed.

Pull yourself together, man!

Archie needed all Sam's wits and none of the unhelpful panic which had gripped him. Rafe, too, needed to see the confident, icy calm of a competent and well-trained physician. The sort who wouldn't make a mistake.

The sort who wouldn't let either of them down.

'Let's take a look at that arm, then, shall we?' He smiled a smile he didn't feel for both their sakes. 'I'm going to leave the tourniquet in place for a minute and cut your sleeve away. It might sting a bit, but I'll be as quick as I can, Archie, I promise.'

He was about to start cutting when Mr Outhwaite skidded through the open door, dressed in just his shirt and breeches and still in his slippers.

'I saw the commotion and have come to help!'

A timely offer, which Sam would have taken up if the older man hadn't balked the second he saw all the blood.

Recognising that Mr Outhwaite might be more of a hindrance than a help, Rafe was quick to divert him. 'Go and fetch my wife from St Hildreth's. Archie will need her.'

'Mine too,' added Sam, without a moment's hesitation, realising that he needed Rose here more than anything. Not only did she face everything head-on, and with no excuses, she was strong and tenacious and he needed both of those attributes now—in spades.

He also just needed her beside him, and right now, when Archie needed him so very much, Sam wasn't going to question why that was.

'You do know that if you made your stitches smaller, your fabric would sit flatter?'

Isobel reached for her stitch-ripper to unpick the haphazard patch that Mrs Fitzherbert had just added to the quilt they were making and the old lady bristled.

'I still do not see why I have to make quilts for the cold and needy of this parish and cannot simply purchase some for them instead.'

'Because this way is more thoughtful, and it is harder to refuse a gift that has been made than it is to turn down one that has been purchased.' Isobel made short work of removing the offending patch and tossing it back. 'The needy of the parish might well be cold and poor, but they still have their pride, and pride always comes before a fall—isn't that right, Rose?'

As the quilts were all Rose's idea, she nodded, a little ashamed that she had badgered the entire Sewing Circle into giving up three evenings this week to the endeavour when they could have just as easily raised some money and purchased them to give out with the food baskets they were also collecting. They had agreed because they were good people and it was a good cause. Only she knew that it was a convenient ploy to help her avoid Sam this week. Until she knew for sure whether she was with child or not, she could not trust herself to keep her anxiety about it to herself.

'It's been a long and bitter winter, and people's reserves are depleted, but most would rather freeze to death than admit it. Nobody likes to feel beholden or a burden to others.'

She certainly didn't. The last thing she wanted was to feel beholden to Sam, and she certainly did not want to become his burden. Not for any longer than they had mutually agreed at least—no matter what occurred or didn't in the next few days.

All her anxiety might well be for nought at this stage

anyway. Yes, her courses were six weeks late, but according to all Sam's medical books it was too early to say for sure that she was pregnant until she had missed two in a row—which wouldn't be for another few days yet. She would have a better idea of her predicament with the next moon. And perhaps it would take even longer than that to be sure, as his books all recommended that to be the time to have it confirmed with a physician's examination, and she certainly couldn't ask for one of those!

She had no clue what to do, and had no forward plan if she was pregnant, but she did know, with absolute certainty, that the last person she wanted to know of her potential predicament was him, when he had been nothing but honest about the depressing fact that he didn't want her in his life any longer than he had to. He didn't want a wife, let alone the additional inconvenience of a child.

Thankfully, after the shocking lie that she still felt so wretched about, he was blissfully ignorant of her turmoil and, rightly or wrongly, she wanted to keep it that way. If she wasn't pregnant, she would leave as planned on the first of April, and if she was, she would probably still leave as planned on that day anyway, leaving him none the wiser.

She already knew that Sam would insist on doing the honourable thing, but would then feel doubly entrapped, and she wouldn't be able to stand that. It was one thing to be unwanted and unloved in the short term, but another entirely to be so for all eternity! If it had been soul-destroying to be jilted by a man she had loved, and then have to watch him find happiness with another, she dreaded to think what living cheek by jowl with a man she loved but who felt nothing but resentment in return would do to her.

Neither of them deserved that misery—and, the honourable thing or not, it didn't strike her as the healthiest environment in which to bring up a child. In which case, the least said, the soonest mended, and she would cross that bridge if she came to it.

Rose did not need to have all the answers figured out yet. She just needed the one answer first—and that wouldn't come until this relentless February finally drew to a close.

Mrs Fitzherbert's bony elbow nudged her out of her reverie. 'You are quiet and contemplative this evening. Are things not going well between you and your handsome doctor? I know the old adage is "marry in haste and repent at leisure" but I have high hopes the pair of you will be the exception to the rule, despite your inauspicious start.'

'I wouldn't put a bet on that if I were you, Mrs Fitzherbert.' If she was leaving in a month regardless, she might as well sow the seeds of their very real discord with her closest friends here. 'Neither of us wanted the marriage, and two months on I am not sure that sentiment has changed. We are still more acquaintances than husband and wife.' Especially now that their friendship was well and truly dead. 'It isn't working and I hold out no hopes that it will.'

There, she'd said it.

'Give it time,' said Sophie as she reached out to squeeze Rose's hand. 'I am sure things will get better. You share a sense of humour, after all, and have always seemed to rub along together well. Perhaps you can build on that?'

Rose pulled a face of disbelief, because they didn't even share any laughter any more, thanks to *that night*. 'That is hardly the most secure of foundations—and how much time do you waste flogging a dead horse?'

Especially when theirs had been shot in the paddock, by mutual agreement, before the race had even started.

'If I were you, I'd give it a bit longer than a few months, because I've always sensed a promising frisson between you both.' A hopeless matchmaker to her core, Isobel wiggled her brows. 'And that will undoubtedly firm up those foundations swiftly if you act upon it.'

'I sincerely doubt that.' Rose couldn't help scoffing, when making love had done nothing but the opposite. Rather than pull them together, it had ripped an enormous chasm between them.

'I sense it too, and I think Isobel is right. Act on the frisson.' Sophie wiggled her own brows. 'Once Rafe and I did, it soon turned into love.'

'It was the frisson that sealed the deal for Ned and me too...' Isobel sighed, then chuckled as if she was remembering something wholly improper. 'A frisson that wouldn't be denied.'

'Not that she tried very hard to deny it.' Mrs Fitzherbert cackled, and then nudged Rose. 'I hope you haven't actually spent the last two months denying it? A decent frisson with a devilishly attractive man should always be acted upon. Especially when two people are married, irrespective of if they want to be, and can legitimately indulge the frisson whenever the urge strikes.'

She cackled some more, and nudged Rose so hard she almost knocked her off her chair.

'Which begs the second obvious question—has the

urge struck yet? Have you allowed your handsome doctor to thoroughly *examine* you?'

'Well... I...er...' Rose's face glowed as red as a beetroot, and then glowed some more when her friends, rather than telling Mrs Fitzherbert off for embarrassing her and asking grossly inappropriate and improper questions, all sat forward, grinning and expectant.

'Well? Has he?' Sophie had at least whispered that, whereas Isobel pointed and laughed.

'Of course he has! The blush never lies, and that one is a particularly guilty one.'

The pointed finger touched Rose's cheek and her outrageous friend made a sizzling sound.

'Our blushing Rose has finally been pricked!'

'Excellent!' Mrs Fitzherbert exclaimed this so loudly all the other sewers stopped to stare at their table. Including Rose's prudish Aunt Agatha. 'And about time too. Five and twenty years is too long to wait for a good pricking.'

'Could you *please* keep your voices down?' Rose hissed, while furiously pretending to the rest of the room that she was focussed on her sewing. She feared the blush on her cheeks, neck and ears had now reached such a level of incendiary ferociousness her hair might actually burst into flames if she touched it. 'Whether he has or he hasn't, it clearly isn't the magical solution you all seem to think, as we are still little better than strangers stuck under the same roof and are both thoroughly miserable to boot.'

Undeterred, and now thoroughly waylaid by thoughts of the actual deed rather than the unfortunate consequences of it, Mrs Fitzherbert spoke with an exaggerated whisper so loud that everyone must hear it.

'Well? Is he as good a lover as we all hoped a man with his medical knowledge would be?'

'Well? Is he?' asked Sophie and Isobel in grinning unison.

'Er...well...um... What difference does it make when we are both still miserable?'

'Sophie, Rose, come quick!' The Reverend Spears suddenly slammed into the village hall and dashed into the centre of the room, with her Uncle William out of breath behind him. 'There has been a dreadful accident—Archie is hurt and you need to go with all haste to the physician's!'

Chapter Eighteen

'I need you all to wait upstairs in the parlour!'

To Sam's relief, Rose shooed the sudden influx of well-meaning onlookers out of the surgery.

'Give poor Archie and my husband some space! And, yes, that does indeed mean you too, Mrs Fitzherbert! The only two people who can stay are Rafe and Sophie!'

She practically pushed the last of them out and went to follow.

'Could you stay too, please, Rose?' He flicked his gaze at their distraught friends, willing her to see that he was in dire need of another level head in this room which currently only possessed one. 'While Sophie and Rafe keep Archie calm, I am going to need an assistant.'

She took one look at Rafe, who was clearly riddled with guilt while he tried to keep his brother still on the examination table, and Sophie, who was cradling the inconsolable Archie to her bosom, and nodded.

'Of course.'

She held up her finger before poking her head back out through the door, where she spoke to someone in hushed tones—mostly likely Isobel—asking her to ensure someone stood guard outside in her stead, then returned, smiling to cover her own anxiety about the situation for their patient's benefit.

'What do you need me to do?'

As she was the second most medically qualified person in the room, albeit in horses rather than humans, and because he wasn't entirely sure himself what needed doing yet and he trusted her, he figured explaining the problem was the best place to start and they would go from there.

He gestured towards the wounded arm in his lap, choosing his words carefully so as not to alarm the others. 'The claws of the trap missed the bone, thank goodness, but they did catch the skin.'

Now that Archie's sleeve had been cut away, and the worst of the wounds cleaned, Sam knew he had a job on his hands.

'These three cuts will need stitching.' They were deep and jagged puncture marks, each about an inch wide and a good half an inch deep. 'This one…' he gently twisted the arm to show her the large chunk of missing flesh which he was most concerned about and her pretty eyes widened '…will need cauterising to stop the bleeding, and that will need to be done first.'

She nodded, grasping the scope of the problem immediately. 'Which cautery do you want me to prepare?'

He answered by widening his thumb and finger several inches. This was going to need one of his substantial old battlefield tools and not the daintier sort he frequently needed here.

'You will find it in the top cupboard to the left.'

Rose retrieved that, and several others, wrapped them in a cloth so Archie did not catch sight of them and hurried out through the door to heat them in the kitchen fire. He was pleased that she'd had the foresight to take them out of this room, as the sight of glowing red metal in here wasn't going to calm anyone.

'I think it's best if we give Archie a bit more laudanum now,' he whispered to Rafe in an aside. 'The less he is aware of what needs to happen next, the better. Once I start, I'm going to need you and Sophie to hold him down.'

Rafe nodded, blanching, because as a former soldier he'd likely seen similar procedures hundreds of times before—but never on his beloved brother. 'Archie's strong, so it might be prudent to tie him down too, once the medicine kicks in.'

'There's some strapping in that drawer over there.'

Good grief, but his profession was brutal sometimes! The fact that Sam was going to have to hurt poor, sweet, gentle Archie to try to heal him made him sick to his stomach, but he had no choice. If he didn't seal that big wound the young man might bleed to death, and even if he did there were no guarantees that he would have done enough.

Once the laudanum was administered, between the three of them they lay Archie flat on the table and prepared both him and themselves for the ordeal to come. By the time Rose slipped back in to check on them, several minutes after leaving, Sam and his patient were as ready as they were going to be. All he had to do was nod his head for Rose to go and fetch the red-hot cautery.

While he composed himself, by getting used to the weight of the iron in his hand, she did something that hadn't ever occurred to him before. She held up a sheet between the business side of the wound and Rafe, Sophie and Archie, and fastened it in place.

'It will be awful enough without having to see it.'

She squeezed her friend's hand and Rafe's shoulder, then came around the other side to rub Sam's back. As if she read his mind, she said exactly what he needed to hear.

'It's what needs to be done, Sam, so don't second guess yourself.'

When he nodded, grateful for the reassurance, she offered him one of her wry, make-the-best-of-it smiles.

'And if it gets too much, or you faint, know that I've branded many a cow and can take over.'

It was almost one in the morning by the time the Hockley carriage left, and everyone was shattered. The sealing of Archie's wounds hadn't taken more than forty minutes, but Sam hadn't allowed Rafe and Sophie to take him home until he was certain that his patient was in a fit enough state to travel. That had meant waiting for the heavy dose of laudanum he had given him to wear off enough that poor Archie was lucid—which had also meant that he was in pain. Pain that was unavoidable under the circumstances, but managed to an extent by the much weaker tincture of laudanum that he had been sent home with. It was still more than Sam was comfortable with.

He was greatly troubled as Rose closed the front door and, as they had on the night when Mrs Anderson had passed, his broad shoulders seemed to bear the entire weight of the world.

'You did an excellent job, Sam. You stopped the bleeding and repaired all the damage.'

She wanted to touch him, to hug him, but couldn't. For a month and a half she had done the best she could not to allow her unreciprocated and unwelcome feelings for him to show, and now that they only had a month together left prudence dictated that she kept it that way.

While she harboured an irrational anger with him for not being able to love her, she also knew that her anger wasn't fair. She had entered this marriage with her eyes wide open, fully aware of the fact that it wasn't a permanent arrangement and that he wasn't capable of ever loving another again. He was too good a man—too good a human being—to be burdened with her predicament. He might not be able to love any more, but he certainly felt a huge responsibility for the people under his care, which she supposed was the category she now sat in, and he was plagued by guilt. Especially for his own perceived limitations and failings.

Rose wasn't going to add to that. She loved him too much to hurt him.

'Once those wounds heal, all Archie will have is a few more scars.'

'*If* those wounds heal.' His entire body sagged as he sighed. 'Unfortunately, we still have a mountain to climb.' At her frown, he sighed again. It was a resigned but frustrated exhalation. 'Infection is the enemy now—just as it always is. It is the curse of medicine. We have learned how to stop bleeding, to an extent, and can to a lesser extent manage pain, but there is nothing in the arsenal to battle infection—and it will be a battle if it sets in.'

'Do you think it will?'

He threw up his palms, his expression fearful. 'That is in the lap of the gods. Archie might be one of the lucky ones who avoids it, but we all need to prepare ourselves that he might not. Like so many things in medicine, there is no rhyme or reason to it. Infection is one of those things that our science is still too primitive to understand, and nobody really knows what causes it. It is arbitrary and ruthless in its selection of victims, and once it's taken hold, it festers quickly. With wounds as large as Archie's, the arm could be gangrenous within days.'

'And if it is?' Rose asked, even though she suspected she knew the answer.

'A swift amputation might stop it.'

Sam's complexion was as green as she felt, and it was obvious it was not something he would find easy to do. Especially to such a gentle, innocent soul as Archie.

'But if the blood is poisoned by it, then…' His voice trailed off and he ran an agitated hand through his hair, looking suddenly so much older than his thirty-four years. 'Let me just say that during the war we lost more men to infections than to bullets. The tiniest injury could be fatal.'

When he had laid it out in such stark terms, she knew that he wouldn't take any comfort from empty platitudes. 'When will we know?'

'The next five days, while the bulk of the healing takes place, will be critical.'

'And the odds?' She had to ask it, even though she dreaded the answer.

'At best, it's evens. In reality, knowing what I know about the unpredictable nature of the beast, Archie has a one in three chance of avoiding it. News I shall have to break to Rafe and Sophie in the morning, when I go and check on him.' He leaned his back against the wall, as if he needed it to support himself. 'I suppose I should have told them tonight, but…'

'Tonight was difficult enough for all concerned, and they didn't need more torment to add to their worries. Do not castigate yourself for sparing them that for a few hours more, Sam.'

'Sophie's expecting again.' He blurted that out as if he needed to purge himself of it. 'Early days, barely eight weeks, so she wants to keep it a secret because she's miscarried before. In truth, I resisted telling them because the stress of something like this so early in her pregnancy might well cause her to miscarry again. The first twelve weeks are always the most precarious while the foetus develops. That is when, metaphorically, it would be the ideal time to wrap the prospective mother in cotton wool.'

Rose suppressed the urge to stroke her own tummy and reassure herself that the child that might be growing in her womb was safe, despite all her fears for Archie. Instead, she gestured for him to follow her to the kitchen and casually asked, 'Does trauma always end in a miscarriage?'

'Not always, but the risks are definitely increased. If she was further along—say four or five months—I would be less worried about the impact of this, but...'

'Then maybe just tell Rafe about the infection risks for now. Sophie doesn't need to know unless the worst happens.'

'I suppose you are right.' He sat at the kitchen table and stared at its surface, lost in thought while she gathered what she needed from the pantry to make them both some hot chocolate. 'Of all the people fate decided to do this to, why Archie? He's never hurt a soul in his life and the scamp does nothing but spread joy.'

'There is no rhyme or reason to it, as you said. Sometimes bad things happen, and often to good people. Life is never plain sailing. Mrs Fitzherbert claims that we need the awful to remind us to celebrate the good.'

'And again I say, why Archie? Why is fate that cruel?'

As his question clearly wasn't just about Archie, Rose couldn't stop herself from reaching out and rubbing his shoulder. 'The only guarantee any of us have in life is that one day it will end. For some, much too soon, and for others too late. All the pondering and philosophising in the world isn't going to make any sense of the reasons why, and perhaps they are not meant to be understood. They just are.'

'To a man of science, that is a very unsatisfactory answer,' he said. He reached up to squeeze her fingers, unaware of the havoc such a simple touch created within her. 'But I suppose the crux of what you are saying has merit, and I suppose I need to learn to accept what nobody yet understands.'

'Or you could continue punishing yourself for things decreed by the cosmos and out of the sphere of your influence so that you will never experience a moment's happiness ever again.'

She hadn't meant that to sound like an accusation, but it had. As he stiffened, she tugged her hand away to pour his drink. 'Here—this will help you sleep.'

'Thank you.' He took the drink with knitted brows. 'But I sincerely doubt an entire vat of this will help me sleep tonight.' He stood. 'I'm going to work through the night instead. Use the insomnia productively and see if I can't find something in my medical journals that will improve Archie's chances.'

He went off at speed, clutching the cup, forcing her to jog to keep up with him.

Rose darted in front of him before he reached the office and blocked the door. 'Oh, no, you are not! You are a brilliant physician, Sam. There is nothing in those books that you do not already know, and probably nowhere near enough in them to encompass all that you do!' She prodded his chest. '*You* are Archie's best chance and he needs you to be at the top of your game tomorrow—not a frazzled, exhausted wreck! So you are going to bed right this minute, even if I have to drag you up those stairs! If sleep eludes you, a few hours of rest will still be more restorative and of more use to Archie than you tormenting yourself trying to find answers that we both already know do not exist!'

For a moment she thought he would argue, but instead he huffed. 'Has anyone ever told you that you are a very bossy woman, Mrs Able?'

'Somebody needs to take care of your physical health, seeing as that is never you.' While she seemed to be winning, she pointed an imperious finger to the stairs. 'Go to bed, Sam—now. Or I will drag you up there by the hair.'

Miraculously, he did as he was told, and within moments they were both on the narrow landing above. Him outside his bedchamber door and her outside hers, directly opposite. Yet instead of heading into the room she had banished him to he lingered, staring at her oddly.

'Thank you,' he said.

'For what?'

'For the chocolate. For nagging me just now. For looking out for me.' He glanced down at the mug in his hands, fingering the handle. 'For all your help tonight with Archie. You were my rock tonight, Rose, when I needed one and…' He winced and stared into the dark depths of his chocolate rather than look at her. 'I don't suppose... No...that's a bad idea. Hugely inappropriate.'

Her pulse quickened. 'You don't suppose what?'

'That you would keep me company.'

His eyes lifted. Locked with hers. They were filled with something akin to yearning. Tortured yearning. As if he was at odds with himself and really didn't want to be feeling any of it.

'I'm not suggesting that we...you know...unless...' His gaze dipped to her lips momentarily, making her want him. 'I'd just like us to talk for a while and...' He blew out a tortured breath, reached out and traced a hesitant finger over her cheek before he twirled it in her hair. 'I've so missed talking to you.'

Rose wanted to lean into his hand. Wanted to touch him. Kiss him. Spend the night with him. Talking with him and making him feel better and making love—which she knew would be inevitable if she followed him through that door. But she also knew that she could only risk the avalanche of emotions that came with that if there was hope.

'Talking and then what?'

He swallowed, and the yearning in his eyes was shuttered. She supposed that said it all. He just wanted a night with her again. The temporary distraction of her body and not all the unpalatable complications that went hand in hand with that.

'Does there have to be a *then*? Can't *now* be good enough for the time being?' he asked.

'For me there does.' She stepped away from his touch. 'I have to leave in a month, and I need to be able to do that knowing exactly where I stand.'

'You don't have to leave in a month.' He closed the

distance again, suddenly too close, but not close enough as he searched her gaze. 'We could extend the deadline and see if…perhaps we can find a way to muddle along together.'

It was the 'if' that did it first. The 'muddle along' was merely the icing on the inedible cake.

'To what point or purpose, Sam? To prolong the agony? To add more layers of complexity to an already untenable situation? You were right the first time—that is a bad idea.'

'Perhaps… But doesn't the fact that I still don't want to let you go count for something? Can't that be enough?'

'No—because you don't want to let Catherine go either, and that's the heart of the problem.'

He jerked back as if she had slapped him, and that was the final nail in their coffin.

'I'm so sick and tired of being the woman a man makes do with, Sam. You are effectively expecting me to agree to always being second-best.'

'You know that I cannot make any sort of—'

She pressed a finger to his lips rather than hear his truth. 'I *do* know, and I'm not asking you to. It wouldn't be fair to you when you have never been anything but brutally honest with me about that. So please do not ask me not to leave next month, as that wouldn't be fair to me. I have to be brutally honest with you too, Sam, as well as with myself. I don't want to "muddle along", or wait and see, or waste my life hoping for more that likely won't come. I deserve to be someone's *everything*, and if the last year has taught me anything, it is that I am not prepared to accept less than everything going forward. No matter what the expectations of others are or the direness of the circumstances. I'd honestly rather spend eternity alone than settle for half-measures ever again.'

It was her truth, and her right, whether she was with child or not. That was a depressing, frightening but still empowering realisation, which made her resolute now.

'I'm sorry, Sam, but there it is, and you need to respect that.'

He nodded, still frowning. 'I shouldn't have asked... I'm sorry.'

Doubtless he wasn't as sorry as she was—but then why would he be when he wouldn't allow his heart to be engaged? And she was in no doubt any more that he still had one. He cared too much about too many things for it to be a dried-up husk in his chest, no matter what he chose to believe to the contrary.

'I just wish that—'

'Don't.' Rose shrugged as she opened her door—because what else was there to say? 'Goodnight, transient husband.'

'Goodnight, temporary wife.'

His answering smile was wry but his eyes...

His haunted, hazel, part-warring, part-molten eyes were suddenly anything but.

Chapter Nineteen

Rose eyed the quarter to noon post to Colchester and wondered for perhaps the fifth time in less than a minute if she shouldn't simply climb on it and go. Call it quits now and escape Whittleston and her temporary marriage a few weeks earlier than planned and just be done with the misery of it all.

Especially as the second new moon had come and gone and there was still no sign of her dratted courses.

Not that she needed the continued absence of them to confirm the worst when her body suddenly wasn't behaving the way it always had for the last quarter-century of her existence. Her breasts were fuller and more tender, her belly was firmer, but rounder, and her skin was positively glowing. And, as bizarre as it sounded, she could feel the life inside her getting stronger by the day.

Therefore, Rose had to immediately face two hard but undeniable facts. Firstly, she needed to accept that she was definitely having Sam's baby, and secondly, for the sake of her own sanity, she needed to have it alone. Preferably without him ever knowing, as the only way her poor, aching heart was going to survive this second bittersweet heartbreak was to never have to see him ever again.

It was a week since he had offered her the lacklustre proposition of muddling through, and each time she saw him she experienced the overwhelming urge to weep. She also felt the overwhelming urge to weep when she didn't see him, because she thought about him constantly, so it was clear that something drastic needed to be done before she did the unthinkable and broke down and wept before him.

She glanced at the quarter to noon post again, as the driver called a warning to the last of the passengers still lingering in the inn that he was off, and almost hurried across the square to join them. And perhaps she would have too, but Mrs Fitzherbert's antiquated barouche box suddenly rattled alongside.

The faded velvet curtains snapped open, closely followed by the door. 'Get in, girl, before you catch a chill!'

'There really is no need when my house is there.' She pointed to the surgery door, feeling slightly pathetic to have been seen avoiding it until Sam's surgery finished and he left for all his afternoon calls. Which was likely imminent. 'Also, I have a few more errands to run.'

She didn't want them to collide in the street. Didn't want to witness that sad but accepting smile which he had developed in the last week. The smile that told her he really didn't want her to leave, but he really couldn't offer more than half-measures and so would respect her decision.

In her current melancholy state, that smile might just be her undoing.

'Urgent errands, are they?' Mrs Fitzherbert's lips flattened. 'Because if they are that begs the question as to why you have been stood on this corner staring wistfully at nought for the last fifteen minutes. And do not dare deny it when I could see you as plain as day from my parlour window, young lady, looking all lost and lonely. So get in! You are clearly miserable and at a loose end—and actively avoiding going home—and I'd appreciate some company.'

As Sam was likely about to burst forth from the front door, Rose climbed in. In case Mrs Fitzherbert continued on her 'lost and lonely' vein, she changed the subject. 'Where are we going?'

'To Hockley Hall. To visit Sophie and Archie.'

'Are they up to visitors?'

'Who knows?' Mrs Fitzherbert threw up her palms. 'I suppose we'll find out once we call upon them.'

The barouche pulled away just as Sam appeared at the front door, but Rose pretended not to notice, pulling one of the many blankets folded on the seat beside her over her lap.

'Isn't it funny how sometimes you do not realise how cold you are until you step out of it?' she said.

'It doesn't help that it's been freezing since November and we've all forgotten what being warm feels like.' The old lady's wizened finger pointed out of the window to the eerie pink-and-grey-hued clouds with a quaking finger. 'Doesn't the Almighty realise that it is March and we are due spring, not more blasted snow? I am sick to the back teeth of all this cold weather.'

'So am I.' Rose relaxed against the seat.

'Marvellous—that's the weather thoroughly discussed, then. Now, let's move on to more pressing things. Like why you've gone shopping every morning this week at eight without fail, have hardly bought a thing, and don't return home until your handsome husband has left it?'

'Well... I...'

'Or, even better, explain why you look constantly sad, and he looks sadder, or why the middle buttons of that fine green pelisse that fitted you like a glove a fort-night ago are suddenly straining?' That wizened finger tapped one of them, while a wily white brow quirked. 'Does he know that he's planted a bun in your oven?'

A week's worth of weeping gathered behind Rose's eyes and then, without a moment's warning, suddenly burst out in a flood of biblical proportions. '*No!* And you c-c-can't tell him! He can n-n-never know!'

'Why ever not?'

'Because we agreed to end our sham marriage on April Fools' Day and s-s-separate. That was always the p-p-plan. We never intended to make a g-g-go of it!'

Then it all came spilling out. Everything from their pre-planned separation to his devotion to his dead wife, and then a painfully abridged retelling of *that night*, her own futile feelings and the chasm both had created, and his subsequent and confusing offer to 'muddle through' when he had needed another distraction. She finished with her current dilemma, confessing that she was sorely tempted to leave early in case Sam spotted the obvious changes happening to her body before March finished.

Throughout it all, Mrs Fitzherbert did not speak. At least not with words. Her expressive face, however, spoke volumes. It was only once Rose had finished the sorry tale and was a quivering, hiccoughing mess that she realised the barouche box had been doing laps up and down the lane to Hockley Hall for goodness knew how long.

'I just don't know what to do.'

'What an unholy mess.' Mrs Fitzherbert shook her head. 'No wonder you are both so miserable.'

The sympathy was all well and good, but what she needed now was the older woman's wisdom. 'If you were me, what would you do?'

'I haven't a clue, dear, but I'll certainly give it some thought.'

Not at all the advice Rose so desperately needed or had hoped for when the confession had been prised out of her.

'In the meantime, let's enjoy a nice cup of tea at Sophie's, shall we?' She rapped on the ceiling of the carriage and smiled. 'I've brought a lovely cake.'

More confused than she had been before she had poured out her heart, Rose had to hurry to repair her face and then paste on a smile in the scant few minutes that it took to pull up on Sophie's drive. Uncertain as to whether their friend would be up to visitors, she tried to hover in the hall while the butler enquired whether or not his mistress was receiving today, but Mrs Fitzherbert wasn't that subtle.

She had already removed her coat and hat and was already halfway to the drawing room when he returned. 'Lady Hockley will be with you presently.'

That was when Rose disrobed. She was barely out of her coat when Fred, Archie's giant dog, galloped down the stairs to greet her. Hot on his heels was the beaming young man himself, and to her untrained eye he appeared to be in the finest of fettles despite his bandaged arm.

'Hello, Rose! I've missed you!' Never one to hide his feelings, Archie was down the stairs like a shot, and flung himself at her and hugged her tight with his good arm. 'Thank you for visiting. I've been so *bored* stuck here indoors I thought I'd die of it!'

'We're in the challenging stage of his convalescence.' Sophie's voice came from the landing. Her friend looked tired, but otherwise well. 'This morning has been particularly trying, so your visit is a timely one as Archie and I are both desperate for diversion.'

'Archibald Peel, come and kiss me this second!'

As he dashed to respond to Mrs Fitzherbert's summons, Rose hugged Sophie. 'He looks well.'

'He *is* well, thank goodness.'

Close up, she could see the shadows around Sophie's eyes and how pale she was. 'And you? How are you bearing up?'

Instinctively, Sophie rubbed her tummy and smiled. 'Much better than I was this time last week. But life does like to toss us these reminders not to take things for granted, so I am grateful that all our worst fears weren't realised and also completely frazzled by Archie's rapid recovery.'

She shot Rose an unamused look.

'Your brilliant husband ordered bedrest, and I am sure you can imagine how well that went down with my exuberant brother-in-law. Rafe threatened to tie him to the bed yesterday. Today, we have both given up trying to keep him horizontal in favour of simply keeping him inside. Suffice to say, after battling him solo for the entire morning, poor Rafe has had to go and chop some wood as he feared he would murder him otherwise. I've managed an hour so far and already need a lie-down.'

'Then allow me and Mrs Fitzherbert to take up the slack while you put your feet up. She's brought a cake.'

They settled in the drawing room with tea and a large slab of fruitcake each. Archie demanded a double slice, because of his war wounds, while Fred gnawed on the enormous bone Mrs Fitzherbert had brought him.

'If you do not mind me saying, you look much too wan and haggard, Sophie.' Never one for tact, Mrs Fitzherbert said this with a scowl. 'Are you coming down with something?'

'I'm going to be an uncle again,' said Archie around a mouthful of cak—before he slapped his forehead. 'Whoops! That was supposed to be a secret, wasn't it?'

'You're pregnant?' The old lady raised her quizzing glass to study Sophie's tummy, then quirked a brow at Rose. 'There must be something in the water as there seems to be a lot of it going around. Congratulations.'

Fortunately, her friend missed that unsubtle hint, and rubbed her barely protruding belly again. 'Thank you—I am delighted, but the morning sickness has been dreadful this time around. It was bad with Lillibet, but nothing like this.'

'Then it's probably a boy,' said Mrs Fitzherbert, giving Rose the side-eye again, as if she should know. 'The male of the species is always the most troublesome, and morning sickness is the devil's work.'

It was a comment which made her question her own pregnancy as she hadn't felt sick once. Did that mean she might not be? And if she wasn't should she be glad rather than sad at the prospect?

'I wouldn't mind if it was confined to the mornings, but it's not. It waxes and wanes throughout the day,' said Sophie.

'It does that,' said Mrs Fitzherbert again, with another pointed glare at Rose. 'And it makes you weepy.'

At least that was reassuring, and probably explained why she felt so tearful. It wasn't all Sam's fault, drat him. Or maybe it was. If he hadn't been so...vigorous, she might not be in this predicament at all, and if he hadn't been so entrenched and devoted to the sainted Catherine maybe she wouldn't be suffering from a chronic case of unrequited love.

As if she'd read her mind, Mrs Fitzherbert dragged him into the conversation. 'What has our eminent local physician prescribed for the nausea?'

'Ginger—in tea or biscuits. Although sadly both make me retch. Along with some sympathy and some jolly good mollycoddling, which does help a bit.' Sophie smiled. 'Sam has been lovely.'

'Then perhaps there is hope for him yet—although I daresay his wife might contradict you, as he's still making her exceedingly miserable.'

Rose contemplated strangling Mrs Fitzherbert before her loose tongue caused irreversible damage, but was denied the chance when she heard Sam's voice out in the hall. In case either of her friends continued the awkward conversation, she placed a finger to her lips for Sophie and shot warning daggers at the nonagenarian to whom she had foolishly confessed all. It seemed to do the trick, and the three of them were all wearing fake smiles when he strode in with Rafe.

He beamed at Sophie—then his step faltered as he realised she was there. Instantly he was uncomfortable. His Adam's apple bobbed twice before he realised his smile had slipped.

'Hello, Archie...ladies.'

Their eyes locked briefly before he snapped his away to address Archie.

'Your brother tells me that you have been an unbear-able patient.'

Archie shrugged, only a little contrite. 'I feel fine, so I don't see why I can't go out.' Then he pouted. 'It's been seven days, Sam. *Seven*. Whole. Days!'

'And if I am not happy, it might be seven more. Give me your arm.' He was about to unwrap it when he seemed to realise he was about to reveal a gory wound in polite company. 'Maybe we should adjourn to another room while the ladies take their tea?'

'Don't mind us,' said Mrs Fitzherbert, shuffling her chair closer to get a better view. 'You do what needs to done. None of us are squeamish.'

'Perhaps I will adjourn to the other room…' Sophie looked bilious. 'Not because of Archie's arm but—' She covered her mouth and bolted, with Rafe just a few steps behind her.

Sam glanced at Rose, a question in his eyes, but it was Mrs Fitzherbert who answered it. 'We all know that she's expecting now, so there's no need to pretend that you don't.'

In case he thought she had betrayed his confidence, Rose was quick to add, 'Archie let the cat out of the bag.'

'Oh.' He visibly relaxed. 'Then you won't mind if I go and see her next. But in the meantime…' He held out one hand and Archie dropped his arm into it in a manner which suggested the pair of them had done this many times in the last week.

Rose knew that he had checked on Archie daily, because it was one of the few essential conversations they had. Usually in the short window of time between him arriving home for his dinner and her leaving him with it. She wanted to know how the lad was faring and he needed to know if there had been any urgent messages for him while he had been out. It was a brief and concise exchange of words that rarely took more than five minutes—which was just as well because anything more than five minutes tended to become excruciating in its awkwardness.

Sam made short work of unravelling the dressing and tossing it in a heap on the side table before he checked on the jagged collection of injuries beneath.

'Everything seems to be healing nicely.' He gently probed the edges of the biggest, cauterised wound, which had now completely scabbed over. 'This one remains nice and dry.'

Which was music to Rose's ears because that was the one which had always been of the most concern.

'All the swelling has gone down.'

'It itches,' complained Archie, trying to scratch it, only to have his hand slapped away.

'Itching equals healing. Scratching leads to trouble, and at least another seven days cooped up inside.' He reached into his medical bag for a clean dressing and Archie groaned.

'The bandage *really* itches!'

'And what does itching equal?' Her transient husband had the patience of a saint with Archie.

'Healing.'

'Then you can suffer it until I take the stitches out in a few more days. Until then, young man, you need to keep these wounds covered and—'

'Urgh!' Archie rolled his eyes like a petulant child. 'Please don't say I need more bedrest, because I'm not doing that!'

'Actually…' Sam dabbed some salve on the stitches

and then briskly set about binding the arm in fresh linen. 'I was going to suggest you could take Fred outside once a day for some fresh air—but only if Rafe is with you and only if you refrain from scratching your arm. However, seeing as you are determined to be stubborn rather than sensible, I might change my mind. Perhaps you are not ready?'

'Oh, I am Sam, and I won't scratch, I promise.'

'Well, all right, then.' The bandage secured, he ruffled Archie's hair as he smiled knowingly at Rose. Mrs Fitzherbert caught her smiling back, and she was forced to take a sip of her tea to hide it.

'In my humble opinion, when the time comes you will make an excellent father, Dr Able.'

While Rose almost choked on her tea, and shot the old lady more daggers over the rim of her cup, Sam struggled to find a suitable response.

'I...um...' Panicked, he glanced to her and assumed— so she hoped—that her stunned reaction was down to the fact that she had no clue how to respond to this rather than suspect anything was amiss. 'Maybe...if we are blessed.'

'I am so glad to hear that you think children a blessing rather than a curse, because they are. In the main. I am sure yours will be delightful, like their affable parents, and far too clever for their own good.' Mrs Fitzherbert sipped her own tea as if butter wouldn't melt in her treacherous, indiscreet mouth. 'And what handsome children you will make too.' The wily old eyes wandered to Rose's belly before they arrowed on Sam. 'Would you prefer boys or girls?'

'Er...no preference. So long as they are healthy I have no preference either way.'

'The correct answer, Dr Able.' Then, as an aside to Rose, she said, 'You married a good one, so make sure you keep hold of him.'

'Well…um…' It was her turn to stutter now, because she had no idea if Mrs Fitzherbert was merely having some fun at their expense, or if she had just advised Rose not to leave.

'Are you able to drop your lovely wife back home? Only it's time for my afternoon nap.' Their aged torturer then stood, as if her work was done.

Hers might be, but Rose's very much wasn't, so she stood too. 'I shall leave with you, Mrs Fitzherbert, if you don't mind. Sam still needs to see Sophie, and then he has more rounds to finish, and I need to get back to the village straight away as I have a long list of things to do.'

Wringing this old lady's neck was at the top of it.

'Suit yourself.' Annoyed at being thwarted, Mrs Fitzherbert curled her lip. 'But you'll need to walk back from my house, as I am very, very tired.'

Rose didn't trust herself to speak until they were alone in the barouche box and cantering along the driveway. 'What do you think you were playing at back there? When I specifically told you that I do not want Sam to know that I am with child!'

'I was testing the ground and observing.'

'By stating aloud that I have found myself "a good one" and need to "keep hold of him"?'

'Oh, that was for his benefit, dear. A test. To see if he deserves you to stay or not. Which he failed.'

'He did?' Her anger giving way to disappointment, Rose slumped back into the seat. 'Then you do *not* think that I should keep hold of him?'

With Mrs Fitzherbert's tendency to talk in riddles, it would make sense to clarify.

'Absolutely not. You have to leave the wretch. In fact, I think your instincts this morning were right, Rose. If I were you, I wouldn't wait until April Fools' Day. I'd leave tomorrow. Nothing can come of you staying, apart from more misery. Not when it's as plain as the nose on your face that he doesn't love you even slightly and isn't ever likely to.'

Rose knew as much, because he had always been up front about it, but it still hurt to hear it. Until she had, she hadn't realised how much she'd harboured the hope that he might change his mind.

'How could you tell?'

'The eyes don't lie, dear, and his were…well…frankly horrified when I suggested that you keep hold of him. And he actually looked disgusted when I mentioned the prospect of children.'

'Disgusted?' All at once Rose wanted to weep again. 'That does not bode well.'

'It bodes awfully, dear. Especially when I get the impression he is as eager to get your sham over with as you are. He'd see the addition of a child to the mix much like the trap that caught Archie last week. He might accept that he has been caught for a short while, out of a misplaced sense of duty, but it won't take long for him to do what all beasts do when they want to be free and chew one of his limbs off to be rid of it.'

'Oh.' It was a blunt and depressing answer that was difficult to hear, but sadly accurate. 'So much for him wanting us to muddle through.'

Mrs Fitzherbert shook her head. 'Men will say anything when they're feeling as frisky as a horse, and you know that deep down, don't you? Or you'd have grate-fully spent the night with the wretch when he asked you to. But you didn't. You turned him down flat and I am proud of you for that. You deserve everything, Rose, and his version of half-measures would ultimately suck all the joy out of your soul.'

Because this brutal dousing with ice-cold water hadn't already rendered her poor soul joyless?

'Then I should leave?'

Why did she keep asking for reassurance when she knew Mrs Fitzherbert's customary bluntness was ac-curate?

'One cannot make a silk purse out of a sow's ear, dear, and you'll get over him quicker if you accept that.' She patted her arm. 'Now, speed is of the essence in your delicate condition.' The old lady eyed her belly, as if it had grown exponentially in the space of the last few hours. 'You need to get away before more snow falls and you are stuck here.' She patted her stomach. 'An-other week and you'll show too much, and our clever doctor is bound to put two and two together to make four. Then his sense of duty will ensure that he never lets you leave, and all three of you will then be doomed to suffer the sow's ear for ever.'

She huffed, her white brows knitted together.

'But how to get you away as fast as possible without putting the cat amongst the pigeons...?'

Chapter Twenty

It was late by the time Sam reached his front door. He was purposely late because he had taken an impromptu trip to Hornchurch to visit the apothecary when he'd run out of afternoon calls to make and hadn't been able to face going home. Or, more accurately, hadn't been able to trust himself to go home and not say something stupid and reckless that he would likely regret or that would make everything worse. Especially when she had, quite rightly, told him that he needed to respect her wishes.

It was constantly on the tip of his tongue to blurt out that she did deserve everything—and he wanted the chance to try and give her it.

It was probably a futile hope. He knew that too. The husk in his chest was too battle-scarred to ever be what she needed it to be, and he was too scared of a thorough resurrection to commit to the cause fully. However, the only thing he knew with any certainty was that, selfishly, he didn't want her to go. At least not on the first of April, as planned. Maybe another month or two might bring more hope, or confirm the futility of it, but he couldn't let her leave until they had both made some effort to fix things.

They had taken vows, after all. They might not have meant them at the time, but some of them definitely resonated with him now.

'To have and to hold', for example, was something he was all for. He also had no issues with 'for better or worse', 'for richer or poorer' and 'in sickness and in health'—that was no less than his duty as a husband and a decent human being. He could also certainly cherish, because he already did cherish Rose. He might have struggled to show her that, but he was thankful for every day they'd had together, and absolutely cherished all the wonderful, unique things that made Rose... Rose. From her sarcasm to her naughty sense of fun. From her lovely smile and lush body to the way she looked after him even though he didn't expect or need her to.

But could he love again? Fully and without reservation? Was he capable of it? Brave enough to risk all of himself again? Allow her to become his everything and then...?

From the reliable way his stomach lurched and he came out in a cold sweat every single time he dared to ponder it, that was probably a no.

So really, pragmatically, there was only one sticking point. Granted, it was the most important one as far as she was concerned, but if he genuinely meant all the rest, and did his best to prove them all to Rose from this day forward, maybe she wouldn't notice?

And maybe pigs might fly, because she had always read him like a book.

But he still had three weeks to ponder and consider, and maybe—if a miracle occurred—he would find a way to keep her with him? Finding better words than the unattractive 'muddling through' might be a good start. He had once been charming, after all. And flirtatious and...fun. Some of that perhaps still existed. If it did, he needed to haul it out of hiding, give it a bit of an airing and then deploy it at the right moment.

But tonight wasn't it.

He wasn't ready, and felt ill-prepared after their stilted encounter earlier at Hockley Hall, when she had made it plain she could think of nothing worse than sharing a curricle with him alone. The look of horror which had skittered across her pretty face had suggested that it might be appropriate for him to lay some proper groundwork before he tried to broach the subject of their future again. The last clumsy attempt had been disastrous. Another might send her running to Suffolk the moment he started speaking.

He pushed on the door and found it locked, which was odd. But as it was past eleven, the porch lamp was lit, and the key was where it always was, he brushed that aside. The lock was stiff, and creaked slightly as it turned, despite him trying to be as quiet as possible. He was hoping she might, in the spirit of her determined avoidance of him, have long gone to bed.

That hope was dashed the moment he stepped into the hall and she appeared on the landing. She was dressed for bed in her prim, knotted robe, and her posture was as stiff and awkward as it could possibly be.

'You're late. You missed dinner.' She fiddled with the knot of her belt, chewing her bottom lip momentarily. 'I was worried.'

Worried was surely a promising sign?

'Can we talk about us, Rose?' The question tumbled out before he could stop it. 'Only, I think—'

She stayed him with her palm, her jaw and spine instantly rigid. 'It's very late, Sam, and I am tired.'

'I know...' He raked a hand through his hair, then started up the stairs. Something within him was screaming at him that if they didn't talk now it would be too late. 'But I have things I need to say and we are running out of time.'

'I think we already have.' She folded her arms, defensive, as his boots hit the landing, and they remained folded when he attempted to reach for her hand. 'No amount of talking is going to change that.'

His hand dropped impotently to his side in defeat and he nodded—then immediately shook his head as his fingers fisted. A sharp pain ripped through his chest. 'But we've still got three weeks, damn it, and I want to at least try!'

'To "muddle through"?'

'To do right by you, Rose!' How to put into words the turmoil churning up his insides? 'I need to do right by you.'

'You have already done right by me, Sam. You married me out of your innate sense of nobility when you really didn't need to. We both know that you were well within your rights not to, when everything that happened was all my fault. From the bet to the flirting to the foal and the night we spent unchaperoned in that blizzard. I was to blame for all of that, and I refused to listen to your repeated cautions to the contrary. You have restored my good reputation and given me the ability to return home with my head held somewhat higher than it was when I left it. I shall be eternally grateful for all of that and require nothing else from you.'

'I want to try. I want to talk—'

Her finger pressed against his lips.

'Not tonight.'

'Tomorrow, then.' His hands found her hips as he stared deep into her eyes, willing her to see that all was not lost. 'Promise me that we can talk about us tomorrow?'

It seemed to take for ever for her to nod. 'Tomorrow.'

But she didn't look convinced that any talk would fix all that needing fixing.

'I want to do right by you, Rose—and that's the honest truth.'

'I know you do.' Then she traced the shape of his mouth and smiled the saddest smile he had ever seen. 'And I want to do right by you too.'

'Then that's a start, isn't it?'

Rather than answer, she pressed her mouth to his, and they both poured everything into a kiss so poignant and sublime that even the dried-up husk in his chest lurched with hope. Because a kiss was a very good start indeed…especially when she seemed to want to prolong it.

When it finally came to an end, neither pulled away and they simply stared deep in to each other's eyes. He wanted to lean in and do it again. Lose himself in her. But that wouldn't be fair when there was still the great unsaid to tackle.

So he smiled down at her and tried to be noble. 'It's very late and you are tired.'

'I am.' She chewed her lip and stared at his. 'But I still want you to make love to me, Sam.'

'Mr Bunion—how can I help?'

Normally the sight of the oily, obnoxious, fusty-smelling solicitor's apprentice in his waiting room would royally spoil Sam's morning, but today he was so filled with sunshine and light he even managed a smile for the man.

His buoyant mood and cheery disposition was undoubtedly all the fault of Rose, who had kept him awake for hours last night, doing all the things to his body that he had yearned for since the first time they had made love. This time he was in no doubt that she had thoroughly enjoyed it, because he had poured his husk of a heart and his soul into showing her that he intended to honour his vows to her.

She had shattered in his arms, or beneath his mouth, four times between midnight and dawn. And as the first rays of the morning had bathed them on his mattress they had made such slow and tender love that it had felt like a rebirth. Without the disguise of darkness, there had also been an honesty to those proceedings that added a new dimension to them. Enough that he had begun to tell her what she meant to him before she'd swallowed his words in a kiss and they had come together.

It had been the fresh start that they had both needed, and it certainly paved the way for some proper honesty when they talked. Which, he thought, with a quick glance at his clock and a smile, he was looking forward to doing in less than fifteen minutes.

He would have happily initiated the conversation as soon as he had awoken again, as all the words had seemed to be there in his head, eager to burst forth, but Rose had already been downstairs and the enticing aroma of bacon had been filling the house. Because she had had to dash to the Friday Sewing Circle, to do something important with quilts, there had been no opportunity to tell her how he was feeling over breakfast. But she had kissed him goodbye as she'd placed his plate in front of him and she had promised that they would talk at luncheon.

'I'm afraid my problem is of a delicate nature,' said Mr Bunion, already unbuttoning his falls, but even that didn't spoil Sam's good mood too much. He'd even find some perverse enjoyment in lancing the enormous boil on the odious fellow's backside, because Mr Bunion had once had the audacity to be rude to his wife, and he figured that the man deserved it.

His wife.

As he washed his hands, Sam realised that it had to be a good sign that he could now think those words without wanting to vomit into a bowl.

There was a brisk rap on his surgery door and Mrs Fitzherbert strolled in, without waiting for him to invite her, and made herself comfortable in the chair. He glanced at the clock again, noted that it was already noon, and almost said something he had never said in all his years as Whittleston-on-the-Water's physician— *Surgery hours are over, so please come back on Monday.* But the woman was ninety-four, and if she was ailing from something she might not last till Monday.

So he swallowed his irritation and smiled. 'How are you, Mrs Fitzherbert?'

'In the finest of fettles, Dr Able, apart from the wicked ache in my bones caused by all this persistent cold. Can you believe that it might snow again?' She shook her head and thumped her cane on the floor. 'Snow! In late March! And all the puddles in the square are so icy it's a wonder nobody has broken their neck this morning. Anyone would think Essex had suddenly turned into Norway.'

'Are you taking the powders I gave you for your rheumatism?'

'Of course not!' She curled her lip in disgust. 'They taste like rotten cabbage! I have to water them down with brandy just to make them palatable.'

'How many times do I have to tell you that brandy isn't a medicine, Mrs Fitzherbert?' Sam knew it was a moot point, because this old lady had always been a law unto herself, but thanks to the Hippocratic Oath he was duty-bound to tell her anyway.

'Until you go blue in the face, Dr Able, as I've managed to get this close to a hundred on the stuff without any issue.'

She made a valid point, he supposed, as she was the oldest patient he had and nothing much ever ailed her. 'Then how about we try some willow bark tea?'

'For what?'

'For your rheumatism, Mrs Fitzherbert.' Sam jumped up to fetch the powders and couldn't resist riling her. 'Or has senility finally set in and you've forgotten what you came to my surgery for?'

'Oh, I didn't come here for my rheumatism, Doctor. I came merely to ask your permission for my man to go upstairs and retrieve Rose's things for her.'

Dread settled like a stone in his stomach. 'I'm sorry?'

'Well, she's gone, hasn't she? Back to Suffolk.'

'Has she?'

'Yes…permanently.' Mrs Fitzherbert pulled an awkward apologetic face. 'She was supposed to leave you a letter. I told her to tell you to your face, but she said she didn't like goodbyes and—'

Blood rushed in his ears as Sam surged to his feet and on unsteady legs dashed to the kitchen. There, in the centre of the table, was nothing but a plate of sandwiches.

A plate of sandwiches only big enough for one.

'Oh, silly me,' said Mrs Fitzherbert, limping in behind him. 'Perhaps I am going senile. She didn't leave the letter here because she didn't want you to find it before the post left. She gave it to me to give to you instead.'

She rummaged in her reticule and finally produced one, then seemed surprised when he snatched it out of her hand.

Chapter Twenty-One

Sam tore the missive open and scanned the contents, then sank into a chair because the ground had suddenly been ripped from beneath his feet.

She had indeed gone to Suffolk—and for good. She thought it was for the best, and she didn't want him to attempt to contact her there because she also thought a clean break was the healthiest thing for them.

A clean break!

After they had spent the night making love!

After she had promised that they would talk!

After the minx had kissed him goodbye this morning!

How dare she do that and give him false hope when she had known it was for the last time?

Mrs Fitzherbert gestured to the crumpled lump of paper in his fist with her cane. 'I hope she mentions in it that she wants me to arrange for her things to be sent on? We thought it most prudent that she travel light, as the quarter to noon post to Colchester is always full. Her decision was last-minute, and we didn't want to risk her not being able to travel today because she had too much baggage.'

'We!' He had the overwhelming urge to grab that cane she had made a point of whacking against the floor with every damned 'we' she uttered and snap it over his knee. 'You knew she was leaving at a bloody quarter to noon today? You knew it and didn't think to tell me so I could stop her?'

'It wasn't my place to tell you, young man, because she did not want to be stopped. And it's not as if your separation wasn't planned—and by both of you to boot, which I must say was very underhanded of the pair of you. All that has changed is the date, and you can hardly blame Rose for bringing that forward when she has been so miserable.'

She prodded him with her cane.

'I cannot imagine how hard it has been for the poor girl to have to live with a man she has fallen hopelessly in love with but who constantly tells her that he is incapable of loving her back! That must be soul-destroying.'

'What?' Now his head was spinning. 'She loves me?' The husk in his chest creaked as it leapt. *'She loves me!'*

And this was how she chose to show it? By abandoning him without a by-your-leave? Without a word? After he'd begged her to talk! To stay! To try! With no mention of that pertinent detail in her bloody awful letter!

'Then why the blazes has she gone?' He probably shouldn't be shouting at a woman in her nineties, no matter how exasperating she was. But with Rose already on the way to Colchester he had nobody else to shoot but the messenger.

The cane jabbed again. 'Because you are a coward, Samuel Able, that's why. A shocking coward and an outrageous liar! Incapable of love, my arse... I cannot think of a bigger-hearted man in the whole of Whittleston! You work all the hours God sends.' The tip of that damn cane found his ribs now. 'Care deeply about every single patient, including the unworthy ones, and punish yourself if you cannot save them! What is that if it is not caring?'

'My job. My duty. My blasted vocation.'

'Poppycock and hogwash. You love your job. Duty is love and so is vocation. A man truly incapable of caring would never have married her in the first place. You're just scared to commit to Rose as she deserves because your first love died. Because the grief was unbearable. Because it's easier to shy away from life than live it to the full, isn't it? Because lightning cannot possibly strike twice, and it cannot possibly be as deep and as meaningful as the first time? Well, shame on you for wasting the life that the good Lord gave you and which he expects you to live to the full! And congratulations for driving your second great love away with your downright insulting offer of "muddling through". Be still my beating heart!'

When her cane hit his breastbone he caught it in his fist to stop the pain—but it didn't stop her verbal assault.

'Did you hear that, coward? For my decrepit old heart still beats and leaps and loves with hope and abandon and I've put three husbands…three great loves…in the ground. And I'd bury another if I could experience the sheer joy of loving a man wholeheartedly again. Because the joy is worth the sacrifice! The pleasure is worth the pain! Because it truly is better to have experienced love and lost it than to have been denied that joy.'

For a moment he thought the old lady might spit in his face, but she spat more vitriol instead.

'It'll serve you right if she does what she intends, and what I have thoroughly encouraged her to do, and finds someone worthy enough to deserve her love back in Suffolk—because only a blithering idiot allows a woman that wonderful to get away!'

'We were supposed to be talking about all that today!' What the blazes had Rose been thinking to just go?

'Before she ran off without giving me the chance to say my piece!'

'Good for her! You don't deserve the opportunity to say it!'

'Well, I am going to!' He pointed a quaking finger at Mrs Fitzherbert as he stalked to the door and grabbed his coat. 'And, as God is my witness—' his finger shook towards the heavens '—my lawful wife is going to bloody well listen!'

The door slammed behind him.

Which was why he didn't see Mrs Fitzherbert holding her sides as she threw her head back and cackled.

Rose watched the spire of St Hildreth's disappear on the murky grey horizon and fought back tears while she tried not to regret her decision. Yes, it was a tragedy, and her heart was breaking to be leaving him, but Mrs Fitzherbert was right. This *was* for the best. You couldn't make a silk purse out of a sow's ear and there really was no point in putting off the inevitable when the pair of them had reached such a momentous impasse.

She wanted everything and he could only give so much, which ultimately would result in them both being unhappy.

Besides, she couldn't risk staying, even though she had been sorely tempted to have the talk Sam had wanted to have, to see if there was any hope. Staying and slowly watching his innate sense of responsibility turning into resentment and then into loathing would be far worse. Therefore this was definitely the right decision.

She also had a child to think of, and while Sam might not be capable of loving it, she was. She already did. Their child would be the one glorious, precious positive she could take away from her short-lived, enforced sow's ear of a marriage.

'Are you all right, miss?' The woman directly opposite her in the cramped and swaying carriage smiled kindly. 'Only you look like you've found a penny but lost a pound.'

'Yes... I'm fine.' Rose forced herself to smile back. 'I'm just a bit sad to be leaving Whittleston after eight months, that's all. It is such a lovely village.'

All the passengers bounced as the carriage hit a bump in the road, then swayed as the driver swerved slightly without slowing at all, clearly determined to get to his next stop in record time.

The older man beside Rose, who was trying to read his newspaper, dropped it and frowned as they clonked through another pothole, and rapped the ceiling in complaint. 'I think they have given us the worst driver in the world,' he said, to nobody in particular, as he snapped his paper back.

'What kept you in Whittleston for eight months?' asked the lady.

'Family.' Old and, she supposed, new.

'Then doubtless they will drag you back there soon enough, so this is only a farewell and not a goodbye.'

Rose nodded, even though she knew that it was goodbye. She couldn't set foot in the place again while Sam lived there. Even if he moved away she would still struggle. Whittleston-on-the-Water held too many memories.

To that end, before she'd left she had spent the entire morning saying her farewells to all the friends she had made. Ned and Isobel had been first, and both had promised to visit her in Suffolk just as soon as she was settled. Sophie, Rafe and Archie had been next, and they had all promised to visit her too. And to write—although letters would be poor second to their actual company. Archie had cried, which of course had set her off, and then that had set Sophie off, and poor Rafe had been stuck in the middle of the three of them, beside himself because he couldn't stop them crying.

Finally, she had gone to say goodbye to her dear aunt and uncle, who had given her refuge at one of the most difficult periods of her life and helped her find her smile again. It might be lost again now, but for the sake of the babe growing inside her she would find it again. She had to search for a new home to raise it in, after all, and then all the unpleasant ties to her past would be cut and she truly could start afresh. It was scary, but it was going to be an adventure, and she was determined to grab it with both hands.

She deserved that. Almost as much as Sam's son or daughter deserved it. It was a thought that warmed her enough that her hand settled contentedly over her belly, despite the film of unshed tears gathering in her eyes.

In a few hours, when this carriage made its first stop in Chelmsford, Mrs Fitzherbert would deliver her letter to him and that would be that. Rose had kept it purposely short, as she had not trusted herself not to pour some of her forlorn hope into it, which might, in turn, force him to feel beholden to come after her. He'd be angry initially, and maybe even a little upset, but once the news had settled he'd be relieved. Then he'd likely bury himself in work to distract himself, and after a respectable amount of time he'd be back to where he'd been before she had turned his ordered life upside down.

Back to working ridiculously long hours, not looking after himself and doubtless living on toast again.

By which time, hopefully, she'd have enough of her own distractions to be able to blot him out of her thoughts. At least for the bulk of her time. Until then he was destined to occupy them and she would mourn the loss of him.

A stray tear tumbled over her lashes, and to hide it from the other five people crowded into this juddering confined space with her she twisted towards the window. The bitter cold outside combined with the warm breath of six people inside had misted the glass with condensation, so she cleared a circle with her glove just in time to see the Dewhursts' farm fly by. Outside was the foal she and Sam had delivered on the fateful night she had been ruined. A few yards away was its mother. Both were covered in blankets and nibbling at the greenery in the meadow.

That was another positive of their sham marriage, and another fond memory she would take back with her to Suffolk to cherish.

They were all pushed sideways as the carriage turned at speed to climb the big hill into Little Ramstead, and the horses slowed briefly with the weight they had to pull. But thanks to their careless and impatient driver and his cracking whip they were soon running at a lick again. Straight through another pothole that had everyone reaching for something to hold on to.

Rose gripped the windowsill as the carriage lurched suddenly to the left with such force that it smashed her head against the window. Pain exploded behind her eyeballs at the impact and a strange mist seemed to engulf her.

She tasted blood in her mouth as she felt the carriage tilt.

Heard the screams of her fellow passengers as it began to roll.

She hit her head hard again, against something that made her see bright, unbearable white.

And then the world went black.

Chapter Twenty-Two

Sam was muttering to himself as he hauled himself into his curricle, so furious with Rose he could barely think straight. Across the square Mrs Outhwaite was eyeing him with blatant hostility, along with a gaggle of ladies who were all tutting in his direction. Clearly all of them had been aware that Rose had left him long before he had. He supposed they had all warranted proper goodbyes this morning. But not him!

No!

All he had been granted was a complete pack of lies and a final kiss that he hadn't realised was final! It was supposed to be men who used a woman in bed and then discarded her without a by-your-leave, but *he* felt used now, damn it! How dared she leave his bed and his life without any warning whatsoever, as if his feelings did not matter? Especially when she apparently loved him!

'Dr Able! Dr Able!'

A cart rattled into the square and on it was none other than Ted Dewhurst.

'You've got to come quick! It's an emergency!'

Sam decided to ignore the cry for help. Someone else would have to deliver the breach foal or calf or pig, or whatever the hell else it was the Dewhursts expected him to be a doctor to now. He was a man on a mission. And as the lad waved his arms, frantic, he snapped his reins and set off.

He was almost free of the square when Ted flung himself in front of his horse, and he had no choice but to come to an abrupt stop. 'Someone had better be about to die, Ted, or you will be!'

'I think someone is.' The lad looked ready to burst into tears. 'There's been an accident. A dreadful accident. The post hit some ice on Little Ramstead hill and overturned.'

'What post?' Ice filled his veins and somehow he knew before Ted confirmed it.

'The Colchester post—and there is blood everywhere!'

Sam had no memory of his journey to the scene, only of the overwhelming compunction to get to it as fast as he could. All the while panic consumed him like a maelstrom. Panic and fear and so much hope he could barely breathe, while over and over in his head he prayed that Rose would be spared.

Please don't take her! Please don't take her!

He had no idea he was repeating that mantra aloud until he saw the devastation on the side of the hill and had to choke the words out.

The carriage was on its side. One wheel was missing and there was baggage strewn everywhere. Clothing spewed from shattered trunks while locals tended to the wounded.

As he scrambled from his curricle he saw a prone body on the ground, surrounded by a crowd of grim faces. So many he could not tell if the ominous black toes of the boots pointing towards the sky belonged to a man or a woman.

The onlookers parted as he ran towards them, and Sam experienced a moment of elation when he realised that it was a man. He was alive, and groaning on the floor.

'Bloody idiot!' Mr Dewhurst was bent near the man's bleeding head, trying to stem the flow with a handkerchief. 'He was running those horses too fast and paying no attention to the ice! He stinks of gin too, the blighter!'

'Who else is hurt?' Sam scanned the scene, frantically looking for Rose. Emotion choked him. Fear mingled with a grief so intense it engulfed him. 'Have you seen my wife?'

'Aye.' Sensing Sam's panic, Mr Dewhurst pointed to his house. 'She's safely in the house with all the others. Thankfully nobody was seriously hurt by this bloody idiot's reckless stupidity.'

'Thank God.' The rush of relief came so fast and so thoroughly Sam struggled move as it flooded his body. Overwhelming tears fell unbidden as he thanked whoever had spared her and ran to the building.

'Rose!'

He flung the door open and burst into the kitchen, his eyes searching, not caring that he must look like a madman to all the blinking people seated around the Dewhursts' kitchen table, gratefully clutching steaming mugs of tea.

'Where is Rose?'

Because she wasn't one of them, and he needed to get to her. To see her. To reassure himself that the woman he had only just realised he loved with all his heart was all right.'

'She's in the parlour.'

He had no idea who said that but barrelled on, slumping in relief when he finally saw Rose, sitting wrapped in a blanket by the fire.

'Oh, my darling...thank God.' He collapsed at her feet to examine her. 'Are you injured anywhere?' He did not care that his profession dictated that he see to the most seriously hurt patients first. That idiot on the grass out there had almost stolen Rose from him, so he felt no guilt. 'Bleeding?'

Her face was as white as a sheet. Her expression stark and sad. 'I bumped my head and blacked out for a few seconds...'

Her fingers went to her hair, to show him the way, and he checked the bump. It was reassuringly hard and the bruise was already angry. He cupped her cheeks, stared deep into her eyes to see if she was concussed. Her pupils were as they should be, so he held up three fingers. 'How many?'

'Three,' she said, as her bottom lip trembled, and he hugged her tight.

'I thought I'd lost you.' He had so much to say. So much she needed to know. 'I thought you were dead... and it broke me, Rose. Shattered me completely. It was just like Lisbon, only worse, because I'd been there before and I couldn't believe that fate would do that to me again. Be so cruel and callous... I am so sorry, my love...because you *are* my love... I didn't realise that I could ever feel again what I felt for Catherine...but I do. I love you. It took almost losing you for me to realise that you are my new everything.'

Her sob exploded against his chest as she held him tight. 'I love you too, Sam, so very much.'

'Then all is good...' He sat back to stare into her soul.

'You'll come home and you'll never, ever think of leaving me again?'

She nodded, struggling to smile through her tears. But then the tears took over and she sobbed for all she was worth. 'I'm pregnant...for now at least...nine weeks.'

She hugged her belly and something else overwhelmed him. Something instinctive and proprietorial.

'But I'm terrified that I am going to miscarry.'

His palm flattened over her belly in wonder while he forced himself to think like a doctor. 'Any pain, cramps or bleeding?'

'Not yet.'

'Then let us hope it stays that way.'

'And if it doesn't?' She was already devastated by the prospect, and he knew he was too, but...

'We will cross that bridge when we come to it— together.' He took her hand, laced his fingers through hers and kissed the wedding ring that he had so reluctantly put on her finger, suddenly grateful that it was there. 'But I do know that this won't be your last pregnancy. If you are game, I think there might just be room in the shrivelled husk in my chest to love a houseful.'

She laughed through the tears and he kissed her.

'I love you, Rose.'

It was bizarre and strange and wonderful, but he was compelled to keep telling her. Not to convince her that he meant it, but to revel in the joy of it. For however long it lasted. Because Mrs Fitzherbert was right. Love was worth the pain of loss, and he was going to revel in every single moment he had been gifted with Rose.

'You are my everything.'

Epilogue

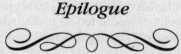

September 1819

St Hildreth's was filled with flowers. In a testament to how much Mrs Fitzherbert was loved, the locals had stripped their quaint corner of Essex of all the last of the summer blooms for today, because Mrs Fitzherbert loved flowers. There were almost as many floral arrangements as there were people crammed into the pews.

Everyone from Whittleston-on-the-Water was there, which wasn't a surprise, but many of the friends she had made elsewhere in her long life had also come. Her three sons, all grey-haired old men themselves, were seated at the front with their wives and grown-up children. Dotted amongst them were grandchildren and great-grandchildren, and every single one of them had inherited that canny, wily, mischievous look from their matriarch. However, despite the enormous crowd, there was hardly any noise, as all of them were oddly quiet and bemused.

Rose was one of them—because all this still hadn't sunk in.

'Ninety-five—almost ninety-six. That's a good innings.' Ned Parker stared at the enormous floral arrangement bursting from behind the altar with a shake of his head. 'We should all be so lucky as to make such old bones.'

Beside him, where they all stood in the porch, his vivacious wife Isobel rubbed a thoughtful circle over her protruding belly. 'I intend to live to a hundred.'

After putting off starting a family for a year, while she established her haberdasher's shop in the village, she was now five months pregnant, and it suited her. It hadn't slowed her down in the slightest. Of all of them, she was probably the most likely to usurp Mrs Fitzherbert's record as the oldest ever person in the village.

'I am going to miss her,' said Sophie, while gently rocking her new born son.

The sleeping Lord Gabriel Peel was a chubby little angel, blessed with his mother's features and Rafe's sandy hair. Which was funny, because his toddling sister Lillibet, who was currently being supervised and entertained by a very frazzled-looking Archie, was the opposite. She was dark, like her mother, but the image of Rafe.

'It's time.' Reverend Spears appeared, clutching his Bible, and Sam nodded.

Reluctantly he passed their baby daughter back to Rose, as Mrs Fitzherbert had expressly stipulated that she wanted him to be part of the service.

'Wish me luck.'

He kissed Rose's cheek tenderly, then bent and did the same to their precious little Violet, whom he was absolutely besotted by. She had only been in the world ten days, and already he could not bear to leave her side.

It had been his idea to call her after another flower. He had said he liked the irony, and after red roses, violets were his favourite.

'Good luck.' Rose squeezed his hand, and he took a deep breath.

'Of all the things that I thought I'd being doing today, this wasn't it.'

She watched him disappear into the vestry and smiled at her remaining friends. 'It's the end of an era, isn't it? Whittleston-on the-Water won't be the same without Mrs Fitzherbert.'

'Oh, do stop talking about me as if I'm dead, girl!' The formidable old lady prodded her with her cane from behind. 'I'm merely moving two miles up the lane!'

'But we are used to you living within spitting distance of the square,' said Isobel.

'Interfering in everything,' muttered Ned under his breath.

'Which I can still do from my new home—and I will.' Then she cackled. 'I was due a new adventure, and living in a windmill will certainly be one. There's something so romantic about a windmill, don't you think?'

'There you are!' A frustrated Sam returned and offered her his arm. 'You were supposed to be waiting for me in the vestry and the Reverend wants to start.'

To prove that, with perfect timing, the organ began to play.

'Well, the Reverend can jolly well wait, can't he?'

She took Sam's arm and then passed her infamous cane to Rafe, who in turn passed her a vivid posy of flowers which matched the wild crown of them on top of her snow-white head.

'It's the bride's prerogative to be late. Besides...' She

cackled again, enjoying herself immensely. 'It will keep my groom on his toes. It'll do the man good to sweat a bit while he wonders if I'm going to turn up. There should always be some mystery in a marriage.'

Sam gave her his arm and Rose and the others took their seats. Standing at the altar beside his son, the aged groom was indeed sweating nervously. But as his bride entered he beamed, and stared at her with such affection he suddenly seemed ten years younger—which was ironic, because at eighty-five he was a decade younger than his new wife-to-be.

The entire village had been surprised at the haste of this marriage. Rose had known that Mr Anderson and Mrs Fitzherbert were old friends, and that she had spent a great deal of time helping him cope with his grief after his wife had died of a stroke last year, but nobody had realised when love had blossomed. The first anyone had known was three Sundays ago, when the first of the banns had been read.

It had been all hands on deck since then, to get this wedding ready so fast, but none of them had minded. Mrs Fitzherbert was right. At ninety-five, she couldn't afford to hang around making preparations. She wanted to get cracking on her fourth marriage straight away. They were even going on a honeymoon tour of Scotland, because neither the bride nor groom had ever seen it. Both were grabbing life by the horns and living it to its fullest.

Mrs Fitzherbert had finally made it all the way down the aisle to the altar, and it was Sam's big moment.

'Who giveth this woman?' asked the Reverend in his loud, commanding voice.

'I do,' he said, handing her over to her groom.

He stepped backwards and quietly took his seat next to Rose. As he did every single time they sat in this church since the carriage accident, he took her hand, laced his fingers through hers and lifted it to his lips so that he could kiss her wedding ring. Then, in a whisper just for her, with love shining in his eyes, he said what he always said, here in the place where they had taken their vows but not intended to mean them.

'I do—and always will—with all my resurrected heart.'

* * * * *

Least Likely To Win A Duke

Emily E K Murdoch

MILLS & BOON

USA TODAY bestselling author **Emily E K Murdoch** is read in multiple languages around the world. Enjoy sweet romances as Emily Murdoch and steamy romances as Emily E K Murdoch. Emily's had a varied career to date: from examining medieval manuscripts to designing museum exhibitions to working as a researcher for the BBC to working for the National Trust. Her books range from England in 1050 to Texas in 1848, and she can't wait for you to fall in love with her heroes and heroines!

Books by Emily E K Murdoch

The Wallflower Academy

Least Likely to Win a Duke

is Emily E K Murdoch's debut for Harlequin Historical.

Look out for more books from Emily E K Murdoch coming soon!

Author Note

This book wouldn't exist without a great number of people. Anyone missed from the list is entirely my error, as are any mistakes that you find (please don't look).

Mary and Gordon Murdoch

My wonderful husband

Stephanie Booth

Amy Rose Bennett

Kathryn Le Veque

Awo Ibrahim

Carly Byrne

Hannah Rossiter

Carolyn Smalley

Krista Oliver

Ruth Machanda

The Harlequin typesetting and proofreading teams

DEDICATION

For my parents,

Who encouraged me to write when I couldn't.

For my husband,

Who emboldened me to write when I wasn't.

And for my wonderful readers,

Who told me to write even more.

Lastly, to PB, PB, BB and BB.

Chapter One

This was absolutely the last place Miss Gwendoline Knox wanted to be—not that she had any choice in the matter.

Murderess wallflowers were rarely wanted at home.

'There y'are,' muttered the coach driver, rather unceremoniously dropping her trunk to the ground. It rolled, mud splattering up one side of the leather case. 'Academy.'

Gwen swallowed and looked up at the large manor house, its beautiful Tudor bricks glowing in the afternoon sun. Imposing chimneys pumped out smoke and the large front door had a highly polished bronze knocker.

'But where am I supposed to—?'

The whip cracked and the horses stepped forward, pulling the coach away and leaving Gwen alone on the drive. Silence quickly spilled into the gardens.

If only her mother had agreed to accompany her, Gwen thought wistfully as she picked up her trunk, leaning slightly thanks to its weight. But that would have meant talking about...the incident. Perhaps this was best.

Besides, this was why she had been sent to the Academy. To get out from under her mother's feet, prevent any hint of scandal and find a husband. Gwen tried to push the unkind thoughts from her mind, but they intruded, nonetheless.

If Mother had been kind enough to come with me, she would not have been so unkind as to send me here.

It was an unpleasant thought, and it was getting her nowhere. The bright autumnal sun was drawing long shadows across the gardens, and a chill in the air hinted at an icy evening.

Stepping forward timidly, Gwen knocked on the door, which was immediately opened by a footman in blue livery.

'Miss Knox,' he said smoothly. 'Miss Pike is expecting you.'

Gwen was certainly not expecting the hall she stepped into, conscious of the mud she was spreading into the magnificent space. High ceilings, a beautiful red carpet, and landscape paintings along the walls: the very picture of elegance.

'Ah, Miss Knox!'

A smiling older woman, perhaps nearing fifty, was approaching rather like a battleship. Gwen took a step backwards.

'How pleasant to make your acquaintance,' said the woman, who could only be Miss Pike. 'The Wallflower Academy welcomes you.'

'And no one will miss you there!'

Her mother's parting words rang through her mind.

'It's not as if women like you deserve happy endings, do you? Not after what you've done...'

Gwen winced. It was bad enough to be labelled a wallflower by one's own mother, but to be sent to such a place! It was scandalously embarrassing.

'I do not want to be here,' she said, the words slipping out before she could stop them.

They did not appear to offend Miss Pike. 'Of course you don't,' she said with a broad smile, waving her hand as though opinions mattered little. 'And you won't be alone.

Matthews, please show Miss Knox to her bedchamber. The end room.'

A flurry of corridors passed Gwen by until she was standing in a small yet genteelly furnished bedchamber. A large bed, a writing desk, a toilette table and a wardrobe were the only items within it, but a large bay window looked out onto the south of the house, towards the rear gardens. She could see kitchen gardens, what appeared to be a walled rose garden, and an abundance of carefully manicured lawn.

She turned. The footman had gone. She had not even noticed his departure.

Breathing out slowly as her heart rate started to slow, Gwen sank onto the end of the bed and closed her eyes. This was not the end of the world. She would manage.

'Goodness, you look terrible,' said a cheerful voice.

Breath caught in her throat, Gwen was unable to say anything as her bedchamber door opened, and a pair of ladies entered.

'Sylvia,' said a woman with black skin and a broad smile.

She had on her arm the hands of another lady, a little older, with milky white eyes.

The door shut and flickers of panic tingled up Gwen's spine. To be so enclosed with unknown people...

'My word, your bedchamber has the most outstanding view,' said Sylvia, leaning towards the window. 'We're all jealous, you know.'

'Oh, I don't know,' said the one with milky eyes, who had been helped to the window seat. 'I don't think I would mind. I'm Marilla. You can call me Rilla.'

Gwen nodded weakly. She was always terrible with names, but she wasn't about to forget Rilla in a hurry. When had she lost her sight? How could she speak of it so calmly?

'I don't hear the new one laughing,' said Rilla mildly. 'Don't you worry about it, whoever you are. I don't—you shouldn't.'

'Gwendoline Knox,' Gwen said weakly, head spinning and in desperate need of solitude. She had risen early for that day's journey. 'You can call me—'

'Do you have any beaus?'

'N-No!' Gwen spluttered, startled into speech by Sylvia's blunt question.

She was still grinning as she leaned against the window. 'I only asked.'

'Don't hound her, Sylvia,' said Rilla.

'I'll hound whoever I want,' said Sylvia brightly. 'I've got to find entertainment somewhere in this place.'

They laughed, and Gwen smiled nervously. As long as she didn't draw attention to herself...

They were not as dull as she had expected. An Academy for Wallflowers...well, her mother had considered it perfect. The perfect place to hide someone. Gwen had tried to imagine the sorts of ladies who were sent to such a place—women no longer wanted by their families, who had tried, and failed, to make a match.

The beginning of the Season had been only a few weeks ago, and Gwen knew precisely what her mother expected of her: to keep her head down and make a good match.

But how was she expected to do so in an Academy full of ladies who could conceive of nothing worse than making light conversation with a handsome gentleman?

'Are we it?' Gwen flushed as laughter resounded around her bedchamber at her question.

'It?' repeated Sylvia with a giggle. 'Were you expecting something far more impressive?'

'Don't tease her, Sylvia,' Rilla said with mock severity. 'You forget, you've been here an entire Season! You can no longer remember how frightened you were when you first arrived.'

A slight pink tinge came to Sylvia's cheeks. 'I suppose not. Yes, Gwen—can I call you Gwen?'

Gwen would have permitted her to call her anything she liked if it meant the focus of the conversation moved on quickly. 'Yes.'

'Yes, Gwen, we are "it"—at least some of it,' said Sylvia with a grin. 'There are—what...? Five of us here now? You make six. I am least likely to be wed—'

'I think I'd agree with you on that one,' muttered Rilla.

'Daphne is least likely to say boo to a mouse—'

'She does this,' Rilla said to a bemused Gwen. 'It's her way of keeping track of us, apparently. Some ladies come and go rather quickly.'

'They...they find husbands?'

Gwen could hardly believe it. For all the wonderful references Miss Pike had sent her mother, it had been hard to fathom how the Academy could marry off so many wallflowers in such a short time.

'Oh, Miss Pike has her ways,' said Rilla dryly.

'She does know what she is doing most of the time,' said Sylvia, glancing at Gwen with a knowing look. 'So, you are here for a husband, are you?'

Gwen wished heat would not immediately flush up her décolletage, wished it would not pinken her cheeks and make her words incomprehensible.

What would she be? Least likely to form a coherent sentence?

'I—I... That is...my mother wants—'

'Oh, mothers,' said Sylvia dismissively. 'I was sent here by my mother.'

'Me by my father,' Rilla said curtly. 'Such as he is. But not for marriage. No, the blackguard believes—'

'Miss Knox does not need to hear our sob stories,' interrupted Sylvia firmly.

Gwen swallowed, curling her fingers around the blanket on the bed. The tension taut in her shoulders and neck was starting to give her a headache, and Sylvia was right. She certainly did not need the histories of the ladies who had invaded her bedchamber.

What she needed was quiet and solitude—a chance to think over all she had heard, all she had seen. All that she might now expect.

She was a prisoner here, sent by her mother after her own scandalous marriage, after the...the incident had become a fact. What she, Gwen, was going to do about it... Well, that was quite another matter. A matter that required due consideration—and she was not going to be able to think with all the noise in here.

But first, Gwen had questions which needed answering. 'What...what happens here? At the Wallflower Academy, I mean? How does she—Miss Pike—how does she... marry us off?'

Rilla chuckled. 'It's all very simple, Miss Knox. You have no need to be concerned. Miss Pike gives us lessons—'

'Lessons in how to be more interesting and charming young ladies,' Sylvia interrupted, rolling her eyes.

'Lessons on attracting a gentleman,' Rilla continued, a smile curling her lips. 'And then eligible gentlemen are invited to come and meet us.'

'View us,' said Sylvia wryly. 'Like specimens. Like animals in a zoo.'

Gwen swallowed. It did not sound particularly appealing. She had never been one to enjoy being looked at— which was all to the good, for her mother had pronounced her plain when she had first started curling her hair and pinning it up.

No, to be invisible. That was the thing. To go through life without being noticed, without attention, was all she desired.

The thought of gentlemen arriving at the Academy to look at them all, as though through a catalogue...

'I will hate it,' she whispered. 'I just want to be left alone.'

'Plenty of opportunities for that,' said Sylvia, and there was little laughter in her tone this time. 'Some of us have been here for years. 'Tis not a given that you will ever be chosen.'

Was that bitterness in her voice? Gwen could hardly tell. There had been such mischief in everything Sylvia had said since barrelling into her bedchamber.

'You will get accustomed to it,' said Rilla quietly. 'We all do.'

Gwen nodded mutely. It sounded awful. So, gentlemen would come to...to examine them.

'We have lessons on how to speak with confidence, how to stand tall, how to select topics of conversation,' Rilla explained, her hands folded in her lap. 'Music, art, languages...the normal things.'

Sylvia rolled her eyes. 'It's completely ridiculous. As though being shy, being a wallflower, is something needing to be cured.'

Only then did a natural smile creep across Gwen's face. Until now, her fears of being forced to change, to be a different person, to lose so much of who she was had overwhelmed her.

'You are not at all the wallflowers I had expected,' Gwen admitted with an awkward laugh.

Rilla grinned, her pale eyes turning in Gwen's direction. 'I am not here as a wallflower, you understand. 'Tis my father's intention—'

'And I'm not a wallflower at all, but a prisoner,' declared Sylvia with a wink. 'My father wants to marry me off without having to bring me out into Society. So here I am, stuck amid all these quiet ones. I manage to gain sufficient conversation at the official dinners, of course. You have missed the first one.'

Official dinners? Gwen's cheeks blazed with heat at the idea she had missed something important. Miss Pike's letter had said that any time was perfect for her arrival, that she should not rush her goodbyes with her family.

It had not prevented her mother from bundling her off as soon as possible...

'Official dinners?' she repeated.

Rilla smiled wearily. 'Miss Pike hosts six dinners throughout the Season. Only the very best and most eligible gentlemen are invited—though of course, they must all be accepting of a wallflower as their bride.'

As their bride.

Gwen's stomach twisted most painfully and her grip on the blanket increased.

Because that was what she was here for, wasn't it? To make a match. To be married off, cast away from her family to make her own way in the world. To be hidden amongst the most unlikely of ladies.

'And I have missed the first?'

A rather wicked smile spread across Sylvia's face. 'You did not miss much—it was a complete disaster! Oh, Gwen, it was awful. The gentlemen Miss Pike had procured were so immensely dull they did not ask us anything, nor start any conversation—and of course this lot said nothing either!'

There was a peal of laughter from Rilla. 'Speak for yourself! I tried to ask Mr Whatshisname something about the meat course, and he said—'

'"I don't speak to wallflowers!"'

Both chorused this, and then fell into peals of giggles, the loudest snort coming from Sylvia.

Gwen looked at the laughing women and tried to smile. It was all too much: too much noise, too much expectation, too much going on. Her mind clouded, her head spun. She tried to make sense of all the information she was being given, but her bones ached from the long carriage ride, and the very last thing she wished to do at this moment was have dinner with what Miss Pike considered to be eligible—

'Don't worry,' said Rilla, a smile still dancing on her lips. 'The second official dinner is this week.'

Gwen's stomach turned horribly, threatening to return the meat pie she had hesitantly accepted at the inn just a few hours ago.

The second official dinner—so soon? She would barely have enough time to settle into the Academy!

The room closed in, as if the air was running out, and Gwen gasped for breath. 'I… I need…'

'Goodness, you sound awful, Gwen,' said Rilla, a slight crease of concern appearing between her eyes. 'Are you quite well?'

Gwen shook her head, unable to speak. Then, remembering Rilla, she said, 'Y-Yes.'

'She needs some air,' said Sylvia firmly. 'A walk in the garden. I will go with you…show you the way—'

But Gwen had already risen and waved a hand. 'Oh, no, I can easily—I—I would like to be alone, if you do not mind.'

Fear seared her heart at the thought of giving offence, but Sylvia only sighed. 'You wallflowers are all the same.'

Gwen swallowed, shame flooding her veins, but a second glance at the beautiful woman showed her Sylvia had meant no harm.

It was just too much. Too many opportunities to reveal the truth.

'I have to...' Gwen tried to speak, but made no effort to continue as she half walked, half stumbled out of the bed-chamber.

It was not difficult to find her way outside. Once she had descended the staircase into the hall, she opened the front door and stepped out into the cold yet welcoming air. There were sufficient borders and hedges here, along the drive, in which to lose herself.

Her skin prickled with the cold, but at least it was cooling. Gwen paced, hardly looking where she was going, entering into one of the portions of the garden lined with hedges.

The Wallflower Academy. It was like a bad jest some-one had made in their cups, and yet it was real. She was here. The tall redbrick building loomed above her. She had no home, no friends—although that might soon change—and no idea what she was going to do with herself at these awful dinners.

If only I was not guilty of something so terrible, Gwen thought bitterly as she turned a corner, her skirts whip-ping because she was walking so fast.

Then she could have asked her mother to allow her to remain at home.

But it was not to be. She had to live with the conse-quences of her actions, and this was far more pleasant than a prison—even if the punishment included being paraded before gentlemen for their enjoyment!

Gwen's eyes filled with tears as she turned hurriedly around the next corner, the hedge brushing against the sleeve of her gown. How could she bear it? What could possibly make the Wallflower Academy endurable?

She turned another corner and walked straight into the most handsome gentleman she had ever seen.

Chapter Two

Percy Devereux, Duke of Knaresby, sighed heavily as his footsteps thudded down the front steps of the dratted Wallflower Academy.

Academy. The cheek of Miss Pike to call it such a thing, when places like Oxford and Cambridge existed in the world. Why, a finishing school concerned with dancing and decorum was hardly an 'academy', in his view.

Besides, Miss Pike was dreadfully dull. If she was any indication of the poor women sent to such a place, it was no wonder the so-called 'wallflowers' found themselves left on the side-lines of every ball and conversation of note.

The bright autumnal air shimmered with the afternoon sun, and Percy watched the merest hint of his breath billowing on the breeze. The Season had begun, and it brought with it little pleasure and less excitement.

It was only down to Staromchor's mother that he had even come at all, cornered at Almack's just days ago. A 'charitable duty'—that was what the Dowager Countess had called it.

A damned nuisance, more like.

That dinner he'd been forced to attend had been outrageously dull, and he had firmly vowed he would only drop by a few times for the look of the thing.

Still, the Academy was only a twenty-minute drive from Town, and it was not so very arduous to make the trip—as long as it was infrequent.

But when there were far more interesting diversions to be had in London—concerts and card parties and riding in the parks—it was impossible to see how he would be dragged out here more than twice in the whole Season.

Percy squared his shoulders and thanked his stars he had performed his duty without having to see a single blushing wallflower. In, five minutes with the dreaded Miss Pike, and out. Not bad.

Striding down the driveway, gravel crunching under his riding boots, Percy pulled on his gloves and tried to calculate what time he would arrive back at the Knaresby townhouse. Almost four o'clock, by his reckoning. Just in time for—

A heavy weight halted his path, so dense and immovable Percy was almost rocked off his feet. But the weight itself was not so fortunate. Down it fell, in a tumble of skirts and ribbons, and to his horror Percy realised he had toppled not some statue unexpectedly in his path…but a woman.

'Dear God,' Percy muttered, shaking his head at the irritating distraction now preventing him from reaching the stables. 'Apologies, I am sure.'

His gruff remark was ignored, however, as was the hand he offered the young lady who had so unceremoniously been toppled to the ground.

A fierce glare came from bright eyes, and unfathomably Percy's breath caught in his throat.

Then his hand was pushed aside and the young lady, dark-haired and apparently furious, rose to her feet, brushing at her skirts.

Ah. One of Pike's wallflowers.

A lazy grin slid onto Percy's face as he waited for the stammering apology he was doubtless about to receive. After all, he was a duke. And though they had not been introduced, it would be clear from his elegantly tailored coat and graceful top hat that he was—

'Why cannot you look where you are going, oaf?'

Percy blinked. The woman before him had just picked a leaf from her skirt and flicked it to the ground, not looking at him as she spoke—but she was looking at him now.

Those bright eyes he had noticed before were now shining with irritation, and a frown creased the otherwise pretty face. Lips were pressed in a rather furious expression, and the lady did not stop there.

'Do us both a favour, Mr Whoever-You-Are, and consider a little when you walk with no thought to your surroundings, for there are others in the world beyond yourself!'

After a ringing silence, the woman clapped her hands to her mouth, eyes wide, cheeks a flaming pink which was, although Percy tried not to notice, most becoming.

Her horror at her own words could not have been more evident, and Percy did the only thing he could: he laughed.

By Jove, he had not expected that! No woman had ever spoken so to him in his life. Admittedly, there must have been a few who had done it behind his back, but still... They all respected the name and the title, never speaking abruptly or disrespectfully.

This was no wallflower—she could not be. What was she doing here, at the Wallflower Academy, with such an unrestrained and violent temper?

'I—I... I do beg...' the woman stammered, her hands not leaving her mouth so her words were muffled.

If only the pink in her cheeks did not make her so alluring, Percy mused, taking a proper look at her as a woman for the first time. An elegant figure, a gown that might have seen many Seasons but was still relatively fashionable, and a large muddy patch on her behind.

A behind that was well formed, even if it was difficult to tell through the fabric…

A lurch in Percy's stomach pulled him to his senses. Now was not the time to be measuring a young lady's assets, impressive though they might be.

Still, his curiosity must be sated. 'What is your name?'

'Nothing,' the woman said hastily, turning away. 'Good day.'

For a moment Percy could hardly believe she had done so. What? No elegant curtsey? No apology for leaving his presence? No flirtatious grin, moreover, and no teasing hint at her name? No invitation for him to call again? No manners at all?

Hardly aware of what his feet were doing, Percy found himself following the woman up the gravel path towards the Academy. Which was foolishness. He was a duke! Ladies were meant to run after him, not the other way around! It was most unaccountable, this need he had to know her name…

'You must have a name,' he said reasonably, his lungs inexplicably tight. 'Everyone does.'

'It is no concern of yours,' came the swift reply over the lady's shoulder.

Remarkable… Since rising to his title Percy had been inundated with ladies, all simpering and smiling, ready to be delighted—something he hardly regretted—but this was the first to actively avoid his presence.

Perhaps it was because she was unaware of his station, his title. That must be it.

Drawing himself up as best he could, while still pacing

after her, Percy said, impressively, 'I am Percy Devereux, Duke of Knaresby.'

A strange noise emitted from the woman before him. It might have been a laugh, or a cough—he could not tell.

'My name is definitely no concern of yours, then,' came the reply.

There was nothing for it. Percy's curiosity was aroused, and despite his better judgment, and all sense of decorum, he reached out.

No woman walked away from him.

'Wait.'

His hand was on her arm, which was covered by her sleeve. There was no reason for the sudden rush of heat, the tingle in his fingers, the sense that it was he who had been knocked over this time.

Everything swayed a little. The world stayed the same, of course, so perhaps it was he who swayed. Perhaps they both did.

The woman had halted, as if unable to walk forward, and was staring as though she had been cornered by a wild dog.

Percy swallowed. He was acting strangely…far out of character. He had not come here to accost young ladies; he had not even wanted to come here at all.

What was such a woman doing at the Wallflower Academy?

'Did you come here to find a husband?'

The words had slipped from his mouth before he could halt them, and Percy found, to his distraction, that they had a rather pleasing effect. Once again the woman's face was tinged with pink, but she looked defiant.

A most intriguing look.

'I do hope, Your Grace, you do not believe I bumped into you merely to gain your notice!'

In truth, Percy had half wondered that very thing—but now she had spoken, now he heard the tremor in her voice, he could not believe it.

'If...if you could release me?' she said softly.

Percy was still holding on to her and had no desire to release her. His curiosity was still piqued, and he was certain she would run off as soon as she was unrestrained. But the connection between them... There was something there. Something he could not explain.

'Unhand me, sir.'

Sir! The audacity!

Very slowly, one finger after another, he released her.

It was like a small bereavement. The connection was cut, the world stopped swaying, and Percy found he had rather enjoyed the dizziness his touching her had produced.

Yet things were not entirely back to normal. The woman had not fled, as he had expected, but was standing before him with wary eyes and hands clasped before her.

Percy examined her. She was no wallflower. He was certain.

The first of Miss Pike's 'official dinners', as she called them, had been one of the most dull affairs of his life. Never before had he been presented with such a quiet bunch of ladies, and although the bolder one, a Miss Sylvia, had attempted conversation, it had been so stilted Percy had left before dessert, his promise to Miss Pike be damned. There was only so much a gentleman should have to do as a favour to his old governess.

He had never met anyone at the Academy like the woman before him now.

Fire lay under that shyness, Percy was sure. He had felt it when she had berated him so heartily for his inattention.

Though the sparks had disappeared, there was something still smouldering under those dark eyes of hers. Something he wanted to fan back into flames.

'Look,' said Percy imperiously, and irritation flushed through his voice, 'I merely wish to know the name of the person I knocked to the ground, that is all. Your name please, miss?'

Unless she was a servant? Surely not. Percy knew enough of good breeding and the clothes of a maid to know one when he saw one.

A tutor, perhaps, at the Academy? He had heard Miss Pike complain that she needed additional help. Was this it?

'I just wish to know you,' Percy said, trying to inject a little of the Knaresby force into his words.

The woman's gaze dropped. 'No, you do not.'

'Are you always this contrary?'

A mere hint of a smile curled across her lips. 'No.'

He chuckled as a cold breeze blew past them. The sun was setting in earnest now, and he would certainly not be back in Town as expected. His mother would have to wait.

'And when people chastise you for that stubborn streak of yours,' he said, 'what do they call you?'

The smile on her face broadened, and Percy's stomach lurched as her beauty blossomed.

Dear God. She was a marvel.

'They…they call me Miss Gwendoline Knox. But mostly they call me Gwen.'

Gwen.

A shiver went down Percy's spine—which he allotted, of course, to the cooling of the afternoon. It had nothing to do with the wallflower before him. It couldn't.

Oh, don't bother lying to yourself, he thought.

It was natural to be attracted to such a woman. She had all the features and form Society expected in a woman to be called pretty, and yet she had…more.

Putting his finger on it would be difficult. And Percy wanted to put more than a finger on her.

Miss Gwendoline Knox. Gwen.

How he dearly wished to call her Gwen. Such an intimacy, of course, would be insupportable. No noble-born gentleman would consider it. No well-bred lady would allow it.

'And now you can be on your way.'

Percy's gaze snapped back. 'Why would I want to?'

Gwen frowned, and glanced back at the manor before saying, 'Well, you cannot wish to stay here in the cold, talking to me.'

Heavens, how little she knew. Percy could see it in her now he came to look closely. The fear of the wallflower... the expectation that she would never be enough. Not entertaining enough, pretty enough, clever enough. The assumption that she would be passed by. The knowledge, deep within her, that no one would wish to know her, that any conversation would be borne of pity, not interest.

What was it like to go through the world in such a way?

'Because you are a wallflower?' he said, with a wry grin.

A flash of sharpness in her eyes, an inclination towards rebellion, then it was gone.

'Yes.'

'At this awful Academy?' Percy said, looking up at the building before him.

A stricken look overcame Gwen's face. 'Is it truly that bad? Is its reputation unfavourable? I only arrived an hour ago.'

Ah.

Percy found it a challenge to consider his words carefully before he spoke again in this woman's presence. He was, after all, a duke. Well, he had been for the last few months. More, he was a Devereux. His family had been bred for careful and considered conversation, for every word to mean something, to convey the very best feelings and hide the rest.

And here, with her, this woman who had berated him just as swiftly as she'd blushed before him, his feelings betrayed him. They offered him nothing but plain truth—something rather dangerous when a duke.

'I did not mean... Not awful,' he said. 'I merely meant... Well, what is the word?'

Gwen looked at him silently. A prickle of discomfort, not unpleasant, crept up his neck. How did she do that? Look at him as though he was merely a servant himself? As though he was not eminently superior to her?

It was uncanny. It was delightful.

'Intense,' Percy landed on, unable to think of anything better. 'Intense, I suppose, for everyone involved. Just a marriage market under a different name.'

'And you are not married?'

It appeared he was not the only one whose tongue was eager to betray its owner. Percy saw a flush cover Gwen's cheeks, but she continued to hold his gaze defiantly.

Interesting... A wallflower with a dash of curiosity as well as a temper. Most interesting... And she found him just as interesting, did she not? Only a woman interested in a gentleman would ask said gentleman about his potential wife, would she not?

Percy found to his surprise that a flicker of pleasure was curling around his heart at the very thought. It appeared Miss Knox was just as intrigued by him as he was her.

Yet it was not possible, of course, for this conversation to go further. Percy straightened his shoulders as the thought, though unwelcome, hit him with its truth.

He was a duke. She was a wallflower. Probably of little family and no real reputation, if her parents had been forced to send her here to find a match.

And Percy Devereux, Duke of Knaresby, was hardly free himself to make a choice in the matter of his own marriage. He had a duty, a responsibility, to marry a woman of excellent breeding, impressive dowry and, most importantly, respectability in Society. He needed someone far more impressive than a mere wallflower.

A shame. This Gwendoline Knox was rather starting to grow on him.

But he had a far more important focus at the moment, and he was late for old Mr Moore. His mother and the solicitor would not wait for ever. James's will had to be read.

Not that he wanted to dwell on such matters, but he was left with little choice after the way he had arrived at his title.

'No,' Percy said with a wry smile. 'No, I am not married. Not for the lack of my mother's efforts, however.'

'Good,' said Gwen. 'I mean—not good! Just…fine. Fine.'

Fine. A mediocre word from a rather extraordinary woman.

Percy saw the interest in her eyes, the desire flushing her cheeks. He watched the way she leaned ever so slightly closer, all thoughts of escaping him clearly gone from her mind.

It was flattering, of course. And it was a relief, in a way, to see the effect he had on women—even those he had rather unceremoniously accosted by way of greeting.

But that did not explain why his body was responding. Why he wished to take a step, bridge the gap between them. Why, when she shivered in the cold of the afternoon, he wished to place an arm around her and pull her near, to share his heat. Wanted to tip her head back and capture those lips and—

Percy cleared his throat.

No, that would not do.

Still, he could not help himself. A little further teasing would do no harm. 'Just "fine"?' he said.

Gwen hesitated, her gaze moving from his eyes to his lips before it fell to her hands. 'Your Grace, you must realise there is a reason I am here. At the Wallflower Academy, I mean.'

'I have no idea,' said Percy honestly. This was no wallflower, he was sure.

'I am not particularly eloquent,' said Gwen to her boots. 'In talking with gentlemen, I mean.'

'We are talking,' he pointed out.

'No,' said Gwen, glancing up with a smile she was evidently trying to hide. 'You are badgering me.'

'Probably.' Percy grinned. 'Rather fun, don't you think?'

He needed to step away. A small part of him knew that, even if it was shrinking at an alarming rate. Step away from the wallflower and return to Town.

'So, you are not here to find a husband?'

Gwen glanced back at the manor house for a moment before saying, 'No. At least, I don't... I am not desperate.'

She said the last word rather too firmly, if Percy was any judge, although he could not understand why. Surely a woman like this would have no trouble in attracting a nice gentleman? A country squire, perhaps? Someone who could keep her comfortable.

A vision of another man touching Gwen rushed through Percy's mind and his heart rebelled. In an instant the image was gone, though his hand was still clenched in a fist.

'Least likely to win a duke, though,' said Gwen quietly. 'Not after what happened at home, I mean.'

'At home?' Percy asked, his curiosity piqued once more. 'What do you mean by—?'

'I must go inside. They will be wondering where I have got to,' said Gwen in a rush. 'Good day, Your Grace. It was…'

Words failing her, Gwen turned and half walked, half ran up the drive to the steps of the Wallflower Academy. Within a moment, she was gone.

Percy stood, unable to move. As swiftly as she had entered his life she had disappeared.

'Least likely to win a duke.'

So she had said. And yet he was intrigued.

Forcing aside the desire which had so quickly blossomed in Gwen's presence, Percy shook his head, as though that would rid him of the confusion miring his mind.

Miss Gwendoline Knox. A wallflower unlike any he had ever met.

Percy smiled. Well, it was only a week until Pike's second official dinner. His invitation had so far gone unanswered. Perhaps it was time to reply and reward himself with more of Gwen. Demonstrate to her just what calibre of man she had been so quick to run from.

Chapter Three

'This dinner,' said Gwen with an awkward smile. 'We truly have to attend?'

Rilla grinned. 'It is not that bad.'

Night had fallen a few hours before, and Gwen's bedchamber had once again become a gathering place for the two wallflowers who had first welcomed her to the Academy.

If anyone had thought to ask Gwen—and no one had—she would have requested they use Sylvia's bedchamber. It was not as well-proportioned as her own, and neither did it have such an impressive view. Nonetheless, Sylvia herself was no wallflower, and revelled in the company of others.

And Gwen...

Sitting in the window seat by the bay window, Gwen looked out at the flickering torches that Miss Pike—or 'the Pike', as she was affectionately yet fearfully known by the other wallflowers—had ordered to be placed along the drive.

In mere moments carriages would be rattling along that driveway, bringing gentlemen of eligible suitability from London to dine at the Wallflower Academy. There would be conversation. There would be attention. There would be expectations.

There might even, Sylvia had teased, be some sort of recital required, when the gentlemen returned to the ladies after their port and cigars.

Gwen's stomach lurched painfully at the mere thought. *Entertainment. Diversion. Singing. God forbid.*

She had been blessed neither with musical talent nor an ear for a tune, and if she was forced to step up to the pianoforte…

Well, there would be no chance of a match for her then. And if Percy should decide to attend—

But Gwen forced that particular thought from her mind. There was no possibility that the Duke of Knaresby—which was how she should consider him—would be attending the second official Wallflower Academy dinner this evening.

Firstly, she told herself sternly, he was a duke, and had no need to hightail it to a house of wallflowers to find a bride. Goodness knew what sort of gentlemen did resort to such a thing.

Secondly, he had no interest in her. A certain curiosity, true—she had seen it in his eyes. A thirst for knowledge, however, did not translate into a hunger for…

And thirdly, Gwen thought hastily, as she tried not to recollect just how delectable the Duke's lips had looked, she was in no rush to be married. Her mother might consider her a problem unless she was darkening someone else's doorway, but she was not eager to be a wife.

'*So, you are not here to find a husband?*'

'*No. At least, I don't… I am not desperate.*'

Her cheeks flamed with heat.

'I can *feel* you worrying.'

Startled, Gwen looked over at the blind woman, who was smiling. 'You can?'

Rilla laughed. 'They really aren't that bad, these dinners of the Pike's.'

'They're not?' said Gwen hopefully.

It was only a dinner. A few hours of good food and polite if a little stilted conversation. A chance for Sylvia, the only one among them who truly wished to shine, to play the pianoforte and sing and dazzle.

And then bed.

The comfort and the sanctuary of her own bedchamber. Gwen swallowed as she looked at its current inhabitants. All she wanted was a bedchamber empty of all others, where she could rest alone and try not to think of the shocked, wide eyes haunting her dreams...

It had been a relief to discover the food was good and the beds comfortable at the Wallflower Academy. Gwen had not been sure that would be the case when she had first entered the Tudor manor, with visions of gruel and slops clouding her mind.

'You're brooding again.'

''Tis all very well for you Rilla,' said Gwen darkly. 'You cannot see all the gentlemen staring at you, wondering why your family was so desperate as to place you here, wondering why you are so unmarriageable.'

'Well,' said Rilla with a dry laugh, 'with me I suppose they can see without needing to wonder.'

Gwen laughed. She could not help herself. Rilla had been encouraging her all week to laugh when she felt like it, rather than censor herself around her merely because she was blind.

'Ah, a laugh!' Rilla grinned, her pearly eyes moving in Gwen's direction. 'You are finally becoming one of us, then, if you are able to laugh at me and with me. Took you long enough.'

'I have been here only a week!' protested Gwen with a laugh of her own, some of the tension in her stomach dissipating. 'And besides, I have never met a blind lady before.'

'Well, we're not special,' said Rilla with a shrug, placing a bracelet on her wrist. 'Which reminds me—do you have a moment?'

She was proffering a letter she had taken from the pocket of her gown.

Gwen took it. 'And this is…?'

'A letter from my father,' said Rilla, with a coldness Gwen had not expected. 'Summarise it for me, would you?'

Blinking down at it, Gwen's gaze took in a medley of affectionate words.

My darling child…hope to hear from you soon…worried for you…think of you daily…

She swallowed. Not phrases *she* had ever received in a letter from a parent. 'You don't want me to read it?'

Rilla shrugged. 'It's always the same. Never mind, give it here.'

Gwen handed it back wordlessly. Oh, to have a father alive! Or a mother who cared enough to write with such warmth, such love…

'Right, then. Are you adorned and ready to descend?'

Gwen's heart skipped a beat. Her first presentation to the eligible bachelors Miss Pike believed would be suitable for her wallflowers. Would she meet their expectations? Would she disappoint them all? Worse, would it be a repeat of the first official dinner, which Sylvia and the others had told her was such a disaster?

'I suppose we have to go?' The question was rhetorical, really, but Gwen had to ask it. 'We cannot… I don't know… Plead a cold, or a headache, or something?'

'Not if you don't want the Pike swimming up here to discover whether you are feigning,' said Rilla wryly. 'Trust me, once you have been subjected to her battery of enquiries you really do have a headache.'

What had occurred in these walls between these wallflowers before she had arrived?

But she'd had no opportunity to ask questions—not that she would have had the boldness to do so and draw attention to herself. There were plenty of secrets in her own past, after all, that she would rather keep hidden.

She would do anything but have the other wallflowers discover what she had done.

Gwen rose. She had not bothered with jewellery or adornment. This was not the time to hope for pleasant conversation. Her mind was still ringing with the words of the Duke who had knocked her to the ground and then taken her breath away in quite another manner.

The thought of conversation with other gentlemen was quite out of the question.

Chatter in the Academy rose as the wallflowers left their bedchambers and descended the stairs. Gwen's foot almost slipped on the next step. She could hear them. The gentlemen.

Gentlemen. Men.

Men she did not know and who would look at her as a piece of meat. What was it Percy—the Duke—had called it?

Just a marriage market under a different name.'

A smile drifted across Gwen's face, although she tried not to think about Percy.

He was not wrong.

'There must be a better way for us to meet eligible bachelors,' she breathed.

Rilla laughed. 'Come on, Gwen. Spend more than one minute thinking about that. Can you imagine us at a ball? Some of us can barely talk to gentlemen, and I am hardly a suitable dance partner.'

Gwen's stomach twisted as she missed the last step and almost pulled Rilla down with her. 'I do apologise!'

'You do remember I am the blind one, don't you?' Rilla said with a laugh, straightening her skirts as she stood at the bottom of the staircase.

Gwen smiled weakly and nodded. Then, remembering Rilla would not see her expression, she said, 'Yes, I will try to remember.'

They had halted in the hall, with its impressive landscape paintings oppressive in the dim, candlelit evening. The door to the drawing room was about ten feet away. Laughter. Chatter. Men's voices. Low, deep, and utterly confident.

Something painful tightened across her chest. If only there was anywhere else Gwen could be in this moment... But no, home was not an option. No longer home, no longer a place she was welcome. She would have to resign herself to the corridors and rooms of the Wallflower Academy.

This was now her home, but Gwen knew not for how long.

'There they are,' one of the wallflowers whispered— rather unnecessarily, in Gwen's opinion.

They all stood there, as if unable to step back and unwilling to go forward. Gwen could guess what they were feeling. If it was anything akin to her own feelings it was a painful mixture of embarrassment, fury at being subjected to such a thing, and fear that the reality would be even worse than her imaginings.

'You will be married!'

Gwen's mother's words echoed painfully in her mind— the last thing she had hurled at her daughter before she had stepped into the coach taking her to the Wallflower Academy.

'You are unlikely to win anyone's affections here, Gwen-

doline, and it is time for you to find your own place in the world. Without me, without scandal following you, and without whispers of what you've done. Any misstep, and I warn you...'

I warn you.

Gwen swallowed, tasting the fear on her tongue. It was infuriating to force down all thoughts and her temper—the part of her that seemed most natural. But then, she had seen what that temper could do. She must never let it out again. Not after shouting at the Duke, anyway.

Even if she would be sorely tempted when certain irritating dukes knocked her to the ground.

'It's just a dinner,' Gwen said aloud into the silence of the hall. 'Just food.'

'If that helps you,' said Rilla with a dry laugh. 'Come on. Let's get this over with.'

The drawing room was brilliant with light, compared to the dull hall. Inside, the room Gwen had seen in the comfort of quiet evenings, with silent reading and gentle conversation between the wallflowers, had been transformed.

Miss Pike truly knew what she was doing, Gwen had to admit. The faded furnishings had been improved dramatically with silk hangings, and there were velvet cushions on every sofa and armchair. Elegant books had been placed carefully around the place, as though to emphasise the wallflowers' reading habits, and someone had—surely on purpose—left a half-finished painting of exquisite beauty near the curtains by the bay window.

A bureau had been opened up to reveal a drinks cabinet for the gentlemen, and the pianoforte had been uncovered. A fire was roaring in the grate, and there were more candles in one room than Gwen had ever seen.

They illuminated…right in the centre, surrounded by a

gaggle of chortling gentlemen... Percy Devereux, Duke of Knaresby.

If it had not been for Rilla on her left, Gwen was fairly certain she would have stopped dead in her tracks. Her heart certainly did, and a painful squeeze followed as it tried desperately to return to its rhythm.

But it couldn't. It pattered painfully in her body. And Gwen could do nothing but stare at the tall, dark and grinning gentleman who was watching her with a possessive expression.

Not, not *possessive*. That was surely her imagination.

Nothing could have prepared her for this moment. It was unthinkable—incomprehensible. Had the Duke not had enough of her foolish conversation that afternoon when she had so thoughtlessly walked into him?

Gwen could not take her eyes from him, and after managing a few steps more came to a halt in the drawing room. Rilla halted too, evidently unwilling for quite different reasons to approach the group of gentlemen.

A roaring rushed through her ears and Gwen blinked, just to ensure she was not seeing things.

But she was not. In fact, it was getting worse the longer she stood here. Percy—*the Duke of Knaresby, she must remember that*—was walking over to her, with that same smile on his lips and an imperious look in his eyes.

'Wh-What are you doing here?' Gwen stammered, hating the hesitancy in her voice but unable to do anything about it, trying desperately to forget how she had yearned to see him.

It was ridiculous. What would a duke need the Wallflower Academy for? Surely he had far more interesting evening entertainments to attend?

Percy raised a quizzical eyebrow. 'Why, I am here to see you, of course.'

Heat blossomed up Gwen's décolletage and she hoped beyond hope he had not noticed. But of course he had. Or did she imagine that twinkle in his eye...a little too know-ing?

'Who is it?' asked Rilla, her unseeing eyes staring at the gentleman before her. 'At least have the good manners to introduce yourself, man.'

Gwen swallowed. The situation was going from bad to worse, but there was nothing she could do to stop it.

Conversation continued around them in the drawing room...mumbled words Gwen was sure were questions being asked about her.

How did a wallflower on speaking terms with a duke arrive at the Academy?

But she could not do anything about the gossip surely circulating at this very moment. Gwen might appear to be a wallflower, but she had a good enough understanding of decorum to know her duty.

'Your Grace, may I have the honour of presenting to you Miss Marilla Newell?' said Gwen, hardly aware of each word that came out of her mouth.

Percy bowed low and Rilla dipped into a curtsey.

'Miss Newell,' said Gwen, swallowing in an attempt to moisten her mouth. 'May I introduce H-His Grace, Percy Devereux, Duke of Knaresby.'

'Duke of—? Well... Very pleased to make your acquain-tance, I'm sure,' said Rilla. 'Very pleased.'

Try as she might, Gwen was unable to keep her eyes from the Duke as he bowed. She wished to goodness she had managed to resist the temptation, for the instant their gazes met he winked.

It was not heat this time, but something rather akin to it that rushed through Gwen's body. A warmth...a prickle of interest—something that drew her to him, pulling a smile across her face against her better judgment.

'Goodness, a duke,' said Rilla conversationally. 'Gwen, why did you bother coming here if you have such a striking circle of acquaintances?'

'I think we are needed over here,' said Sylvia, stepping forward hastily. 'Come on, Rilla. Your servant, Your Grace.'

After dipping the fastest curtsey Gwen had ever seen, Sylvia shepherded Rilla away and left Gwen alone with the handsome Duke.

Not that she thought him handsome. Obviously.

That would be foolish, Gwen told herself, *for he certainly does not consider you any such thing.*

But after convincing herself over the last six days that she had seen the last of the Duke, it was rather discomforting to find him not only at an evening dinner which she would be forced to sit through, but to be accosted by him the moment she entered the room...

'Well, you have made your point, turned up and surprised me,' she said quietly, so only Percy could hear. 'You can go now—back to your companions or back to Town, which is where I suppose you will go.'

'Nonsense,' said Percy briskly. 'I came for dinner, and I am very much looking forward to the conversation of my dinner companion.'

A little of the tension in Gwen's shoulders seeped away at these words. With five wallflowers, and seemingly double the number of gentlemen—the Pike had outdone herself—there was little chance she would be seated beside this particular gentleman, who made her whole body shiver whenever he came close.

A knowing smile teased across Percy's lips. 'I have, of course, applied to Pike to ensure you are seated beside me.'

Gwen's mouth fell open, and she saw with some surprise that the Duke's gaze followed her lower lip. 'You—you haven't?'

His eyes glittered. 'She's my old governess—you didn't know? She thinks my conversation would be good for you.'

Governess? It was rather difficult to picture the Pike anywhere but here. 'Your governess?'

The Duke was prevented from replying by the resounding gong echoing from the hall. Instead, he moved to her side and put out his arm without speaking, a haughty look on his face.

Speaking was not necessary; his meaning was clear. He intended to accompany her into the dining room and she was supposed to be grateful for the honour.

Entering the second official dinner of the Wallflower Academy that Season on the arm of a duke!

Gwen could never have dreamed of such a thing—would never have expected such attentions from any gentleman, let alone one with a title!

But there was something strange about this man. The pomposity was to be expected, she thought dryly, because he was a duke. There was the arrogance she'd always thought dukes would have, the expectation that anyone in his presence should be thanking him on bended knee for paying them any attention whatsoever.

Could there be any more to him than superciliousness?

Percy cleared his throat. Gwen's heart tightened for a moment, but the warmth created by his presence was spreading through her body and she could do nothing but take his arm.

'Thank you,' she said in a small voice.

He nodded.

As they stepped forward together Gwen was conscious of every eye in the room upon her, wallflowers and gentlemen alike. That must account for the strange tingling in her stomach and just below. There could be no other explanation.

And then he hesitated.

She glanced up at Percy. His eyes were roving the table. He was evidently unsure where he should sit.

Unsure? A duke? Did they not always have the greatest precedence?

His hand tightened on hers. 'I… Uh…'

'Over here, Your Grace!' The angelic tones of Miss Pike. She was gesturing to the head of the table. 'Only the best seat for our most esteemed, our most…'

Her words washed in and out of Gwen's ears unheard as Percy resumed his pace and helped her to the seat beside his.

As he did so, the wallflower opposite her picked up a spoon, immediately dropped it with a clatter onto her wine glass, and flushed crimson.

Sylvia leaned past two of the gentlemen without offering either a glance. 'All these wallflowers!'

'Hush!' Miss Pike frowned.

Gwen's stomach turned, but Sylvia merely flashed a grin. 'Rilla and I rather hoped you wouldn't be a true wallflower, Gwen, but I can see by your flush that you're just like them!'

It was all Gwen could do to smile and say nothing. Well, she had managed it, then. In just one week she had put aside her temper and faded into the background. As her mother had always wished.

They sat in silence until the first course was brought out—some sort of soup. Pea soup? Normally Gwen would not care for such a thing, but she eagerly picked up her spoon and began to eat.

If she was eating, she could not be expected to maintain conversation.

'You look very…nice.'

Gwen choked, spewing green soup across the crisp white linen tablecloth. *Nice?*

'Do not tease me,' she said in a low tone.

She was fortunate tonight. Miss Pike had evidently endeavoured to find a few talkative gentlemen, for a pair of them were having a spirited conversation about the latest horse racing at one end of the table, and Sylvia was engaged in a debate on poetry with a man three seats along.

No one seemed to have noticed her shameful soup spurt…although a footman was looking at her rather despairingly.

Surrounded by the noise of the conversation, Gwen glared at the Duke beside her.

'I am not teasing,' said Percy amiably. 'If I was teasing you…'

He put down his spoon and twisted in his seat to face her. Gwen tried to ignore him, to take another mouthful of soup, but her hands did not obey her. Quite contrary to her desire, she also twisted, the better to face the Duke.

His face was a picture of solemnity, and when he spoke it was in a low voice—so low only Gwen could hear him. 'If I was teasing you, I would say you are the most…the most beautiful woman I have ever seen.'

Scalding heat seared Gwen's face.

The cheek! Did he wish to offend her, then? Was this all some game? Some trick to entertain him?

'So that's not true, then?' she asked fiercely. The arrogance of the man!

'Oh, no, it's all true,' said Percy lightly. His eyes did not waver. 'A duke never lies. I just wanted to tease you.'

Gwen swallowed, soup entirely forgotten. How was it possible for a gentleman to make her feel like this? As though…as though her skin was waking up for the first time, tingling, aching for something she did not understand?

She glanced across the table and saw Miss Pike nodding encouragingly at the pair of them. 'You do know what the Pike will think, don't you? Now you've insisted on sitting next to me at dinner, I mean.'

Percy shrugged nonchalantly. Evidently to him the opinions of a woman like Miss Pike were inconsequential. 'Let her think what she wants. I certainly know what *I* want.'

This was ridiculous!

Gwen tried to turn away, but for some reason her body did not wish to comply. On the contrary, it wished to be nearer. Gwen found herself leaning closer, and to her great surprise Percy did not move back.

'This is ridiculous,' she said in an undertone. 'You are a duke and I am—'

'Nothing,' Percy said quietly, all laughter gone from his voice. 'I remember what you said, Gwen. And, despite my turning up here in my best cravat and most elegantly embroidered waistcoat, you are not impressed by me, are you?'

How easily they did it, Gwen thought with a shot of pain through her heart.

The way gentlemen flirted, responded so quickly, with such wit. Just like they did in novels. It was most unfair. She had no knowledge of the world, no knowledge of men or their ways. How was she supposed to spar with him?

'Impressed? No,' Gwen said quietly.

Was that a flash of anger she saw in those commanding eyes? 'Why the devil not?'

'Because you have done nothing impressive, Your Grace, save bearing a title you inherited and did not earn.'

Not for the first time in his presence Gwen raised her hands to her mouth in horror at what she had said. When would she learn that her temper had to be hidden away, never permitted to surface?

Percy did not look offended, but he hardly looked delighted. 'I see.'

'And besides, if…if my father was alive, he would ask you…' Gwen licked her lips as she hesitated, and saw with wonder the flash of desire in Percy's eyes. 'He d-died just a few months ago. Suddenly. He would wonder, as I am, why you, a duke, are noticing a mere commoner like myself?'

'I am asking myself the same question.'

'And he would ask you what your intentions are.'

It was a bold statement, and Gwen could hardly believe she had spoken it. But Percy did not look away. And even though a shiver rushed up Gwen's spine, she did not break the connection either.

'Well,' said Percy, 'if your father was alive, I would tell him.'

She laughed—and immediately clapped her hands over her mouth as most of those at the table looked at her.

It took a moment—it seemed an age—but eventually they all returned either to their soup or their conversations.

Except one.

Percy was chuckling under his breath. 'You are not really a wallflower, are you?'

Well, perhaps this is rather enjoyable, Gwen thought as she took in the handsome, strong jaw of this man who seemed unable to leave her alone.

Why not flirt with a duke? It would certainly not lead anywhere. She could consider it practice. A distraction.

'And you?' she said lightly. 'Are you really a duke? I only have your word for it, after all.'

Gwen had thought her remark rather witty, but it had a most unexpected effect on the gentleman. A shadow swept over his face, and a flash of anger, of fury, and for the first time since they had been seated at the table he looked away.

'I apologise,' Gwen said quickly. Whatever she had said, she had clearly offended him.

Percy laughed dryly. 'You do not know what you are apologising for. Do you?'

It was too much. Gwen was all at sea in their conversation—which always seemed to be the case whenever she was in the company of the Duke of Knaresby. Percy did something to her—something she could not understand but could only guess at.

She liked him. She was attracted to him. She found him most irresistible, even if his manners were incorrigible and his conversation haughty. Was this why she was acting so strangely…as though drawn like a moth to a flame?

'No,' Gwen said helplessly. 'I do not. I am sorry.'

Somehow that was the right answer. A teasing smile on his lips, Percy reached towards her and took her hand in his.

Gwen almost gasped aloud as he raised it to his lips and kissed the very tips of her fingers. Oh, to feel those lips, to feel the warmth of them… The pooling desire in her body was crying out for it. Such a simple movement, yet one so heightened with promise of more.

'Gwendoline Knox,' said Percy quietly, her hand still in his, 'when I make you do something that requires an apology, you will really need to mean it.'

Chapter Four

'Then I realised it was in my pocket the entire time! Reminds me of the time I went hunting with Buxhill and Lindham—you know them, of course? Fine gentlemen, but not so good with a horse. Did I ever tell you where I got my filly from? Lovely ride, really pleasant manner—though when I first purchased her naturally...'

Percy's chin almost touched his chest and he jerked up, sleep swiftly pushed back. Never mind that the impending slumber would have been appreciated, it would not do to be seen napping while Westerleigh chatted away at White's.

That was the trouble with the gentlemen's club, Percy thought, as he nodded vaguely at whatever the old boy was saying and leaned forward to pick up his cup of tea. It was cold.

White's was all very well—a sterling establishment, and he wouldn't hear a word against it—and yet... There was just something rather old-fashioned about it. Percy glanced about the Blue Drawing Room, where he had settled himself not an hour ago. Decorated in the finest furnishings the seventeen-seventies could lavishly permit, there was a rather tired air about the place. The leather was worn to skin in some places on the armchairs, and each of the little tables upon which the gentlemen rested their cups—tea, whisky, or other—were chipped.

In truth, Percy thought, stretching in an attempt not to show Westerleigh that he was bored by his monologue, there was nothing interesting at White's. When it boiled down to it—and the meat here was dreadfully boiled—it was all about the people one interacted with.

And when one of them was Westerleigh…

A yawn threatened to reveal his boredom, but Percy managed to stifle it just as a gap appeared in the conversation. 'Yes, indeed,' he said.

The Earl of Westerleigh nodded pompously, evidently unaware that his dull monologue was putting his companion to sleep. 'And, of course, there was nothing for it but to continue! When I spoke to the man in question, he told me…'

Percy could not have recounted precisely what this anecdote was about for love nor money, having totally lost the train of the conversation, but that was rather an advantage. It left him free to think about a more pleasant topic.

Like Miss Gwendoline Knox, for example, and the way candlelight illuminated her face when she was embarrassed—or aroused.

Percy swallowed, but saw that old Westerleigh hadn't a clue. No one in the place was listening to a word he said, and he had not noticed that his young companion had quite another thing on his mind.

A young lady with dark, almost black hair curling around her bright, expressive eyes. Eyes that had danced with confusion and mischief as they had conversed at that Wallflower Academy dinner.

And to think he nearly hadn't attended.

Percy dreaded to think how he might have spent that evening talking to some of his mother's dull friends, listening to dull tales like Westerleigh's, eating dull food…

Instead he had been treated to the most delightful display of restrained irritation he had ever seen. Why, if they had been alone, Percy was willing to bet Gwen would have walloped him for the things he had said—and quite rightly, too, in some cases.

'Gwendoline Knox, when I make you do something that requires an apology, you will really need to mean it.'

He shivered at the very thought. Oh, the things he would like to do to Gwendoline Knox... It was almost criminal, how delectable she was. Far more interesting than old Westerleigh, though Percy was not so unpolitic as to say so.

It was strange, though. Any other Thursday in Town, Percy would have expected some of his acquaintances to be here—rather than this old friend of his father who was boring him at present, his moustache bristling in the almost continuous speech.

'I thought to meself, *This is it, young chap!* Of course in those days gentlemen had far more opportunities for adventure—none of this Grand Tour nonsense you chaps dally with. No, it was to war for me, and I discovered to my surprise...'

Percy nodded. On any other day Westerleigh's new topic might have lifted him out of his listlessness, but not today.

No, unless a certain lady walked into White's, with a delicate air and a fierce temper...

Percy was smiling—a most uncommon occurrence in White's. One did not come here to be entertained. One came to escape the world. The trouble was, he did not particularly wish to escape the world today. At least, not one particular part of it.

Not that he should.

He folded his hands firmly in his lap, as though that would prevent him from being rash. It wasn't *his* reputation, after all, that would be harmed. It would be Gwen's.

Their unequal stations, her innocence, his lack of honourable intentions...

Gwen would take a great risk in just being seen speaking to him, Percy knew. The censure of Society... But then,
he would risk the wrath of his mother. It was almost the
same thing.

'And then I—Knaresby, old thing. Where are you
going?' Westerleigh blinked in surprise.

Percy pulled his coat straight and nodded politely to the
older man. 'Duty calls, my dear chap.'

'Ah... Well, duty and all that,' said the older gentleman
comfortably, reaching for the glass of brandy which had
been refilled subtly, without request, by a footman as soon
as it had been emptied. 'Quite understand.'

Percy was impressed—because he certainly didn't understand. He could not comprehend why he was walking
out of White's at this early hour, why he was instructing
his man to ready his horse, and why he was directing that
horse out of Town.

'Your Grace?'

In fact, he—

'Your Grace? Devereux?'

Percy halted. Of course. *He* was 'Your Grace'. It was
still taking a bit of getting used to.

The demure words had been spoken by a footman in
White's colours, his hands clasped together before him
almost as a supplicant.

What on earth did he want?

'Yes?' Percy prompted.

The footman smiled awkwardly. 'It is only... I need to
speak to your steward, Your Grace.'

Percy blinked. 'My steward?'

What on earth for? There had never been any need for
his steward to be involved in his White's membership.

The footman inclined his head. 'To organise your bill, Your Grace. 'Tis a small matter...'

'Oh, that's easy enough,' said Percy, his shoulders relaxing. 'You had me worried there! Here, how much is my tab?'

He pulled his pocketbook from inside his jacket, and saw with surprise that the footman looked genuinely flummoxed.

'I... You... Your steward,' muttered the man. He cleared his throat. 'Dukes do not carry money!'

Heat flushed Percy's cheeks. 'They...they don't?'

No one had told him that. But then, there were so many hidden rules, weren't there? So many things others just seemed to do without thinking, as easily as breathing.

Whereas every breath he took was a determined gasp.

'I must speak with your steward,' the footman said firmly, carefully avoiding looking at the pound notes in Percy's hands. 'That is the proper way of doing things.'

Proper way of doing things? *Well, that's as may be,* Percy thought, as he gave his steward's name to the clearly embarrassed footman.

James wouldn't have allowed a mere servant to talk to him like that—make him feel the fool. Besides, he had never been one to enjoy 'the proper way' of doing things. Not before the title, not after.

Why else, he thought as the autumnal air whipped past him, chilling his ears and giving him a greater desire to arrive, *would I be so intrigued by Gwen?*

Why else would he be arriving unannounced at the Wallflower Academy?

It was not so far out of London that a visit was unwarranted or surprising, but as far as he knew there were no planned events this afternoon. No teas, no music recitals, no card games, no dinner—and certainly no ball.

A wry smile slipped across Percy's face as he surveyed

the old manor house as it appeared around a corner. That was a thought... Gwen at a ball.

Miss Knox.

He really needed to remember the bounds of propriety, Percy reminded himself as he slipped off his horse and handed over the reins to a stableboy who had rushed forward.

He might have called Gwen by her first name at the dinner, and he might have looked as though he wished to slowly unwrap each and every piece of her clothing, wanted to kiss every inch of her skin...

But that didn't mean he was going to do anything foolish. Except turn up here unannounced, of course.

His knock on the front door of the Wallflower Academy was therefore accidental. He had not meant to do it. His feet had just meandered to the door, and now he was there it seemed ridiculous not to knock.

Precisely what he intended to do, Percy was not sure. His thoughts were not forming properly. For some reason his heart was thumping loudly. He could hear it in his ears, feel the tight pressure in his chest.

When a footman finally answered the door, Percy astonished himself and the servant by barking, 'Gwen!'

The footman blinked. 'I beg your pardon, Your Grace?'

Percy shifted on his feet, as though that might help him remember both his manners and his senses.

You are not falling in love with a mere wallflower, he told himself sternly. *After everything you have been through to get here, you do not need any complication. You know the sort of woman you must marry. You know the criteria. You are just being polite. You are visiting the Academy. You could be visiting any of them.*

The array of wallflowers currently in residence at the Academy rushed through his mind.

Perhaps not. None of them attracted him as Gwen did. None of them drove a need in him…a want that was starting to affect his judgment.

Percy jutted out his jaw imperiously—or at least as imperiously as he could muster. 'I thought I would visit the wallflowers.'

This was evidently an unusual statement. The footman looked a little concerned, and swallowed hard before saying, 'Is…is there an invitation upon your person, Your Grace, that I could see?'

'Invitation?' repeated Percy, completely bemused. 'What would I need an invitation for?'

'Well, you see, it's a matter of…of delicacy,' muttered the footman, his boldness deserting him. 'Having gentlemen in the house unaccompanied…'tis not right…'

Percy cleared his throat, but said nothing.

The man had a point.

Miss Pike had probably created the rule after a difficult situation. One that should certainly not have occurred. A scandalous one. Involving a wallflower and a rake, no doubt.

Someone entirely different from him.

'I think, in the circumstances, you can make an exception,' Percy said, smiling and taking a step forward.

It was a step he had to immediately retract, as the footman did not budge.

'Circumstances, Your Grace?'

The man knew him and yet was determined to refuse him access! The blackguard!

'I am a duke,' Percy said pointedly.

'And I am a footman,' said the footman stoutly, not looking Percy in the eye, but rather gazing at something just beyond his left shoulder. 'I know my place, and I am sorry to say, Your Grace, my place is in here and yours is out there. Unless you have an invitation...'

Percy stared at the man helplessly. Foiled—and by a footman. no less! It was most infuriating. Just beyond this man was a woman who was bold and brash and a wallflower. She was also shy, and a multitude of complexities Percy had still to understand.

And once he understood her he could leave her alone and get back to his primary goal this Season: finding a wife.

It was simple as that.

Understand Gwen, then leave her.

The twist in his stomach told Percy he was attempting to fool himself, but he ignored it and instead directed all his ire towards the unfortunate footman before him.

'Miss Pike,' Percy said in a cold tone, 'will hear about this.'

The servant drew himself up. 'I hope so, Your Grace.'

Muttering curses under his breath against servants in general and footmen in particular, Percy turned away from the man and walked down the steps.

It was galling to be so close to Gwen and yet be unable to see her...

A slow smile crept over Percy's face as he stepped towards the stables and he halted in his tracks. If he skirted around the other side of the house—not towards the stables but towards the orangery—there was a very real chance he would be able to see her.

But that would be a foolish thing to do. Something only a lovesick mule would do. Percy knew better. He would get his horse and ride straight home. That would be the sensible thing to do.

Stepping lightly across the gravel, and hoping the dratted footman was not watching, Percy crept away from the stables and towards the westerly side of the house where the large orangery stood. A little dilapidated now, it none-theless offered a perfect view into the dining room and the drawing room of the house.

Surely Gwen would be in one of those at this time of day...?

Highly conscious that he had no idea whatsoever what the wallflowers imprisoned inside the Academy found to fill their time, Percy crept through a rather cumbersome hedge and across a border, ruffling a rose.

Soon he found himself at one end of the orangery.

And was rewarded.

Looking through the orangery and into the room be-yond, Percy could make out Gwen and the other wallflow-ers, evidently having a lesson in dinner etiquette.

They were all seated at the dining room table with places set and a plethora of knives and forks before them. An irate-looking Miss Pike was striding up and down, de-livering a monologue perhaps not unlike the one he had been subjected to by Westerleigh.

The reactions of the wallflowers, at least, looked the same as his. From where Percy was standing, it appeared that the black wallflower—Sylvia, wasn't it?—was try-ing to stifle giggles.

Percy smiled as he watched Gwen attempting to pay attention despite the obvious tedium.

How had a woman like Gwen ended up in a place like this?

True, she was shy—but there was a real temper under that hesitancy. Her beauty, her conversation... It did not seem possible that Gwen could not find a match. Percy was cer-tainly finding her far more interesting than he should be...

He gasped. Gwen had looked up, right into his eyes, her gaze fierce, sharp, as though she had heard his thought. As though she had not approved of it.

Taking a hurried step backwards, Percy felt his foot slip on some mud, toppling him to the ground. The wind knocked out of him, he gazed up at the gloomy grey sky and wondered what it was about this woman she managed to cause someone to be tipped to the ground every time they came near to each other.

When he'd managed to right himself, brushing off as much mud as possible, Percy looked up to see Gwen red-faced and the other wallflowers giggling around the table.

Blast. He had obviously embarrassed not only himself, but Gwen too.

What had overcome him? Bringing him to the Wallflower Academy without an invitation, skulking around like a common cad, slipping over with shock when a mere glance met his eye?

He was a damned duke! He had responsibilities—duties in Town unable to be ignored. So why was he here, pulled towards this woman?

It was a question Percy could not answer, but he would soon need to.

After exchanging a few words with Miss Pike, Gwen rose, curtsied, then started towards him.

Oh, hell. What was he supposed to say? How was he supposed to explain why a duke was hiding in hedges and falling beside orangeries, all to see a wallflower he must not pursue?

'Well,' said Gwen quietly, opening the door of the orangery and leaning against the doorframe. 'You seem to have made your acquaintance with the ground.'

Percy glared. How did she do it? There was no malice in her tone, no coquettish teasing as he had learned to expect from eligible young ladies. Instead, Gwen appeared to be…earnest. Honest. It was a strange thing to see in a lady of marriageable age, and Percy found himself rather undone by the entire experience.

'I… I fell,' he snapped.

By Jove, he needed to gather his thoughts and tame his tongue, or he would be making even more of a fool of himself than he already had!

The damp from his fall had started to seep through his breeches.

'Yes, I saw,' said Gwen, still quietly.

There was mischief in her eyes, but it was held back by a reticence Percy did not quite understand.

'There is a front door, you know. I've walked through it myself. 'Tis not too arduous.'

Percy forced himself to speak. 'I wasn't permitted entry.'

Gwen stared. 'Goodness, why on earth not?'

He shrugged, as though that explained the situation. When it became apparent from Gwen's waiting expression that it did not, Percy tried to make the entire thing far more impressive than it actually was.

'I was forbidden entry because…because it was believed the place would not be safe with me in it,' he said, waving an arm expressively. 'That you wallflowers would not be safe with me. Have to fight me off with a stick, I suppose.'

Gwen's cheeks flushed scarlet and she glanced behind her, presumably at someone carefully listening in. Decorum had to be upheld. They could not be alone.

It was instantaneous. He'd crossed a line—some line Percy had had no idea was there—and she'd closed herself off.

The mischievous air was gone, replaced only by the demeanour of a quiet, uninterested wallflower.

'Well, I will say good day, then,' said Gwen, and moved to shut the door.

'Wait!' Percy acted on instinct, his desire to impress disappearing, subsumed by the need to keep her with him.

He looked down. He had placed his hand on hers, and even through his riding glove he could once again sense that strange, yet enjoyable tingling that typically preceded one of his beddings.

Percy was no innocent. He did not have to wonder what this meant. He wanted her—badly. Needed to know every inch of her...to tease pleasure from those lips now parting in wonder at his presumption in touching her. Then he'd leave her behind.

But Gwen did not know that—and it was best she never knew. Percy might take the pleasures of courtesans, but he was not one to take the innocence of a wallflower—not one under the protection of a lady as fearsome as Miss Pike, anyway.

Carefully, and slowly, as though any sudden movement might break the connection between them, Percy removed his hand and moved back.

'Your Grace, I do not understand why—'

'Come with me.'

Gwen's eyes widened, her breath catching in her throat, and Percy stepped towards her, his desire to dominate her will forcing him forward. He wanted to see the change in her as she spoke. Not just hear her words, but sense the change in her breath, feel the heat of her skin.

'I... I beg your pardon?' Gwen whispered.

'On a ride,' Percy said high-handedly. 'I have my mare here, and I am sure there are horses in the Academy's stables. Come with me. On a ride.'

For a heady moment he thought he had convinced her. Gwen examined him, her eyes appraising, and Percy felt scrutinised as never before. What was she looking for? Trustworthiness? A sense of his being a rake?

She would find both—and more besides, Percy thought with a wry smile. But what he was far more interested in was what *he* would find when spending more time with her.

Gwen Knox. There was something about her...something he could not put his finger on though he very much wished to. Something she was hiding. Something more than was natural for a wallflower.

Something that one day he would uncover.

'No,' she said firmly, though her lips curled into a smile. 'You are jesting with me.'

'I am not jesting with you,' said Percy, piqued at her immediate refusal. 'Come riding with me.'

'You came all this way from Town to ask me to go on a ride?'

'I came all this way to see you.'

Percy could think of no better way to put it. It was the truth. She had drawn him here inexorably, against his better judgement and seemingly against the wishes of the footman who guarded the door.

But he was here, and so was she.

Gwen had had no need to leave her lesson to speak with him—she had chosen to do that of her own volition. She wanted him. Percy could sense it.

The fact was it was absolutely impossible—foolish, even—for a duke and a wallflower to be conversing like this...

Well, Percy would deal with his conscience later.

'Do you not need to marry a woman of—of good fortune and connections?'

Percy blanched. The bold question from Gwen had come from nowhere, her words clear and without malice.

And she was right.

Percy wished to contradict her immediately, tell her that

his choices were his own, and he could wed—or bed—whomever he wished.

But it would be a lie. A boldfaced lie and one she would discover soon enough. Gwen had seen the need in him. For Percy certainly did need to find a wife with a dowry and a good reputation.

Needed to far more than she could ever realise.

'I see the truth in your eyes, you know. You cannot hide it.'

'I...' Percy said, but words failed him.

This was ridiculous—words never failed him. He was a master at wit and at wooing, but when it came to Gwen... she undid him. It was most unfair, for he had never wished to impress anyone more.

'Well, when you work out the answer,' said Gwen gently, 'come and tell me. I cannot help but feel, Your Grace, you are teasing yourself far more than you are teasing me. Good day.'

And with that she closed the door of the orangery and returned not merely to her seat in the dining room, but further into the Academy and out of sight.

Percy leaned heavily against the glass of the orangery—then hastily stood as it made an awful creaking sound.

This woman was going to be the death of him.

How had Gwen put it?

'Least likely to win a duke.'

Percy shook his head with a smile. *Least likely?* That was not precisely how he would have put it.

Chapter Five

Monday slid into Tuesday, which was very much like Wednesday, and before Gwen knew it she had been at the Wallflower Academy almost two weeks.

Days repeated each other in the same tired, dull routine she was already accustomed to, and it was difficult to see how some of the other wallflowers, who had been resident in the place for months, if not years, suffered such boredom.

Breakfast, and then a little light reading was expected from all the wallflowers—but not too much. Gwen had been subjected to a lecture one day from Miss Pike, on how too much reading was wont to make a woman a blue-stocking.

'And if there is one thing worse than a wallflower,' the indefatigable Miss Pike had said sternly, 'it is a blue-stocking.'

Gwen had spotted out of the corner of her eye a particularly irritated scowl, but no one had been bold enough to contradict the owner of the Wallflower Academy.

Which was probably all to the good. Gwen had no desire to bring attention to herself, or to challenge the fearsome Pike and have even a hint of a suggestion of returning home to her mother.

Not after the chaos she had endured at home. She had left that behind. She would never face that again.

After breakfast and light reading came lessons—something Gwen was resigned to.

Lessons. The Academy made her feel as if she was back in the schoolroom, learning her alphabet and practising her handwriting, but these lessons were irritatingly childish.

Small talk and conversation. Napkin folding. Disagreeing with one's conversational partner. Using forks and spoons. Walking with one's head at the correct angle. The appropriate way to speak of the weather. Identifying a person's rank at a distance. Music appreciation.

If Gwen had had anywhere else to go, she would have packed her things and been off within three days of arriving at the austere Academy.

By Thursday afternoon, several days after Percy—the Duke of Knaresby...she really must remember to give him his correct title—had arrived so strangely at the Wallflower Academy and played some sort of jest upon her at the orangery, Gwen could not remove his words from her mind.

'Come riding with me.'

If she was truly so desirous of leaving, Gwen thought painfully, as she sat in silence in the quiet of the afternoon with the other wallflowers, some reading, some embroidering, Rilla just gazing sightlessly into space, then why had she not accepted Percy's invitation?

A ride... Something she had forgone since she had left home. An opportunity to see some of the countryside about the place. More, a chance to leave the confines of the Wallflower Academy for more than five minutes in the garden.

It would have been heavenly.

It would have been glorious.

It would have been far too much of a temptation to bear.

Which was why Gwen was rather surprised to find herself bundled into a dog cart at this awful time in the morning.

It was all Sylvia's fault, of course.

'Sylvia, what on earth is this about?' Gwen had asked, yawning, after being dragged out of bed by Sylvia, who had already been dressed. She had got into her own gown and been pulled down the servants' staircase to this dog cart waiting by the side of the Academy. 'Have you lost your senses?'

She certainly had.

The morning air was freezing, and Gwen's mind had whirled at such an unexpected turn of events.

What was Sylvia thinking?

Sylvia's expression was sharp and determined. 'I'm not staying here to rot for ever. I don't care what the Pike says. I'm not going to be married off, and my parents won't take me back—not my father, at any rate.'

Gwen tried to follow her rapid words. 'But that doesn't explain—'

'I'm running away,' Sylvia pronounced proudly. 'On!'

The dog cart jerked forward as Gwen attempted to take in the words just spoken. Running away?

'So what am I doing here with you?' It was all she could manage.

The day was so early, her breath blossomed before them.

Sylvia grinned. 'You're no wallflower.'

Gwen swallowed. 'Y-yes, I am.'

The lie tasted bitter, but she had no choice. She could not be found out. She had to fade into the background and—

'No, you're not,' Sylvia said, quite calmly, leaning back in the dog cart as if she frequently drove such a conveyance. 'And though that place is no prison, let's be honest. Our families don't want us. They can call it an academy as much as they want, but it's just a place where unwanted daughters are left and abandoned.'

Gwen tried to think of words to counter Sylvia's argument, but she could not. Was she herself not a perfect example of this?

'No, the whole world is out there, and I am tired of being treated like a child, ordered about by the Pike as though I have no idea what I'm doing,' Sylvia said firmly.

'And so...a dog cart?' asked Gwen helplessly. 'And abducting me, I suppose? Is that the plan?'

Sylvia's grin was bold. 'All part of the plan. You can get out, if you prefer, but I thought you'd be interested in getting out of this place.'

Gwen's gaze flickered up to the tall manor house slowly disappearing into the distance.

She had no wish to be there, it was true. But where else could she go?

And Sylvia was no fool. Though she had not shared the information, she must have a plan. They must be meeting someone, wherever they were going. She must have some family who would take her.

Gwen sighed. 'This is ridiculous.'

'This is an adventure!' beamed Sylvia. 'Finally!'

It did not feel like much of an adventure when the dog cart brought them to a loud, noisy and most definitely stench-filled street. There were countless people meandering up and down, carts, dogs, a man on a horse, a woman leaning out of a window shouting something...

It was overwhelming. Intoxicating.

And the dog cart had disappeared into the melee.

'Is...is this London?' Gwen asked in wonder.

Sylvia snorted. 'This place? No, just a small town where I thought I could find...'

Her voice trailed away and Gwen narrowed her eyes. 'I thought you had a plan.'

'I did,' Sylvia said, though her defiance was lacking now. 'I planned to leave the Wallflower Academy. Now I have—'

'Sylvia Bryant, you have no idea what to do next, do you?' Gwen said, with dawning comprehension and panic rising in her chest.

She was in a strange town she'd never heard of, with a woman with no plan at all, no luggage, no money—what on earth were they going to do?

The panic started to solidify into shame. Her mother had ordered her to be obedient and not to draw any attention to herself! And here she was, bound to get into trouble with the Pike when they got back.

If they could get back...

Sylvia looked wretched. 'I... Well, I didn't expect it to be so—'

'No one wants us, Sylvia,' Gwen found herself saying, the shame and panic mingling to bring her temper out. 'We're at the Academy because we have nowhere else to go! It's not a prison if you have no alternative!'

Sylvia's cheeks were reddening. 'I never said—'

'Gwen? Sylvia?'

Against all the odds, a voice was calling their names— a voice that came from a coach.

Gwen's stomach twisted as a face appeared in the window of that coach. Of all the people—

'What are you doing here?' asked Percy brightly.

Her heart skipped a beat. This was most untoward— what on earth was *he* doing here? And how was she supposed to explain?

'It's your duke, Gwen!' Sylvia said eagerly. 'My word, do you think he could take us—?'

'He'll take us straight back to the Academy, and you

must pray the Pike hasn't noticed our absence,' Gwen said, far more firmly than she felt.

If they were lucky, they could slip back in and pretend the whole thing had never happened.

As long as Percy could be trusted to keep his mouth shut...

A lopsided lazy grin slipped over the Duke's face as he clambered out of his carriage. 'I didn't think to see you here!'

His words were directed at Gwen, who refused to meet his eye. It was going to be painful, asking him this, but—

'Can we have a lift?' Sylvia asked cheerfully.

Gwen blinked. How did she do it? Speak so boldly, without any care, to a duke?

'Sylvia,' she hissed under her breath. 'I think—'

'Oh, I'm more than happy to take you back to the Academy,' said Percy, though his gaze was firmly fixed not on Sylvia, but on Gwen. She could feel the intensity of his gaze even without looking up. 'Come on. I'll—'

'I don't think so, Y'Grace.'

Gwen looked up. A man's voice had spoken—one she did not recognise. Now she had looked up, she could see it was Percy's driver.

He looked a little embarrassed, but it was nothing to the surprise on Percy's face. 'Why in heaven's not?' he asked.

'Well, because...because dukes don't pick women up off the street,' said the shamefaced driver. 'Not in daylight, anyway.'

Heat blossomed across Gwen's chest. Was the man insinuating—?

'This duke does,' Percy said firmly, offering a hand to Sylvia. 'A gentleman always rescues a lady, my man, and in this case there are two. Gwen?'

She had no choice but to accept his hand into the coach.

Settling beside Sylvia, Gwen gave her a stern look that received nothing but a grin in reply—and then Percy himself seated himself in the carriage.

'You're running away, aren't you?' he asked conversationally.

Before Gwen could do anything, Sylvia nodded blithely. 'Gwen tried to stop me, but I was determined.'

'Yes, I can see that,' said Percy softly.

Gwen looked at her hands, clasped together in her lap, as the carriage jerked forward.

This was outrageous! It was all Sylvia's fault—running away, indeed—and Percy would never let her hear the end of it, she was sure. Why, he would—

'I think it's best,' came Percy's quiet voice, 'if we say no more about it. We'll be at the Academy in less than twenty minutes, and you can slip back in. It's still early.'

Gwen swallowed, and managed to force herself to look up in gratitude.

Her breath caught in her throat. How did he look like... like *that*?

As though it was his greatest pleasure to rescue her.

As though he had hoped for nothing more when he awoke that morning.

As though spending just a few stolen minutes with her, even in the company of Sylvia, was a gift she could have bestowed upon no more grateful recipient.

Gwen forced herself to breathe. She was seeing far more in that look than existed, she was sure.

And he was right. In an inordinately swift amount of time the Academy could be seen through the carriage window, and Sylvia's shoulders had slumped.

'Not a word,' Gwen said firmly as the carriage came to a halt.

And, most surprisingly, Sylvia obeyed.

The two of them said nothing to Percy as they descended from his carriage, nothing to each other as they slipped through a side door and walked the familiar route to the drawing room, and nothing to the wallflowers who looked up curiously as they entered.

Gwen stepped over to an empty seat after retrieving her embroidery from the box. Her heart was thundering as she pulled out her needle and examined her progress.

What a disaster the morning might have been!

'Miss Knox?'

Besides, Gwen told herself firmly, her gaze drifting over the crimson thread slowly forming a rose on the embroidery hoop between her fingers, *a carriage ride with a duke is not simple. And it was Sylvia's fault, entirely.*

And it meant something. She was sure it did. If not to her, then to Percy. Certainly to the Pike, if she ever found out.

'Miss Knox!'

Startled, Gwen dropped her embroidery hoop. It slipped to the floor with a low *thunk*, and after she'd leaned down to pick it up the mirage of the Pike before her did not disappear.

'Miss Knox, you do not attend!'

Gwen swallowed. It was one of the most common critiques she had to endure from the sharp eyes of Miss Pike: not attending.

As though it was that easy.

As though she could force from her mind the face of Percy Devereux.

As though she could forget the way he had spoken to her at the dinner, the way he had held her hand, skin to skin, something Gwen had never done with any gentleman before.

As though she could pretend she had not seen him that morning.

Their connection was something she longed for. A connection which drew something out of her she did not understand. Yet she knew where it led...

Oh, she knew.

'Yes, Miss Pike,' Gwen said hastily, conscious that the owner of the Wallflower Academy was waiting for a response. 'I do apologise, Miss Pike. I was thinking about... about the next rose.'

'Rose?' Miss Pike raised an eyebrow.

Gwen lifted her embroidery. 'Yellow or white?'

For a moment Miss Pike glared, as though attempting to discover whether there was an impertinence somewhere in the wallflower's remark.

Eventually it appeared she could find none. She sniffed. 'White. There is a letter for you.'

Her hand shot out and Gwen stared at the letter within it. Cheap paper and no seal—just a dot of sealing wax. Her heart sank, all hopes that it might have been a note from a certain gentleman disappearing in an instant.

There was only one person that letter could be from.

'You know, Miss Knox, I believe you are doing well in your comportment classes,' said Miss Pike stiffly, as though it physically pained her to say something pleasant.

Sylvia was seated behind Miss Pike, and Gwen saw her grin, and then make a silly face behind the older woman's back. Gwen stifled a laugh. She would not permit Sylvia to get her into trouble, no matter the inducement. Not even when she had dragged Gwen into a dog cart to run away from the Academy.

'But I wish you would try harder in your dining etiquette,' continued Miss Pike, a creasing frown appearing between her grey eyes. 'Really...disappearing off in the last fork lesson... I was most displeased.'

Gwen swallowed. Percy's face swam into view—that

teasing smile, that shamed expression when he'd been caught slipping over in the mud by the orangery.

He was a delight.

He was a torment.

He was a duke. Certainly not someone she should be thinking of.

'Yes,' said Gwen quietly, taking the letter from Miss Pike's hand and choosing not to comment on the negative remark. 'Thank you for your kind words, Miss Pike.'

If possible, the Pike's frown deepened as she examined her, and Gwen did not attempt to hold her gaze. It would be a fruitless task. Not only because her natural shyness did not permit it, but because Miss Pike clearly had decades of practice in fearsome gazes.

Gwen's gaze slipped instead to the roses in the embroidery in her hands, one complete, one half finished, the other a mere outline. She swallowed hard, forcing down the remembrance of that strange encounter.

What had Percy been thinking? Sneaking around the side of the Academy, looking in at them from the orangery, and then saying such strange things to her—almost flirting with her. As though she was a prize to be won, a lady to be courted, a prospective bride...

The thought was unconscionable. No gentleman would consider her a worthy match, Gwen was sure. No dowry, no real family name, no spirit or conversation to recommend her.

Only a temper which, once unleashed, could be deadly.

Her throat was dry, and no matter how many times she swallowed Gwen could not regain her composure.

She was being ridiculous.

Likely as not, dukes flirted with anything that moved. She was not special. She had not attracted him for any particular reason.

She was here because it had been impossible for her to remain at home after the scandal.

But that did not explain why he had come here, all the way from London, a full twenty-minute ride. Gwen could not comprehend it. Surely he would be inundated with invitations for parties and concerts, opportunities to visit Court, to see old friends and make new acquaintances…

What did it all mean?

'I see you have made quite an impression on the Duke of Knaresby.'

Gwen's eyes snapped back to Miss Pike, whose frown had disappeared and been replaced by an expression she could not place for a moment.

Then it became clear. Greed. Of course.

Miss Pike would be well rewarded by my Mother, Gwen thought darkly, *if she marries me off to a duke.*

It would be quite a coup for the Wallflower Academy. She doubted whether anything so wild had ever occurred in the place.

'I think you have done well with him so far, Miss Knox,' said Miss Pike calmly, utterly unable to see the flush on her charge's face—or simply ignoring it. 'I would have had you pegged as the least likely to win a duke. But I believe more conversation is required to hook him. You will need to put in more effort.'

Gwen could hardly believe those words were being spoken—and in the drawing room before all the other wallflowers, too! She could only see Sylvia and Rilla's expressions, to be sure, but if they were indicative of the others' she would soon be under a most direct interrogation.

'I cannot… I will not… I do not believe the Duke will be returning,' Gwen managed.

At least she was almost certain those words had come out of her mouth. She had intended them to do so.

'Nonsense,' said Miss Pike cheerfully. 'I will ensure he receives every invitation.'

If only she had a little bravery, a little determination—anything to force her mouth to move and her thoughts to pour into the conversation. If only she could make it clear to Miss Pike that she had no desire whatsoever to see Percy—the Duke—again.

Except she did.

Gwen could not lie to herself, even if she wished to lie to others. Seeing Percy was the only potential event of interest on her horizon—a horizon that stretched out seemingly for ever, littered with boring lessons, dull afternoon teas, insipid conversations at dinner and nothing else.

Nothing until she found a husband.

But she never would.

Gwen could confide in no one at the Academy—not yet. But she did not need the opinion of others to know that her secret would be ruinous to any potential husband, let alone a duke.

She would not put Percy and his family name through such scandal.

Not, Gwen thought hastily, her cheeks searing with heat, *that Percy was even considering her in such a manner.*

This was all Miss Pike's fantasy. She wished to see something that was not there, Gwen told herself firmly. It was not. At least, not from his side.

Miss Pike sighed. 'Why do you not go outside, Miss Knox, and read your letter there? I believe you are in great need of fresh air…you look most flushed.'

It was all she could do to nod mutely, rise, place her embroidery on her seat, and leave the room without falling over. As she stepped away the room spun, which to Gwen's mind was most unhelpful. And each step was a leaden beat against the drum of her own heart, which did not appear to be beating properly.

'You look most flushed.'

Well, it was no wonder she looked flushed. As Gwen opened the front door and stepped into the blessed cool of the afternoon's autumnal air, she tried not to think of Miss Pike's critique, her words of encouragement in Percy's direction, the gaze of all the other wallflowers and, worst of all, the letter in her hand.

The letter she knew she would have to read.

Gwen walked around the house, past the orangery, the sight of which at least tugged her lips into a wry smile, and continued across the lawn towards the ornamental gardens. The one just before the kitchen garden had a nook she had made her own, between a corner of the redbrick walls and a growing evergreen tree which gave her protection from the wind.

It was there, on a small bench which must have been placed there at least a decade ago, if the growing moss upon it was anything to go by, that Gwen seated herself and slowly cracked open the sealing wax to unfold the letter.

It was, as she had expected, from her mother. It was short, cruel, and to the point. Just like every one of the almost daily letters she was receiving.

Gwendoline,
Goodness, I have never been so entertained in all my life as when the Crawfords come to visit. Their company is most welcome now that I have removed you from the house, and their son pays me such flattering compliments—nothing, of course, my dear Walter could complain at, and in fairness it appears there is little gentlemen of real taste can do in my presence but praise it.

Why, I had to be quite forceful with the Major just last week when he kissed my hand, and in public too! I soon put him to rights, but I am sorry to say it only seems to have increased his passion.

That is the benefit of marrying a man like Walter. He recognises that my beauty cannot be diminished by his affections. I really was the most fortunate of ladies to have snared him.

The inn is doing well, though you did not ask. We are thinking of renaming it. Naturally we simply cannot let it be known as the Golden Hind any longer.

I receive very few reports of your conduct at the Wallflower Academy, so I must presume it is bad. I am disappointed, Gwendoline, but not surprised. You always were a most contrary thing.

While I have made not one, but two impressive marriages, you are lagging behind in your duty to me. When will you find a gentleman prepared to have you? I am sure Miss Pike does all she can, so it must be your deficiencies, your faults prevent it.

Remember, this secret of yours is one I could spill at a moment's notice, and if I am led to believe by Miss Pike's reports that you have been disobliging, I am willing to share it.

Even if it leads to the ruin of us both.

Keep me informed of any gentlemen you believe worthy of your attentions, if you are able to find any. I hope you enjoy your long sojourn at the Wallflower Academy.

Your Mother

PS I have redecorated your bedchamber and made it my sewing room. Why did you never say the light was so delightful? You cruel thing, keeping such a pleasant place from me.

Gwen leaned against the crumbling brick wall and exhaled slowly, but it did nothing to relieve the tension in her shoulders, which was creeping across her skin like a wire, prickling painfully, tightening her chest, making every breath more difficult.

She should not have read the letter. She probably shouldn't read any of them. She had known before the seal had been broken that it would contain words such as this. Words that hurt. Words that pained deeper than any cut.

Despite her better judgment, Gwen looked again at the letter. Each capital had been elegantly curled. Her mother's handwriting was so like her own. It was as though her own words were biting back at her.

'Gwen—I mean, Miss Knox?'

Gwen stared at the approaching figure of Percy Devereux, who was stepping around the borders with purpose towards her.

No. It could not be.

She had dreamed him up…his appearance was only a figment of her imagination. She had been thinking about him too much over the last few days, that was all. She had not expected to see him, had assumed he had returned to whatever business had taken him from London. She had dwelt too much on his face, on the way his lips curled when he looked at her, that tantalising scent that was his and his alone.

But she was not dreaming him. She could not be—not with the few other wallflowers taking a walk around the gardens staring so curiously at him.

Percy stopped before her, his gaze dancing to the letter in her hands and then back to her face.

Gwen swallowed, the tension in her shoulders spreading to her throat, making it difficult to speak. What could she say? Her mind was swimming with the harsh words of her mother, preventing her from breathing calmly, from even thinking clearly.

> *Keep me informed of any gentlemen you believe worthy of your attentions, if you are able to find any.*

Well, she had certainly found one.

'A letter, I see,' said Percy. 'From your mother?'

Gwen's heart skipped a painful beat. 'How did you know?' She had spoken too quickly—an accusation, not a question.

Percy shrugged, as though he had not noticed the fear within her. 'Well, you mentioned that your father had died just recently, and you have not spoken of any sibling. *Is* it from your mother?'

Frantic thoughts did Gwen no service, offering her no possible reply save, 'Yes.'

She had to get rid of it. Even the smallest chance that Percy might catch a glimpse of some of her mother's words... It did not bear thinking about. But she had brought no reticule.

'I did not expect to see you here,' she said as calmly as she could manage, quickly folding the letter and placing it in the one place she could be certain no one would touch: down the front of her corset. 'I would have thought you'd return to London.'

Only then did Gwen realise that Percy's cheeks had pinkened and his gaze was most inexplicably focused on her breasts.

Ah.

The action of placing something in one's corset did not raise any comment in an Academy designed for wallflowers. They were all ladies there, and often without a reticule… Before a gentleman, however, it was rather a scandalous thing to do.

Gwen rose, her only thought to distract the Duke from the rather hussy-like thing she had just done. 'Will you walk with me?'

'Walk?' repeated Percy in a dazed voice, as though he had been hit over the head with a mallet. He blinked, then his eyes focused. 'Walk. Yes, as you wish. Walk…'

It was all Gwen could do to keep her breathing calm as she stood at Percy's side and started to walk slowly through the gardens. He was so close; if she was not careful her fingers would graze his own.

She could feel the heat of him, the intensity of his presence—or was that merely her imagination? Whatever it was, it was overpowering. Intoxicating. Painful. Thank goodness they were not technically alone, what with the other wallflowers gawping at them across the flowerbeds.

To be so close and yet not to touch…to feel the incompleteness of her desire… Gwen knew it was scandalous even to think such things, but she was sorely tempted. Just to know…

'I am beginning to think,' she said quietly, 'that you never leave the Academy.'

Percy chuckled, and picked at the dead head of a seed pod as they passed a border. 'Not with you stuck here. I prefer to be here.'

It was mere politeness, that was all, Gwen told herself.

It was foolish to think Percy would not say such a thing to any lady he was walking with.

Still. It was pleasant to hear such things.

'Ensure Miss Pike does not hear you say that,' Gwen tried to say lightly. 'She will consider you a gentleman wallflower and may seek to imprison you here alongside us.'

'I can see compensations in that,' came the quick reply.

Gwen looked aside. How was he able to do it? Was Percy an unusual gentleman, able to return any flattery with a quip of his own? Or were all gentlemen, and dukes in particular, trained in such fawning?

'It was from your mother, wasn't it?' asked Percy quietly as they turned a corner to walk in the rose garden, where a few splendid white blooms were still fragrant on the air. 'The letter? I saw the way you flushed, Gwen, I hope you do not mind me saying so.'

Gwen swallowed. 'And what if it was?'

She had not intended to be so combative, but it was difficult not to be. What did he want with her, this duke who surely had offers of far more interesting conversation elsewhere?

'Nothing. I just…' Percy's voice trailed away, and Gwen was astonished to see in his face what appeared to be genuine curiosity. 'I am interested. In the letter. In you. In— Damn.'

Gwen waited for further clarification, but it did not appear to be forthcoming.

It did not make sense—*he* did not make sense. A duke would hardly interest himself in the affairs of a wallflower—particularly one with no name and little prestige.

Yet there was something about him. Something that drew words from her Gwen could not imagine revealing to any other. Something that made her trust him more than anyone else she had ever met.

'It was from my mother,' she admitted. She paused at a rose bush, reaching out to cup a blossom. It would make an excellent model for her embroidery. 'She…she has remarried, and is rather pleased to have me removed from under her feet.'

That was putting it politely.

Gwen had to congratulate herself on her restraint, especially when Percy asked a most interesting question.

'I suppose she is encouraging you to be wed yourself, then?'

The tightness that had emerged in her shoulders the moment she had started to read the letter started to lessen. Though she could not explain it, there was relief in speaking the words aloud, even to someone like Percy. Someone who looked at her with such... Well... In anyone else, Gwen would have called it longing.

'No one wants to marry me.'

The words had been spoken before Gwen could call them back, and highly conscious that she was discussing her marriage prospects with a duke, she forced herself to laugh and continue walking through the gardens.

'I mean to say, all wallflowers are a rather difficult prospect,' she said swiftly, babbling, 'and I do not believe myself any different from any other wallflower. I merely speak the truth of the situation in which we all find—'

'Gwen.'

She halted. The single syllable from the Duke was sufficient to stem both the tide of her words and the movement of her feet.

Percy was smiling. That roguish grin she was starting to depend on more than anything was dancing across his lips. 'I would not be so sure that no one wishes to marry you, you know. I mean, not myself, obviously. I have a reputation to—Certain criteria must be met before I—'

Her hands were in his. Gwen was unsure how it had happened—she had certainly not stepped forward and reached for him. But that left only the possibility that he had stepped towards her and claimed her hands with his own.

And that could not be.

As Gwen's heart pattered most painfully in her chest, her breath short and her mind spiralling, she knew she must be mistaken.

Percy was right beside her, inches away. Why, if she just stepped forward she would close the gap between them… feel not only the strength of his hands around hers but the movement of his chest with each breath, the power of his body…

And that was when Gwen knew she was in trouble.

As she gazed, speechless, into the dark eyes of this Duke who so easily bewitched her, a desire rose within her that she could not and would not contain.

A desire she had never felt before.

A desire to be kissed, and to kiss in return.

To be held close, closer than was acceptable for a gentleman and a lady…a duke and a wallflower.

'I wondered…' breathed Percy, and Gwen shivered at the warmth of his breath on her skin. 'I wondered whether you would permit…'

His voice trailed away and Gwen unconsciously leaned closer, desperate for him to continue. In this moment she would have given him anything.

'Yes?' she whispered.

And there it was—the same desire that rushed through her veins was in his eyes. He wanted something she could not give.

'Permit me to take you on a carriage ride next week?'

Gwen blinked. There did not appear to be any teasing in his eyes, but he could not be serious.

A carriage ride with a duke?

He had said himself, just moments ago, that she was most unsuitable for him. *Certain criteria,* or something.

What would Miss Pike say? What would Society say,

seeing a wallflower from the Academy out with a duke in the intimacy of a carriage?

'How can I refuse?' said Gwen with a wry smile. 'What day suits you best?'

Chapter Six

It was not the incorrect day. Percy knew this to be impossible. He had been counting down the hours, not merely the days, since Gwen had agreed to come with him for a carriage ride.

Sunday after church, that had been the day agreed, at two o'clock. Plenty of time for Gwen to finish her luncheon, Percy had theorised, although his own stomach had incomprehensibly rebelled at the thought of food when it came to his own meal.

'And where are you going?' asked his mother sharply, as Percy pulled on his greatcoat and hunted for his favourite top hat.

Percy missed only a beat before he replied lightly, 'Oh, taking a lady out in the barouche. You know how it is…'

He smiled at his mother, a finely dressed, impressive-looking lady. She had been pretty as a young girl. Percy knew that from the portrait on the landing upstairs in their London townhouse, but she had become a far more handsome woman.

A woman who was now frowning. 'I see.'

Was it the fluttering of discomfort he felt at his mother's look, or something else curling within his stomach? Perhaps it was hunger. Percy had been unable to eat anything, despite his mother's glares at the dining table.

'I must be off, Mother,' Percy said, a little too brightly, opening the front door. 'I know you would hate for me to be late!'

'Hmph…'

That was the only sound he heard before the door closed behind him.

Percy grinned. And the grin did not fade as he grew closer to the Wallflower Academy, or when its redbrick frontage appeared at the end of the drive. Yet below the smile was something else…something that worried him.

It was a strange sort of gnawing at his stomach that recalled the sensation of hunger yet could not be the sole reason.

It was only when Percy drew back the reins and slowed his barouche to a stop outside the Wallflower Academy that he was able put his finger on precisely what it was.

Still. It was so unlike him.

Nerves?

He had never been nervous with a lady before in his life.

No, as Percy jumped down from the barouche, and admired the coat of arms so recently painted on its doors, he knew it was foolish to be nervous.

What did he have to be afraid of?

It was only a drive with the most beautiful woman he had ever met.

Only a wallflower with a temper like a tiger.

Only a suggestion to the world at large and Society in particular that he was courting said woman…a woman he could never marry.

Percy cleared his throat and attempted to push aside his rebellious thoughts. It was madness. If his mother knew he had not called upon Miss Middlesborough, or Lady Rose, or the Honourable Miss Maynard…well, there would be trouble.

Trouble for another time. For now, his thoughts and heart were filled with one woman, and as Percy strode forward to knock smartly on the front door of the Academy he was filled with the foolish hope that it would be Gwen herself who would open it.

Of course that was not the case.

'Hmm…' said the footman, in a remarkably similar tone to Percy's mother not half an hour ago. 'Miss Knox, I presume?'

'The Duke of Knaresby, actually,' said Percy, with what he hoped was a winning smile.

Neither the smile nor the jest appeared to have much impact on the footman. Indeed, it had rather the reverse effect from the one Percy had intended: the footman glowered, then slammed the door.

Taken aback, Percy turned and looked at his barouche.

He could not have mistaken the day.

He had even gone so far as to pencil the date into his diary—a most unusual event.

No other lady required such attention.

No other lady, Percy could not help but think, *was Miss Gwendoline Knox.*

The knot in his stomach had risen and was now in his throat. He should get back inside the barouche and leave. It was a ridiculous proposition to have made to a wallflower with no name and no dowry.

Percy knew what was due to him as a duke, to be sure, but he was equally cognisant of what he owed to the Dukedom.

Heirs.

The next generation did not spring out of nowhere. One had to create it, and with a woman who had the breeding and elegance one expected in a duchess.

Gwen was not that woman.

Percy hated the thought, but could not deny its veracity. Gwen was a wallflower, far below his station, with no family to recommend her nor any position in Society to protect and elevate his own.

She was, in short, precisely the sort of woman his mother would not be impressed by.

A prickle of excitement seared his heart. Perhaps, if Percy was honest with himself, that was part of the attraction. Gwen was beautiful, yes, with a temper that only flashed when she allowed herself to be provoked, and she made Percy wish to bed her immediately, if only to remove this all-consuming desire from his body.

But that could not be. His… Well, his rather unusual rise to the Dukedom of Knaresby required him to avoid all potential for scandal and find a wife with enough prestige in Society to paper over the cracks of his own respectability.

Oh, he hadn't caused any true scandals. Not really. But as a man he had been reckless, thoughtless of consequences, easy to befriend and easy to egg on… It was a miracle, really, that he hadn't got into more trouble.

And he certainly couldn't bed Gwen just to get her out of his system, no matter how much he might wish to.

Gwen was no courtesan, happy to exchange her body for coin or the protection of his name. She was different. Precious. He'd seen that in the flush of her cheeks whenever he looked at her, whenever his growing desire slipped into his words.

Percy's jaw tightened. Besides, she was protected by the iron fist of the Pike, as he had started calling her in the privacy of his mind—ever since Gwen had mentioned the nickname.

The Pike would certainly not permit any of her ladies to be taken in such a way.

No, Percy was a fool and he knew it.

As the wind rustled in the trees around him, their leaves starting to fall and their golden colouring splashing the drive with their red and yellow hues, he turned to the barouche.

This had been a mistake. He should leave before he made even more of a fool of himself.

He therefore had to perform a rather uncomfortable twist to face the Academy once again, when the sound of the front door opening and the swishing of skirts met his ears.

'Gwen—Miss Knox,' Percy corrected hastily as he almost fell over in his haste.

The smile which had already started to creep across his lips disappeared in an instant. There was Gwen, beautiful as ever, with a simple yet elegant pelisse around her shoulders. The painful lurch in Percy's stomach informed him, with very little potential for misunderstanding, that although he could neither wed nor bed the pretty wallflower, that fact did not prevent desire.

And there was Miss Pike. She stood beside her charge, a frown deep across her forehead and a glower on her face.

Percy smiled weakly. 'Ah... Hello, Pike—Miss Pike.'

Blast. If only he could maintain some sort of decorum. Percy tried not to notice Gwen stifling a giggle, nor the additional creases appearing on Miss Pike's forehead.

'Indeed,' she said, with a deference he knew her wallflowers did not often see in the woman. 'Your Grace. I have to say I am surprised—a barouche?'

Percy waited for more information, but there did not appear to be any. 'I assure you it is in most excellent repair, and will provide a smooth and gentle ride for Miss Knox.'

Damn his searing cheeks and the unexpected twist in his stomach! It was hardly Percy's fault, was it, that the innuendo was right there for anyone to see?

Gwen had certainly seen it—that, or there was another reason why her cheeks had darkened and her gaze dropped.

He really could not make her out. Sometimes wallflower…sometimes impassioned woman, Gwen was a medley of things Percy found rather intoxicating.

'I am sure it is a most impressive barouche,' said Miss Pike with a fawning laugh, 'but I was given to understand that this would be a carriage ride of a different nature.'

Percy stared. *Different nature?* Surely she did not believe him to be so much a cad as all that? If he'd had nefarious intentions, he would not have collected Gwen from the front of the Academy!

'Different nature?' he repeated, as an awkward silence crept between the three of them.

Gwen cleared her throat and spoke to the ground. 'I believe what Miss Pike intends to say is that a barouche can only carry two.'

Once again Percy waited for the rest of the explanation, but it was not forthcoming. 'I invited you, Miss Knox, and no other. Was I supposed to provide a second barouche for your companions?'

Miss Pike rolled her eyes with a smile. 'Really, Your Grace, I thought I had taught you better! I should have thought it obvious that your carriage requires sufficient room for a chaperone!'

Ah… Too late, Percy realised what the two ladies had assumed about this journey, and why Miss Pike was wearing a rather severe pelisse of her own, with no adornment of any kind.

Yes, it should have been obvious—and to any gentleman of real merit it would have been clear. Taking Gwen out on her own would be a recipe for scandal if they were spotted, and Percy could expect that someone would inform his mother immediately of the unknown woman in his company.

Alone with him. In his barouche.

But it was rarely a concern for a man of low rank, and it had never been of concern to Mr Percy Devereux, when he had been that man. It seemed a long time ago now. No woman had ever attempted to compromise him into matrimony then. There had been no point.

But now…

'Such an honour…such a pleasure to have you gracing us with your presence,' Miss Pike was saying, with an ingratiating smile on her face as she curtseyed again. 'So wonderful to…'

Percy allowed her to continue. It was nothing he hadn't heard before; the woman had been fond of him for years. Although admittedly the Pike's reverence had dramatically increased upon his ascension to the title. It was astonishing, really, just how welcome his presence was wherever he went now that he was a duke. No one had been much interested in his company before.

'Ah, there you are,' said Miss Pike, turning back to the door which had just reopened.

Percy glanced at it too, and was astonished to see Miss Marilla Newell appear, guided by a footman. Another wallflower?

'Miss Pike,' said Miss Newell firmly. 'I think you must admit, once and for all, that I hardly meet the requirements to be a chaperone. It might have escaped your notice, but I am blind.'

A shot of embarrassment flooded through Percy's bones and he looked away, even though he knew the lady could not see his gaze—but Gwen laughed and stepped forward towards him.

'Do not mind Rilla,' she said in an undertone as the

blind wallflower and Miss Pike began a heated argument in murmured whispers. 'She rather enjoys teasing people, and she is not shy at all about her blindness. It is…it is most agreeable to see you.'

Percy smiled weakly. 'Right. Yes. Good.'

'And furthermore, Miss Newell, you must consider your future here at the Academy!' Miss Pike's words had risen in volume, only increasing Percy's embarrassment at the whole situation. 'Why, you have been here three years and…'

'We could just…go…' said Gwen quietly.

Percy blinked. The wallflower had a rather scandalous look about her—a mischievous twinkle in her eye he had only glimpsed once before, when she had attempted to flirt with him at the dining table.

It did something rather strange to him. Not unpleasant— no, Percy would not describe this sensation as unpleasant. But it was…different. He had bedded ladies before…even dallied with the idea of having a mistress, before deciding it was probably more trouble than it was worth. Expensive things, mistresses.

He knew desire, knew passion.

Knew what it was to make love to someone.

But this was not that feeling.

True, it was similar—a rising stirring in his stomach that both dropped to his manhood and rose to his heart. But it was different. Warmer. Deeper. And a twinge of pain came with it…a bittersweet sort of knowledge that something was not quite right.

'We could,' said Percy with a smile. Raising his voice, he turned to the arguing ladies on the doorstep of the Academy. 'Miss Pike, Miss Newell—I promise not to kiss Miss Knox, if that is what it takes for you to trust me. I shall bring her back within the hour and we shall keep to the country lanes. No visits to Town. Will that do?'

There were splotchy red patches across both Miss Pike's and Miss Newell's cheeks.

'Well, really!' said Miss Pike. 'Percy Devereux, I have never heard the—'

'Excellent,' said Percy cheerfully. 'Come on, Miss Knox.'

To his great disappointment, Gwen was wearing gloves. And after Percy had helped her into his barouche, though there was the pleasure of being close to her, of having been of some small service, there was no opportunity to touch her again. Not as he would like, anyway.

Leaving behind the astonished voice of Miss Pike and the laughter of Miss Newell, Percy tapped the horses with his whip and the barouche moved forward, crunching along the drive.

Only then was he able to lose himself in his delectable consciousness of Gwen seated beside him. That was the real benefit of a barouche, Percy thought gleefully, as the horses settled into a gentle trot and they reached the road, taking a left to meander along a country lane. It might not offer the most comfort, nor the most elegance—but, goodness, did it offer an opportunity for intimacy!

Gwen was seated beside him, her hips pressed against his own. With every movement of the carriage Percy could feel her. His arm, now dropped to his side, nestled against hers.

It was enough to stir something hungry within him, something Percy immediately forced down.

This was not that sort of carriage ride.

'I...' Gwen swallowed when Percy glanced at her. 'I have never been in a carriage before. With a gentleman, I mean. Alone.'

It was perhaps the most endearing thing he had ever

heard. Percy saw the hesitancy in her, the nervousness at being around him, and it spurred on his feelings of power.

How delightful to be around a woman who was so easily impressed, so easily won over.

'Well, I would not concern yourself,' Percy said brightly, in an attempt to put Gwen at ease. 'I have been in plenty.'

Only as the words left his mouth did Percy see his mistake—too late. Gwen's face fell, her gaze dropping to her hands, and he saw tension creeping around her mouth as her lips pressed together.

'I see,' she said quietly.

'No, you don't,' said Percy quickly, hating himself for speaking so thoughtlessly. 'I meant… Well, there is no trick to it—no brilliance one has to offer. You just have to enjoy yourself. The responsibility to entertain is upon myself.'

A smile crept over Gwen's face at this pronouncement. 'Something you are well practised in, I would think?'

'Yes. I mean, no.'

'Well? Which is it?'

The temptation to say nothing—to sweep this awkward moment away and focus instead on the beauty of the countryside and the woman beside him, anything except be honest—weighed heavily on Percy's heart.

Gentlemen were not honest. Dukes certainly weren't. Very few occasions in their life required them to be.

It was often easier to just ignore one's feelings, push aside all and any desires against Society's expectations, and instead laugh.

Percy sighed. 'My mother arranges carriage rides for me with eligible young ladies—but you cannot be surprised, surely? I am the Duke of Knaresby.'

By God, he would have to do better. Percy hated the twisting pathetic words he had used instead of the direct honest ones he wanted to. Words ringing in his heart as well as his mind.

This is different, Gwen, because you are different. You are special. You are becoming more special to me with every visit, and I don't know what to do with myself when I am without you.

Percy cleared his throat. Words he could not say.

'In a way, then,' said Gwen, 'we are under the same pressures, the same obligations. We both live in houses with older women who are determined to marry us off.'

He could not help but laugh at that characterisation of his mother. 'Something like that, yes—only in my case... Well... What do you know of the Duchy of Knaresby?'

Gwen stared, obviously surprised.

Percy was a little surprised himself. As he directed the barouche along another country lane, not meeting a single person along the way, he wondered what had possessed him to start on this topic.

He had never spoken openly about it before.

Why now?

'In truth, I had never heard of it until we met,' said Gwen. 'Why?'

Percy sighed. 'Many reasons... My father was not the Duke of Knaresby.'

For a moment he hesitated. There was no need to tell Gwen his sorry tale, was there? Only a woman who might have a permanent connection with him needed to hear it, and Gwen was certainly not that woman.

Marry Gwen? A woman with no connections, no name, and no opportunity to better Percy's position in Society? A woman who did not fit James's criteria?

Ridiculous.

Still, he continued. 'The Duke was my uncle—my father's brother. He died along with his two sons, in a terrible accident, and just months later my brother...'

His throat tightened and he found he could not continue.

When was the last time he had spoken about James?

Not since the funeral. Not since they had laid his brother in the cold, damp earth.

'I am sorry to hear of your loss.'

Gwen's voice was sweet, gentle, soothing to his soul.

Percy cleared his throat and found he had the strength to continue.

'I am the last Devereux—the last male in the line, anyway... I never thought I would... No man should face such a thing. My brother was the most...the best brother anyone could have...'

Percy cleared his throat once more, and blinked rather rapidly at the road ahead of them.

He was not about to permit himself to show something as uncivilised as emotion!

'He taught me almost everything I know about being a man, a gentleman,' he continued, in a rather more controlled tone. 'He was eleven years older than me, and our father died when I was very young. Indeed, my brother was the one who taught me what a gentleman should look for in a wife.'

The words hung in the air most uncomfortably, and Percy wondered what in the name of goodness had come over him.

A subtle glance at his companion showed him that Gwen had raised an eyebrow. 'Indeed?'

'Indeed,' said Percy, retreating into the haughtiness which was his fortress in difficult conversations. 'Elegance, of course, and beauty. Good manners, a good family—far more important now I have inherited the title.'

'Indeed,' repeated Gwen.

A prickle of discomfort seared across Percy's chest, but he refused to pay it any heed.

'Blonde, naturally,' Percy continued blithely. 'And a good singer, with only one sibling—'

'And here I am, an only child,' Gwen interrupted with a wry smile. 'And not blonde, to boot. Though I think I am unlikely to make a match for...for other reasons.'

Percy flushed. God above, it was not as though no other gentleman in Society had dissimilar requirements! He was just more honest about them. Did he not deserve such a wife?

'My brother taught me the criteria, and now he is gone,' Percy said stiffly. 'And the last time I saw him...'

His voice failed him. The last time he had seen James neither of them had known it would be. Just a hunting party... just an evening spent talking and laughing and drinking and smoking. As any father and son would. At times, it had been hard to recall that James wasn't Percy's father.

And what had his brother said?

'Now, you must promise me, Percival...'

Percy had grinned adoringly at his elder brother.

'Not to marry a woman who does not fit my require-ments. I won't have just anyone joining this family!'

'I have no thoughts of matrimony—' Percy had tried to say.

But James had cut across him.

'Promise me, Percy. Promise me you will marry some-one who fits these conditions exactly. Promise me!'

And Percy had swallowed. *'I promise.'*

'I promised him,' he said aloud to the waiting Gwen, his cheeks red. 'Promised I would marry someone he would have approved of. It was the last thing I ever said to him.'

Gwen looked at him curiously. 'Almost a deathbed prom-ise, then?'

Percy's jaw tightened. He was not going to cry. 'I honour him by seeking out a woman of whom he would have approved.'

He tried not to glance once more at Gwen. *Blast.* A woman James certainly would *not* have approved of.

Grief threatened to overwhelm him, just for a moment, but Percy pushed it back. He would honour his brother's wishes. He would speak calmly and matter-of-factly with the wallflower, then he would take her home. This had been a mistake.

He cleared his throat. 'Neither James nor I expected that a title would be our fortune. Consequently, as you might imagine, I was not raised to be a duke, nor even a duke's brother.' Percy laughed bitterly. 'Many in Society do not consider me to have the upbringing—nor, in truth, the breeding—to be a duke. Least likely to distinguish myself, I suppose.'

'Well,' said Gwen, nudging him gently and making Percy's stomach lurch most uncomfortably, 'I certainly have not seen you display the decorum I would expect in a duke.'

Their laughter mingled in the cool autumnal air and Percy was enchanted despite himself. There was no denying it. She was beautiful, witty, kind, all wrapped up into one. But James would not have liked her because of her low breeding and lack of title, her dark hair and surely half a dozen other reasons…

His traitorous heart ached at the thought of disappointing his dead brother. Did Gwen know how rare a gift she was?

Percy pulled back on the reins and slowed the barouche to a stop. Enjoyable though the journey was, for this he wanted to be stationary. He wanted to look into Gwen's eyes…see her reaction to him.

He wanted to know whether what was sparking in his heart was sparking in hers.

'You know,' he said quietly, glancing at her, 'we are truly not that different.'

A mocking smile teased at Gwen's lips. 'Yes, I suppose so. I must marry someone—anyone who will have me. I am least likely to make a good match, let alone win a…a man's heart. Whereas you…you must wed a beautiful, wealthy, well-connected someone. Not so very different.'

Painfully conscious of her arm resting beside his own, Percy turned in the barouche towards her.

Gwen's gaze did not drop, meeting the fire of his own.

'Well, you meet one of the criteria, at least,' Percy whispered.

Something was happening. Something he could not explain and had no wish to halt.

He had to—

He shouldn't.

Drawn to her inexplicably, unable to stay away, Percy leaned slowly towards her, not moving his hands, bringing his head closer to hers. His lips closer to her lips.

He could not stop looking at them, could not understand why he was not already kissing her when this desire had grown inside him so passionately.

For a heart-stopping moment Percy was certain she'd permit the indelicacy…lift her lips to his own and claim him as he wished to claim her.

A few inches…not even an inch…and Percy stared at the delicately delicious lips which were now mere seconds away from touching his own.

Gwen pulled away.

'I don't think—W-We shouldn't…' she said breathlessly, looking away to the horses, her fingers tightly wound in her lap. 'You promised the Pike.'

Percy could hardly help himself. He wanted to ignore the world and its expectations, push aside all memories of James and what he would demand of his little brother, and instead…

He knew he should lean back, give her space, give her a moment to compose herself—but he didn't want her composed. He wanted her underneath him, begging for more, desperate for his touch.

He forced that image of Gwen away but the reality of Gwen remained before him.

Dear Lord, such a pretty temptation.

'Perhaps we shouldn't,' he murmured. 'But I want to.'

Gwen's laughter was gentle as she raised a hand to his cheek. Percy leaned into it, desperate for her touch—anything to quench the growing desires within him. But it did nothing but augment them.

'I think,' said Gwen quietly, 'that you should return me to the Wallflower Academy.'

Percy groaned. 'You're no wallflower…you're a torturer.'

'You chose your own method,' said Gwen lightly, removing her hand and clearing her throat. 'Well, Your Grace. I think it is best you take me home. Then you can return to London and seek out this perfect wife your brother prepared you for.'

Chapter Seven

'And, of course, there are many elements that might make a conversation dry. The first thing that can make a conversation dry is the topic itself. The second thing that will make a conversation dull is the primary narrator. The third thing that makes a conversation boring...'

'This whole conversation is boring,' muttered Sylvia under her breath.

Gwen tried not to giggle, though it was a difficult task. After all, Miss Pike had been monologuing about the difficulties of entering, maintaining and refreshing a dull conversation for at least ten minutes—with, it appeared, little awareness that her own soliloquy was perhaps just as dull as the conversations she was encouraging them to avoid.

'So, when a gentleman chooses a topic you have little interest in, what should you do?' asked Miss Pike, rearranging her skirts in the pew, as the large church grew busy with people and noise. 'Miss Sylvia?'

'Leave him in the dust and—'

'Now, there is nothing worse,' said Miss Pike, turning to her wallflowers and speaking over the grinning young woman, 'than a lady who is unable to show interest in a gentleman's conversation—even, as I have said, if it is most dull. I assure you there will be topics gentlemen wish to discuss which border on the banal!'

'Nothing could be worse than this lecture,' Sylvia breathed to Gwen, who was seated beside her on the pew behind Miss Pike.

Gwen was forced to turn her giggle into a cough. At least this lecture could not go on for ever—the gentleman at the front of the nave had just risen, and the vicar was nodding approvingly.

Miss Pike turned swiftly. 'Another cough, Miss Knox? I would hate to think you had caught a chill on your carriage ride with His Grace. I should have forbidden it.'

'No, no, just a tickle in my throat,' Gwen said hastily.

She was still a little unclear just how much power Miss Pike had over them, but if it was anything like she feared, the older woman could send any of the wallflowers to bed without any supper if they so much as hinted at having a cold.

And then she would have no opportunity to see Percy.

The thought flashed through her mind unconsciously. Gwen half smiled as she noticed it. Not that she had any plans to see Percy. It would be ridiculous to expect to see him again so soon after yesterday's carriage ride.

So soon after yesterday's revelations about his marital expectations. And his brother's requirements. Requirements that were understandable, in Percy's position. And even more understandable after hearing about the loss of his brother.

After yesterday's almost-kiss...

'I think I will leave you,' said Miss Pike severely. 'This wedding is one of my greatest triumphs, and I should rightly be seated behind the bride. A gentleman with two thousand a year! Any of you should be grateful even for the idea of being so well married. Good afternoon, ladies.

Enjoy the wedding, and we will continue this conversation later.'

The wallflowers inclined their heads politely as the owner of the Wallflower Academy elegantly swept across the church. Only when the footsteps of the Pike halted, as she sat imperiously at the front of the church, did all the heads turn in one direction.

Heat seared Gwen's cheeks.

All were turning to her.

'Well?' Sylvia demanded.

Gwen blinked. She could not be asking what she thought she was, could she? She would not be so indecorous, and in a church—

'Tell us everything about this duke of yours!' Sylvia said eagerly. 'And when I say "everything", I mean *everything*! Quickly… Lizzie could be marching down the aisle at any moment!'

'Do not skimp on the details,' said Rilla. 'I can do without any description of the Duke, though.'

'Speak for yourself! I need to hear about every iota of conversation, every touch, every thought that flew through your head,' said Sylvia with a laugh. 'Come on, Gwen— we will live vicariously through you! Oh, that handsome duke!'

Her stomach stirring uncomfortably, Gwen groaned, dropping her face into her hands as raucous laughter filled the church, along with a cry from Rilla that no one had told her he was handsome.

'You didn't want a description!' Gwen said into her hands.

Rilla snorted. 'You know I did not mean it!'

Other clamours echoed around the church as all the wallflowers demanded the full story, though there were a few pink cheeks as other congregants glanced over at them and the Pike glared over her shoulder.

It was all too much. Gwen had known she was a woman who found no delight in the attention of others for most of her life. But she had a temper—a temper unbecoming in any woman, let alone a wallflower.

The idea that all her new friends—friends who really hardly knew her, and who saw her as naught but a fellow wallflower, like them, with no dark secrets—wanted to hear about each moment she had spent with Percy, those precious moments…so unexpected…

If she spoke of them aloud they would surely disappear into the ether like vapor, gone like mist on a winter's morning.

'There is really not much to tell,' Gwen said weakly as she lifted her face from her hands and saw, much to her disappointment, that the wallflowers had, if anything, grown closer.

Sylvia raised an eyebrow. 'So the Duke did not invite you on a carriage ride?'

Gwen's stomach twisted. 'Well—'

'And he did not force Miss Pike to permit you to go alone, despite the provision of a perfectly good chaperone?' asked Rilla dryly.

Gwen smiled weakly. If this had been happening to any other person—anyone other than her—she knew she would perhaps be barraging that wallflower with the very same questions she was being subjected to. She would want to know all the details. How it had felt to be so singled out, to be in the presence of a gentleman with such a grand title, to feel his hand on her own, to feel him move closer and closer, inch by inch, his fierce gaze softening as it focused on her lips…

Gwen swallowed.

Her heart was not fluttering, she told herself firmly. She was merely tired.

And not tired because she had been unable to sleep last night, desperately trying to understand what on earth Percy had been about. Kissing her in a carriage? All alone in a country lane? The man had his reputation to think of, irrespective of her own!

'But Gwen—'

'Hush! Here she is!'

The organ music had changed, the sound half lost in the rush of skirts as the congregation rose. Gwen quickly joined them, peering around to see a blushing bride in a delicate pink gown walk down the aisle.

A wallflower wedding...

Miss Pike was correct, in a way. It was a triumph. Gwen could hardly believe it had been achieved, but the proof was right before her.

As Lizzie reached her equally blushing husband-to-be, and the congregation took their seats, the voice of the vicar washed over her.

'We are gathered here today...'

A wedding. Gwen had never considered—or not with any seriousness—quite what that would mean. Standing there beside Percy, vowing to—

Beside Percy?

Now, where had that thought come from?

The vows were over far more swiftly than she had imagined, and Gwen rose hastily as the clearly ecstatic newlyweds swept down the aisle in a rush of lace. The church emptied slowly and the wallflowers were buffeted about. When Gwen finally made it outside, she stepped to one side of the porch and leaned against the wall.

There. She had managed to attend a wallflower wedding without drawing any attention to herself. She should be congratulated, really.

Someone nudged her shoulder.

'A duke!' Sylvia looked remarkably impressed. 'My word, Gwen, I must admit I did not think you had it in you when you first arrived at the Academy.'

'It is not like that,' Gwen attempted to say—but it was no use.

It was quite clear the wallflowers had had precious little opportunity to see one of their own attracting any attention—now they needed to revel in all the details.

'Well, whatever it is like,' said Rilla, leaning on Sylvia's arm with a mischievous grin, 'I recommend seducing him as soon as possible.'

Sylvia and Rilla collapsed into hysterics as astonished gasps came from those around them.

'You know,' said a different, deeper voice, 'that is a wonderful idea.'

Gwen froze. Her heart stopped, her fingers turning to ice, as she turned very slowly to look past the crowd who had gathered around the happy couple, to where the voice had emanated from.

Leaning against the church door with a wide grin on his face, cutting an impressively majestic figure in coat and breeches, was Percy.

Gwen's legs quivered, and her mind was unable to think about what she might possibly do next. Run? Flee the churchyard? Flee the Wallflower Academy and never return?

There could be no other option. How would she ever live with herself, knowing that Percy had overheard such nonsense? How could she possibly return to the Academy, knowing they all believed her to be courted by a duke when she knew full well he could not offer her anything?

Worse, how would she ever be able to look Percy in the eyes, knowing he had said such words?

Sylvia's laughter had faded swiftly. The other wallflowers had disappeared, which Gwen thought impressive, for she had not noticed them leave, and Rilla was looking in his direction, he head tilted to one side.

'Do my ears deceive me?' she asked in a low voice. 'Is that the Duke in question?'

'Yes…' breathed Gwen.

How long has he been standing there?

How much of the conversation had he heard?

Gwen tried desperately to run through all the wild and inappropriate words.

His hearing even one statement would be too much, but there was naught she could do now.

Besides, if she was not careful Sylvia would start pestering Percy with uncomfortable questions. Gwen might only have known her for a few weeks, but she knew there was nothing that woman would not ask.

'Excuse me,' Gwen said quietly, stepping away from the church wall towards where Percy still stood, a wide grin on his face.

Forcing herself to ignore the whispered conversation now occurring behind her, between Rilla and Sylvia, Gwen tried to step past Percy and go back into the church. Into sanctuary. Surely nothing untoward could occur there?

He did not budge.

'Why, hello, Gwen,' Percy said, his smile still broad. 'How pleasant to see you.'

'Let me pass, please,' said Gwen.

It was most irritating. He was doing it on purpose merely to annoy her, she knew, and the trouble was it was working.

Percy Devereux, Duke of Knaresby, had a particular skill in gaining a rise out of her, and the worst of it was the sensation was not pure irritation. That would be far too simple. Added in was a medley of desire, desperation, and…

Percy straightened up only slightly, leaving a gap just small enough for her to pass through if she brushed past him.

The sensation of her gown moving against his coat would be heavenly, but Gwen attempted to ignore the thought of it. What would Miss Pike say if she saw such shenanigans? Surely she would reprimand her, and there could even be a letter home to her mother.

A mother with far too much power over her.

'Your Grace…' Gwen said, as the murmurs behind her increased in volume.

'Percy,' he said, his smile faltering. 'I think…no, I am sure… I want you to call me Percy.'

Gwen's heart had only just started racing again, and now it skipped a painful beat.

Percy? How could he expect her to address a gentleman—a duke, no less—by his Christian name!

It was outrageous. It was intimate.

It was precisely what she wanted.

'I only call my friends by their Christian names,' said Gwen with a raised eyebrow as she remained by the church doorway. 'And a friend would move aside so I could step through.'

Was he surprised by her response? Gwen could hardly tell. Her mind was whirling, trying to understand what on earth he was doing here, hoping he would ignore—or forget—Rilla's comment.

Percy nodded. 'I suppose a friend would. But I, Gwen, am not your friend.'

Gwen's stomach twisted painfully.

And there it was.

The confirmation she should not have needed. The Duke

was merely playing with her. Teasing her. She was entertainment, that was all. Really, she should be grateful to receive any attention form him whatsoever. It was far more than she had expected, and drastically more than she had deserved.

'I see,' she said dully.

'No... "Friend" would not be the right word,' said Percy, dropping his voice under the medley of congratulations and conversations about the wedding.

At least they were not alone, Gwen tried to tell herself. That truly would be scandalous.

'What would be the right word?'

His face flickered. Gwen could see the war within him between what he wanted to say and what he knew he should not.

'Gwen, despite my better judgement, I want far more than friendship from you. And friendship would not be sufficient to describe what I feel about you.'

Gwen swallowed and looked into his face. A dark sort of seriousness had overcome Percy now, and she could see a flicker of uncertainty, of doubt, that she had never seen in that proud face before.

It stoked something in her...something new.

Hardly aware where this boldness was coming from, and certain she would regret this later, Gwen stepped forward. Her chest brushed up against his and for a wild moment she felt his breathing, felt it in tune with her own. She could feel his heartbeat—although perhaps that was her own pulse, racing frantically as she moved her face to within a single inch from his.

Then it was over.

Gwen stepped through into the church, where sunlight was streaming through the stained-glass windows, and although her breath was inexplicably ragged, she was still standing.

Two small pink dots had appeared in Percy's cheeks and his hands were clenched, as though he had forced himself not to reach out and touch her.

Mere fancy, Gwen reminded herself as she took in the several people still in the church, chattering away. She was seeing what she wished to see. Percy certainly would not have desired to do such a thing. He was merely teasing.

He stepped closer and whistled. 'Dear God, Gwen, what do you want to do to me? Drive me mad?'

Gwen flushed. There was no helping it. There had been desire in his words in the doorway—there was no possibility of mistaking it for anything else.

He desired her.

Matrimony was out of the question, and it would be far better for her if she could put it entirely out of her head. The spectre of his brother would loom over his choice.

A pair of ladies ceased their conversation and moved towards the door, glancing at the two of them curiously. Gwen stepped out of their path, carefully not looking at Percy, now standing on the other side of the aisle. If Miss Pike was to find her here, with the Duke, having a private conversation...

Well, there was no limit to what the owner of the Wallflower Academy might think.

Gwen half smiled at the memory of the almost-kiss she and Percy had shared in his barouche just four and twenty hours ago. Perhaps Miss Pike would not have a completely erroneous idea of what was happening, after all...

'I have no intention of driving you mad, Your—Percy,' Gwen said hesitantly, stepping towards him and keeping her voice low. His name sounded sweet on her lips. Sweet, and yet shockingly forbidden. 'You have said I do not meet your criteria, that your brother would not approve. You were the one eavesdropping on my conversation.'

My private conversation, Gwen thought as Percy stepped towards her, closing the careful gap she had left.

Not that she would have shared her true feelings with the other wallflowers. No, Gwen was still trying to ascertain precisely what they were, and she could not yet comprehend sharing them with anyone else.

She had feelings for him, undeniably. Feelings that swirled and mingled. Fear, desire, and a need to be felt and seen and heard as she never had been before.

And they were real feelings. These were not imagined emotions after reading a novel, or hearing from her mother about yet another lady of her acquaintance who had found a match.

No, these feelings stemmed from a gentleman whose voice made the hair on the back of her neck stand up and every part of her want to be closer to him. Closer than was appropriate.

Gwen swallowed. This was ridiculous. Percy was a duke. He needed to marry well—far better than her level. Had he not been open with her, and honest about the qualities his wife would need to have? And the truth of why she was at the Academy... Well, that scandal would be the last thing a gentleman like Percy needed.

'I rather enjoyed hearing you and your friends discuss me, I will admit,' said Percy cheerfully.

A knot tightened in Gwen's throat. 'I—I wasn't talking about you.'

Percy raised an eyebrow. 'Goodness, should I be worried?'

'You should not have been eavesdropping in the first place,' said Gwen, choosing to sidestep his question. ''Tis hardly a gentlemanly thing to do. And outside a church!'

He shrugged with all the lack of care of a titled nobleman. 'If the conversation is about me, does it truly count as eavesdropping? I do not believe so.'

It was a careless counter, but Gwen found it difficult to argue with. The conversation had, after all, been about Percy.

She supposed she should be grateful she had not been overheard saying anything personal. Why, if she had even attempted to explain to the wallflowers how she felt about him…the attraction in every word he spoke, the way he had almost kissed her…and his kindness. The way he looked at her not as a wallflower, but as a woman.

Gwen swallowed. 'I think, g-given the kind of woman you must marry, and the woman I am—'

'A wallflower, you mean?'

It would be too easy to merely agree with him. Gwen tried to formulate the word 'murderess' but decided against it.

Too much honesty would be the end of her.

'Yes, a wallflower,' she said quietly. 'I just think… Well… You and I, Percy—'

'I like that,' Percy interrupted, and Gwen realised with a start that he was now merely inches away. How had he moved without her notice? She needed to step back, but her feet weren't working. '"You and I".'

There was a sound—a movement out of the corner of her eye. Gwen took a hasty step back from the Duke as a gentleman stalked past them, glaring at Percy most irritably.

'What on earth…?' Gwen murmured as the gentleman stepped out of the church.

Percy chuckled. 'Oh, he's just sore because I won a bet against him just a few weeks ago. Now, will I be seeing you for dinner?'

Percy? At the Academy for dinner?

Panic flushed through Gwen's veins like boiling tar, searing her heart and her stomach alike with painful dread.

Another dinner? She was not aware of any formal dinner that evening—and if she was going to suffer through another official Wallflower Academy dinner she would have appreciated more time to prepare.

Prepare for what, she could not think.

'There's one tonight? A dinner, I mean?'

Percy frowned. 'I had thought you would eat dinner every night.'

There was nothing Gwen could do to prevent the flush searing her cheeks. 'So…there is no formal dinner? It will just be you?'

The words echoed around the church in a most disobliging way, but there was naught Gwen could do to stop them.

Percy hesitated for a moment before replying, 'As much as I would wish it…no. The wallflowers will be there, of course. And the Pike.'

That at least forced a smile to Gwen's face. 'I… I asked you once what—what your intentions were. You did not answer me then.'

That boldness she did not recognise within herself had risen once more to the fore, and this time she did not look away from Percy's face as she spoke the words—not really a question, but a statement of confusion. A need to know more.

But the bravado typically within Percy's face had disappeared, replaced by something akin to uncertainty. He shifted his feet, and when he finally replied it was in a soft whisper. 'I don't know.'

Gwen stared. It was not the answer she had expected at all—far from it.

'I should not be here, waiting after a wedding service to see you. I should not want to—My brother would never have encouraged—All I know is that I cannot stay away from you, Gwen,' said Percy urgently, reaching for her hand. 'That I will not.'

'I do not want you to. Stay away, I mean.'

Her heart was racing, but there was nothing she could do to stop it. Was his racing too? Were the same desperate confusions whirling around his mind? If only Gwen could read Percy's thoughts and know whether this was a trick, a jest, or something more. Something deeper.

'I do not know where this is going...' Gwen breathed weakly.

Percy smiled. 'You know, for the first time, I wholeheartedly agree with you.'

Chapter Eight

It was the ride, Percy told himself as he slowed his barouche along the drive towards the Wallflower Academy.

It was the ride. That must be it. There could be no other explanation for why his heart was pattering so painfully, why he could not concentrate on more than one thing for a matter of minutes before his mind meandered again.

Meandered to Gwen.

Percy clenched his jaw as the horses trotted along the gravel drive, but he could not help breaking out into a smile.

Gwen. Well, there was no point in trying to lie to himself, at least not in the privacy of his own mind.

He knew why his body was on fire, his mind unable to stop returning to the woman who had become the reason for his entire existence since he had first seen her.

Before he knew it, Percy had found himself visiting her almost every day. Playing cards, walking in the gardens, even putting up with those awful musical recitals from other wallflowers.

His stomach lurched. He was spending, in summary, far too much time here and not nearly enough time doing what he should be doing. Seeking a suitable wife.

Even now his desire had got the better of him. Approaching the Wallflower Academy with this wild idea? It was foolhardy.

Percy could not explain to himself why it was so important that he keep returning to the Wallflower Academy, but it was becoming increasingly painful for him to be away. The new idea, of course, had come to him only an hour ago, and it should have been immediately pushed aside. James would never have countenanced it. No, tonight's plan, concocted an hour ago, just as dusk had been falling, was far more audacious.

Which was why his presence here was just as much a surprise to himself as anyone else.

Percy pulled up his barouche outside the stables to the left of the main house. He was beginning to sound ridiculous even in his own head.

A stableboy scampered out of the stables as Percy's boots hit the gravel. 'Y'Grace!'

'Hello, Tom,' said Percy with a wry smile.

It was bad indeed that he was on first-name terms with some of the servants here at the Academy. But he was one step closer to Gwen. To seeing her, listening to her. Making her laugh, if he was fortunate. To making an even bigger fool of himself than he had already, if unfortunate.

'Back again, Y'Grace?' commented the stable lad with no shame. 'You're here an awful lot, aren't you?'

Percy glared. 'Not very often, I think.'

'At least three times a week at my count,' continued Tom with little fear. 'Don't you have other places to be, a great lord like you?'

Percy laughed weakly, but he could see the boy was not speaking to flatter. It was an honest question, one he would have to answer eventually—at the very least to his mother.

For he had not yet verbalised, even within himself, just why he could not stay away from Gwen. Why his chest tightened whenever he was away, as though his very lungs were unwilling to breathe air she did not breathe.

Why, his dreams were starting to become so scandalous it was surely not right for him to be coming to see Gwen at all. Not when the last time he had seen her in his mind she had been without clothes, without shame, and desperate...

Percy swallowed. The stable boy was still staring, wide-eyed, clearly intrigued by this strange duke who considered the Wallflower Academy the height of entertainment.

And the boy was right. He did have other places to be. Places his mother was expecting him to attend to meet the very best of eligible young ladies. He needed to find a wife—one who would confirm his place in Society now he'd inherited the title.

Well, he'd soon find himself in one of those places...

'I like it here,' he found himself saying to the boy. 'Tom, look after my horses, will you? I pushed them hard on the road.'

Because I was desperate to get here.

Percy made sure he did not say that.

Because every minute I am away from this place, I cannot help but wonder why. And being away from Gwen...

Percy clenched his jaw to ensure none of those words slipped out. The last thing he needed was the whole household thinking him a fool—not just the wallflowers. A grimace covered his face for a moment as he thought of the conversation he had overheard...

'I recommend seducing him as soon as possible.'

It was difficult to know who was more the fool: Gwen, for permitting his attentions when she knew there was nothing he could do about them, or himself for continuing to return, time and time again, to the woman he craved more than any other.

Craved, but must not have.

'I'll look after them,' said Tom placidly, clearly unaware of the turmoil within the Duke before him. 'Good day, Y'Grace.'

Percy blinked. He could not stay standing in the stable all day. He had to go and be a gentleman—and whisk Gwen away from the Wallflower Academy in a very non-gentlemanly manner.

How long he stood there before the redbrick manor house, his heart thumping painfully and his mind unable to decide whether to simply return home and avoid the shame inevitably coming his way, or enter and spend as many precious minutes with Gwen as he could...

Percy could not tell. He was sliding into trouble, he knew. No other lady of his acquaintance made him feel like this, made him question himself like this. Made him wonder whether it was worth it to throw it all away, leave the title and glory behind, and make Gwen his wife.

Gwen...his wife.

It was a heady thought. Percy found his fingers tingling and he clenched them, as though refusing to permit the sensation.

He was being ridiculous. Worst of all, he was playing not only with his heart but with Gwen's. What was he doing, if not hurting them both?

'Percy?'

He started. He had not noticed her step out, attired in an evening gown for dinner. *Excellent.*

'Marvellous, you're suitably dressed.'

Gwen frowned. 'Suitably dressed for—?'

'An academy dinner, I suppose?' Percy said, unable to help his interruption as excitement coursed through him. 'Tell Miss Pike you've received an invitation to Town for this evening,' he ordered.

She bristled. 'Who are you to be ordering me—?'

'I'm no one…no one to you,' he said, the words spilling from him. 'But I want to be.'

Gwen's eyes were wide, but she disappeared back into the Wallflower Academy without another word.

This was foolishness to the extreme! Percy knew he was running a risk with this plan, that it was one he should not even be contemplating, but there was too much reward to be gained. Besides, she had obeyed him. Not that he wished to make frequent demands of her…but surely if she had no wish for his company she would not have complied?

By the time Gwen stepped out again, a pelisse hugging her shoulders and a confused expression still in her eyes, Percy had made up his mind. Society be damned. He would take her.

'Where on earth are we—?'

'I'll explain when we get there,' said Percy, certain that Gwen would argue with him if he was so foolish as to reveal all now. 'Come on.'

The journey was swift, and for some unknown reason he found their silence more comforting than any conversation might have been. When was the last time he had truly enjoyed the company of a woman like this? In a delicate, unassuming way? It was most odd.

Only when his barouche rattled down King Street did Gwen turn to him with wide eyes. 'You have brought me to London!'

'I would have thought that was obvious,' said Percy with a snort.

Her cheeks darkened to crimson. 'I just—Well… Perhaps obvious to you. I have never been here before.'

Percy could not prevent his jaw from dropping. Never been to—? But London was the centre of the world—it was where everyone was! Anyone of importance, anyway.

'Never been to—?'

'It may have passed you by, Your Grace,' came the snapping retort, 'but the world does not revolve around London.'

Percy swallowed his indignation. The way she spoke to him sometimes—as though he was nothing! Well, this evening he would show her just how a woman should address a duke.

And then, whispered the irritating voice in the back of his mind, *you'll take her back to the Wallflower Academy and never see her again? Because this is a mistake. Your brother James would never have sanctioned this!*

'Well, here we are,' Percy said aloud, drawing the carriage to a halt. 'Almack's.'

It was Gwen's turn for her face to fall. 'No, you have not…? Almack's?'

'I have indeed,' said Percy with a grin. Dear God, it was pleasant to be rich. Rich, powerful, able to do whatever he wanted! 'I'm sneaking you in, so you had better be on your best—'

'But you can't—'

'There is nothing I cannot do,' said Percy easily, jumping down from the carriage. 'You'll soon see.'

He was rather pleased with himself. Almack's was, after all, one of the most delightful and exclusive assembly halls in London. Vouchers were issued by strict invitation by the most respected in Society. To be seen in Almack's was to be a part of the *ton.*

He offered his hand, but for some inexplicable reason Gwen did not take it. Stranger still, she was glaring.

'Don't you want to get out of that Academy?' he said.

She hesitated. 'Yes, but—'

'And haven't you always wanted to see how the better classes live?'

Percy had not meant his words to wound, but he saw a

spark of anger in Gwen's eyes, glittering with the reflection of candles.

'I've seen enough already,' she said darkly.

Percy blinked. Now, what on earth did she mean by—?

'Come on, then, let us get it over with,' said Gwen with a sigh, disembarking from the carriage while studiously ignoring Percy's proffered hand.

'Over with?'

Gwen marched up the steps, leaving Percy to suddenly realise he had been left behind.

How did this woman never cease to surprise him?

She was handing her pelisse to a footman with very bad grace by the time Percy reached her. He threw his great-coat to the same man.

'Gwen, I—'

'I think you'll find it's Miss Knox here,' Gwen said, arching an eyebrow. 'I suppose you have some sort of pretence for my being here?'

Percy hesitated. He supposed he should do, but—

'Devereux? I thought it was you. It was so kind of you to wait. Your mother has asked you to accompany me.'

His heart froze. He turned slowly on his heel towards the sound of the imperious voice, and his stomach lurched painfully when he saw it was indeed the woman he had feared.

The Dowager Countess of Staromchor. Finlay Jellicoe's mother. He was a friend from childhood—a rather elevated one at the time, considering Percy had had no title, but strangely lesser than him now when it came to rank.

Percy almost laughed. The vagaries of Society could alter so dramatically with just a few deaths.

But he had certainly not intended to meet the Dowager Countess here. What was she doing—and why was she so convinced his mother had asked him to go with her?

'Come now, sir, offer me your arm!'

He felt something strange and stiff brace within him. 'It's Your Grace, actually.'

'Oh…' The Dowager Countess raised an eyebrow, looking far too amused for Percy's liking. 'I suppose it is.'

Percy felt Gwen's eyes on him, but could say nothing.

The Dowager had done it on purpose, of course. All the old aristocratic families had been astonished when he had been elevated to their rank, and some were none too happy about it.

Not that they would say so outright, naturally.

'My darling boy is sadly occupied this evening, so it was not possible for him to accompany me,' said the Dowager Countess impressively as she dropped her pelisse onto the now almost buried footman. She leaned against the cane clasped in her left hand. 'You are here to make a match, I suppose? And quite right too. Almack's is the only place to find a woman of suitable breeding. And you are…?'

Percy opened his mouth but, traitorously, no sound came out.

'Miss Gwendoline Knox, my lady,' said Gwen, curtseying low.

It was painful to watch the Dowager Countess sneer so openly at a woman she evidently believed inferior to her—and not without cause.

Percy's stomach dropped. Had he made a grave error by bringing Gwen here? And the Dowager Countess was still holding out her hand to him, as though it was natural Percy that would abandon his companion and accompany her.

'My lady…' he said aloud.

Well, what choice did he have?

'I don't know what you are doing, loitering here in the hall, we will be much warmer inside,' said the Dowager

Countess, striding on impressively now she had her balance. 'You may have my arm.'

Percy put out his own automatically—well, he was not a complete cad—but he could not help but regret finding himself in this corner.

How was he supposed to speak with Gwen now?

Just out of the corner of his eye he could see her, watching him curiously. Oh, damn it all to—

'I must say, I have been reading such dreadful things about your family, Your Grace,' the Dowager Countess said happily. 'I can see why you need to wed—and swiftly. Your brother's death…what a scandal! Have they caught the culprit yet?'

Percy's jaw tightened. 'No, my lady. Investigations are ongoing.'

'Indeed? An inn, I heard? Though where such a place could be found I do not know.'

He said nothing—not even to correct her. His mother was right, though: he needed to marry. He should not be here, should not be dallying with wallflowers when he needed a bride, and a wedding to distract the gossips of London.

That certainty did not help now—particularly with Gwen following them so demurely. Knowing her place, Percy thought darkly.

When it became clear that he was not going to speak, the Dowager Countess said, 'I thought I might see you at the Wallflower Academy, for I hear gossip that you have made yourself rather popular there.'

Percy's jaw tightened. Dear God, the speed at which rumours could spread in this town! Now he would have to hope beyond hope that his reputation was not sullied by the connection, and that he would still manage to find a woman of whom James would have approved.

He was highly conscious of the heat on the back of his neck. Undoubtedly it was being warmed by the gaze of Gwen...

'Yes, I always knew being a patroness of the Wallflower Academy would provide me with sufficient entertainment,' the Dowager Countess continued as they walked towards double doors which opened to reveal spectacle and noise as they approached. 'But I had no comprehension it would be so thrilling. They are little darlings, aren't they?'

Percy smiled weakly, but held his tongue despite great provocation.

It was, after all, most infuriating. Not only was he being forced to remain by the Dowager Countess's side—unable to speak to Gwen at all, let alone privately—but he was also being forced to endure the banal conversation of a woman who clearly considered the wallflowers mere playthings.

Playthings! He would like her to spend more than five minutes in their company, Percy thought darkly. Sylvia had a tongue that could lash just as well as the Dowager Countess's, and Rilla was sharper than half the men in his acquaintance.

'They are most eloquent women,' Percy said as they stepped into the dance hall.

Much like White's, Almack's was unchanged. He couldn't imagine it being any different from the way it had been since the first time he had been given his vouchers: the elegant pillars, the tables covered in food and large punch bowls. A set of musicians were tuning their instruments at one end of the room, while Mamas cooed after their daughters, newly entering Society, at the other.

'Eloquent? I do not believe I have heard any of them string three words together,' said the Dowager Countess impressively, inclining her head at someone who had approached in a rush of fawning. 'Apparently there is a new one to view…most interesting. No real family, of course, and no connections. No real beauty either, I'm told.'

Percy's stomach twisted painfully and he could not help himself—he looked over his shoulder at Gwen.

She was furious. The same fury he had seen when he had accidentally knocked her down was visible in her eyes, and Percy could understand why.

Not that he could say anything. Oh, perhaps a man *born* the son of a duke…who'd had a duke's education, had been taught a duke's mannerisms, pride…perhaps he would be bold enough to directly challenge a woman like the Dowager Countess.

It was, after all, mostly true. Gwen had no family and no connections. She was a most unsuitable companion for a duke. She had beauty, yes, but Percy was not foolish enough to think that sufficient.

Perhaps, if James had not died…

Percy swallowed. Then he would not have been the Duke. Wouldn't have risen to the title under a cloud of scandal. Wouldn't need his advice at all.

But he was gone.

Percy's heart hardened. He was not about to disgrace his memory.

It was fortunate indeed that the Dowager Countess had released his arm to move away and chatter with the person who had approached. He was relieved not to have to disgrace both himself and Gwen by a half-hearted breathless defence.

No real beauty? Gwen? What idiot had shared *that* message? Percy could not conceive of anyone looking at Gwen, with her dark eyes, the cleverness within their pupils, the way her lips curled into a smile when she believed she was not being observed…

Percy's stomach lurched painfully.

Not beautiful?

'Well...' said Gwen quietly. 'That is breeding.'

A rush of exasperation roared through him. 'I cannot defend the indefensible, but you should think twice before speaking in such a way of your betters!'

Speaking to anyone in such a way a few months ago... it would not even have crossed his mind.

But he had changed, somehow, and it was only now that Percy realised it. Betters? Almost everyone had been his 'better' before the Duchy had fallen most unexpectedly into his lap.

Something curdled painfully in his chest.

Now they were words he might have spoken to anyone who had uttered such a disrespectful sentence. So why did Percy feel so traitorous saying them to Gwen?

They might have been such a perfect match. Before his title, before Society's expectations, before his mother had demanded the world...

Gwen would have been perfect. Bold, clever, elegant. Beautiful. Well-born enough for a man with no real fortune and no ambitions to nobility.

Indecision washed through him.

He should leave.

He should turn around, apologise to the Dowager Countess and her companion, if he could find the patience, and leave. Take Gwen back to the Academy. Forget about her.

Percy had come not to hear gossip but to be with Gwen—to get her on her own if he could. To make her laugh if he could. To dance with her scandalously before the *ton*, who would not know her humble origins. To lean close, breathe her in, finally kiss her, taste her lips...

'My betters? Right... So long as I know my place,' Gwen said with a glare. 'Well, we are here now—unless you wish to return me to the Academy at once. What does one do at Almack's?'

A pair of gentlemen overheard her question and shot her a puzzled, disapproving look.

Percy grimaced. He felt so foolish now. What had he been thinking, bringing her here?

'I'm sorry,' he said stiffly.

For a moment Gwen merely examined him, as though she could see within his mind, within his heart. Could she see the regret? Feel the anguish of the words which had slipped out?

'You don't even know the meaning—Forget it... You are forgiven,' she said quietly.

Percy frowned, examining her closely. 'Don't know the meaning of what?'

For some strange reason, Gwen would not meet his eye. 'It doesn't matter.'

'Anything you wish to say to me matters,' he said softly, his chest painful when she refused to look at him. 'Gwen!'

There was something intangible flickering under the surface. A passion, an intellect...something more. Something he had underestimated. There was far more to Gwen's thoughts than her mere words.

Gwen continued to talk, but he could not take in a word. He had acted rashly, yes, but they were here now, weren't they? Was it better to stay, attempt to make the best of the evening...? Or return her to the Academy? And what had she been about to say?

'Your Grace?'

Indecision paralysed him, preventing him from retreating, getting out of the place, or moving forward to dance with Gwen before the floor grew too crowded.

After all, there was always the danger that his mother might change her mind and attend tonight...

'Per—Your Grace?'

Percy blinked. Gwen was looking at him with a rather strange smile.

'I said, are you ready to accompany me in the next set?'

Percy swallowed. He should not even be countenancing such—

Fingers, warm and certain, slipped into his. He looked down. Gwen had taken his hand.

'I know I shall never come here again,' Gwen said in a low voice as the musicians played their opening notes. 'So I think it only right you dance once with me before we leave.'

His stomach relaxed and his heart sang as his eyes met hers.

Gwen.

It was criminal, the way he was being tempted. By God, Percy knew full well that he should leave. He certainly should not tempt Gwen's temper again. Once unleashed, it made her as fearsome and as eloquent as any man, let alone any lady of good Society.

Percy's feet took him closer, unconsciously. A flush crept across her cheeks.

'Well?'

'Oh, you must not mind His Grace,' said the Dowager Countess airily, waving a hand at Percy as she leaned away from her conversation partner. 'He is a duke, true, and far above your station, but you may speak to him if you wish.'

The colour in Gwen's cheeks was now a radiant crimson, and Percy would have done anything to help her escape. Every nerve in his body was on edge, but there was naught he could do. How could he disrupt Almack's? His reputation was only just being remade after his brother's outrageous death—he could not risk…

'I'll bear that in mind, thank you,' said Gwen sweetly,

before pulling Percy towards the set now being made in the centre of the room.

His heart was beating so rapidly he could barely hear the music—but that did not seem to matter. Gwen released his hand as she passed him, leaving him to stand in the line of gentlemen, and it was agony—agony to be without her.

This was too much...he was going too deep. He needed to step away and—

The dance began and the line of ladies moved forward. Percy's heart caught in his throat as Gwen smiled, her eyes flashing with mischief, and he knew then this was the most delightful mistake he had ever made.

He raised his hand and his stomach lurched as she met it with hers. It wasn't meant to feel like this, was it? He had danced before with countless ladies, all of them far superior in station to Gwen. At least, Percy supposed they had been. It was hard to concentrate on any other ladies now, with Gwen's hands in his as they promenaded down the set.

'You are so beautiful...' he breathed.

He could not keep the thought in; she had to know.

Gwen smiled ruefully. 'Is this the part of the dance where you compliment your partner?'

Percy swallowed. 'No, this is the part of the dance where I am supposed to find my senses.'

Because his hands burned as he touched her waist and ached as they left it. His heart was thumping so loudly he was certain she would hear it, and if he was not very much mistaken...

Oh, he would need an ice-cold bath after this.

Gwen glanced up through dark eyelashes as they stood at the end of the line, watching the other dancers promenade down the set. 'What did you expect, Your Grace, by bringing me here?'

Percy did not know. All he knew was that the mistake

was a glorious one. One never to be repeated, and so to be revelled in.

'Aren't you afraid?' she asked.

His stomach lurched as he lied, 'No.'

'Someone could recognise you…spread rumours…ruin your reputation,' Gwen said with a knowing smile as she stepped towards him.

Heat rushed through Percy as their bodies grew closer again. Recognise him? He had already crossed words with the Dowager Countess—it was too late for that. He would simply have to hope their conversation would not be mentioned to his mother.

Besides, he was not yet so famed in the *ton* to have his face noticed in a crowd.

'If they do, they will see naught but me dancing with a beautiful woman,' he said smoothly.

'A woman you cannot marry, though. Or even consider.'

'Of course not,' Percy said instinctively. 'You don't meet the—I mean…'

Damn. He had spoken without thought, giving the correct answer—the only response he could possibly give. And yet they tasted bitter in his mouth, those words which he would have said to any other woman who did not meet James's standards. And why did looking at Gwen make the words hollow?

And then the dance was over. The music stopped. Percy blinked, and heard gentle applause echoing around the room.

Gwen shook her head with a smile as she took Percy's unhesitating arm. 'I think we are agreed that I am not your future bride. So let us forget that. I had always worried I would never be able to dance in public.'

'In public?' repeated Percy, as though he had been hit over the head with a cricket bat. 'Yes…'

They were walking back to the side of the room—unfortunately, Percy saw too late, to where the Dowager Countess was now standing.

'I've never done such a thing at the Academy, anyway, and—'

'The Academy?'

Percy groaned inwardly as the Dowager Countess looked over at them.

'I know you cannot be talking about the Wallflower Academy. His Grace would never be so foolish as to risk his reputation by giving one of those girls any expectations,' the Dowager Countess said with a laugh that filled the whole room. 'Besides, they have little to recommend them, do they not?'

Bitter fire rose in Percy's throat. 'I believe the purpose of the Academy is to teach—'

'Oh, but you cannot teach the ability to talk to people, no matter what that woman says,' interrupted the Dowager Countess. 'What's her name? Miss Perch? Miss Pickle? And that must leave the wallflowers in a sorry position, must it not? Not that I am saying *you* are such a thing, Miss… I would never presume to insult you so. I mean to say, who would marry a wallflower?'

Percy could barely see, he was so furious, so desperate for this moment to be over. It was excruciating, standing before Gwen in such a conversation.

'I believe that with many wallflowers, as you call them, it is only confidence which is lacking,' he said quietly, trying not to catch Gwen's eye. 'With a little confidence—'

'Confidence comes from breeding, not lessons,' said the Dowager Countess curtly. 'Not that you'd know anything about that.'

Now it was Percy's turn to flush.

Of all the things she could have said—it was an out-rage! Just because he had not been born to the Dukedom...

But he could say nothing. His mother's desire to re-main in polite Society, let alone his own, required that he accepted the whispers and the murmurs about his sudden rise to the aristocracy. Why else was his mother so fixated on him making a 'proper' marriage?

'Have you nothing to say for yourself? Why are you so dull?' the Dowager Countess said lightly, flicking a finger at Gwen.

Percy's blood boiled—but he had no right to feel that way. He was not Gwen's relation, not father nor brother, to protect her reputation. He was not her betrothed and nor— Percy's stomach lurched—her husband to stand by her.

But by God he wished he was.

Mortified did not adequately explain the feeling in Percy's system, yet no words rose to Gwen's defence.

What could he say—what could he do?

Cause more rumours to flutter about London, to reach his mother's hearing, that he had fallen for a wallflower? Allow the whole of Society to believe he had been taken in by a woman who, in public, was unable to string more than two words together?

Worst of all, he might give Gwen hope that he would one day offer her something Percy knew he could never give her.

Gwen smiled coldly, no warmth reaching her eyes. 'My apologies, my lady, Your Grace, for being so devastatingly dull as to be considered a wallflower.'

'No, don't—don't say that,' said Percy wretchedly. 'Gwen—'

'You must understand, Your Grace, we are simply not prepared to speak to people of your elevated rank.'

Gwen's words were so icy she might have given his

mother lessons. Percy hated the way she spoke—without hope, without any belief that she was worth so much more than this rotten treatment.

'Do not say that,' said Percy again, stepping towards her. He wanted to be much closer, to bring Gwen into his arms, but he managed to restrain himself. Almack's was not the place for such expressions of passion. 'It is just that people of my rank, you know…we must speak the—'

'Truth?' interjected Gwen with a raised eyebrow. 'It is true. You and your kind, Percy—my apologies, *Your Grace*—look at us as like animals in a zoo. That's all we are to you—entertainment. Well, I have no desire to entertain you further today. I want to go home—I mean, to the Academy.'

Without another word, Gwen strode off towards the double doors, though she had the presence of mind not to slam them.

Percy stood there, hating himself and the situation he had allowed himself to be pulled into. Because Gwen was right. To others of his kind, the Wallflower Academy *was* merely entertainment—a way to be amused on a quiet day. His mother would certainly agree. He had been absolutely round the twist to bring her to Almack's. His father would never—

The thought halted in Percy's racing mind. Now he came to think about it, he wasn't sure what his father would have done. The man was a distant memory, faded, based primarily on the portrait of him in the hall. The man himself… It was James who had stepped into that role. James who had fleshed out the figure now living in Percy's mind, doling out judgement.

Percy swallowed. So what would James advise in this scenario?

And what was he to do with these growing affections?

Chapter Nine

'*Have you nothing to say for yourself? Why are you so dull?*'

Gwen swallowed and pushed away the painful memory from the day before and the fit of rage threatening to surface. She was not going to allow one conversation to overtake her mind, nor permit the words of one woman to colour her day.

But it isn't just one person's opinion, is it? a horrible, cruel voice in her mind reminded her, as each passing day brought more elevenses, luncheons, teas, dinners—though, thank goodness, no balls.

One after another they would continue, she knew, until she had managed to make a match her mother could be proud of.

Or, Gwen thought dully as she tried to focus on Miss Pike, *until her mother gave up hope of her marrying at all.*

How long? A Season? A year? Rilla had been here three years, she had revealed to Gwen, and her family had all but given up hope of a match.

'They have far more nefarious plans for me now,' Rilla had said darkly, only that morning, but though Gwen had questioned her politely she had been unwilling to say more.

'And the left foot forward!' Miss Pike said fiercely.

Gwen cleared her throat and moved her left foot, matching the other wallflowers in the line. That was the trouble with this particular class at the Academy. One could pretend to be attending when one was being lectured on etiquette. The ladies could have their own conversations when pretending to practise small talk. Even when learning the refinements expected at a dining table it was possible to ignore much of what Miss Pike said.

But not, evidently, in dancing lessons.

'Really, Miss Knox, I expected better of you,' said Miss Pike severely.

She was standing before the line of wallflowers in a room that anywhere else Gwen would have been described as a ballroom, though she had never seen it used in such a fashion. Still, the wooden floor was sprung, there were candelabras all along the walls and a magnificent chandelier above—at least, Gwen was sure it was magnificent. It was for the moment covered in a dustsheet.

'I do apologise, Miss Pike,' Gwen said quietly to the floor.

She tried not to notice the intrigued looks Sylvia was giving her, just to her right. As long as she prevented her mind from slipping back to the day before, when she had danced in a very different room and with a very different partner...

'Now—right hand up, palm straight, for you to meet the palm of your partner,' said Miss Pike, demonstrating.

Gwen started. She had become lost in her thoughts again—an inconvenient and all too repetitive problem of late.

That was the trouble with almost kissing dukes, she told herself sternly. And this particular duke had rather got into her head.

Still, it was not as though he had almost kissed her

yesterday—nor put up much of a defence at the Dowager Countess's words.

Gwen sighed and lifted her hand in the manner Miss Pike indicated. How they were supposed to learn to dance without partners, she had no idea. If only they could bring in a few gentlemen to dance with.

Any gentleman but Percy.

Even the thought felt like a betrayal. Though anger still roared in her veins, hot and sparking along her fingertips, she could not entirely quash the memory of his fingers on her skin, those tantalisingly unbidden desires—

She mustn't.

Yet the thoughts did not diminish.

Gwen's heart leapt at the prospect of dancing with the dashing Duke again. His hand pressed up against her, his steps following hers, that wonderful moment when he'd place his hand on her back, around her waist, and she'd look into his eyes and know...

Know.

Know what he wanted of her. What he felt.

It did not appear that Percy knew what he felt, but Gwen could not blame him. She hardly knew herself.

Besides, it was not likely she and Percy would ever dance together again. The Wallflower Academy never had balls—at least, Rilla had never known one in three years—and there was no possibility of returning to Almack's.

Gwen shivered. She needed to concentrate. Percy Devereux, Duke of Knaresby, was not her ticket out of the Wallflower Academy and she needed to remember that. If she wished to make a match—a respectable match, any match—she would need to leave Percy alone at the next afternoon tea or formal dinner and speak to other gentlemen.

Even if they did not raise her heartbeat like Percy did.

Even though they did not make her feel warm like Percy did. Did not make her long to be touched, to be held.

It made her realise he was one of the first people ever to have truly listened to her...

'One, two, three, four. One, two—Are you paying attention, Miss Knox?'

'Yes, are you paying attention?' whispered Sylvia with a wicked grin. 'Or are you thinking about that duke of yours?'

Gwen flushed. 'I am not—he is not my duke!'

'Enough talking there!' Miss Pike looked flushed herself. It appeared counting and moving was far more than her solid constitution could bear. 'Well, you know the steps now. Let me see what you can do. One, two, three, four...'

It was all rather dull, thought Gwen morosely as she stepped forward and back, lifting and dropping her hands on the correct beats. Pretend-dancing in preparation for gentlemen they'd never speak to and balls they would never be invited to.

It was all nonsense. All foolishness.

How did Miss Pike expect any of them to get married if they were never permitted to see any gentlemen truly as themselves? One could not simply transform a wallflower...

Perhaps it would be best if she did not see Percy again.

Gwen rebelled at the thought, but a part of her knew it was best. The best way to avoid pain and to reduce the agony of separation when Percy grew tired of coming here.

Because he would. He had almost said so himself. He could not marry her, could not court her—not properly. He had to make an impressive match. And she? She was a murderess. Hardly a suitable bride for a duke.

Gwen's heart contracted painfully, but she could not deny the truth of her thoughts. From today, she vowed, she would ensure she did naught to attract Percy's attention. If he even returned after that excruciating conversation between him and the Dowager Countess...

Trust her to make a fool of herself before a dowager countess!

No, from now on Percy could have nothing to do with—

'Good morning, Miss Pike...ladies,' said Percy brightly as he stepped into the ballroom. 'Practising a country dance, I see? My favourite.'

A slow smile crept over Rilla's face. 'My, my...' she said with clear satisfaction. 'Is that Gwen's duke I can hear?'

'He is not my duke,' Gwen hissed, hoping beyond hope that Percy had not heard those words—though it was too much to hope for if the grin on his face was anything to go by.

'I wouldn't be so sure, Gwen,' said Sylvia with a laugh.

'Ladies!' spluttered Miss Pike, astonished. 'Really!'

'Oh, I would not concern yourself, Miss Pike. They say far worse things about me when I am not around,' said Percy cheerfully. 'Well, we'll be off, then.'

Before Gwen could say anything, or even think about the confusion around her, Percy had leaned forward, taken her hand in his, and was pulling her towards the door.

'Off?' Miss Pike's stern voice echoed impressively around the room. '*Off*, Your Grace? Who do you think you are—stop manhandling my wallflower!'

Even with their difference in social station, it appeared the Duke could not resist a direct order spoken in Miss Pike's ringing tones.

Perhaps it was something to do with her being his governess, Gwen thought wryly as she stood, confused, by his side. All gentlemen of his class were raised by governesses, weren't they? Strong, determined, educated women, with stern voices carrying absolute command.

Perhaps Miss Pike had left her true calling.

'A problem, Miss Pike?' Percy asked mildly.

Gwen told herself she was not going to look at him—then immediately did so and regretted it. Why was the man so irritatingly handsome?

It wouldn't be difficult to resist his allure, his charming presence, if Percy was not so pleasant to look at—but as it was, she found herself utterly captivated.

He was everything she wanted.

Everything she knew she could not have.

'Y-You cannot simply abduct one of my wallflowers!' Miss Pike strode towards him, lowering her voice into a hiss, as though there were others within the room who might overhear and be shocked.

As it was, the other wallflowers looked remarkably entertained. Gwen tried not to look, but was then faced with two increasingly difficult options: gazing at Percy again, and allowing her heart to race most painfully in her chest, or looking at the ire of Miss Pike.

She compromised by staring at the floor between them.

'I cannot?' Percy raised an eyebrow. 'They are hardly prisoners. I promise to bring her back, Miss Pike, but beyond that I do not believe you can stop me.'

Once again, he took Gwen's hand in his own, and this time, with a thrill of excitement because she was both to leave the claustrophobic atmosphere of the Wallflower Academy for a time and spend time with Percy, she allowed herself to be pulled.

'Where are we going?' she asked breathlessly as Percy charged down the corridor and turned a corner.

He grinned as he glanced back. 'Anywhere but here.'

Gwen's heart soared, though there was a tinge of worry. What would her mother say if she was informed?

But there were moments—and this was one of them—

when she knew Percy understood her...really knew her. He understood her growing frustration at being cooped up like a child who had misbehaved. Why else had he taken her last night to Almack's?

Still, there was a prickle of discontent in Gwen's heart that she could not ignore as they reached the hallway and the protesting footman, who was roundly ignored by the Duke.

It had been not quite four and twenty hours since she had thrown angry words at him, and though she burned to think of them, Gwen did not regret their utterance.

She'd meant every last word.

There was too much to divide them, too much to keep them apart, even if Percy evidently did not wish it. Their stations in life and what was expected of them—and her dark past, which Percy simply could not guess—all should prevent any sort of attachment between them.

Gwen swallowed as she saw the Knaresby barouche once again stationed outside the Academy, horses snuffling in the cold air, their breath blossoming before them.

Only the smallest portion of her temper had been lost yesterday, and what had she done? Shouted at a duke, berated him for trying—and failing—to defend her from a dowager countess, then stormed out of Almack's, doubtless causing great upset and scandalous whispers.

It was a small mercy she had not raised her hand to him, Gwen thought wildly.

She was dangerous. She should not be spending any time with a gentleman like Percy, even if he was so arrogant. For his sake.

'Up you get,' said Percy briskly, lifting his hand and placing Gwen in the carriage before she could protest. 'There.' He strode around the barouche and within a moment was seated beside her. 'Off we go.'

Where they were to go, Gwen could not comprehend. Knowing not the lanes around the Wallflower Academy, it was impossible to guess. She could ask, to be sure, but after her outburst the previous day she found her words stuck in her throat.

How could she face him?

It did not appear, however, that Percy had much to say either. For a full twenty minutes, as London grew closer, they sat in silence as the hedgerows passed them at an ever-increasing pace, frost still picking at the corners of their golden leaves. They gave out as more streets emerged, and the clatter and noise of London roared about them.

Eventually, Gwen could stand it no longer. 'Where... where are we going?'

She shivered, though whether from cold or from uncertainty, she was not sure. If only she'd had time to collect her pelisse... If only she'd had time to ask more questions...

Yet time was not the problem here. Had she not, within this very hour, promised herself she would not spend any more time with the Duke who was fast securing her heart?

'I don't know,' said Percy shortly.

A thrill of horror rushed through Gwen's mind as the barouche turned a corner and rumbled down another street. She had believed Miss Pike to be far too agitated when she had accused Percy of abducting one of her wallflowers, but there was so much about Percy she did not know—huge swathes of his life she had never seen.

What was the Duke of Knaresby like when not at the Wallflower Academy? Was he taking her to his townhouse, where they would talk—where he would try to seduce her?

Gwen swallowed as her body warmed at the thought.

You are not supposed to desire such things, she told herself sternly.

Least of all with a duke who certainly could offer her nothing in the way of matrimony.

If only she had permitted him to kiss her when they had last been in his barouche…

It was a scandalous thought, but one Gwen could not help. The idea of being ravished by Percy, making love to him, his fingers on her skin… Though guilt clouded her mind, it did not diminish her desire.

A young lady should not want such things, she knew. A young lady should be chaste, and innocent, almost ignorant.

Gwen glanced at the gentleman beside her, highly conscious of his knee pressed up against hers. How would it feel if her skirts and his breeches were not in the way?

'You are cold,' said Percy regretfully, as she shivered again. 'I should have brought blankets. I did not… I just… I had to see you.'

That was perhaps the most endearing thing about Percy. When she had pictured a duke in her childhood days, even before she had arrived at the Wallflower Academy, she had envisaged an aloof, dry gentleman who never admitted fault and always blamed others.

But Percy was not like that. At least, he was sometimes. Arrogant and imperious and absolutely convinced he was in the right, no matter the subject of conversation. But at the same time he was…different. Warmer. Exactly what she wanted from a gentleman. From a husband. From a lover.

'We'll stop here.'

Gwen started as Percy nudged the horses to the side of the street and pulled them to a halt. Stop here? Where were they? And why had he brought her here?

Percy tossed a penny at a boy who was loitering on the pavement. 'See to my horses,' he said easily, 'and if they are well when I return I shall give you a crown.'

As she laughed at the boy's wide eyes, Gwen's cheeks were hot.

Here she was, in London, alone with a gentleman—with a duke, no less! What would her mother think?

'Rotten Row is just there—we'll go for a walk,' said Percy briskly. 'Come on.'

He seemed to be saying that a lot recently, Gwen thought sombrely, as she clambered down from the barouche, conscious of stares from those walking along the pavement. Well, he was a gentleman accustomed to barking orders. His rudeness was not rehearsed, but inbuilt.

'Here,' Percy said, moving his arm around her and pulling her close as he guided her forward towards what appeared to be the entrance to a great park.

Gwen's eyelashes fluttered as she was overwhelmed with the intensity of the intimacy. His warmth flooded her body as she was drawn to his chest. She could feel his heartbeat and it echoed hers—fast and frantic and untamed.

It was the most intimate she had ever been with a gentleman, and she wanted more. Unsatiated, Gwen knew that what she wanted was unthinkable. Yet it was certainly not unimaginable.

They passed through wrought-iron gates and she saw that there was, indeed, a park before them. A long path made predominantly of sand wended its way to the left, and it was there that Percy pulled her.

A number of other couples—all of excellent breeding, from what Gwen could tell from their outer garments—were walking in a similar manner.

Well, she thought wildly. *This is what it means to be a part of Society!*

How much time passed before either of them spoke again, Gwen was unsure. Her gaze drifted past the spires of churches and the roofs of tall buildings, looming against the autumnal sky. Other walkers looked at her curiously, their gazes flicking between her and Percy.

Her cheeks darkened. Of course they were wondering what she was doing with a gentleman like him!

'London,' said Percy with a sigh. 'I thought... Well, I thought it would be a chance to do something different.'

'I have never been to Town before. Except for last night, I mean.'

'Truly never been? I thought you were jesting.'

It appeared the idea was unthinkable to him, but Percy evidently had something else on his mind, for he asked no further questions.

Instead, after a minute of silence between them as they continued to walk, he said quietly, 'I must apologise for my behaviour yesterday. It was... There is no excuse. I can only ask for your forgiveness.'

There was clear tension in him as he spoke. Evidently the Duke had been punishing himself most severely for the way he had treated her and was unwilling to continue without an apology.

She swallowed. It all seemed like a dream now. The brilliance of the candles at Almack's, the silk gowns, the powdered hair, the sweeping movement of the dance...

Something of the way he had spoken echoed in her mind, and Gwen smiled. Her temper demanded that she rage, shout, even shove him to prove just how furious she was.

And she had been.

But no longer.

'You once said to me, at the first dinner we attended together, that when I had something to apologise for I would know it. You should recognise that in yourself, you know. And this...this isn't it. You have nothing to apologise for,

Percy. It was…regrettable. Regrettable, indeed. But not your fault.'

Percy sighed deeply and Gwen could almost sense the tension leaving his body. It was a surprise to see how greatly his apology had affected him, just as it had her. Why had he cared so much?

Why, if it came to that, were they in Town?

A terrifying thought struck Gwen.

He wasn't…he wasn't about to introduce her to his mother, was he?

Though the prospect frightened and intrigued her in equal measure, it soon became clear that Percy had no real idea of why he had brought her to Town at all. They meandered along Rotten Row and Gwen stared around her at London, loud and cacophonous, full of people and shouting and animals and noise.

'I thought of showing you the Queen's Palace,' said Percy with a dry laugh, 'but now I am wondering whether you would just like to stare at the people!'

Gwen's cheeks burned. 'I just—I had no idea London was so busy!'

'Far too busy, if you ask me,' Percy said with a shake of his head. 'Here, let us turn off here and I can take you through some of the busiest streets for your amusement.'

With the well-practised ease of a gentleman who had done it a thousand times, Percy guided her across the path of those well-dressed others walking along Rotten Row, out of the park, and onto the pavement of a bustling street.

Hawkers peddled their wares, someone was attempting to sell newspapers, a vicar stood on a box yelling at passers-by, and every minute another barouche or a chaise or a mail coach rushed past them.

Gwen could hardly take it all in, and fear curled at her heart. What if someone saw them? What rumours would flourish if the handsome, eligible new Duke of Knaresby was seen in public with a woman without a chaperon?

'Well, where shall we begin?' asked Percy, clapping his hands together.

Gwen laughed at her own ignorance. 'I just—Well, seeing anything, just the people in London, the noise, the excitement—'tis too much!'

Percy smiled as they started to meander. 'Truly, there is no particular spectacle you wish to see?'

'Sometimes you underestimate just how ordinary I am, Your Grace,' said Gwen with a teasing tone as they turned a corner onto a street that was, if possible, even busier. 'Most of us did not grow up as heirs to a dukedom.'

She had believed he would laugh, say something amusing about London and the people within it. What she did not expect was the dark expression that crossed Percy's face, as if a shadow had passed over the sun of his life.

'I... I thought that even if both my cousins had died without issue it would be James who...'

Gwen wished she could take back her words. Of course—how could she have forgotten? It was only by familial tragedy that his title had been inherited. How could she have been so thoughtless?

Percy laughed at the look on her face and shook his head. 'That is the trouble with you, Gwen,' he said quietly. 'Whenever I am with you I wish to remain in the present, not dwell on the past.'

'If it is too painful—'

'Oh, I can think on it quite well now,' Percy said easily, though Gwen was not entirely sure that was true. There was a catch in his voice suggesting otherwise. ''Tis only that... Well, I told you my uncle and cousins died most unexpectedly, and then my brother, and I inherited the title. But I did not mention in detail... I told you about him, my brother—my elder brother? He was a great deal older than me, so I saw little of him, and his death was quite sudden. Mysterious circumstances, to tell the truth. There were whispers of foul play, but obviously that was just talk. It was an accident. One of those accidents one can never predict.'

Gwen's heart seared with pain and she looked away. Was her life to be marked by such accidents? By these deaths of which at least one could be ascribed to her door?

She had not meant to—but then, had she? And he had died, that man. She was dangerous, that was what she was, and she should steer clear of any man she cared for.

If only she could stay away...

She had to get back. The Wallflower Academy might be dull, but it was safety. She must return.

'Gwen?'

Percy sounded astonished as Gwen removed her hand from his arm and turned around, pacing back the way they had come.

It was this way, wasn't it? Every street looked the same, and she had not been paying much attention to where they were going, most of her attention taken by the company she was keeping. She had to find her way back to the barouche...

'Gwen, what is wrong?' Percy caught up with her easily, a look of concern across his face.

'Nothing,' said Gwen, dropping her gaze so she did not have to look at him. She would not reveal the truth—not to him, not to anyone. Through a flustered breath, she said, 'The carriage—where is the barouche?'

'Gwen, come here.'

Gwen almost cried out as Percy pulled her suddenly to one side, into an alleyway she had not noticed. It was hardly wide enough for the two of them to stand in, and

Gwen leaned against the wall, ignoring its dirt, as her legs shook.

'You confuse me most heartily,' said Percy, his eyes searching her own.

Gwen could not look away. 'You confuse me every moment I am with you…'

Her breath was short in her lungs, and the world was spiralling, but for some reason concentrating on him, on Percy, kept Gwen grounded. His hands were cupping her face now, and she could not think how they had got there, only knew they felt as if they were home.

'Gwen…' breathed Percy, closing the gap between them and pressing against her, making it even more difficult for Gwen to draw breath. 'Gwen, I cannot stop—I cannot stop thinking about that kiss.'

Gwen swallowed, and Percy groaned as she whispered, 'Wh-What kiss?'

'The kiss that never was,' Percy said softly. 'The kiss we almost had in the carriage. The kiss I would take now, if you would let me. Oh, Gwen…'

It was hearing her name on his lips that did it. Overturning all her reason, Gwen gave herself up to the feelings she had so long suppressed and lifted her lips to be kissed. Percy moaned her name once more, and captured her lips with his own, gently at first.

The sudden shock of a gentleman's lips on hers was quickly overcome, and Gwen lifted her hands to clasp them around Percy's neck. And that was when the kiss deepened. He tilted her face, allowing his tongue to tease along her lips, one hand moving to her waist to pull her even closer, and Gwen's whole body tingled at the sudden pleasure rippling through her as she allowed him in.

'Gwen…' Percy moaned as he deepened the kiss, his tongue ravishing her even as his lips possessed hers.

And Gwen wanted more.

More of whatever he could give her, whatever they could share.

And even though she knew it was scandalous, kissing a duke in an alleyway as the rest of London passed them by, Gwen lost herself in the passionate embrace.

Eventually the kiss ended. Far too soon.

Percy looked into her gaze with a shaky smile. 'What have you done to me, you wallflower? You've made me want you all the more.'

Chapter Ten

Gwen tried to concentrate. She really did. And it was not a lack of willingness to pay attention, but more an inability to—

'Miss Knox! Kindly refrain from permitting your horse to meander. We are keeping to the path!'

Gritting her teeth, and attempting not to tell the Pike precisely how difficult it was to direct a horse one had only met an hour ago, Gwen tried to smile sweetly. 'Yes, Miss Pike.'

The autumnal air made their breath blossom like steam, and perhaps in any other circumstances Gwen would have enjoyed the ride. After all, it was pleasant to leave the confines of the Wallflower Academy, even if she could still just about see the Tudor manor from where they were. Mostly it was hidden by the wide oaks, their leaves almost gone, and it was almost possible to believe she had escaped the place—though Miss Pike's continuous presence rather challenged that, unfortunately.

'Ladies!'

Her heart stopped. No, not stopped—but it skipped a beat most painfully. So painfully Gwen brought a hand to her chest.

It was as though she had dreamed Percy into existence as a perfect picture of genteel masculinity, with the breeze tugging at his riding coat and a haughty yet warm smile on his lips.

Percy Devereux, the Duke of Knaresby, rode towards the gaggle of wallflowers on a steed at least three hands larger than their own. Gwen heard a gasp. For a moment she thought it had been Sylvia's, but then she realised it was her own.

'Well met,' said Percy, still grinning as he brought his horse alongside Gwen's. 'What a fortuitous chance that we meet, Miss Pike.'

Miss Pike seemed utterly lost for words. Her gaze snapped to the Duke on his horse and the wallflower he was beside.

Gwen tried to hold the woman's gaze as boldly as possible, but she could no longer do so after a few moments. How could she when she was in the presence of both the woman who had been instructed by her mother to help her find a husband and the one man she…?

But she had to put those sorts of thoughts out of her mind. It would not do even to permit them, Gwen told herself firmly.

'Y-Your Grace,' stammered Miss Pike, evidently thrown by the sudden appearance of a man of such nobility. 'You honour us with your presence!'

'So I see,' said Percy, winking at Sylvia, who giggled. 'I wonder whether you will permit me to assist?'

'Assist?' repeated not only Miss Pike, but also Gwen.

She was staring at the man who, the last time she had seen him, had been kissing her senseless in an alley before they returned to the Wallflower Academy.

Just what did Percy think he was up to?

'Assist,' repeated Percy, his smile unwavering. 'It appears you are giving the ladies some practice at horseback riding, and I would imagine the addition of a gentleman for them to speak to would greatly enhance the challenge of the exercise. Why don't I take…oh, Miss Knox, say… on a route into the woodlands, and we can practise the art of conversation?'

Heat blossomed through Gwen's body and she hoped beyond hope that it would not be obvious to the eye.

Practise the art of conversation? She would have laughed aloud if she had not been so mortified. Did he really think the Pike so foolish as to—?

'What a wonderful idea, Your Grace,' simpered Miss Pike, inclining her head as though unable to withstand such cleverness. 'Miss Knox, I require you to attend on the Duke.'

'But—'

'*Now,* Miss Knox,' came the firm direction.

And what did it matter anyway? Gwen wondered, as she gently nudged her horse to follow Percy's down a path she had never explored before. What sort of argument could she possibly put up to prevent such an action?

If she even wished to…

The voice of Sylvia echoed behind them as Gwen followed Percy wordlessly into the woodland. The trees grew closer here, obscuring house, Sylvia and the Pike until they were alone.

Gwen shivered despite herself. Alone with Percy. Again. With a man who kissed like the devil yet made her feel like an angel.

Percy breathed a laugh as he slowed his horse to walk slowly beside hers. 'Goodness, what a stroke of luck.'

'You were too bold,' Gwen pointed out, her heart pattering painfully in her chest and a smile creasing her lips despite her surprise at seeing him. 'I never would have thought the Pike—Miss Pike, I mean—would agree to such a scheme.'

'What? Because your innocence might be in danger?'

The words were shot back so quickly Gwen hardly knew what to say in response. All she could do was look at Percy, see the desire and hunger in his eyes, and swallow.

Was it just as obvious in her own expression just how dearly she wished to be kissed again?

Which was a nonsense—because where could this go?

Oh, the woodland path would undoubtedly stretch for miles, disappearing off into the wilderness. Gwen was certain the two of them could endeavour to 'get lost' if they really put their minds to it, and Miss Pike would never think to question such an excuse if it gave one of her wallflowers additional time with a gentleman such as a duke.

But after that?

Gwen's mind whirled frantically as she attempted to understand.

One more kiss, yes—but what then? Percy could hardly make an offer to her. He had made that perfectly clear...

Until he had kissed her. Then he had been perfectly *un*clear.

'Did you hear that?'

'What?' Gwen said, turning.

There did not seem to be any movement in the trees, nor any sound to be heard. But Percy was looking around, his gaze narrowed, as though expecting to see someone's shadow flickering through the trees.

'Nothing, I just thought...' Percy swallowed. 'My mother says I'm getting paranoid. Expecting people to be talking about me.'

'And they're not?'

'Oh, they are,' he said with a wry smile. 'But my mother assures me it's only good things.'

Gwen tried to smile. Only good things… That was what she wanted from Percy, but even she could not explain what she meant. *Good things.* What would 'good' look like with Percy? What was possible? They were so different. So—

'Gwen?'

Gwen started. Percy had not only halted his own horse, but hers, too. His hand had reached out, unbeknownst to her, and caught the reins of her mare, drawing her to a stop. There was a look of deep concern on his face and, try as she might, it was difficult to ignore just how handsome he was.

She smiled weakly. 'Percy…'

'Walk with me,' he said quietly, dismounting.

'But I am supposed to be practising—'

'A pox on your practising,' Percy said, holding out a hand.

Gwen hesitated only for a moment. She liked riding, but the opportunity to walk with Percy, close to him, far closer than would be possible while they were mounted… it was too much to resist.

Gently sliding from her mare, Gwen found to her utter distraction that Percy had been standing so close she was now firmly wedged between the unmoving horse and his broad chest.

Her breath caught in her throat, her gaze was caught by his own, and there was a fiery look within his eyes she had never noticed before.

Or was it simply that it had not been there before?

'I have missed you, Gwen…' Percy breathed softly.

Gwen swallowed. She should not say anything, certainly not agree… 'I have missed you too.'

This kiss was different from those they had shared in the alley. Yesterday they had been unrestrained, hot, passionate, demanding of Gwen everything she was, and she had given herself willingly.

But this was different. Softer, gentler, no less passionate but with a different flavour of desire. More reverent.

Still, it fair took Gwen's breath away, and made it near impossible for her to stand. She would have fallen if she had not been so heavily pressed between man and mare.

'Come on,' said Percy quietly.

'You have a habit of saying that, you know?'

'I wouldn't need to if you would just follow me.'

Placing her arm in his, Percy gently tied the reins of both horses to a large oak tree and started to walk Gwen deeper into the woods.

'You have never kissed anyone before me, have you?' he asked.

Gwen's cheeks immediately flared with heat. 'What makes you say—?'

'Oh, I have no complaints,' said Percy quickly. His arm tightened around her own. 'Dear God, quite the opposite… No, it's just… I can tell. Something in the way you cling to me.'

This was going from bad to worse! How was Gwen supposed to keep a calm head on her shoulders with such—such a conversation between them?

'I was kissed once,' said Gwen, the words tripping off her tongue no matter how much she attempted to halt them. 'But I did not like it.'

What on earth had possessed her to say such a thing? They had vowed, she and her mother, that they would never speak of that night—not with anyone. Not even between themselves. Not ever again.

It had been painful enough to do so the first time.

Why would either of them wish to do such a thing a second time?

But something about Percy was drawing it out of her like…like poison from a wound.

Gwen had read once about drawing out the poison when one had been attacked by a snake in the wilds of India. And was this not the same? Had not poison settled in her heart, her treacherous heart, and would she not be whole again if it could be removed?

Percy was frowning. 'Dear me, was the gentleman unskilled?'

Gwen took a deep breath. 'The man—I will not call him a gentleman—was...was forceful.'

Forceful. That was all she could manage, all she was willing to say, but even uttering the word seemed to quieten a part of her soul she had not realised had been broken.

'Forceful?' repeated Percy, and then his eyes darkened. 'Gwen, you don't mean—?'

'I am still an innocent,' said Gwen hastily, her cheeks still pink. 'He did not—But he was forceful. I did not enjoy—I did not want—'

'The blackguard—I'll cut him through! I'll call him out! I'll face him across a field at dawn!' spat Percy, and she could feel the rage boiling within him. 'The brute! Who was it?'

Gwen swallowed, remembering the darkness of that night, the chaos, the desperate need to be free, to escape from the clutches of a man who smelt of drink and pain. How she had struggled, desperate, her temper rising, outraged at his treatment, overwhelmed until she'd pushed—

'I don't know,' she admitted.

It was the truth, even if Percy glowered. 'You do not have to protect him...'

'I know,' Gwen said softly.

She swallowed, tried not to think about the crack of the—

'I know,' she repeated. 'And I do not keep his name from you to protect him. I simply do not know it.'

'No gentleman would ever—The blackguard! Is he here? At the Wallflower Acad—?'

'No!' Gwen interrupted, her heart pattering painfully still. Oh, she should never have admitted such a thing. Her temper that flared and caused such terrible things to happen. 'No, it was b-before.'

After all, how had her mother put it?

'Where's the best place to hide a murderess, Gwen? In a garden of wallflowers...'

Percy's breath was still tight as leaves crunched under their feet. 'Well, I am glad you are well rid of him, Gwen.'

It was difficult not to exclaim at this, but Gwen managed it. 'Well rid of him, indeed. It is the way of the world; I am not unique.'

'And to think it happened to you! You, of all people!' Percy continued.

Gwen's stomach twisted as he spoke.

'I remember when my brother James first talked to me about women. Told me what to look for...what to admire. Why, he was such a gentleman. He knew the ladies far better than I ever could.'

A small smile crept across Gwen's face. Something had changed in Percy. She had felt it as well as seen it. It was as if a gentle relaxing, a warmth, was flooding through him. Comfort...a sense of peace.

'You truly admired him, did you not?' she asked.

'Oh, I don't think anyone who met James did not admire him, even if they didn't like him,' said Percy, chuckling under his breath. 'He was taller than me, yet one did not feel overawed by the man. He was generous with his time—arguably to a fault. There are times, you know... times when I think I shall never live up to him. To his charm, his cleverness. His memory. Why, I remember this one time...'

Gwen's stomach slowly began to unclench as Percy chattered happily about the brother he had so clearly adored. Well, she had managed it. It was as close a conversation as she'd had about the truth, and she had not revealed the shameful end.

Perhaps—just perhaps—she could go through the rest of her life without consequences. Without having to face the awful thing she had—

'Gwen?'

Gwen blinked. Percy had halted, and her own footsteps had halted too, but she had not noticed. His expression was strange, hard to read, though intensely focused on her in a way she found most disconcerting.

'Percy?' she said.

A smile spread across his lips. 'I like it when you say my name. You weren't listening, were you?'

Shame flashed through her heart. 'Yes, I—'

'So what did my brother purchase for my last birthday?'

Gwen opened her mouth, knew there was no hope of her guessing, and closed it again. 'You know I haven't the faintest idea.'

Percy snorted. 'Well, at least that's honest. What's distracted you, Gwen?'

She hesitated before answering. It would not be right, would it, to admit to the topic that had truly entangled her mind away from his company? And in truth there was more than one distraction in her heart, and one of them was standing right before her.

'You.'

It was a simple syllable, one hardly requiring any thought. It flowed from her, from the truth of her heart, and something changed in Percy's eyes.

'You know I would never do anything you did not wish me to do, don't you?' he said quietly, dropping her arm but only doing so, it seemed, to clasp her hand in his. 'You are…precious to me, Gwen.'

The moment between them was unlike anything Gwen had ever known. Safety and danger. The heat within her meeting the cold air in a rushing twist of desire she knew she should not give in to, but—

'Kiss me…' she breathed.

It appeared Percy needed no additional invitation. Pulling her into his arms, he kissed her exquisitely on the mouth, his ardour forcing Gwen to take a few steps backwards as she clung to him desperately, her body tingling as prickles of pleasure rushed through her.

And then she was pressed up against a tree, and she gasped as Percy's tongue met hers in a tantalising tangle of lust and something deeper, something far softer. She moaned…

'Gwen,' murmured Percy, his lips moving to her neck, trailing kisses to the collar of her pelisse as Gwen tilted her head back, unable to stop herself, eager for more. 'Oh, Gwen…'

'Percy!' she gasped, unable to say anything more, hardly able to think. 'Percy, I want—'

But any specific request—even if her brain had been able to think of one—was wrenched from her mind as Percy seemed to act on her very thoughts.

If she had been able to think such a scandalous thing, of course…

While his lips continued to worship her neck she melted into his arms. This was what it should be like, she could not help but think wildly, as memories of that less pleasant encounter were overwritten by his softness, his gentleness.

There was passion there, yes, but it was controlled. Determined, but not demanding. Eager, but not exacting.

Desire rose within her…a desire which had never been

sparked before. And she wanted to tell him, show him, just how greatly she desired him.

Without a word, he seemed to know.

Percy's fingers reached for her gown. Somehow—Gwen was not sure how, pleasure having removed all senses but touch—he had pulled up her skirts past her knee, and his hand now rested on her upper thigh—her actual thigh.

Gwen moaned. The sense of his fingers on her skin was overwhelming, intoxicating, and there was nothing she could do but cling to him and hope this moment would never end.

'Tell me if you want me to stop,' Percy managed on a jagged breath. 'You understand, don't you, Gwen?'

'Don't stop…' Gwen moaned.

All thought that they might be found, discovered perhaps even by Miss Pike herself, had been driven from her mind. All she wanted was to lose herself in this moment as Percy—

'Percy!'

She had not shouted—there was not enough air in her lungs—but Gwen had been unable to help herself exclaiming as he gently brushed her curls with his fingers.

Such a jolt of decadent pleasure, such an overwhelming sensation, Gwen had never known before. Head spinning, hardly aware how she was still standing, she whimpered with joy as Percy's fingers grazed her again.

'Gwen—'

'More…' That was all she could manage. 'More!'

He needed nothing else.

As Percy's lips returned to her own, capturing both them and her whimpers, his fingers grew bolder, one of them slipping into her secret place. Gwen could see stars, feel an aching heat building in her such as she had never known before, could never have imagined her body could contain, and then suddenly—

'Percy!'

That was what Gwen had tried to shout, but her mouth had been utterly captured by the man she now knew she loved, and as Percy's fingers stroked her into ecstasy there was nothing she could do but hold on…hold on to the man she had given everything to, would give anything to.

As the pleasure slowly receded like a tide, Gwen managed to open her eyes.

Percy was gazing adoringly straight into hers. 'Gwen—'

'Percy…' she breathed, hardly able to believe she had permitted him to do such a thing. 'I—'

'Hush…'

Gwen blinked up, unsure why, after such lofty heights, Percy had had to bring her back to earth. He was looking around as if he had seen something, heard something, though what she could not—

'Gwen? Gwen, the Pike says we must return to the Academy in time for dining practice. Where are you?'

Reality was a rather disappointing thing to discover after such sensual decadence. Gwen breathed out a laugh, dropping her head onto Percy's chest, and wished they'd had a little more time. More time to talk, to kiss, to—

'Damn,' said Percy dryly, neatly capturing her feelings in one word.

'Damn, indeed,' Gwen said, the bold word sharp on her tongue. 'I had hoped—'

'I should probably take you back,' he said, sighing, allowing her skirts to fall back to the ground. 'Although I would really—Gwen, I hope that was pleasurable for you?'

'Pleasurable?' she repeated.

How could the man be in any doubt?

A flicker of uncertainty tinged his face. 'I am sorry if—'

'Percy Devereux, I could happily have you do that to me every hour, on the hour, for the rest of my life,' said Gwen quietly, pushing aside the thought that her future could never contain that. She was dangerous; she would not hurt him. And his promise to his brother would divide them for ever. 'If I could—'

'Gwen? Gwen, can you hear me?' The indefatigable voice of Sylvia came through the trees.

Percy groaned. 'Gwen, I don't want you to go.'

Her heart was racing, and the temptation to tell him she had no wish to return either was teasing her heart. They could leave. They had two horses...they could make their own way in the world...

But they couldn't. She couldn't.

There was already one scandal in her past that she was attempting to escape from. It would not do to tempt fate and cause another.

'Your Grace,' she said primly, almost laughing at the groan Percy uttered as she released him. 'I believe it is time for you to return me to the Academy.'

'Blasted Academy.'

'Yes, that one,' said Gwen with a laugh.

Oh, it was glorious to see how disappointed he was, to see how very viscerally he wished to keep her... But it was no use.

'Oh. There you are.'

Gwen whirled around, stepping as far away from Percy as she could without it being too obvious—*was* it too obvious?

Perhaps. There was an uncomfortably knowing look on Sylvia's face as she beamed at the two of them.

'My apologies, Your Grace, for disturbing you, but I am afraid Miss Knox must return with me.'

'Of course,' said Percy smoothly, and Gwen both hated and loved it that he could so swiftly act as though nothing had happened between them when everything had—everything. 'Let me help you onto your horse, Miss Knox.'

Gwen tried not to notice how her fingers tingled as Percy helped her mount her mare.

'I shall see you soon, will I not, Your Grace?' she asked in a low voice as Sylvia turned her own steed around, heading back towards the Academy.

Percy's eyes twinkled. 'Soon? Oh, very soon. As soon as I can make it.'

Chapter Eleven

The first day, Gwen did not worry. Her mind was full of memories of tantalising touches, of kisses that lingered—and those that did not.

'Gwen!'

Gwen started. A piece of fried egg slipped from the fork she had been holding before her, evidently for some minutes, her mind entirely on other things.

Sylvia was staring, utterly bemused. 'What on earth has got into you?'

'Nothing,' Gwen said hastily.

The last thing she wished to do was reveal to the wallflowers precisely what had happened between her and Percy.

He had not needed to gain a promise from her of secrecy. The very idea of sharing the most intimate moment of her life with others...

'Is it just me, or is Gwen rather quiet this morning?' asked Rilla as another wallflower helped her with her breakfast.

'I am not—'

'Silence, ladies!' Miss Pike, at the head of the breakfast table, glared at them. 'I will not have bickering at breakfast. It is far too early for all that.'

And so Gwen moved through the day dreamily, even with Sylvia's uncertain looks upon her.

The second day, Gwen did not worry either. Well, it had only been a day, and Percy surely had commitments in Town that he was required to fulfil.

He is a duke after all, Gwen thought dreamily when she was supposed to be working on some embroidery.

'Ladies should always have a talent to discuss,' Miss Pike had said firmly, that very afternoon. 'And the only appropriate talents are music, embroidery, watercolour painting or remarking upon the weather.'

The embroidery of roses that Gwen was supposed to be completing had seen no change, however, in the hour during which she and the other ladies had been seated, ostensibly at their needlework, in the orangery as slow afternoon sunlight poured through the glass.

Her needle poked into the embroidery circle but then abandoned, Gwen smiled wistfully at the thought of the way Percy had kissed her.

He must care for her. She had not expected such affection from any gentleman, so to find it from him, a man so kind, so gentle... And yet on first meeting his haughtiness! His determination that his position required the perfect wife!

It was therefore on the third day that a prickle of concern started to creep around Gwen's heart. It was, after all, a long time to go without hearing a word from the man one had shared such a scandalous moment with. A very long time indeed after one had given him one's heart—and rather more.

No note.

Gwen had looked up eagerly when the post had been brought in that morning, but her shoulders had slumped as only one letter had been placed before her, her mother's handwriting adorning the front.

Gwen had given it little thought. She knew what it would contain. More crowing over her mother's neighbours, more exhortation for Gwen to marry well—but not too well— and more vague threats about revealing their secret.

It was still unopened upstairs in her bedchamber as she sat downstairs in the drawing room, listening to the dull monologue Miss Pike was now giving the wallflowers about the correct mode of address.

'Naturally, as wallflowers, you are nervous, and there-fore more likely to make mistakes,' Miss Pike was saying so cheerfully. 'The best thing to do, if you are unsure, is wait until someone else has made reference to the person in question. Then you can see…'

On the fourth day, Gwen awoke with panic settled in her stomach. Why did Percy stay away? Worse, why did he send her no word?

She had been happy to acquiesce to silence, to secrecy, but not to solitude. The rambling Tudor manor felt acutely discomforting, both home and prison.

Perhaps she should have asked him more precise ques-tions, Gwen could not help but wonder as she stood in a line in the ballroom that afternoon, trying to follow Miss Pike's erratic instructions for a new country dance.

Perhaps she should have clarified what they would do next.

Or perhaps there was no plan? Perhaps Percy had no intention of seeing her until he was bored with Town?

The very thought curdled in her stomach.

Gwen swallowed and turned left as the other wallflow-ers turned right.

'Really, Miss Knox, pay attention!'

'Apologies, Miss Pike,' said Gwen quietly, her gaze fixed on the floor.

'It's that duke of hers,' said Rilla. She had a ribbon in

her hand, her sightless eyes fixed towards the sound of the wallflowers attempting to learn new steps. 'He has been away a few days, now I come to think about it.'

Gwen's heart contracted painfully.

She would do anything not to hear her new friends discuss such things!

'He has probably gone to his estate for the shoot,' Miss Pike said soothingly, and Gwen looked up to see the owner of the Wallflower Academy doing a rare thing: smiling. 'I must say I did not think you had it in you, Miss Knox, but you certainly seem to have attracted his attention.'

Heat crept across Gwen's cheeks, but she said nothing.

Why, if Miss Pike could even guess what had truly occurred between herself and Percy!

It was on the fifth day that Gwen truly started to panic. Had she upset or offended him in some way? Worse, had he discovered the truth of her past?

When that thought occurred to her, as she was reading and Sylvia read aloud to Rilla, on the evening of the fifth day since she had seen him, Gwen was certain for an instant that she was going to be sick. The very idea that Percy might have discovered her terrible crime… She was dangerous and, worse, a danger to his reputation…

'You are very quiet.'

Gwen looked up. Not a single word on the page of her book had been taken in, and she was surprised to see not only the windows dark, but the lamps lit.

'What?' she said, distracted.

'I have noticed,' said Rilla. 'Something has changed in you, Gwen, and do not say it has not, for I am quite capable of knowing when I am being lied to.'

Gwen looked at her book rather than meet Sylvia's penetrating gaze. 'It's nothing.'

Sylvia snorted. 'Nonsense.'

Could...could they tell?

Gwen was not aware that feeling the heights of ecstasy thanks to a gentleman's fingers could change one's appearance, and she had attempted to participate in all the lessons at the Academy over the last few days. They should not be able to tell she was any different—at least, not by looking at her.

'You are upset,' said Rilla quietly, 'for you have not seen your duke in a while. Am I right?'

Thankful that Rilla was unable to see the flush that was surely on her cheeks, and hoping Sylvia would not remark upon it, Gwen said, 'He is not my duke.'

'Are you so sure?'

Gwen focused her gaze on the other wallflowers talking at the far end of the room—anything rather than give credence to Rilla's words.

But she could not help it. Rilla was right, even if she did not wish to say it. Percy was hers—her duke.

The idea of her having a duke was most ridiculous, and Gwen could not help but smile at the thought. But it was true. She owned him—or at least, she owned him as much as he owned her. He had possessed her now, body and soul, and she could as easily remove her own heart as untangle it from his.

'What I do not understand,' said Rilla, 'is what you are doing now.'

Gwen blinked. 'Now?'

Rilla nodded. 'He has not been here for several days. You are clearly eager to see him. Why are you waiting for him to come to you?'

It was only when her companion said the words that Gwen realised she had no idea. Why was she here, waiting for Percy to arrive at the Wallflower Academy, when she was no true wallflower?

Just because she had been sent to the Wallflower Academy it did not mean she had to wait for her life to start, unseeingly accepting whatever hand was dealt to her.

Her life—her real life... It could begin now. This moment.

Gwen smiled at the thought.

'I need to go,' she said, rising with a swish of her skirts.

Rilla smiled. 'I thought you might. Miss Pike mentioned she would be in her study upstairs, if you wish to speak to her.'

Gwen's shoulders tightened at the thought of the lie she would have to tell, but she jutted out her chin. 'Thank you, Rilla.'

'Anything to match a wallflower,' came the quiet reply. 'It is all I'm good for at my age.'

If Gwen had thought about it, she would have remained a moment, to ask Rilla precisely what she meant. But her heart had leapt at the thought of seeing Percy, so she did not pause when leaving the drawing room, and flew up the stairs towards Miss Pike's study.

Only when she reached her door did she hesitate. She knew the room's location, naturally—she had had it pointed out to her on her second day. But she had never received an invitation—or an order—to enter Miss Pike's study before. It was territory unlike the rest of the Academy: a place for Miss Pike and Miss Pike alone.

This was where the matches were agreed.

Swallowing hard, Gwen knocked on the door.

'Come!'

The door opened into a small but elegantly furnished room, rather like a small sitting room, but with an impressive desk in one corner. Upon the desk were piles of letters and paperwork—neat piles, but piles nonetheless.

Miss Pike was seated by a small fire, knitting needles

in her hands and a rather impressive shawl trailing to her feet. Her eyebrows rose.

'Goodness, Miss Knox,' she said languidly, not ceasing her knitting. 'What a surprise. How may I help you?'

Gwen swallowed, as though that might calm the frantic beating of her heart. It made no difference.

'I… I have received a letter. From my mother,' Gwen said hesitantly.

She did not like lying. It was something she did infrequently—especially since the night that had changed her life for ever and ended a man's life.

But still, it was hardly a lie. She had, after all, received a letter from her mother.

'I would like to borrow a carriage and go to Town,' Gwen said in a rush.

Miss Pike raised an eyebrow. 'Your mother would like to meet you in Town? She does not wish to visit you here?'

Gwen swallowed.

Everything she was saying was true.

'I would appreciate the loan of the carriage, Miss Pike, but I understand if it is not possible. I will merely write to my mother to inform her.'

It was delicately done, to be sure—but was it enough? Gwen could not tell. Miss Pike certainly would not wish any of her wallflowers to write home to their families to say they were not being given the opportunity to go to Town, especially when it was to visit a family member.

'When?' came the clipped question.

'Tomorrow,' Gwen said, with reluctance.

It was too late today, but the sooner she saw Percy, the better. Her heart needed to be soothed, and he was the only one who could achieve it.

Miss Pike examined her closely. 'The Duke of Knaresby

is in Town at the moment, perhaps? And your mother? Both of them?'

Gwen swallowed. So that was what the owner of the Wallflower Academy assumed. That she was orchestrating a meeting between her mother and the Duke who had marked her out as a favourite.

'I believe the Duke is in Town,' Gwen said, dropping her gaze to her clasped hands.

A moment of silence, then... 'I have no wish to speak out of turn, but from your mother's correspondence...' Miss Pike's voice trailed off. 'Well, I do not have the impression that she is an easy woman to please.'

Heat blossomed up Gwen's chest. It was an understatement. Her mother was demanding, cruel, argumentative... and the holder of her great secret. A secret she had held over her head more than once, with delicate threats as to what might happen to disobliging daughters.

'You have my permission to borrow the carriage,' said Miss Pike impressively, not waiting for her to reply. 'Well done, Miss Knox. Well done, indeed.'

Gwen left the study quickly and quashed all concerns about lying, deceit and being caught out.

As soon as breakfast was over the next morning, she was outside and the carriage was waiting.

'Thank you,' she said breathlessly as the driver helped her up into the chaise and four. 'The Duke of Knaresby's residence, please.'

It was all Gwen could do to calm herself as the carriage rumbled along the road, slowing as the noise of London rose around it. She was almost there. After almost a week—a terribly long week without the sight of Percy's face—she was surely only minutes from seeing him. The man she loved.

'Here y'go, miss.'

Gwen started.

They could not possibly have arrived already, could they?

The driver turned and poked his head through the small opening at the front of the carriage. 'Shall I wait here, then?'

'I—I… Yes, please. Thank you,' mumbled Gwen.

She had given no thought to the driver at all, in truth. All her thoughts had been focused on one man. But those thoughts were chased away now, as she stared up at the building.

The door was imposing. Tall, wide, painted a beautiful red and with a shining brass knocker, it sat at the centre of four large bay windows.

Gwen swallowed. This townhouse of Percy's—his second home, or perhaps even his third—why, it was larger than her own home…larger than the inn itself.

A prickle of hesitation caused her hand to stay before knocking. He lived such a different life from her. In a different world…in the spotlight. Was she truly ready to risk it all—scandal, perhaps imprisonment—by drawing attention to herself and stepping into his circle?

But impulse pushed her forward and she knocked. She had to see him. She could not bear to be without him any longer.

When the door opened, Gwen said impetuously, 'Percy!'

An elderly man in servant's livery blinked. 'I beg your pardon, young lady?'

Gwen flushed. 'I—I mean… I have come to see the Duke.'

The servant, probably a butler, stared. 'Indeed? And who shall I say is calling?'

If only she had considered this beforehand. There had been plenty of time in the carriage, if she had put her mind to it, and yet she could think of nothing to say beyond the obvious.

'Say…say it is a lady.'

The butler nodded—and closed the door in her face. Gwen blinked. Was that intended as a reproof, a rejection of her request? Or was it common practice for a butler to close the door before a guest entered?

Uncertainty stirred in her stomach.

Just another example of how very different they were, Gwen thought wretchedly. The more she tried to ignore their differences in station, the more obvious they appeared.

When the door was opened again it was by Percy, who looked confused—then horrified.

'Percy!' Gwen said with a wide smile. 'I thought I would surprise you!'

It was indeed a surprise. Gwen could see the astonishment on the Duke's face. But it was mired by rather different emotions: panic, confusion, and…

And something akin to embarrassment.

Her gaze dropped and the excitement that had filled her ebbed away.

'I… I did not know when I was going to see you again,' she said, filling the awkward silence that Percy did not appear to have any wish to end. 'So I… I thought you might like to go for a walk. See the Queen's Palace, as we did not see it last time. Or…or visit any alleys or trees which are close by.'

That had been rather daring of her, it was true, but Gwen's boldness rose whenever she was with Percy. He made her more herself, somehow.

Yet the Percy she knew did not appear to be present today.

Flushing darkly, he stepped out of the house and closed the door behind him.

Gwen stared. *Was she not going to be invited inside?*

'You have to go.'

Percy's voice was low, soft, as though he was terrified of someone overhearing him.

His words did not make sense to Gwen—so little that she repeated just one. 'Go?'

'Yes, go,' said Percy, just as quietly. 'Now.'

'I… I came all this way to see you,' said Gwen, confusion twisting her heart. 'Why would I go before I have properly seen you?'

'It is a shame, but unfortunately you have arrived at a most inopportune time,' said Percy quickly, his voice low. 'I am sorry to say I have another appointment.'

Another appointment. *Of course he does,* Gwen thought dully.

It would be far too much to assume that Percy would have nothing to do today, or any day. He was a duke. There would be many calls on his time, unlike on hers.

'Go, now,' said Percy, turning her around by the shoulders and pushing her forward, back on to the pavement. 'I… I will come to see you.'

'Soon?' asked Gwen, unable to understand quite what was happening. 'Percy?'

'As soon as I am able,' said Percy, glancing back at the house as though concerned they were being watched.

Gwen looked up at the large bay windows.

Were they?

'Go, Miss Knox,' said Percy in clipped tones. 'Good day.'

The door had opened and closed again, swallowing the Duke up with it, before Gwen could say another word, and she stood there in astonished silence.

Percy did not wish to see her.

More, he had made no definite appointment day or time to see her at the Academy. Worse, there had been no declaration of love, which Gwen had not only hoped for, but expected.

A flicker of doubt circled her heart, followed by that rise of that terrible temper of hers. Gwen tried to breathe, tried to ignore the rising passion tempting her to slam her fists on the door and demand to be let in.

It was all very strange. But then, he was a duke, and she a wallflower—at least in his eyes. Perhaps this was how a courtship of this kind was carried out…

Chapter Twelve

'You mustn't!'

'I have,' said Sylvia with apparent glee. 'And there is no point attempting to talk me out of it, so don't even bother. My half-brother says this was the best trick he ever played at his club!'

Gwen stifled a laugh as she sat by the fire in the drawing room, watching the imperious Sylvia raise a dark eyebrow at the other wallflowers.

'But you mustn't!' said Rilla with a snort. 'Sylvia, you'll be caught—and Miss Pike will be furious when she—'

'The Pike could do with loosening up a little. Not all of us are wallflowers, waiting around for our lives to begin,' said Sylvia smartly as she adjusted the door, left it slightly ajar, and beamed at her creation. 'No offence.'

'None taken,' said Rilla wryly. 'Describe it to me again.'

Gwen smiled, despite herself. 'Sylvia has got it into her head to play a childish practical joke upon our benefactress.'

'Benefactress?' Sylvia snorted as she stepped away from the door and dropped heavily into an armchair. 'Jailor, rather.'

'Either way…' said Gwen hastily. Anything to avoid an argument, with Sylvia clearly feeling particularly bold today. 'Sylvia has carefully balanced a bucket of water over the door—'

'Ice-cold water,' Sylvia interrupted with apparent relish.

Rilla laughed dryly. 'You are always one for the dramatic, Sylvia.'

'Well, if not now, when?' the prankster demanded. 'Here we are, stuck inside unless we are able to catch the eye of a duke—and Gwen still won't reveal how she managed that.'

'And when the door opens for Miss Pike as she joins us before dinner…' Gwen said hastily.

The less said about Percy, the better.

She still could not get that kiss from her mind, nor the way he had spoken to her…

'The door will open, the bucket will fall, and the poor thing will be absolutely drenched.'

'I am not sure I would characterise her as a "poor thing",' said Rilla with a mischievous smile. 'Not after her nonsense yesterday about me not being able to dance. Has she even seen me attempt it?'

'No, she has not,' Sylvia said emphatically as a smile crept over Rilla's face. 'This will serve her right, I say— and all of you must swear not to reveal that it was I, or it will be the same for you when you are least expecting it!'

'You really shouldn't!' said Gwen.

But she knew well enough not to attempt to change the young woman's mind. With a smile across her lips and a knowing glint in her dark, almost black eyes, Sylvia was not a woman to have her mind changed for her.

'I'm bored,' Sylvia said dramatically. 'Bored with waiting around for gentlemen to come and view us as though we are pastries in a shop, deciding to choose which one of us to be their boring wives. I'm just trying to bring a bit of merriment into our lives.'

'Even if we wished to stop you,' Rilla said softly, 'could we?'

Gwen glanced at Sylvia, who grinned. 'No. Miss Pike will get wet—and it's only water. She can go upstairs and change easily enough.'

'Then the real fun will begin,' said Rilla, a hint of trouble in her tones. 'A card party this evening, isn't it?'

Gwen sighed. 'A card party? I truly do not understand how I will bear it. Gentlemen playing at cards…trying to pretend we are in any way interesting to them…'

Her voice trailed away. She had not thought to ask if Percy was attending. Her thoughts had wended in quite a different direction. How had he dared speak to her like that? Why hadn't he invited her inside? Had his deathbed vow to his brother finally come between them?

Then at other times—when she permitted herself to forget that he was a duke, forget the promise he'd made to his brother, forget her past—she would wonder whether they could find again that little nook in the woodland near the Wallflower Academy, where they'd shared more passionate kisses… She would think of the way he'd touched her under that tree…ponder if those kisses would ever lead anywhere…

Despite the heat of the fire, a greater fire rushed through Gwen, turning her cheeks pink and making it impossible for her to contribute to the ongoing conversation.

Rilla was laughing. 'You're acting like a child, Sylvia!'

'Perhaps I am. But I'm tired of being stuck here, tired of never getting my own way, tired of being treated like a child by the Pike!' Sylvia retorted. 'We're adults! We're ladies, women of wit…'

Gwen only half listened. If the other wallflowers knew just what she and Percy had done… It had grown, hadn't it? Grown into something far more than a lady of good repute should even conceive of!

Young ladies did not kiss dukes in carriages—and certainly not in alleyways. Wallflowers did not get taken to ecstasy after a horseback ride, with a gentleman's body pressed up against her.

Gwen had been able to do nothing but cling on for her very life as Percy had taken her on an adventure to pleasure she had never known possible…

And, worse, Gwen was certain there was more. So much more. More that she and Percy would inevitably never share.

'Shush—shush! Here she comes!'

Gwen blinked. Sylvia was waving her hands around to get the others to stop talking, and now they could all hear footsteps approaching across the hall.

Her heart leaping into her mouth, Gwen could not help but glance between Sylvia and the ajar door as the footsteps grew closer. Any moment now the door would open, and Miss Pike would receive the shock of her life!

There was indeed a startled yelp as the door opened and the bucket of freezing water fell onto the unsuspecting entrant into the room—but it was no lady in skirts unexpectedly doused.

Percy blinked through his sodden hair as the bucket fell to the floor with a clatter. 'Wh-What…? Water…?'

Gwen gasped as Rilla fell into raucous giggles. The Duke was absolutely soaked: his jacket drenched, his cravat dripping, his breeches covered in water.

'My—Your Grace!' Sylvia rose, mortification across her features. 'I did not—I thought it was—You are so wet!'

'So very wet,' said Percy with a laugh, pulling at his cravat and twisting it before him so that water ran down onto the carpet. 'Oh, dear, Miss Pike won't like her carpet being so damp…'

Rilla snorted. 'Am I to suppose Sylvia's victim is not who we thought?'

'Sylvia's victim, you say?' Percy raised an eyebrow through his wet hair and turned a sardonic look at the woman now spluttering incomprehensively. 'Is it you, Miss Bryant, I have to thank for this sudden bath?'

Even Gwen had to laugh.

Really, it was most ridiculous!

How had they not considered it might be a gentleman arriving for the card party who might fall victim to Sylvia's trap?

Percy shook his head and flicked water across the wallpaper. 'I do not suppose there is somewhere I can change?'

Rilla was laughing too much to be of any help. Sylvia appeared unable to replicate human speech, and the other wallflowers had all looked away in astonished embarrassment. That left...*her*.

'Here,' Gwen said quietly, rising. 'I can show you somewhere you can remove those wet things.'

Why did her cheeks have to flush at such a statement? It was hardly as if she had offered her own bedchamber, which certainly would have been outrageous.

Yet even though she knew she was doing nothing wrong, Gwen could not help but feel disgraceful as she approached the dripping wet Duke.

'Thank you. That would be most welcome,' said Percy, brushing the water out of his eyes and grinning at Sylvia. 'And you and I, Miss Bryant, will talk about this another time. For now, I would suggest you remove the bucket. Anything to avoid awkward questions from the Pike, I am sure.'

He strode out of the room, squelching on the carpet, and Gwen followed him, trying not to laugh.

'You are laughing at me, Gwen,' Percy said ruefully as he walked soggily beside her up the stairs.

Gwen giggled. 'Serves you right after the way you sent me away.'

She had not intended to speak so directly, but her words did not appear to upset him. Quite to the contrary.

Percy smiled ruefully. 'I deserved that,' he said, shaking his hands. Water scattered about him. 'Well, not this, but your reprimand. My…my mother was visiting me, and she is quite…well.'

Gwen nodded. That was all that needed to be said. His mother would certainly have got the wrong impression if she had walked in—after all, there was no future between herself and Percy. Not unless his brother came back from the grave and changed his mind.

'I… I understand. You are here for the card party, I suppose? I shall enjoy watching you explain the damp patch on your seat to Miss Pike.'

'Perhaps you will,' he countered, although there was no anger in his voice. 'Dear me, what am I going to wear?'

'The only thing I can think of is something from the footmen's store,' said Gwen, thinking quickly.

It took her but a moment to retrieve a footman's outfit from the cupboard at the end of the corridor, though Percy frowned rather doubtfully at the breeches, shirt, waistcoat and jacket she handed him.

'So I can be footman and bar the door to all other gentlemen?'

Gwen grinned. 'Do you want to?'

She should not have spoken so boldly. Percy affixed her with such a serious look that Gwen was forced to look away and walk down the corridor.

How did he do that? Look at her with such intensity her whole body reacted?

'Here,' she said, hardly aware of what she was thinking, led by instinct. 'You can change in here.'

She had opened the door before she could stop herself and Percy had walked in.

The Duke looked around the small room, It was her bedchamber, with its large bed and bay window.

'A pleasant aspect in the daytime, I am sure,' Percy said quietly, placing the footman's clothes on a chair in the corner. 'Whose chamber is it?'

Gwen swallowed, her lungs tight in her chest. 'Mine.'

Silence fell between them, A silence Gwen desperately wanted to break, but could not think how. What had she done? She had invited a duke—Percy, the man she wished to be kissing right at this moment—into her bedchamber.

Percy smiled. 'Well, I thank you. And now, if you do not mind…?'

He glanced at the clothes and, cheeks flushed, Gwen nodded.

Leaving the room without saying another word, she reached out to close the door behind her—but something outrageous within her slowed her movements, until the door was only almost closed, leaving a small crack through which she could see.

It was a perfect view. Percy had already ripped off his jacket, waistcoat and shirt—all sodden, all dropped to the floor. Gwen tried not to gasp, but it was difficult. Even in this small sliver of a view, she could see that Percy was a handsome man down to his skin. Broad shoulders, a strength in his arms she had felt but never seen, a smattering of hair trailing down his chest towards his breeches…

Gwen swallowed. Something was stirring within her—something she did not quite understand. But she wanted more.

Oh, so much more.

There was a twist, a change, a gasp—and Percy looked up and caught her gaze.

Gwen gasped too. At the sudden shock of being caught out. Caught staring at a half-naked duke.

It was quite clear from the look on Gwen's face that she was horrified at being caught—but Percy could not think of anything better.

There it was. The desire he knew was inside her, just waiting to come out. He'd seen it once and was desperate to see it again. First the temper, then the tension, now the temptation.

Excitement rushed through Percy as he saw Gwen's wide eyes. So she had been watching him, had she? And had she liked what she had seen?

After weeks of restraint, after stolen kisses in alleyways and in carriages, after being desperate to know her—all of her—this was his chance.

His chance to...talk.

Striding over to the door and opening it fully, Percy leaned against the doorframe and gave the woman before him a lopsided grin. 'Was there more you wanted to say, Miss Knox?'

'I shouldn't have—I should go. I should return downstairs,' Gwen babbled.

Percy caught her hand in his as she turned and started to walk away. There was a tension in that hand...a fierce passion held back. He shivered. Dear Lord, if there was such desire in her now, just from looking at him, just from knowing what he could do when he kissed her...what more could she promise?

'Come on,' he muttered in a low voice.

Gwen did not need encouragement. She slipped into the room with soft footsteps, and when Percy closed the door and leaned against it he saw a woman who knew both what she wanted, and the fact that it was forbidden.

Percy swallowed. He would have to tread carefully here. Just because he knew Gwen Knox had been won over almost from the first moment he had met her, that did not mean Gwen knew herself what she was craving.

Or just how far she was willing to go to get it.

It was time to be a little more direct. A little more obvious about his own desires, Percy mused. And James be damned. Oh, his brother had meant well, certainly—but with Gwen constantly on his mind Percy had to admit that perhaps his brother, in a very small and insignificant way, had been wrong about women such as her. About ladies in general.

He did not have to seek someone who fitted the perfect list of criteria.

He had found Gwen.

'Does it give you pleasure?' he said quietly. 'To look at me?'

To his great surprise, he heard his own heart thumping wildly and loudly in his ears. Percy looked carefully at the woman before him, at the delicate elegance, the shyness that had swiftly returned to Gwen's features the moment she'd realised she had been caught.

Yes, she was a wallflower. But there was something far more here than just a wallflower. Gwen was more than a simple label that diminished her.

Gwen was a wallflower and a warrior. A scandalous woman in some ways, and a most proper one in others. Percy was not sure he would ever get tired of trying to understand the layers of this woman. But he certainly wished to become better acquainted with some of the layers she was wearing!

Though Gwen was clearly scandalised by his question, and Percy knew she had every right to be, he could not help himself. She was a woman so lovely, so interesting—far more interesting than any of the insipid chits his mother had attempted to introduce him to.

Gwen remained silent, though unusually she had not looked away. So Percy decided to attempt a different tack: honesty.

'It gives me pleasure to look at you,' he said quietly. 'Though I admit not as much pleasure as touching you would.'

Gwen's lips parted, almost unconsciously, but she said nothing. Yet still she did not look away, her gaze affixed on his.

Her desires had won, Percy realised, excitement growing in his stomach and descending to his manhood, which was even now trying to stand to attention. She wanted him to speak like this to her...to tease her, perhaps even to touch her. To caress her.

'What do you want, Gwen?' Percy asked as he took a few steps towards her. When she said nothing, he said softly, 'I can tell you what *I* want. I want to kiss you. Touch you. Hold your hands—hold you close to me. Closer than you could possibly imagine.'

'Why are you doing this?' Gwen's voice held no reproach, just confusion and desire.

Percy smiled as he took another step closer. 'Because I... I was wrong.'

She stared. 'Wrong?'

It was as unnatural for him to say it as it was for her to hear it, Percy realised with a twist in his chest. But then, gentlemen of his breeding were rarely ever told they were wrong, were they?

And since he had inherited the title... Well, since then he could not recall ever being told he was wrong!

'I... There isn't a perfect list for what a woman is, Gwen,' Percy found himself saying. 'My brother was wrong in this one regard, I think, and it is a most important thing for me to realise. Oh, Gwen, I cannot stay away from you! I think no one has ever told you how winning you are, Gwen. How desirable you are. I want more than I think you can give me—certainly more than you should...'

He watched her swallow, watched her pupils dilate as he came closer. By God, she wanted him.

'I knew it when I sent you away,' he said quietly. 'I knew it as I bitterly regretted watching you get back into that carriage—that I never wanted you to do that again. And James...'

Percy hesitated. It was difficult to articulate, even to himself, but he had to try. Gwen deserved that. *He* deserved that.

'James would not want me to be unhappy,' he said, his voice breaking. 'My brother...he created the criteria, made me promise because he thought it would make me happy. But you do, Gwen. It's you.'

He saw the flicker of astonishment in her eyes, the amazement at his revelation—and the excitement at what might come next.

'I would like to kiss you, taste you...know precisely how you moan when I give you pleasure,' said Percy softly. He was standing before her now, probably too close—or perhaps not close enough.

Gwen took a small step forward. They were mere inches away from each other now. 'And...and what then?' she asked.

It was all Percy could do not to crush her to him, desperate as he was to end this tension, this dance they had been doing around each other. But not yet. *Not yet.*

'Then...' he said, in half a voice, half a growl. 'Then I would like to take off your gown and kiss every inch of you.'

'I like the sound of that,' whispered Gwen, her mouth

curling into a smile. A tantalising smile which made Percy wish he had the restraint he should have—*any* restraint. For the words in his heart were threatening to spill out, to shock both of them, in a rush of certainty he had never known before.

Marry me, Gwen. Make me happy. Let me make you happy.

If he'd had restraint, he would not have said the words that would take them past a turning point: once they'd passed it, there would be no turning back.

What was it she had once said? *'Least likely to win a duke.'*

'Why don't I show you just how likely you are to win me?' he asked.

Chapter Thirteen

Gwen stared at the man who had asked her such a dangerous and delicious question.

She knew what it was now—this strange sensation in her chest, this anticipatory tingling across her body, the warmth between her legs.

Arousal.

She wanted Percy to make love to her, to kiss her and touch her and do all the delectable things he had said.

'I would like to kiss you, taste you…know precisely how you moan when I give you pleasure.'

But something held Gwen back, despite all the memories of tantalising pleasure, despite her imaginings of forbidden pleasure to come. Something that confused her.

It took a moment to understand what it was.

Fear.

As Gwen looked into Percy's eyes, his honest face, she knew it was not enough.

It was not sufficient to merely want another, to desire their touch. She cared for Percy deeply, and only now could she admit what those feelings amounted to.

Love.

She loved him.

It was a strange, new, imperfect love, to be sure—one that if she had been a titled lady might have grown into something precious and beautiful.

But she was not. She was a murderess—someone with no beauty nor wealth nor position in Society. And they were all precisely what Percy needed. She knew it; he knew it.

So when he offered her such things, such wonderful delights, it was as a mistress.

Gwen's stomach twisted painfully at the thought, but she could not ignore it.

While she might want to be his wife, marry him, spend the rest of her days falling more and more in love with the man before her... He did not want that. Percy needed to marry as a duke married, and those marital limitations pained her more than she could say.

It was too much. Too painful. Too excruciating.

Gwen knew she should step away...remove herself from such temptation.

But Percy's intoxicating presence was too much. His words were too much. His admission that his brother had been wrong, that he chose instead to be happy...

Although they were not even touching, Gwen was dazzled by the prospect of such intimacy. His naked chest was before her, crying out for her touch.

'Then I would like to take off your gown and kiss every inch of you.'

Something warm and aching slipped from her heart to between her legs. Gwen knew what she wanted: Percy. All of him. Not just his kisses, nor even his lovemaking, but his heart.

Something she knew he simply could not give her.

Besides, it would be scandalous to give in to such hedonistic desires! She was supposed to be a wallflower, not a wanton! No lady could permit herself to simply take the pleasures offered by dukes—even if they were as handsome and alluring as Percy.

'Gwen?' Percy said quietly. 'Are you quite well?'

Gwen opened her mouth, but nothing came out.

How could she speak? What could she say? It was impossible to conceive of any words that would make any sense to a man like him.

Surely he had experience in such matters?

At that very thought Gwen's gaze dropped, unbidden images of Percy with other women cutting through her thoughts.

The movement of her gaze did not help, however. Before it had been affixed to his eyes, something Gwen had thought far too intense, but now she was looking at the trail of hair disappearing into his breeches, under which there appeared to be a rather prominent bulge...

Ah.

Gwen's cheeks seared with heat as she realised what it was. Percy's manhood. He wanted her. His desire was obvious. This was no teasing trick.

But no duke should desire her in this way. Gwen was sure of that.

'I know why you are hesitating.'

Gwen could not help but laugh dryly at Percy's words. 'I do not think you do.'

How could he? Could a duke, or any gentleman, understand what it was to be so utterly overwhelmed? To be on the one hand overcome with desire for a gentleman— a desire Gwen knew she should not be feeling—and on the other hand believe that even if that gentleman made love to her it would not be meaningful unless it came with certain promises?

Promises Gwen knew Percy could not make.

She should never have shown him to any bedchamber,

let alone her own. She should not have watched while he removed his clothing.

She certainly should not have permitted such sensual conversation.

'I think I do,' said Percy. 'You want this to mean something. To be deeper than just physicality, I mean. A connection not just of bodies, but of hearts, minds, souls.'

Gwen looked up. Percy was not teasing her. 'You…you are right.'

How could she put it into words—or did she need to if he already understood?

Tempting as it was to reach out and touch that handsome chest, Gwen took a deep breath and tried to concentrate. It was important, explaining to him how she felt. He needed to know. There might never be anyone else she could explain this to.

'The…the act of lovemaking…' said Gwen. Her cheeks were flushing, but there was nothing she could do about it. 'Kissing, touching, c-caressing…any of that. All of it. I believe it should be…well, between two people who truly care for each other. Who are committed to each other.'

Had she said too much? Gwen's heart was pattering lightly but rapidly in her chest, making it difficult to think, to breathe, to know whether she had spoken too brashly.

There was a rather too knowing smile dancing across Percy's lips. 'You did not say that when you were kissing me in that alley, nor when I pushed you up against that tree.'

Gwen laughed weakly as he lifted a hand to push back one of the curls that had fallen over her forehead. Every inch of her skin came alive when he brushed it, as though for the first time. As though she would die if he did not touch her again.

'I did think it,' Gwen admitted in a breathless voice.

'It was just… I wanted you to keep kissing me so much I did not say anything.'

A flash of something she did not recognise seared across Percy's face. Was it desire? Desperation? Glory? A sense of achievement—or something else?

'I wish you had said,' Percy said. 'It… Gwen, it matters to me that you are comfortable with me kissing you. Touching you.'

Gwen's heart rose. He was a good man. She had known it before but had not been able to put it into words, nor had it demonstrated so clearly.

Gwen said quietly, 'I know. I… I truly care for you, Percy.'

Percy took a step backwards, widening the gap between them as he examined her. Gwen could almost feel the change in the air, the change in temperature as he retreated.

She should not have spoken so openly. Nothing good came of her voicing her opinions or letting loose her temper—Gwen knew that. And just at the moment when it was most important for her to be near him, to feel the reassuring presence of him being close, he had stepped away.

Of course he had, Gwen thought dully.

Dukes did not want wallflowers admitting they had feelings for them. They looked for quick and meaningless relief—pleasure, not partnership.

'Forget my words,' Gwen said hastily, turning away. 'I should not have said—'

'I will never forget them.'

Gwen's heart stopped, skipping a beat almost painfully. She turned back to look at Percy.

'I am relieved to hear you say those words,' he said softly, 'because…because I have known for too long that I care too much for you. Too long and too much.'

It took a moment for Gwen to take in what he had said.

It could not be.

Did the handsome man before her really care for her? It must be a trick of her hearing, even with those words about ignoring his promise to his brother ringing in her ears. Yet Gwen could not imagine what words she must have mistaken for such a declaration of affection.

'Could...could you say that again?'

Percy chuckled softly as he stepped forward. 'You wish me to make another declaration of my fondness for you?'

'Are...are you in love with me?' Gwen asked shyly, stepping into his arms and almost crying out as Percy's arms curled around her and pulled her close.

This was where she was supposed to be. After all this time, wondering why her mother had seen fit to send her to such a joyless place, now Gwen knew why she had been sent to the Wallflower Academy.

To meet him. Percy. To know him. To stand here, in his arms, as his smile became bashful upon hearing her words.

'Oh, I don't think I said that aloud,' Percy said, his gaze slipping from hers.

Gwen smiled, joy flooding her heart. Everything she might attempt to say now could be communicated in a much more delicious way.

This time when Gwen lifted up her lips to be kissed Percy did not start gently. No, he possessed her mouth as a thirsty man reached water...as though without it he would surely die.

Gwen gasped into his mouth, heady sensations overwhelming her rapidly as Percy's naked chest pressed against her clothed one.

Just a few layers of silk, she could not help thinking, as her hands returned to the nape of his neck, as they had done when they had kissed in that alleyway. Just one gown, easily moved aside as it had been when he'd touched her by that tree. Just a few inches of silk and their skin would touch, would meet with the same passion and reverence they had enjoyed then.

The kiss ended, and still Percy looked bashful.

'You did not say it aloud,' said Gwen hesitantly, certain she should not speak these words, but knowing she would never forgive herself if she did not. 'But do...do you feel it? In your heart?'

At first it appeared as though Percy would avoid the question. But he certainly did not avoid another chance to kiss her lips, and Gwen shivered as his tongue teased greater pleasure from her than ever before.

But when he pulled away, eyes blazing and mouth clearly hungry for more, he murmured, 'Yes. Oh, yes, Gwen—I love you. I did not know it until it was too late to do anything about it, and even then...even then I did not want to. I love you, Gwen.'

It was everything Gwen had ever hoped the moment would be and more. Nestled in Percy's arms, with his strong hands on her waist, slipping towards her buttocks, her hands around his neck, keeping his mouth close, was precisely where she wanted to be, his words ringing in her ears...

He loved her.

Happiness was searing her heart, branding it and branding this moment in her mind as one she would never forget.

He loved her.

'I love you, Percy,' Gwen said shyly, growing in confidence with every syllable. 'I love you even if you are a duke.'

Percy laughed. 'Is that a problem?'

'No! No, I just meant...' Gwen tried to explain, then laughed when she saw his teasing smile. 'You are a most irritating man, Percy Devereux.'

'And you are a most tantalising woman, Gwen Knox,'

said Percy with a groan, his fingers finally reaching her buttocks, cupping them and pulling her towards him. 'I don't know how you've done it, but you've won me over.'

Gwen smiled, delight almost overwhelming her. She loved him. She loved Percy, and he loved her.

'Does this mean,' asked Percy, 'that you will permit me to do what I want?'

Her smile quickly disappearing, Gwen swallowed and tried to think calmly—something that would be far easier if she was not in the warm embrace of a half-naked duke.

What he wanted?

What he wanted was everything, as far as Gwen could tell. She was hardly well versed in the art of making love, but touching, caressing, touching every part of her skin...?

It would be a line crossed that she could never uncross. A departure from her life of good manners and well-behaved solitude. It would mean giving up any chance of keeping that part of herself for her wedding night.

The thought scorched her mind, but Gwen pushed it aside. She loved Percy and he loved her. To all intents and purposes this *was* her wedding night. Their wedding night.

'They'll come looking for us...' she breathed. 'The Pike. The card party—'

'I did not return my invitation, and I'm sure she'll be far too distracted by Sylvia to think of anything else,' Percy said, his gaze hungry.

Gwen nodded, easily convinced by his words. Yes, they were alone, and they would be left alone. And if she could not give herself to the man she loved, what was the point of all this growing love and affection within her?

'I want you,' said Gwen softly, 'to kiss me...everywhere.'

Percy's eyes widened.

She laughed. 'Ladies have desires too, you know.'

'Yes, well, that's all very well... But...everywhere?' Percy said in a half-whisper.

It was as though he could not quite believe his ears.

Gwen could hardly believe she had spoken the words herself, except she knew they had sprung from her own heart, her own desires.

If she could not be open and honest now, with the man she loved, when could she?

'I love you,' said Gwen quietly. 'And I want you.'

Percy did not need greater encouragement. Returning his lips to hers in an ardent yet reverential kiss, he moved his fingers from her buttocks—to Gwen's regret—and started to untie the delicate ribbons along the side of her gown.

Lost in the heady sensations of nibbling lips and searing hot tongues, Gwen was so lost in the pleasure of the moment she barely noticed when Percy had finished his work. It was only when her gown slipped to the floor, leaving her in naught but her stays and under-shift, that Gwen gasped.

'There,' Percy said, kissing just below Gwen's ear, making her shiver. 'And now...'

It was all Gwen could do not to moan as Percy's lips moved across her bare shoulder. Every inch of contact branded her as his and Percy claimed her...all the parts of her no one else had touched.

Now, no one else ever would.

'Percy!' Gwen gasped as his swift and knowledgeable fingers removed her stays and under-shift in but a moment, leaving her utterly naked.

It was a strange sensation. Gwen had never been so vulnerable before another person—had never had a gentleman see any part of her, let alone all of her.

Moving her hands to hide herself, she glanced nervously at Percy. There was such potent desire in his gaze that

Gwen found all her nerves melting away. It was not a disapproving look...

'I never imagined... You are so beautiful, Gwen. I can't stop myself—tell me if you want me to stop.'

There was no sense of demand in his voice, and Gwen could not think what he meant—until he stepped forward and gently pulled her across the room and against the door.

'Percy...?' Gwen whispered, conscious of only this narrow block of wood keeping them from the corridor.

But he did not reply—at least, not in words. Kissing her lips with a passionate moan, Percy left her mouth and kissed down her neck towards her breasts.

Barely able to stand, Gwen grasped the door handle and quickly turned the key in the lock. Her entire body quivered as pleasure soared between each kiss, peaking to an unimaginable height as Percy captured one of her nipples in his mouth, arching his tongue slowly around it.

'Oh, Percy!'

Gwen tried to stay quiet, she really did, but it was impossible once Percy descended to his knees, his kisses moving down her stomach and suddenly to her secret place. Through her curls, his tongue entered her, and Gwen arched her back against the door at the sudden rush of ecstasy consuming her body.

'Percy!' she gasped, hardly aware of what she was saying.

This was too much. When he had said he wanted to kiss her everywhere...

Percy seemed to take her quivering, twisting pleasure as encouragement to continue, and Gwen moaned and sobbed, clutching desperately at the door handle as his tongue twisted within her, sucked and then built a rhythm, bringing her closer and closer to a peak she remembered and ached for, until eventually Gwen cried out his name, with no thought to who might hear her, as her climax shook her entire body.

'Percy!'

His hands reached her hips, holding her there, preventing her from collapsing. Stars appeared in her eyes, and for a moment she was not entirely sure where she was.

After blinking several times, Gwen looked down to see Percy looking up, a desperate hunger on his face.

'I wanted to hear you come,' he whispered, 'and now I need to feel it. Get on the bed.'

Gwen obeyed—not because there was any threat in his request, but because she wished to please him. Oh, she wanted to please the man who could make her feel like that...

Percy had stripped off his boots and breeches by the time he joined her on the bed, and Gwen tried not to stare at that part of him she had never expected to see.

His manhood. Large, hard, stiff as Percy settled himself between her legs and into her welcoming embrace.

'I will go slowly,' Percy promised, kissing her lightly on the corner of her mouth.

Slowly? Gwen did not want to go slowly. She wanted the fast, desperate, hungry pace Percy had given her with his tongue, deep inside her. She was wet with desire as he slipped into her and started to build a rhythm she now recognised—the same rhythm which had taken her body to such heights only moments before—and Gwen's heart quickly rose in excitement at the thought of feeling that again.

At feeling everything again.

Everything he could give her.

'Damn, Gwen, you feel so good,' moaned Percy as he plunged himself into her once more, causing twinges of pleasure to ripple through Gwen's body.

She clung to his shoulders, unsure whether she should say something but actually unable to speak a word. Not when she was experiencing such pleasure—a pleasure that was building and building, as it had done before, and she wanted it, craved it, craved him, Percy, the man she loved—

'Percy...oh, yes!'

Gwen could not help it. She cried out for a second time as ecstasy overwhelmed her, and it appeared Percy had reached the same peak, for he thrust into her rapidly and then collapsed.

Clutching him, pulling him into her arms, Gwen tried to think, tried to concentrate on the breathing that felt difficult in this moment.

To think such things were possible...such sensation was just at arm's reach. How did anyone, once knowing the pleasure such desire could bring, manage to stay away from it?

'I could never have imagined it...' Gwen breathed, unable to help herself. 'Losing my innocence in such a way. In such a...a heated, delicious encounter that fulfilled all my wildest dreams.'

And more, she wanted to say, for she could never have dreamt of such sensuality.

Percy chuckled as he moved onto the bed beside her, pulling her into his arms. 'Good,' he said sleepily, his eyelashes fluttering shut. 'And now I have you right where I want you...'

Gwen snuggled into him, placing her face on his chest. His heartbeat was just as frantic as her own.

'Oh? And where is that?'

'Right in my arms,' said Percy quietly. 'And in my heart.'

Chapter Fourteen

It was cruel that he had to depart.

Percy told himself another few minutes would not matter. Why not stay here, in the comforting warmth of Gwen's bed, with her naked form beside him, lost in slumber?

He had awoken early—so early the sun was still not up. Birdsong drifted through the bay window, its curtains open. They had been so lost in their lovemaking, then fallen asleep swiftly.

Gwen's gentle breathing moved the blanket Percy had drawn over her and he watched, marvelling at her beauty. To think that he had seen, touched, those delicate fingers, those sensual breasts…had taken and given pleasure of all kinds with such a woman.

It was more than he had ever expected. Perhaps more than he deserved. Certainly more than he should have done. He had thrown out all decorum, Society's expectations, his brother's precepts, and his own knowledge of what he needed to do to cement his title's reputation.

But Percy knew there was little he could keep from Gwen now, even if he wanted to, now he had given her his heart.

His heart contracted, then relaxed, expanding with his devotion. She was a wallflower, yes, but a passionate one.

A woman who understood him, who cared for him—who loved him.

Joy blossomed through him. Love—something he had not expected and yet had found with this precious, beautiful woman. If only he could stay. If only this moment, these early hours, with the Wallflower Academy silent and their secret still their own, could continue for ever.

Percy sighed, his breath ruffling Gwen's long dark hair, draped over her shoulders and the pillow.

But it could not be. He had to leave—and quickly, if he was not to be spotted. And that meant leaving Gwen. His stomach rebelled, aching both from hunger and agitation at the thought of leaving her.

There was no other choice.

Percy reached out a hand and softly brushed away the hair from Gwen's shoulder. She stirred, her head twisting, and murmured gently, though her eyes stayed closed.

He smiled.

So, Gwen was not a morning person.

There was still so much to learn about her…so much to discover. He would never grow bored with this tempestuous wallflower.

'Gwen…' Percy whispered.

That seemed to be enough to draw the drowsy woman from sleep. Gently, Gwen's eyelashes fluttered, and she looked up. For a moment there was stillness, and then a broad smile crept across her face.

'Percy…' she breathed.

'Hello, my love,' said Percy.

It was instinct leading him to speak in such a way. Why not speak words of love to the woman to whom he had given his heart? And he had been offered hers so openly in return.

Difficult though it was to accept that they must now be apart, Percy clenched his jaw and forced himself to say the words he knew must be said—even if they pained him. 'I must go.'

Gwen blinked, and then a sharpness appeared in her pupils and a line appeared between her eyes. 'Go? Now? Why?'

Percy jerked his head towards the window. 'Day breaks, and if I am to leave the Academy without anyone seeing it must be now.'

For a moment it appeared Gwen would disagree, debate the fact, but then a look of sorrowful resignation covered her face.

'I suppose so,' she said, but then a mischievous smile crept across her lips. 'Although if you stayed here I could always make it worth your while.'

Her fingers crept towards him, pulling him closer, and Percy groaned.

What had he unleashed within this woman?

Heavens, if he was not careful, he would make love to her again, and doubtless wake the whole household with her cries of pleasure.

His manhood jerked. It was not the worst idea he'd ever had...

'No—no, Gwen,' Percy said regretfully as he captured her fingers in his and held them tight. 'I really must go.'

Gwen's mischievous smile softened. 'I will miss you.'

'I know,' said Percy heavily, wishing he could remain here for ever, in the safety and sanctuary of her affections. 'I will miss you too.'

He allowed himself one kiss, one dipped moment of connection, and his whole body quivered as his lips touched hers. This was more than love, more than affection. It was an intimacy he could never have conceived of...beautiful, perfect.

It was with great regret that Percy broke the kiss. Gwen

appeared to feel the same, leaning up in an attempt to prolong the connection for as long as possible.

'Gwen...' said Percy quietly.

'Percy...' said Gwen, leaning up for another kiss.

He leaned back. This was important, and it could not
be said in the middle of sleep, nor while affectionate
kisses were addling their minds. He had to make sure she
understood—or there would be consequences, and not
ones he could control.

Percy took a deep breath. 'Gwen, we will need to keep
this...what's between us...between us. Do you understand?'

Perhaps he should explain more clearly, he thought
wryly. It was, after all, very early in the morning, and
Gwen had given him no sign of being particularly awake
yet.

She frowned. 'Keep what's between us, between us?'

Percy swallowed. 'I mean...our lovemaking...the fact
we love each other—'

'I do love you,' said Gwen with a sleepy smile.

Percy's stomach twisted. James's list of conditions for
a wife—to be elegant, refined, distant, wealthy—had always seemed right, naturally. It was James's list. Only now
could Percy see just how cold and isolating a woman like
that would have been.

A woman James would have approved of...

He could not imagine her now. Not with Gwen before
him.

She was everything he wanted: gentle and loving, passionate and wild. So ready to accept his touch, All the
things he had never expected to find in one woman—let
alone one so beautiful.

'Gwen,' Percy said firmly, half to get her attention, half
to focus his own. 'No one can know—do you understand?
It's not the right time. Not yet. This must stay between us.

'Our lovemaking, our declarations of love…they must stay a secret. For the moment.'

Because, Percy thought darkly as he watched the words sink into Gwen's sleepy mind, *he had no idea as yet just how to broach this with his mother.*

The idea of telling her that her son, her only remaining son, had given himself away to a chit of a wallflower with no connections nor refinements…

He would find a way, Percy told himself, and then he would declare his passion and affections for Gwen and they would be married. It would all come right, eventually. They just needed to be patient.

'I suppose that makes sense,' said Gwen quietly, yawning. 'We will need to think about how to tell my mother, and Miss Pike—goodness, and *your* mother, I suppose.'

The knot of tension which had been building in Percy's stomach had not consciously been noticed by him before—not until Gwen spoke those words and the knot started to fade away. She understood.

'Precisely,' he said with a sigh of relief. 'Thank you, Gwen.'

Percy kissed her again, unable to resist the allure of those soft, inviting lips, and groaned as Gwen placed her hands around his neck to pull him closer.

'No—no, Gwen. I must away,' Percy said regretfully.

Gwen sighed as she nestled herself into the pillows. 'I suppose you are right.'

'I am not so sure,' Percy said ruefully as he entwined his fingers with hers. 'The very last thing I wish is to leave you here, but I… I have no choice.'

And that was the truth, Percy thought as he looked at the most beautiful woman he had ever seen. *No choice.* No choice but to love her…no choice but to be devoted.

Even if his mother would never have made this choice.

Even if it was going to be one of the most difficult conversations he had ever had, trying to convince his mother to accept Gwen as her daughter-in-law.

And if she did not? If she refused to give her permission? Refused to accept that Percy was going to invest his marital prospects—the prospects of a duke, no less!—in a woman with no dowry, family or prestige?

What if—heaven forbid—he received the Cut from Society? And his mother, in similar fashion, was cut from her friends, her connections, her very reason for living?

The knot of tension had returned, but Percy could do naught about it. He had no idea how he would solve that problem, and a problem it was.

He swallowed, then kissed Gwen lightly on the nose. 'We'll see each other again soon. Last night...you won my devotion, Gwen.'

'I already had it,' Gwen said sleepily, her eyes closing as she drifted back to sleep.

Percy's heart fluttered painfully before continuing in a regular beat.

He might not have started this with...well, with the best of intentions. When everything within him had told him being near Gwen was both terribly wrong and painfully right. But there was nothing he could do now to prevent the loss of his heart.

He would have her. No matter what happened.

Gwen had almost fallen asleep by the time Percy slipped out of the bed into the cold morning air. It took him but a few moments to put on the footman's outfit, finding the breeches a little short but otherwise sufficient. It was a pain, truly, that his clothes were still damp.

But then, Percy thought, *I did not exactly spend much time last night worrying about drying them.*

He had been far too interested in removing Gwen's clothes than looking to his own.

Percy almost made it to the stall where his mare had been lodged overnight without discovery, but as he opened the door to the stables a young voice shouted after him.

'Hi, there!'

Percy sighed. It had been too much, it appeared, to expect to be able to leave without detection.

Turning on his heel, he saw Tom, the stable boy, approaching him with a frown.

'You're not a footman here,' the boy said in an accusatory tone. 'Who are you? A thief come to steal from the house using your trickery?'

Percy stared. It was incomprehensible that the boy should not recognise him—but then he was dressed very differently from the way he had been in their previous encounters.

Oh, the shame...to be taken not even for a footman but for a thief!

''Tis I, Tom,' Percy said in a low voice.

The stable boy frowned, evidently recognising the voice but unable to place it. 'You? Who *are* you?'

Swallowing heavily, Percy saw there was nothing for it. He would have to reveal himself and hope for Tom's natural deference.

'The Duke of Knaresby,' Percy said softly, as though a lower volume would make it less scandalous. 'I had to— My clothes were ruined. I needed to borrow... Just let me get to my horse!'

Striding past the astonished stable boy, Percy reached for the tack and quickly saddled his horse. Tom appeared to be so utterly astonished he was unable to speak. Only when Percy had mounted the mare, wincing slightly as the footman's breeches stretched painfully, did Tom finally say something.

'But...but why are you dressed like a footman?'

Percy sighed. How on earth was he to explain the series of events which had led him to be dressed like this?

Well, he should probably start at the beginning.

'Sylvia—'

'Say no more, Your Grace,' said Tom hastily, cheeks flushing. 'I quite understand.'

That was remarkably simple, Percy thought as he nudged his horse forward.

'Marvellous,' he said in a low voice. 'And no word to Miss Pike, if you please.'

Tom nodded, and was rewarded with a smile—Percy, of course had no coin to give him. Everything was still in his waistcoat, tucked under his arm. He would have to remember on his next visit.

The ride back to London was unpleasant, to say the least. Percy made a variety of discoveries while on his horse in the freezing cold morning air. Firstly, he knew that he would never criticise his tailor again, for he now knew the value of well-fitting clothes. Secondly, footmen had rather a difficult lot, being forced to wear these ridiculous clothes. And thirdly, he could manage to trot down the streets of London to his home and pass the reins to his astonished stable master so early almost no one would be up.

His good fortune, however, did not last. Percy ought to have expected something to go wrong, but his confidence peaked as he slipped into his London townhouse by the back door, closed it as quietly as he could manage, and leaned, exhausted, against the wall.

Well, he was home.

In less than half an hour he could be in a hot bath, left to think only of his delightfully disreputable encounter with Gwen Knox. And he had managed it all without his mother—

'Percival William Devereux—what are you wearing?'

Percy straightened hastily, pulling the ill-fitting jacket down, and smiled weakly at his mother, who was striding down the corridor towards him.

Ah. Now there was a morning person—more was the pity. It would be difficult to explain this away to her as easily as to Tom, the stable boy.

'Good morning, Mother,' Percy said brightly, as though cheerfulness might prevent his mother from seeing the state he was in. 'It is very early, is it not?'

'You are wearing the clothes of a servant, Percy—and not a servant of this house,' said Lady Devereux severely, stopping before him and frowning. 'Dear me, this is a livery I admit I do not recognise. What interesting piping on the sleeves.'

Percy's smile froze on his face. 'Ah. Yes, well, the thing is—'

'Dear Lord, is that the livery of the Wallflower Academy?' The frown on his mother's face deepened as Percy's stomach twisted. 'Percival William Devereux—what on earth were you doing there? I thought you were attending the Kenceysham ball last night?'

'Well…' said Percy awkwardly. 'The thing is—'

'And returning in a servant's outfit!' Lady Devereux shook her head. 'Percy, what am I to do with you? You spend far too much time at that place. If I have said it before, I have said it a thousand times!'

'You have indeed,' said Percy heavily.

'And with all this threat of scandal in the newspapers, your brother's death still unexplained, I would have thought you would take your responsibilities as the new Duke of Knaresby more seriously!'

'I am,' said Percy urgently. Did she think he did not care? 'Which reminds me… I thought I would go to the inn where James was killed—the Golden Hind, I think it was called—and ask—'

'No,' said his mother firmly. 'No. I forbid it.'

Frustration stirred in his chest. Did she not wish to know more? Questions about his brother's last moments had always whirled through his mind. 'I have never understood why you have no wish to know—'

'Is this what you call taking your requirement to marry well *seriously*? Wearing the clothes of a servant? Percy, really!'

Blast. It was too much to hope that his mother would understand the hilarious circumstances in which the wearing of the outfit had occurred.

Explaining about Gwen, he thought darkly, *was not a good idea—not now.*

He would shelve that for another time.

'You see, the thing was,' he said, with what he hoped was a light-hearted smile, 'one of the wallflowers—a Miss Sylvia Bryant—played a trick involving—'

'I do not want to hear it,' his mother said sharply. 'I hardly need further proof that you should not be visiting the Academy—if one could even call it that. You are better than that, Percy. Always were. And especially now. You have your title to think of!'

Percy swallowed, but said nothing. He well knew his mother's opinion, and could only guess the response he would receive if he revealed that he had fallen for one of the Academy's occupants.

Fallen and fallen hard.

Love is a powerful force, Percy thought. *Oh, yes, Gwen— I love you. I did not know it until it was too late to do any-*

thing about it, and even then…even then I would not have wanted to. I love you, Gwen.

Something stirred within his heart—something bold, brash—and he determined to make a clean breast of it to his mother. He loved Gwen. That was not going to change. And the sooner his mother could start reconciling herself to that truth, the better.

'Mother,' Percy said firmly. 'I must tell you. I have decided I will marry—'

'Yes, yes, I know. And all we have to do is find the right lady,' said Lady Devereux, waving a hand. 'That is precisely why you need to hurry.'

Percy smiled. 'Well, actually, there is no need to hurry. I have already found—'

'When I say you need to hurry, I say it advisedly,' said his mother sharply. 'Go now, upstairs, and get changed. They'll be here in less than an hour, and I cannot have you wandering around looking like a servant.'

Percy blinked. 'Who will be here in an hour?'

'*Now,* Percy!'

Kissing his mother on the cheek, he nodded. Well, what else was there to do? Arguing with his mother was rather like shouting at a mountain: one might feel better afterwards, but the mountain would be unchanged.

A bath, however, would be welcome.

Sinking into its almost scalding embrace, Percy sighed heavily and leaned back. It was strange to think how far he had come in only the last few hours. This time yesterday he'd had no thought of revealing his feelings to Gwen.

In truth, he'd had no idea how deeply they went until he had seen her watching him undress.

There is such an attraction, he mused, *in seeing attraction in another.*

Now he had shared his affections, and Gwen hers, and

they had shared in delightful lovemaking, all he had to do was find the right time to speak to his mother.

With guests arriving in less than an hour, now was certainly not the right time…

After a quick shave from his valet, and the relief of getting dressed in his own clothes, Percy felt a little more human again. He descended the stairs hastily as he looked at his pocket watch. Almost eleven o'clock—an early visit, indeed. But then his mother had never seen the point in wasting the day away.

'Well, Mother,' Percy said as he entered the morning room. 'I hope you will find this outfit more accept…'

Eyes wide, he stared at the scene before him and wondered whether he had entered the wrong room—the wrong house. This appeared to be far more like a scene from the Wallflower Academy than his own home.

His mother was seated in an armchair by a small table, where a tea tray had been laid, and was smiling broadly. Opposite her, standing in a line, were three young ladies, all dressed in their finest gowns. One had even put a flower in her hair. They were staring as though they had been waiting for hours. One was flushed. Another fluttered her eyelashes coquettishly.

'Ah, there you are, Knaresby,' said Lady Devereux smartly, using his title name as they were in company. 'See—I have three very eligible young ladies for your viewing.'

Percy opened his mouth, but no words came out. How could he speak? What could he say to such nonsense? To such a way of shoving him towards an appropriate marriage?

What on earth was his mother doing, speaking about these ladies as though they were not here?

'Now, the Honourable Miss Maynard—that's the one on

the left—she comes from a very good family, with suffi- cient dowry but nothing too impressive,' began his mother, pointing at the first young lady.

Percy saw Miss Maynard's cheeks flush as his mother spoke of her so callously.

'Whereas Lady Rose has a very impressive dowry, but rather unimpressive brothers,' continued Lady Devereux, with a knowing look at her son. 'If you chose her, you would have to do something about their behaviour, I de- clare. For one of them would soon bring us down in Soci- ety if left unchecked. And Miss Middlesborough—'

'Mother!' Percy said, mortified, as he shut the door be- hind him and strode towards the seated women. 'Really!'

This was awful—worse than the way the Wallflower Academy treated its inhabitants. Why, what was she think- ing, having them standing there, listening to her nonsense, lining them up as though at a cattle market!

'Oh, you care too much,' said his mother, tapping him lightly on the shoulder. 'These young ladies knew what to expect when they received my invitation—did you not, ladies?'

'Yes, m'lady,' came the murmured replies.

Percy's stomach clenched. 'Nonetheless—'

'Nonetheless, nothing,' said his mother sharply, her eyes affixed on her son. 'Mark my words, Percy—Knaresby. When a duke marries, he must consider all these things. He marries not for himself but for the betterment of the fam- ily and the title. There is a great weight of responsibility upon him. 'Tis not as though you will have a love match. We seek a marriage to benefit both parties.'

Percy opened his mouth, but his typically eloquent tongue failed him. How could he speak when his mind was clouded not with reasonable arguments against the

nonsense before him, but instead on how each of these ladies was nothing compared to Gwen?

He found them wanting, despite their superior breeding
and their dowries. He felt nothing for them. There was no
comparison to Gwen.

'And besides,' his mother said, her gaze still fierce, 'it
is what your father would have wanted. Would have *expected.*'

Percy closed his mouth as his heart sank. He would?

In his vague recollections of his father he had never
spoken to him of such things. Why would he? Percy had
been nothing but a child when his father had died.

'What would James have wanted?' he blurted out.

His mother's eyebrows rose. 'James? What on earth
does your brother have to do with this?'

Percy hesitated. He knew he could never express to her
the tumultuous emotions turbulent in his heart. How was
he ever to explain them to his mother, who surely would
never accept a mere wallflower?

Chapter Fifteen

'We are going out for afternoon tea,' Miss Pike announced grandly, as though she had just given the wallflowers a precious gift as they sat around the luncheon table. 'With members of the aristocracy.'

Sylvia's eyes widened.

Miss Pike nodded approvingly. 'Indeed, you may look impressed, Miss Bryant,' she said grandly. 'I have worked especially hard for this afternoon tea to be a perfect opportunity for you ladies to make an impression on a gentleman with a title—take a leaf, perhaps, out of Miss Knox's book.'

Gwen flushed as the owner of the Wallflower Academy nodded impressively in her direction. Her hands twisted in her lap, her plate of cured ham and potatoes abandoned.

How could she eat? How could she act as though everything was normal, as though her life was perfectly ordinary, when she knew it was not?

Worse, the one thing Miss Pike was apt to praise her for—attracting the attentions of a duke—made her heart so unsure of the future?

The remembrance of Percy's heated touches, his clever fingers, crowded Gwen's mind and made it impossible for her to follow the conversation now circling around the table.

'Gentlemen of note do not all need to have titles, surely?' Sylvia was saying.

Rilla laughed. 'Are you honestly telling me you would decline the advances of a gentleman merely because he had a title?'

'That is not what I am saying at all…'

Titles, Gwen thought wryly. True, when she had been a little younger, a little more foolish, she had daydreamed about being taken away by a gentleman with more riches and titles than he knew what to do with.

Until that fateful night.

Until the whole of her world had fallen around her because of what she had done.

Until her mother had discovered her.

Since then, it had been easiest to keep her head down and be silent. A wallflower, indeed, even if it was merely because she was afraid of being found out.

But Percy was that imagined perfect gentleman, was he not? Wealthy, with a title, but kind, too. With something deeper in him she had never discovered in any other man.

Of course they would not wish to announce their engagement before he had spoken with his mother—so did his absence mean Percy's mother had taken against her? It had, after all, been almost a week.

Seven days without him. Without a word. After giving herself to him so willingly…

Perhaps she had been foolish to consider herself worthy of him, to think their union would not be endangered by the truth of the past. But she loved him. Oh, how she loved him. And a very real pain twisted in her stomach at the idea of never seeing him again.

From the moment Gwen had seen Percy—admittedly

she had been on the gravel of the drive—she had been unable to resist him. Resist his presence. Resist the growing attraction budding inside her...

Even when he had acted so haughtily against any union between them at the start.

And after giving herself to Percy it was a cruel separation.

'Many members of the aristocracy—at least ten—have confirmed their attendance at tea, and there are more I hope will attend,' Miss Pike was saying. 'We will enter the carriages half an hour after luncheon.'

Something stirred in Gwen's memory.

'We'll see each other again soon.'

Was this what he had meant? Gwen's heart fluttered at the hopeful thought which now invaded her mind. Had he been thinking of this afternoon tea?

A smile graced Gwen's lips, if only for a moment.

Oh, if only he would be in attendance today.

She had not paid attention to the place where they were going, only taking in the fact that it was a lady's home in London. A chance, Miss Pike had said, to practise their manners.

And if Percy was there...

They would have the opportunity to talk, to laugh. Perhaps he would move his fingers across hers. A sense of anticipation rushed through her. Perhaps, if they were very careful, they would be able to slip away together.

Gwen swallowed the scandalous thought, but now it had occurred there was no way to ignore it.

Picking up her knife and fork in the hope that the other wallflowers and Miss Pike would not notice anything amiss, Gwen lost herself for a few minutes in delightful imaginings of Percy pulling her aside while no one was looking, the two of them running up the stairs hand in hand, slipping into a bedchamber and making love, hastily and passionately, trying desperately to muffle their moans of joy...

And then, Gwen thought wistfully, *they would talk— properly talk.*

Talk of when their wedding would be, and where they would live, and how happy they would be. For they would be happy, wouldn't they? It would be glorious to be together for the rest of their lives.

A prickle of guilt interrupted these pleasant thoughts.

As long as the truth of her past could remain hidden.

That was vital, of course—but what was the point in waiting? They had given themselves to each other, Gwen thought with a smile. What was left but their marriage?

'Gwendoline Knox!'

Gwen started. 'What?'

Miss Pike was shaking her head. 'You really are lost in the clouds at the moment, aren't you? I asked how was your visit with your mother and your...gentleman friend? You never did tell me, but I have not forgotten.'

Gwen swallowed. So far she had been able to relate the details of her excursion without lying. Only Rilla knew the truth of her intentions, and even she did not know the awkward reality of her journey.

'It was without incident,' Gwen said quietly, looking to the expectant face of Miss Pike, who now nodded approvingly.

'That is what I like to hear. Take notice, ladies! "Without incident" is a great accomplishment for any wallflower. Next, I would appreciate a little announcement, Miss Knox...you know the sort I mean. After all, you know whose home we are visiting today...'

Cringing inwardly at this pointed reference to a wallflower's inability to navigate social situations without embarrassing herself, and still utterly at a loss as to where they were going, Gwen held her tongue rather than add to the Pike's irritation.

Thirty minutes did not feel adequate to prepare herself for returning once more to London—to the place where she had danced with Percy, had been kissed by him for the first time.

But this would be different, wouldn't it?

Gwen tried to convince herself of that as she and the other wallflowers gathered outside the Academy, taking turns to step into the carriages waiting to take them to Town.

As it happened, the first carriage was full, so she stepped towards the second, where Rilla stood waiting.

'There you are, Gwen,' she said.

'How did you know?'

Rilla snorted. 'You think I cannot hear someone coming? I often don't know who they are until they speak, but Miss Pike said you'd be in my carriage. Here, help me up.'

It was a relief to be settled in the carriage with Rilla and no questioning Miss Pike or Sylvia, Gwen thought ruefully.

With a sudden jerk, the carriage moved forward.

'Well, then—are you ready to talk?' asked Rilla.

Gwen swallowed. 'I don't know what you mean...'

Rilla snorted. 'Wallflowers usually hide in their bedchambers before this sort of thing, but I think you need someone to talk to. Something's changed, hasn't it?'

Gwen flushed at the very idea of someone as innocent as Rilla knowing that she had lost her own innocence. Why, it was wild indeed just to have done it—but for it to be *known*!

'Look,' said Rilla quietly as the carriage rattled on, 'I am blind. And that does not mean I become a savant in the other senses—that is just a story told to children. But

I do have other senses, and, Gwen, I smelt the Duke's cigars on you the day after he was soaked by Sylvia's jest. I am not mistaken, am I?'

It had been delicately done, but that did not mean Gwen was not mortified. Rilla had smelt Percy's cigars on her... Well, of course she had—he had been pressed up against her! Even now she could remember his heady scent.

'And you did not come downstairs to the card party after you showed the Duke upstairs,' Rilla continued in a low voice—so low that Gwen could only just hear her. 'The following morning you said you'd had a headache, and no one questioned you, but...'

Her voice trailed away delicately, and Gwen's heart thumped so painfully it echoed in her ears.

'You...you won't tell anyone?' she managed. 'Please, Rilla—'

'I will not betray you, I promise—'tis not my secret to tell,' said the blind woman with a smile. 'And I do not believe anyone else has noticed. At least, they have said nothing to me, and I am sure if Sylvia even suspected it would be all she could speak of.'

Gwen laughed weakly. Yes, that was a fair comment. If Sylvia had any inkling that the newest arrival at the Wallflower Academy was now no longer an innocent it would be her primary—perhaps only—topic of conversation.

Streets were starting to appear through the carriage windows, and the clouds of the wintry day were heavy in the sky.

'The question is, what are you going to do about it?'

'Do about it?' repeated Gwen. The idea of *her* doing anything, when Percy was a duke... 'I... I don't know.'

What was a wallflower—a murderess wallflower, no less—supposed to do after such an encounter? When they had shared their mutual love not only in words but in ecstasy?

The carriage was drawing to a stop. They were here, and that meant she might only be a few minutes away from seeing—

'Wallflowers!'

Gwen winced as Miss Pike's cry echoed up the street. Surely it was bad enough that they had been brought here under the inauspicious description of a wallflower. Did Miss Pike really have to shout out such a moniker right in front of the row of impressive townhouses they had halted by?

'Well, I suppose it's time…' murmured Rilla.

The carriage door was opened by the driver, and Gwen helped Rilla out. The other wallflowers had collected by the front door, nervously standing close to each other. She could see the fear on their faces.

Another day…another set of forced encounters with eligible gentlemen.

Another expectation of gaining a proposal.

Gwen's heart pounded painfully in her chest.

Another hope of seeing Percy.

'Here we go again,' said Sylvia with a dry laugh, stepping over to them. 'Will we be seeing your duke, Gwen?'

'He is not my duke,' Gwen said, with the strange sensation that she had said that phrase too many times.

It was not as though she did not want him to be her duke.

She did. Desperately.

But it was all so complicated, and she'd had no word from Percy as to what they would do next.

Gwen squared her shoulders. 'Let us see what type of gentlemen Miss Pike has managed to accumulate for us.'

Sylvia laughed as Miss Pike led the wallflowers towards the door and rang the bell. 'If there *are* any gentlemen.'

Rilla frowned. 'What do you mean?'

'Well, did you notice Miss Pike used her words very carefully?' Sylvia said as they walked forward, entering an impressive hall. A chandelier tinkled above them as the door was shut. '"Aristocracy", not gentlemen. We could be about to attend a gathering of ladies, not men.'

It appeared Sylvia's suspicions were well founded.

When they were ushered into a drawing room there were elegant piles of cakes and sweets on platters around the room, along with steaming teapots and many cups.

There was also a plethora of ladies.

'Hmm…' said Sylvia knowingly, glancing at Rilla and Gwen.

Gwen's shoulders slumped. From what she could see there were a number of older women seated around the room, their conversation halting, clearly talking about the wallflowers as they entered.

But no gentlemen.

More importantly, no Percy.

He was nowhere to be seen and Gwen's heart sank.

Well, she would merely have to enjoy this opportunity to escape the Academy—and the room where they stood was certainly elegant and refined. The latest in printed paper adorned the walls—a delicate blue with a flower motif. A console table made of marble hosted several teapots, cups and saucers, and the rug by the fire looked to be antique, from what Gwen could make out.

Yes, here were all the trappings of respectability and wealth.

So, whose home were they in?

'There's our hostess,' Miss Pike hissed, her cheeks slightly flushed and her hands waving in the general direction of at least four finely dressed ladies. 'Gwen will introduce you, I am sure. Won't you, Gwen? Go and thank her, ladies, for she is doing you an eminent service by—No, Sylvia, absolutely not!'

Miss Pike strode off to pull Sylvia away from the window, where she was waving at the passers-by, before clarifying who precisely it was who had invited them. Gwen was mystified. Why on earth would *she* be able to introduce their hostess to the wallflowers? She knew no one in London.

Besides, every moment was pointless if Percy was not in it with her.

Would this feeling ever pass? she wondered as she took up a position by another of the large windows overlooking the bustling street. Or would it fade over time as they became more accustomed to each other?

As we live happily together, Gwen thought with a brief smile, *how will that happiness change?*

The door opened and she turned eagerly towards it— but a gentleman she did not recognise, with large teeth and a haughty laugh, entered. After two successive entrances by gentlemen, she was still disappointed.

It appeared the Duke of Knaresby would not be attending this particular gathering.

It was only when she had reconciled herself to the fact that he would not be attending, and she would simply have to learn to be patient, that Gwen was finally rewarded.

'Ah, Knaresby!' The large-toothed gentleman strode forward to clap Percy's shoulder as he came in and Gwen's heart leapt. 'Never expected to receive an invitation from your mother. What an honour!'

Curiosity overcome her shyness, and Gwen peered across the room at the woman who would soon be her mother-in-law.

Impressive. That was the only word Gwen could think of when looking at the woman who stood beside Percy wearing a conceited expression. She was dressed in the most fabulous gown, with more ruffles and delicate embroidery than Gwen had ever seen on a single skirt. There was a string of pearls around her neck, and she looked around the room as if she was rather displeased.

'Yes, I should think it *is* an honour,' said Lady Devereux imperiously. 'But then I am always doing what I can for the unfortunate. Inviting these poor wallflowers to Mayfair House is nothing at all. Percy, bring me some tea.'

No one appeared astonished at the lady of the house ordering her son about, rather than calling a footman. Perhaps that was just how it was with nobility.

Delight tempered with astonishment curled at the edges of Gwen's heart as she watched the man she loved step across the room to pour his mother some tea.

Mayfair House…this was Lady Devereux's home? Oh, now there could be no mistaking it. This tea party was a kindness for her, surely! Percy must have told her, quietly, and the two of them had cooked up this excuse to meet her.

Gwen's stomach lurched at the very idea.

He was here.

With his mother, admittedly, which Gwen had not foreseen.

Miss Pike had surely not mentioned it was Lady Devereux who had invited them for afternoon tea—but that was no matter…not now.

It would certainly be a discomforting sort of encounter, this first time—and in public too. And she had not prepared herself emotionally for meeting the mother of the man she loved—but still… It was a start.

After all, Percy had had ample time to acquaint his mother with the truth of their affection.

Although, Gwen thought hastily, *not perhaps the whole truth.*

Just enough for Lady Devereux to know she would soon be acquiring a daughter-in-law.

And that meant eventually Percy would have to meet her own mother.

The thought caused a shudder to rush through Gwen, which she forced aside. She would not enjoy that.

Perhaps Percy was uncomfortable—perhaps that explained why he had not looked over at her, or taken the chance to introduce them immediately.

Gwen took a deep breath, smoothed her skirts, and tried to ready herself for what was to come.

Her first meeting with Lady Devereux.

All she could hope was that it would go well.

It was about as bad as Percy could imagine—and he had imagined some rather awful scenarios. But this was the worst, and it was all his doing. His dishonesty. His idiocy.

He had not even mentioned Gwen by name to his mother, nor referred to her in any way.

This whole afternoon was a mistake—and he had been unable to convince his mother to call it off when she had first revealed what she had done not an hour ago.

'But you cannot! Mother, you must send a messenger to the Wallflower Academy immediately and rescind the invitation,' Percy had argued vehemently.

His mother had only raised an eyebrow. 'What a thing to say, my boy. Rescind my invitation? I have never done such a thing in my life and see no reason to start now.'

Now Percy swallowed, his heart thumping, as he saw the wallflowers in his mother's drawing room. This was a mistake—and now there was no opportunity to stop Gwen as she meandered her way towards them.

If Gwen was about to do what he thought she was—introduce herself to his mother, on the assumption that the introduction would be welcome—everything would fall apart.

Tension crept across his neck, and Percy's heart pounded painfully in his chest, but nothing could stir him to move. His mother sat on the sofa beside Lady Windsor, and just as Gwen reached them Percy spoke, words he could not hold back spilling out of his mouth.

'Are you quite comfortable, Mother?'

Lady Devereux looked up. 'Comfortable? Well, as comfortable as I could hope to be, I suppose, surrounded by such people.'

The tension around his neck increased. Percy could almost feel the indignation rising in Gwen, but could neither acknowledge her nor comfort her.

This had to go well—but how could it be anything but a disaster?

'Indeed, I reconsidered whether this was something I wished to do. After all, the parks in London are teeming with the very best of people,' Lady Devereux continued, even as Percy winced at her disdain for those around her. 'But then, you are a duke now, and must do your best for the unfortunate.'

Out of the corner of his eye Percy saw Sylvia bristle at those words. He stepped to the right, to prevent his mother from seeing the ire she was creating in the wallflowers of the Academy, but unfortunately that took him further away from Gwen. From the one person in the room who could give him any sense of peace. If only they could be alone…

'All these unwanted daughters,' his mother said loudly, taking a sip of tea.

'Mother,' said Percy hastily, trying not to look at Gwen. 'Really!'

'Do not attempt to say they are otherwise, Knaresby. It does you no benefit to pretend they are other than what they are,' said his mother impressively. She nudged her companion on the sofa. 'Some poor gentlemen will eventually be trapped by them, I suppose…'

If only the ground would swallow him up here and now, thought Percy desperately, preferably taking Gwen with him—or, better, if only it would swallow up his mother!

The room was starting to quieten as people listened to the harsh words his mother was saying, and Percy tried to laugh loudly as a way to distract them. That was the trouble with hosting an afternoon tea; people were wont to actually pay heed to your words.

If she could just stop there, he thought frantically, glancing at Gwen and seeing the rising anger he knew dwelled within her. *If his mother could just hold her impertinent opinions—*

'What did you say, Your Ladyship?' asked Miss Sylvia Bryant sweetly, stepping around Percy despite his best efforts to get in her way. 'I am sorry, Your Ladyship, did you say we are here to entrap gentlemen? We came on *your* invitation.'

Now everyone in the room was listening. Percy felt the pressure of their gazes, and the discomfort of his stomach stirred as he tried not to notice the whispers of the gentlemen.

This was precisely what he had not wished for.

'I am sure that is not what you meant, Mother, is it?' Percy said pointedly, conscious that his mother had not replied. 'There are many ladies of quality here, and—'

Percy was not sure how, but his mother managed to cut him off with a sniff.

'Well,' she said coldly. 'I am not so sure, my dear. This is an occasion for charity, not matchmaking. I doubt very much that a wallflower could entrap a duke, even if she wished to. A wallflower is not an appropriate wife for a duke, and I should not have to be the one to tell you that.'

A movement just out of the corner of his eye made Percy turn and he saw that Gwen had taken a step back, as though retreat was the only option when facing such an onslaught.

Perhaps she's right, Percy thought wildly. Perhaps he and Gwen should just leave, abandon his mother to her terrible opinions and—and run away together!

But he did not move. Despite knowing what his mother had said was rude, arrogant and hurtful, he said nothing. James would have agreed with his mother, likely as not, and the idea of forming a contrary opinion to his brother was painful in a way Percy had not expected.

Lips clamped shut, mouth dry, heart pounding, he found he could not contradict his mother in public. Not in her own home. Could not bring shame upon her when all she had done ever since he had ascended to his title was attempt to calm the rumours about his brother.

'Wallflowers,' Lady Devereux said then, 'can be very pretty things—and a few are, I see. But they are decoration, Knaresby. One plants wallflowers for a season, and then one grows tired of them and they are replaced. They are not what one has a garden *for*. They are not roses.'

Percy's pulse was ringing in his ears, and his gaze was pulled inexorably to the one person he did not wish to hear such things: Gwen.

She was pale—far paler than he had ever seen her. Her eyes were wide, flickering between him and his mother as though she was expecting him to do something.

Yes, do something, Percy's mind craved, and yet he stood motionless.

Perhaps this was his punishment. If he had just been brave enough to speak to his mother before the wallflowers had arrived, at any point in the last few days, he would not be suffering the agony of bringing Gwen this hurt.

But he had not spoken to her. Years of obedience... years of following James and never having to make a stand against his mother... Only now did he realise what that had bred into him.

Inaction.

Well, no longer.

Percy swallowed. No. He would not allow it. 'Mother, I must say—'

'Lady Devereux, these cakes are delicious,' Miss Pike said hastily, rushing over to their hostess, cheeks crimson. 'Your cook must tell mine precisely how the delicate sponge is able to—'

Percy could wait no longer. His mother's attention was diverted, if only for a moment, and this was his best and perhaps only chance to speak to Gwen. He took her hand, pulled her away. Ignoring Sylvia's gasp and questioning look, he opened the nearest door, stepped through it, and took Gwen with him.

It was the dining room.

Percy shut the door heavily and did what he had wanted to do the moment he had seen Gwen by the window. Cupping her face with his hands, he kissed her desperately, as though everything could be wiped away as long as they were together. As long as their love was at the centre.

But the kiss did not last long.

Gwen pushed him away violently, cheeks now scarlet. 'How can you kiss me?' Gwen hissed, even as murmurs of the conversation in the next room flowed under the door. 'How can you kiss me after permitting your mother to... to speak about me like that?'

Percy shrugged helplessly, his hand rubbing absentmindedly at where she had shoved him. Quite forcefully, as it happened.

Respect, honour, love, affection... They were at war within him. He could not respect and honour his mother while also loving Gwen.

She waited for him to say something, a quizzical eyebrow raised, and then her expression changed. Her fury hardened into something more akin to coldness.

'I am wanted back in the drawing room, I am sure,' she said icily as she strode past.

'You are wanted here!' Percy said desperately.

How could he make her see how impossible this was? Make her understand that it was difficult, and would take time. Time he knew he didn't deserve, but so very desperately hoped she would give him.

Gwen examined his face for a moment, then shook her head. 'I am not so sure. After all the things you said...after what we shared... I am wanted, you say? I am accustomed to being the least likely to win your true affections, Percy. Be sure, next time I see you. Be sure of what you want. I would hate for that meeting to be our last.'

The door snapped shut.

Percy leaned against the wall, his chest tight, as uninvited emotions swirled within him. This didn't feel like winning the heart of his future wife...

Chapter Sixteen

'*Wallflowers can be very pretty things, and a few are, I see. But they are decoration, Knaresby. One plants wallflowers for a season, and then one grows tired of them and they are replaced. They are not what one has a garden for. They are not roses.*'

No matter what she did, Gwen could not prevent Lady Devereux's cruel words ringing in her ears.

Over and over again, even as the days slipped by, the words would not leave her alone. They were relentless, appearing in her dreams, preventing her from rest and paining her heart as she saw the completely insurmountable pressure that was on their love.

She cleared her throat, as though that would clear the painful remembrances from her mind, but it was no use. They plagued her.

It was as if the library echoed with the sound, then the book-lined walls absorbed the noise and left Gwen once again in silence.

Silence and solitude. That was what she craved.

Ever since the afternoon tea party Gwen had attracted the great ire of Miss Pike—for her impertinence and her stubbornness.

'You have refused to attend even one of my evening parties for five days now!' Miss Pike had snapped at dinner the evening before. 'Really! It is most unbecoming of you to be so rebellious, Miss Knox. I never would have expected this from a wallflower! I should write to your mother!'

Gwen had clenched her jaw, tightened her grip on her fork, but said nothing.

What could she say?

That she had never been a wallflower to begin with, but had been sent here because her mother knew her to be a murderess?

That she had no intention of ever attending another of the Pike's foolish events, for if there was even one single chance she could see Percy again...

Gwen snapped shut the book in her hands. She was barely taking in a word anyway—and besides, the library had been stocked with severely dull books that Miss Pike evidently thought wallflowers should be interested in.

There was nothing more Gwen needed to learn about how lace was made in the French style, or the way roses needed to be arranged, and everything else was dull, dull, dull.

Standing and meandering down the shelves, Gwen gently brushed the spines of the books with her fingertips. There must be *something* interesting in this library that would capture her attention for at least half an hour. Distract her from the thoughts that were swiftly overpowering her.

Gwen swallowed. It was not enough, it appeared, that Percy's mother had spoken so harshly—words that could have come from her own mother's mouth...a feat remarkable in itself. No. The encounter had also reinforced all her fears about Percy and their love for each other—a love fragmented as soon as it had formed. He wanted her, yes. But not for marriage. For a tup.

She would not see him again.

Gwen knew that deep within herself, and although it pained her to be away from him it was surely a lesser agony than what she would suffer if she was in his presence again.

Whatever they had, it could not be love. Lust, perhaps. Desire, certainly. But nothing that could last, or surmount the growing pressures of parents and prestige. Her past would not permit it.

Gwen sat heavily in an armchair by the bay window and looked listlessly at the gardens. Winter had arrived with a vengeance, and the trees were now almost bare. The wind rattled them, shaking the last few leaves which had managed to cling on.

Her parents had never been particularly demonstrative in their affection for each other. She had hoped, foolishly, for a match of happiness. That would bring her something...*more*.

'This is the library, isn't it?'

Rilla was standing in the doorway, the cane she used to feel her way around the corridors when alone in her right hand.

'It is,' said Gwen with a wry smile.

Even when she wanted to be alone it was impossible. Discovered by a blind woman—who would have thought it?

'Ah, there you are, Gwen,' said Rilla with a laugh as she stepped into the library. 'Any possibility of helping me to the sofa?'

Gwen rose. 'Of course.'

When Rilla was seated, she patted the space beside her. 'Come, join me.'

Gwen hesitated, not immediately accepting the invitation. It was solitude she sought, not company—rather ironic, now she came to think about it, as she would likely be spending the rest of her life alone.

Still, it would be rude not to join Rilla.

Gwen sat slowly on the sofa and folded her hands in her lap. She knew sometimes Rilla merely wished to have the sense of someone's presence around her. It did not necessarily mean she wished to talk about anything, let alone—

'Your duke is by the front door, you know,' Rilla said conversationally.

Gwen sighed heavily, her shoulders slumping as she fell back into the sofa. 'He is not my duke.'

'So you keep saying,' said Rilla. 'I am astonished that you keep protesting, you know. No one believes you.'

Gwen took advantage of the woman's blindness to glare at her.

'Don't give me that look.'

It was impossible not to splutter at Rilla's retort. 'How did you—?'

'You think I need to see to know precisely how you will react?' Rilla laughed. 'I'm blind, not mute. You are, if you will forgive me for saying so, Gwen, a rather predictable character. Now you're going to tell me that you do not want to see him.'

'But I don't want to—'

'Protesting again?' cut in Rilla with a smile.

Gwen frowned, a growing knot of irritation twisting her stomach. 'So if I say I do not want to see him, and that he is not my duke, that merely means I do want to see him because he is?'

Her companion smiled. 'I know… It is rather a contradiction in terms.'

Gwen had never considered the matter much but, if asked, she would have said it would be easier to lie to a blind person than someone with sight. So many clues in one's body language, one's face, would be missed. It did not appear that mattered to Rilla.

'I truly have no wish to see the Duke of Knaresby,' she said finally, as aloofly as she could.

'I do not need to see to know you are lying.'

'You heard what his mother said!' Gwen could not help her outburst, and they were alone in the library. 'You heard her! All that talk about wallflowers trapping men, and being useless, a-and—'

'And a lot of other things we wallflowers have heard our entire lives,' Rilla completed.

'You heard what Lady Devereux said,' Gwen repeated, her heart contracting painfully at the memory.

Rilla was quiet for a moment. 'Yes. But I did not hear her son say it.'

Gwen stared. Although Percy had never said anything of the kind, his silence had cut deeper than any blade.

'He has almost knocked down the front door, you know,' Rilla said quietly. 'The footman says he demands to speak to you. The Pike is furious that you won't see him.'

Gwen almost smiled. Oh, if only that passion, that desire, could have come from *Mister* Percy Devereux—the same man, but without all the challenges that came with a title, without a reputation to maintain, a dead brother to honour, a mother to please. Just a man who could love her. A man without the need to protect his nobility.

'He has brought you a letter. I have it here.'

Startled, Gwen looked around. 'What does it say? I mean—' She had to laugh. 'I do apologise, Rilla.'

But her friend merely smiled. 'Oh, it does not matter—but I too am intrigued by the contents. Will you do me the honour of reading it?'

Gwen tried not to think about what the letter might contain as she took the small envelope from Rilla. It was sealed with a wax dollop formed into the shape of a very elegant K intertwined with a D.

Knaresby. Devereux.

Gwen swallowed. It was disgraceful, receiving a letter from a gentleman to whom one was not formally engaged— but then, their…entanglement, for want of a better word, was far more intimate than many engagements.

It could not be wrong, could it, to receive and read such a letter?

'I don't hear any opening of a letter.'

Gwen sighed and shook her head. 'You are a menace, you know.'

'I know,' said Rilla cheerfully. 'Perennially underesti-mated—that's me.'

When Gwen had pulled apart the seal and removed the letter from the envelope her first emotion was disappoint-ment. The letter was short—a scrawl, really—clearly writ-ten in haste and with terrible penmanship.

> *Gwen—*
>
> > *You must let me explain.*
> >
> > *Let me apologise.*
> >
> > *I know not how to convince you that nothing my mother said was…*
> >
> > *I am still navigating my responsibilities as a duke, and the expectations placed upon me, but one thing I do know, and that is I have always been forbidden from contradicting either of my parents in public. It is a hard habit to break.*
> >
> > *But I am not a child now, I am a man, and I should have defended you. If I could take back her words—*
> >
> > *Perhaps that would not be enough.*
> >
> > *Meet with me, and I will show you just how de-voted I am,*
>
> *Your humble servant,*
> *Percy*

Gwen's throat constricted.

How could she believe a single thing he had written? How could she countenance the idea of meeting with a gentleman who gave her so little respect?

No, Percy had been pained by her parting words when he had written this, but that did not mean he could make any change within his circumstances to make this...this love...this marriage...a possibility.

Pain seared Gwen's heart, but she knew she could do nothing about it. She had given her heart, entirely, to a gentleman who could not keep it.

Percy was a duke.

She was a false wallflower with a secret in her past that would risk not only her reputation in Society but his own. The wife he needed was one with wealth and connections, and she had none.

Worse, her secret...what she had done that fateful night...it was too much. She would ruin not only Percy, but the Knaresby name. There were too many obstacles. Too many walls to breach if they even attempted to seriously consider a future together.

Something strange tugged at her memory and Gwen glanced at the letter again. Although Percy had only written a short amount, almost all of it was taken up with his mother. There was no declaration of love, no formal offer of marriage, no commitment of any kind.

Worse, his request to see her was surely only an attempt to seduce her once again!

Matrimony was a topic never mentioned by either of them, Gwen thought, and wondered, her heart pattering painfully, that she had never noticed before.

How had she permitted herself to be so undone, so vulnerable—giving away her innocence, the most precious thing she could bring into a marriage—without any sort of promise?

Yes, he had spoken of love, Gwen thought wildly, and of wanting, of desire…but not anything more tangible.

She was a fool. A fool easily taken in by a handsome face and a dream of marriage to a man so delicious as the Duke.

'Miss Gwendoline Knox!'

Gwen rose hurriedly from the sofa, heart racing, to see an irate Miss Pike glaring from the doorway.

'Miss Pike…?' she ventured.

What could she have possibly done this time?

'There is a duke at my front door,' said Miss Pike, her eyebrows raised.

Gwen fought the desire to snap that it was not her fault. 'I am aware, Miss Pike.'

'What I am aware of is the fact that you have not seen him!'

Of course, Gwen thought darkly. No one would understand why she was not falling over herself to secure a duke.

'He is damaging my front door!' Miss Pike glared at Gwen. 'I command you to speak to him. He is a *duke*, for goodness' sake!'

'That is no reason why I should speak to him,' Gwen said, as calmly as she could.

Rilla moved her head from side to side, following the sound of the conversation.

But Miss Pike was not finished. Affixing Gwen with a glare, she hissed, 'This is the entire reason you, Miss Knox, were sent to the Wallflower Academy in the first place! To find a husband! Do you not think a duke might be a suitable option?'

Gwen opened her mouth, hesitated, and closed it again. What could she say? It was true—any lady would consider herself lucky to receive the attentions of a duke—any duke—and Percy was a very likeable gentleman.

If only it was not so complicated.

Gwen was not sure she could even explain it fully to herself.

Still, that left her with but one option.

'Fine,' she said testily, returning Miss Pike's glare with her own. 'I will see him.'

Miss Pike breathed out slowly, as though she had been fighting a great beast, and placed a hand on Rilla's shoulder. 'Come away, Miss Newell.'

Rilla said nothing, but rose and followed Miss Pike's guidance out of the library. Gwen beseeched her with her expression to stay, but there was nothing she could say in Miss Pike's presence and the door was shut behind them.

It did not remain shut for long. Given hardly a minute to compose herself, Gwen gasped as the door slammed open and Percy appeared.

'Gwen,' he said, shutting the door behind him and stepping forward.

Gwen curtsied low. 'Your Grace.'

'Don't give me that. We have never treated each other—'

'Perhaps that was our first mistake,' interrupted Gwen, hating herself for doing so, but knowing it was the only way. She had to show him how impossible this was. 'Perhaps if I had treated you as a duke and you had treated me as a wallflower—'

'I no more think all men should be treated one way than that all wallflowers should either,' Percy said, with a grin that unfortunately made him incredibly handsome. 'Come on, Gwen, you know I am not like that.'

Gwen glared, but said nothing for a moment. This conversation had to be brief, to the point, and above all without tears. If that was possible.

'Your Grace,' she began stiffly, 'when your mother—'

'Forget my mother.'

'You think I can so easily do such a thing?' Gwen snapped, her temper rising. 'You think it is easy for me to brush aside the indignities spoken to me? To all of us?'

It was clear Percy regretted his words. Biting the corner of his lip, he said, 'I have already apologised for her. I regret to tell you I think it unlikely she will offer an apology herself.'

'It is not your mother I am…upset with,' said Gwen, heat whirling in her throat, making it difficult for her to speak. 'It is you.' Gwen's temper flared. 'You should have defended me, Percy—Your Grace—and I don't buy your story of always obeying your mother as a child, because you are not a child, you are a grown man, and your mother was rude!'

'I should have said something…'

Gwen waited for more, her heart desperate, willing him to share something that would convince her, that would put the entire situation in a different light.

But nothing came.

'You are the sort of gentleman who always gets what he wants,' Gwen said with a dry laugh, her bitter temper finally unleashed. 'But in this situation you should have known better. Another duke would have known better—hell, any gentleman would have known better.'

It was as though she had physically slapped him.

Percy's mouth fell open, his eyes went wide with pain, and he took a staggering step back.

'I had not known your temper was so violent,' Percy said quietly.

Gwen blanched. That he would say such a thing—and to her! But then he did not know, did he? No one did. She had been sure, when she came to the Wallflower Academy, that no one knew of her terrible past.

'Dear God,' said Percy, a puzzled expression on his face. 'Why do you react so?'

'Because…' Gwen knew she should not answer, knew she should keep her counsel, but it was too much. Her heart was breaking, and her head hurt, and the tirade she knew she should not let loose came pouring from her lips. 'Because earlier this year I killed a man!'

She clasped her hands over her mouth in horror, but it was too late. The words were said.

Percy stared at her as though unseeing for several seconds in silence, then said, 'Killed a man?'

'I did not mean to, but he…he had stolen from us… my family…'

Gwen knew not from where these words came—knew she should laugh, pretend it was all a jest, make Percy love her again. But he could not love her. He could not love a murderess.

'My family's inn…the Golden Hind. My mother said she saw the body…she knows I did it! He stole from us and then he tried to kiss me, to force me to—I told you before. I fought him off.'

'The Golden Hind?'

Gwen stared. Of all the things she had said, the admissions she had made, the confession that she was a murderess… And Percy was more interested in the location of where her crime had taken place?

She nodded. 'My parents' inn—my mother's now, I suppose—'

'The Golden Hind in Sussex?' Percy said urgently, stepping away.

Gwen nodded again. What did it matter? The deed was done, the man was dead—not because she'd wished to do it, but to protect herself.

'You killed my brother.'

Gwen blinked. She could not have heard those words. She had imagined them.

'You killed James,' said Percy dully. 'Oh, God… To think for all these months we have wondered… He was found outside the Golden Hind inn…dead from a blow to the head. Murdered by a common harlot.'

'It was not like that,' whispered Gwen, feeling stinging tears enter her eyes. 'The man would not pay…and he grabbed me…he tried to kiss me. His hands were all over me—I told you before—and I pushed him. And when he fell—'

'I have heard enough.'

Percy's gaze had slipped away, was now focused on a point just above her shoulder. He straightened his jacket.

'Dear God, I never would have expected… Thank you for this information, Miss Knox, it will finally put my mother's heart at rest. We will not meet again. Good day.'

Chapter Seventeen

Well, he should have guessed he would end up here, Percy thought hazily as he hiccupped for a second time in a row.

Did not all dukes end up this way eventually?

Was it not the one direction every duke took: towards drink?

The glass in his hand was resting upon his stomach as Percy sat lazily in his armchair by the fire. It was seemingly empty. That could not be. He had filled it with brandy but five minutes ago... Was it five minutes ago?

Percy glanced at the grandfather clock in the corner and was astonished to find the clock was moving.

No—no, wait. That was him. He was moving.

After reaching to clutch at the arm of the chair, Percy was struck by the unfortunate realisation that neither himself nor the clock were moving. But his room was.

How many brandies had he had?

Percy reached to the floor, where he had left the brandy bottle, and was surprised at the ease with which he could lift it up to his eyeline.

That was because it was empty.

'Dear God...' Percy groaned into the silence of his study,

and wondered whether his hangover would be as bad as he was already imagining.

Probably. Perhaps worse.

Perhaps then his body would feel as awful as his heart, with that twisting pain, the agony and the heaviness he could not shift from his soul. Perhaps then it would all align and he would feel as appalling as he knew he should.

Rising in a swift movement, then staggering forward, Percy sighed and sat down again. Maybe retrieving another bottle of brandy was not a good idea. Perhaps it was safer to merely sit here, alone, watching the dying embers of the fire disappear, taking the warmth with them.

When so much was wrong with the world, why not sit and experience the simple things?

'Because earlier this year I killed a man!'

Percy's jaw tightened. He should have known. He should have known the minute he had walked into Gwen and received her tirade for knocking her down.

It was all too good to be true.

A wallflower with that sort of temper…the way Gwen's eyes brightened when she became passionate…the way she became more beautiful when aroused…

All too good to be true.

And just when he'd thought he was close to happiness—finding that Gwen desired him just as much as he desired her, and that their mutual attraction sparked into a pleasure that was riveting—his inability to stop his mother talking had led to a revelation he could hardly ignore.

Percy dropped his head into his hands. He had thought the most difficult challenge to surmount would be his mother and Gwen never seeing eye to eye—but to find himself face to face with the woman he loved, who was also his brother's murderess!

It was too much. No one would blame him for finding a little liquid solace.

Not when the woman he wanted to hold on to for dear life…the woman he knew, loved, had bedded…was not just a wallflower with a temper…

No. Gwen was so much more.

Percy would never have been lumbered with this title and all the rules and restrictions that came with it if it had not been for Gwen.

It couldn't be.

There had been times, in the five days since Gwen had made her startling revelation, when Percy had believed himself confused. He must have misheard her, he had tried to convince himself in the dead of night, with sleep eluding him.

What word sounded like murderess?

Countess?

Actress?

No. No, it was no good. Percy knew himself to be a fool, certainly, but not that kind of fool. He had not misheard. He just did not wish to believe, as well he might not, that the woman who was still overtaking his thoughts at every moment was the woman who had taken the life of his brother.

That temper of hers.

That fiery blaze, always just underneath the surface.

Percy laughed bitterly as he sat up and shook his head, looking into the fire. He had seen it—it had been there the whole time. Not always visible, but when one knew where to look—there it was.

He had known she was no wallflower from the very beginning. He should have trusted his instincts. But instead of doing so he had fallen in love. There was this pain in his heart, this twisted devotion, this desire to see her even now…even after knowing she had murdered James…

What else could it be, if not love?

Percy sighed and wondered what the time was. Glancing at the grandfather clock, he saw to his relief that it had stopped its merry dance and was now showing near eleven o'clock.

He had given his heart to a woman who could hate as strongly as she could love, whom he certainly should not love, and he was late.

Percy chuckled in the darkness, the only light the amber flickering of the fire.

Late? He was far more than late. Terminally late.

Lady Rose would surely have put the card tables away by now…disappointed, he was sure, at missing her chance of hooking the Duke of Knaresby.

Well, he was in no mood to be accepting pretty compliments or agreeable charms. Not when he wanted to see the delicately frustrated expression of Gwen, when debating with him about the right way to drive a horse, or laughing at the way Miss Pike attempted to orchestrate impossible matches.

His stomach twisted and he placed a hand upon it. He would never recover. Gwen had a piece of his heart now, even if he did wish to have it back.

'More brandy, I think,' Percy muttered.

The door to his study opened behind him.

'Do not disturb me,' he snapped at whatever servant had entered the room.

'There is no need to speak to me like that,' said Lady Devereux curtly as she stepped around him to glare into the eyes of her son.

Percy swallowed. There was an unwritten rule in the townhouse that he would not enter the parlour without his mother's permission and she would not enter the study without his. Having Mayfair House made that easier. Most of the time his mother stayed there.

It was entirely different at the estate in the country, of course. Percy was still learning his way around the place, more in need of a map than mere directions, and his mother had an entire wing to herself. Apparently the Dower House was insufficient.

But here, in Town, it was important to have different spaces.

It avoided awkward scenarios like this, for example, he thought darkly as he placed his empty glass hastily down beside the empty brandy bottle and hoped his mother would not notice.

'Ah,' he said aloud, as though that would clarify things.

Lady Devereux raised an eyebrow. 'Ah, indeed.'

Well, it was his own fault for being the worse for wear, Percy thought awkwardly as his mother settled herself in a chair opposite him.

'Well, you were greatly missed at Lady Alice's, of course—but then you know that,' said his mother impressively, her gaze still affixed to his own.

Percy swallowed. 'I do.'

'You do,' said Lady Devereux pointedly, 'because you were not there.'

Blast and damn it. He should have known better than to think his absence would go unnoticed. He should have attended for half an hour or so and then slipped away, convincing his mother later that he had merely been in a different room.

As it was...

'What is wrong, then?' asked his mother curtly. 'Come on—out with it.'

Percy knew what the correct answer was, of course. 'Nothing is wrong. I merely felt tired and wished to—'

'Poppycock.'

Percy's eyes widened but his mother said nothing, waiting for him to continue.

As though he could continue.

What was Percy supposed to do? Admit to his own mother that he had fallen in love not merely with a wallflower—a type of person she clearly disliked—and not only with a woman with no title, no connections, nor anything to offer the Knaresby title, but with the murderess of her eldest son?

No. Percy was not a cruel man, and he saw no reason to inflict this pain upon her. Lady Devereux had buried her brother-in-law and her son in the last year. He would not force her to bury all her hopes for his marriage.

''Tis as I say,' Percy said stiffly. 'Nothing.'

Lady Devereux examined him for a moment, and when she spoke again it was in a far softer voice than he had expected. 'I am your mother, you know.'

It was such a different line of attack—one Percy had not been expecting—that he found he had once again dropped his head into his hands.

'Nothing is wrong,' he said, his voice muffled, knowing how ridiculous it was. His mother was no fool.

She snorted. 'I raised you, Percy Devereux, long before you were ever destined to become a duke. I know when you are lying. Now, I demand to know what the problem is. It surely cannot be any worse than my imaginings.'

Percy lifted his face and looked straight into the eyes of his mother. Could she understand? Would he ever be able to make her see just how awful the whole thing was?

Lady Devereux blanched. 'Perhaps it *is* worse than my imaginings.'

'I...' Percy hesitated, but he knew the truth had to come out eventually.

She would need to know why he wanted to shut up the London townhouses and disappear to their country estate. There would be questions. Society would talk…wonder why. At least this way his mother would have answers.

Unless she decided to stay, of course, and face them.

Percy took a deep breath. 'I… I have broken things off with a woman I… I truly cared about. There. Now you know.'

Lady Devereux gasped, a hand moving to her chest. 'A woman you—? Percy Devereux, had you offered marriage to this woman?'

'Yes—No,' corrected Percy quickly, his mind whirling.

How had that never occurred to him before? He had never noticed till now, but in truth he had never mentioned matrimony to Gwen. It had seemed so obvious, so clear that he wished for it. Had she expected him to offer directly? Had she been pained, perhaps, that he had not spoken the words?

He pushed aside his concerns. What did it matter? She'd killed his brother. Gwen did not deserve such loyalty, such consideration.

'But I did not know you were even courting anyone!' Lady Devereux looked most put out. 'There I was, parading ladies before you for your choice, when you had already made it!'

'Well, I have unmade it,' said Percy hastily, and felt a wrench pulling through his heart. 'Which should make you happy.'

His mother was silent for a moment. 'And the young lady in question was…?'

Percy did not know what made him do it. He only knew he must keep the truth of Gwen's identity to himself. What good would it do now, to name her to his mother, when she was not only no longer to be her daughter-in-law, but was confirmed as her son's killer?

Still, it was impossible to withstand the glare his mother was subjecting him to for long, and Percy found himself saying, in some sort of defence, 'One of Miss Pike's ladies.'

Percy waited for the onslaught of criticism. He should never have gone in the first place...should never have talked to those ladies...should never have compromised his affections...

He could well imagine the criticism his mother was about to level at him.

As he'd expected, Lady Devereux groaned. What was unexpected, however, was her words.

'Oh, Percy, I wish you had said something at the time! I must have offended her so deeply—I do hope the breach between you is not on my account!'

Percy blinked. He waited for the words to realign themselves and mean something different, with more clarity, more like what he'd been expecting.

But they did not. And now he came to look more closely Percy realised there was a flush of something that might be shame upon his mother's cheeks.

What on earth was going on?

'Oh, I have deeply regretted my words since that afternoon tea ended,' said his mother, shifting uncomfortably in her seat. 'I wish I had spoken differently, to be sure, and that was even before I knew I could be doing you such harm.'

'What—? Harm?' Percy could not help himself; he was bewildered. 'What do you...? Mother, I have never known you to regret speaking in your life!'

'When you have lived as long as I have, my boy,' said his mother sharply, 'you will find there are more than sufficient ways to embarrass yourself. But I had hoped I was past the worst.'

Percy could not understand it. Perhaps it was the brandy, but he was certain that in living memory his mother had never apologised for anything she had said or done.

And this was to be the first time?

'The truth is, I always feel a little awkward around wall-flowers,' his mother said with a heavy sigh. 'They never do or say anything, do they?'

Memories of Gwen flashed before Percy's eyes: Gwen laughing, Gwen challenging him to a game of cards, Gwen teasing him at the dinner table or in the carriage, telling him how much she cared for him...

'Well,' he said dully, 'you do not have to worry on that score any longer. As I said, I have broken things off with her.'

'And why, precisely, is that?'

Percy tried not to laugh, but it was difficult not to. It was not a laugh of joy, but one of desperation. How could his life have descended into this...this pit of despair?

'Because she has no dowry, no title of any kind, no family, no connections and no prestige in Society. She does not fit any of the criteria James would have wanted, and she also,' Percy said quietly, unsure if he was brave enough to speak these words, 'has guilt on her hands.'

Lady Devereux frowned. 'Guilt on her hands?'

Percy nodded.

His dear Gwen...the woman he had given his heart to...

'She is a murderess.'

His mother's mouth fell open. She sat for almost a full minute, then managed, 'I—I beg your pardon?'

Nodding again, Percy found he could say nothing else. There was nothing more to be said. The woman he loved— a woman he could never have imagined doing such a ter-rible thing—had committed one of the most heinous acts a person could.

She had taken a life—and not just any life. The life of his brother.

'And who, precisely,' asked Lady Devereux icily, 'was the woman in question?'

Percy swallowed. 'Miss Gwendoline Knox.'

He had no real expectation of what his mother would do with this information—which was why it was most alarming when his mother's cheeks turned pale and she rose so hastily that her gloves fell to the floor.

She strode across the room, opened the drinks cabinet, and pulled out a bottle of whisky and a glass.

'Hang on, there,' protested Percy, 'that is my whisky you are—'

'It is for both of us,' interrupted Lady Devereux calmly, returning to her seat and opening the bottle. 'Pass me your glass.'

Percy obeyed wordlessly. His mother drank alcohol, of course, just like any lady with taste. But it was usually a delicate sweet wine in a small glass, on a Sunday evening after supper.

He watched in silence as his mother poured a generous helping of the amber liquid into each of their glasses, drank hers in one, then replenished it.

'Steady on, Mother,' Percy said quietly. 'I do not think there is any need for—'

'You have just told me you've fallen in love with a woman you believe has killed,' said Lady Devereux succinctly. 'Killed, as I suspect you know, your brother. I believe there is every need.'

Percy blinked. He was dreaming. That was it. He had fallen asleep on the sofa after his brandy. Though even he would never have expected his mind to concoct such nonsense.

How on earth did his mother know?

'Oh, Percy, you were always such an innocent,' said his mother heavily.

Percy straightened up on the sofa. 'I would not say I was—'

'I am your mother. I shall decide,' Lady Devereux said smartly. 'And you always did idolise your brother, no matter the... Well, the rather unsavoury habits he developed as he grew up. He was so much older than you, wasn't he? Eleven years... What a difference that can make.'

Percy swallowed. James had been quite a bit older than him, it was true. It had felt like an insurmountable distance when they were boys, but as they had both grown Percy had hoped to spend more time with him.

Then it had been too late.

'James was away so often—at Cambridge, then the Inns of Court as a lawyer,' Percy said hoarsely. 'There was never much time to—'

'He was not at Cambridge,' interrupted Lady Devereux, a painful note in her voice. 'Not for long, anyway. Nor at the Inns of Court, I am afraid. All lies. All untrue.'

Percy stared. It was not possible. 'But James said—'

'He was not a good man, Percy. It pains me to say it, but there it is,' said his mother. 'Sometimes one has to accept that the boy one has borne and raised is not the man one would have hoped he'd be. He got himself into... difficulties.'

Percy leaned forward. He had believed Gwen's revelation to be the greatest shock of his life, but clearly he had been wrong. 'Difficulties?'

A nerve twitched in Lady Devereux's jaw. 'With money. With ladies. He was...disrespectful. He attempted to... Well, the less said about that the better. But I was forced to give quite large sums of money to ladies who had suffered his attentions being pressed just a little too hard.'

Nausea rose in Percy's stomach and mixed with the brandy, making his head spin. No. No, it was not possible, James would never—

'He was not a good man, Percy,' Lady Devereux said again. 'Lord knows, I should have spoken to you about this earlier. His behaviour... I would not call it merely bad. Criminal, perhaps.'

Percy could not speak—he could barely breathe. James had never thought much of obeying the rules, to be sure. And there had been that streak in him... Not cruelty. Not exactly...

'When his body was discovered outside an inn, a gash across his head and a rock—an immovable rock, mark you—stained with his blood,' said Lady Devereux calmly, 'with the daughter of the house hysterical and shouting about how she would not permit him to touch her... Well. That was an end to it.'

Silence fell in the study, although Percy was sure he could hear the pumping of his heart, the twisting of his lungs as they worked hard to keep him alive.

Gwen.

Gwen and James.

He had tried to...

'It was her,' Percy mumbled. 'Gwen. He tried—'

'The important thing is that he did not,' said his mother curtly. 'I looked into the matter, of course. The Knox family—mother and daughter. The daughter was well spoken of, well liked, though very shy and quiet, and withdrawn after the...the incident. I had thought her kept quietly at home...'

'But she was sent to the Wallflower Academy,' said Percy, his eyes wide. 'And that is where she met—'

'You.' Lady Devereux sighed. 'Oh, Percy, I hope I did not

offend her. I wish you had told me of her before you went bumbling in and got the wrong end of the stick.'

Percy stared at his mother.

She could not be serious.

How was this his fault? All he had done was fall in love. Was that his doing? How could he have prevented such a thing from occurring?

'You are a fool,' said his mother.

'Me a fool?' Percy spluttered. 'Why on earth do you say—?'

'I have heard about your Miss Knox, and from a very reputable source,' said his mother with a dry laugh. 'Yes, Miss Pike cannot stop singing her praises. Rather unusual for that woman. I now see why. She obviously believed I knew of your feelings. You would be lucky to have her, Percy.'

He was definitely dreaming. Percy could well remember all the lectures he had endured from his mother about how to find a wife who would further the Knaresby name, a woman who had the elegant breeding of the very best of Society, with money to boot.

'But all the gossip…the newspaper reports and the questions about whether I am a suitable heir to the line,' Percy continued wildly. 'Do you think marrying a woman with nothing to recommend her will help?'

'No, but—'

'You were the one who said I needed to marry for the Knaresby line,' Percy reminded his mother. 'For money and prestige all the things Gwen does not have!'

Lady Devereux fixed him with a beady eye. 'Yes, I did, didn't I? But I married for love…and it brought me nothing but happiness with your father.'

Percy smiled ruefully. His father. Gone these seven and ten years now. His memories of his parents together had faded, yes, but the colour had not gone from them. Neither had the sense of happiness.

'That was different,' he said weakly.

His mother raised an eyebrow. 'You are right. You are a duke now. You have responsibilities and you currently have no heir. I have seen arranged marriages blossom into love, and I have seen arranged marriages wither with no children, for they could barely stand the sight of each other. Answer me this, Percy. How will the Knaresby line continue if you do not marry someone you truly love?'

Chapter Eighteen

Gwen had never looked at the ceiling of the orangery before. It was not the sort of thing one paid a huge amount of attention to, not really, but as she lay there on the cold, calming floor, she was remarkably impressed by the intricacy of the lattice work.

'You are overreacting.'

'I am not overreacting,' said Gwen firmly from the comfort of the floor. If anything, she was underreacting. She had just admitted to murder, to a duke—the duke she had fallen in love with, no less—only to discover that the killed man in question had been his own brother.

What a disaster.

She could not have imagined a more devastating blow to the growing love they had been desperately trying to keep alive—and it was too late now. It was over.

Movement.

Her gaze flickered away from the orangery ceiling to see the face of Sylvia.

'You don't have to lie there, you know,' she pointed out as she looked down.

Gwen shrugged from her prone position on the floor. 'I

don't have to lie anywhere. I don't have to do anything. Nothing changes anything. Nothing matters.'

The dull ache in her heart had settled there the moment Percy had turned his back on her, refusing to hear her explanation—as though it would have made any difference—and disappearing from her life.

After holding him at arm's length for days, for fear of him not being able to love her, and fear of his mother's disapproval, Gwen thought it was poetic justice that it was her own actions which had finally torn them apart.

And she hadn't cried. No matter how much she had attempted it, alone in bed at night, upstairs in her lonely bedchamber, Gwen had not been able to force a single tear to fall.

Perhaps that was why she felt so adrift in the sea of life. What did it matter whether gentlemen came to the Wallflower Academy to view them, take tea with them, dine with them?

None was Percy.

None would ever accept a murderess for a wife.

She was going to be here, at the Wallflower Academy, for the rest of her life.

A foot nudged her—not painfully, but enough for Gwen to wince. 'Ouch!'

'Didn't see you there,' said Rilla placidly, from her seat beside Gwen on the floor. 'And I don't know what you're so upset about.'

Gwen glared, though she knew it had little effect. 'You don't?'

'It is not as though you would ever have been able to convince Lady Devereux of your suitability for her son,' Rilla said plainly, her face expressionless. 'Even if you hadn't revealed whatever it was that made the Duke leave so suddenly.'

A heavy weight settled in Gwen's stomach. 'You are not very comforting, you know.'

'I am doing my best,' countered Rilla. 'You've not given me much to go on.'

Gwen sighed and turned back to look at the ceiling of the orangery. That was certainly true, but nothing any of the wallflowers said would convince her to reveal precisely why Percy, after banging on the front door for nearly an hour and demanding to see her, had spent less than ten minutes with her before storming out.

He had not returned to the Wallflower Academy.

He never would, Gwen was sure.

'Perhaps it was best to break things off,' said Rilla, her voice softer now. 'I mean...before things became too serious.'

A tear welled up in Gwen's eye and slowly trickled into her hair.

Too serious.

Rilla had only guessed at what she and Percy had shared in her bedchamber—and she had clearly underestimated just how intimate they had been.

Too serious.

Gwen could not imagine anything more serious than her feelings for Percy, complicated as they were, tinged with sadness and confusion after his mother's words, affection and desire after their conversations and kisses, pain at his brother's death, frustration and hurt...

'I am doing all I can,' muttered Rilla above her. She was speaking to Sylvia, who was whispering rapidly into her ear. 'No, I will not tell her to buck up!'

Gwen sighed. No matter how hard the other wallflowers tried, she knew it was not possible to restore her spirits.

'Well, does she *look* comforted?' Rilla's voice was irritable. Evidently she was exasperated by the harassment Sylvia was subjecting her to.

'You should have a good cry,' said Sylvia, matter-of-factly, as though she had survived several heartbreaks and lived to tell the tale. 'A good cry will do you the world of good. Then eat cake. All the cake we can find.'

Gwen blinked. It was not the worst idea she had ever heard. Truth be told, of all the wallflowers at the Academy at the moment, Sylvia was the last one she had expected to be so...so understanding.

She looked up at the concerned face of the woman.

Sylvia smiled wryly, her black eyes glittering with what might have been tears. 'You are not the only one of us to have had her heart broken. It happens to all of us eventually.'

Gwen opened her mouth to ask the question. Had she had her own heart broken?

But approaching footsteps, smart and purposeful, halted her tongue. There was only one person who walked like that at the Wallflower Academy.

'Miss Gwendoline Knox,' said Miss Pike sternly, leaning over her wallflower. 'What are you doing?'

Gwen's heart sank. It was not enough that she was to be heartbroken, left here to fester as a wallflower until the end of her days. No, she had to be criticised for it into the bargain.

'When can we expect the pleasure of His Grace's company again?'

Gwen swallowed, tasting bitterness on her tongue. It was all over. It was too cruel, too harsh to make her say it again, but she would. She would say it until the rest of them believed her. Percy was never coming back, and in a way she could not blame him.

She had no siblings, no one to protect or feel protective of. But Percy had adored his brother.

There was no possibility that Percy would find it in his heart to forgive her—none at all. The more she hoped for it, the less likely it would be.

She needed to come to peace with it, Gwen thought as she drew in a deep breath, *and that meant being frank.*

Until she could speak openly about it without tears, without fear of overwhelming emotion, she would be a captive to this pain.

'I am sorry to inform you, Miss Pike,' said Gwen quietly, still lying on the floor—well, she had not been instructed to rise, had she?—'that I have broken things off with the Duke of Knaresby. I do not believe he will be visiting the Academy again. He will wed another.'

The thought cracked her heart in two.

She had not considered it until the words had tripped out of her mouth, but that was likely, wasn't it? Whether he found her here at the Wallflower Academy, or at Almack's, or in someone's dining room, or at a card party, Percy would meet someone else. Another lady he would learn to love, who would not have the ignominious past of having murdered someone he loved.

'B-But...if an invitation was sent to him—'

Gwen sighed. 'Miss Pike, I regret it, but there it is. I do not believe an invitation even from your own hand would be sufficient to entice the Duke of Knaresby back to the Wallflower Academy. That is my opinion, of course, but I share it advisedly.'

Not after revealing my terrible secret, she thought wretchedly, tears threatening and prickling at the corners of her eyes again. Not after she had finally answered the question which had clearly plagued Percy for many a month: who, precisely, had murdered his brother?

If only it had never happened. But Gwen had known, deep down, that the moment would one day come back to haunt her. She could not be let off with merely the fear of being discovered; she would be punished, somehow, and now she knew how.

In a strange way, it was a relief. Now at least she would not have to concern herself with the fear of being found out. The worst had already happened. Percy would be protected from her and her terrible temper. She would never have to fear that one day she would lash out and hurt him, too.

Who knew what scandal might have occurred if she had married him? The Duchess of Knaresby...murdering the heir to the Knaresby line. It would have been terrible.

'Miss Knox, I am ashamed of you!'

Gwen's gaze focused on Miss Pike as her words echoed around the orangery like a death knell. 'A-Ashamed?'

Miss Pike rose to her full height, which from the floor of the orangery was a great deal, and affixed a most malignant stare to the unfortunate wallflower. 'Miss Knox, I cannot prevent myself from berating you, you shameless woman! Losing the affections of a duke...perhaps the best marriage offer you could ever have had!'

Out of the corner of her eye, Gwen noticed that Sylvia had taken Rilla's hand and quietly begun leading her out of the orangery.

Evidently they had no wish to be witnesses to another scene of Gwen's shame. She could not blame them. She did not particularly wish to witness it herself.

'And to think the only reason you are here is because your mother wishes you to find a husband!' continued Miss Pike, eyes blazing. 'What ingratitude to show her...when you were on the brink of securing for yourself the finest husband any wallflower here has ever attained!'

Gwen bristled and sat up to glare directly at Miss Pike.

Well, really!

Her mother had only wished to be rid of her, and if Miss Pike had ever taken the time to get to know her she would have known that her mother would be mortified if her daughter had married someone as impressive as a duke! Her daughter? Outrank her? It was not to be borne!

Besides, it was scandalous, the way Miss Pike was talking. She spoke of husbands like—like fish! Specimens to be caught—to be mesmerised into falling onto hooks, scooped up out of the water and displayed like prizes!

Percy—if she had been fortunate enough to become his wife—would have been far more! Far more than just a trophy…a prize to crow over with other women!

'You may have lost,' said Miss Pike, lowering her voice but losing none of her intensity, 'the one and only chance you will ever have at happiness.'

And that was it.

Gwen could take no more.

Her heart had been bruised, battered, squeezed beyond belief, then broken. She had tried desperately to cry tears of agony, had railed against the darkness of her life, had wished she had never even been there that night at the Golden Hind.

But this was too far. How dared Miss Pike criticise her for her own heartbreak?

Though her heart had been ripped from her chest, while it was still beating, Gwen was still certain she had done the right thing.

Her confession had spared Percy from a lifetime of misery as her husband—and through it all she loved him. She loved him too much to condemn him to a lifetime of defending himself against a scandal he had never been informed of.

Percy deserved better. That was her gift to him.

'I am very disappointed in you,' said Miss Pike, with feeling.

Gwen rose to her feet. Every inch of her body was humming with rage, a rage she could barely keep inside, but she would do her utmost to make sure she was calm and collected.

She had a certain few things to say to Miss Pike, and as they were alone this was the perfect opportunity.

A small smile crept across Gwen's face. She was going to enjoy this. Her temper rarely had an opportunity to be released, particularly since the incident at the inn, and it had been fizzing inside her for far too long.

She would relish the chance to tell Miss Pike a few home truths.

'The trouble with you, Miss Pike,' Gwen said quietly, 'is that you think there is nothing more important in the world than mere marriage.'

Miss Pike blinked, startled. She had evidently never heard such a measured, yet forceful statement. 'I—I... I beg your pardon?'

'The Wallflower Academy is not the be-all and end-all of the world, Miss Pike,' said Gwen triumphantly, warming to her theme.

Oh, it felt wonderful to finally stand up for herself. She could not recall doing so since first arriving at the Academy, when...when Percy had knocked her down.

Speaking her mind, her true opinions, with no malice but merely honesty, was a balm for her broken heart.

'Yes, I have lost the affection of the Duke of Knaresby, and arguably for good reason,' Gwen said calmly, hoping beyond hope that Miss Pike would not enquire just what that reason was. 'And, yes, I loved him—still love him, in fact, far too much to tie him to me when he is unwilling. But he is not my last chance of happiness!'

Miss Pike's mouth was opening and shutting in the same fashion as her namesake, but no words came out.

Gwen took a step forward. Power crackled in her bones, as though she had been given the gift of speech after being forced to be mute for decades.

It was wonderful to say these things—but it was even more wonderful to mean them.

'One's happiness is not merely tied to a husband. One should not be defined by one's connection to a man! They do not own us—we are not possessions! I admit I would have loved to be Percy's wife,' said Gwen, a little emotion tremoring in her voice. Miss Pike's eyes had widened at her use of the Duke's first name, but Gwen continued onward before the owner of the Wallflower Academy could interrupt her. 'Perhaps I may not marry, and I will find a different kind of happiness then, but there is every chance someone else will want me. They will. Because I am a fine match for—for anyone. Duke or not! I may be the least likely to win a duke, but perhaps a duke is least likely to win me!'

Her last words echoed around the orangery, and Gwen could not help but feel victorious as she spoke them. Because she was only now starting to believe it. Someone, one day, would recognise her worth, her value. See that she was a good person, and could be an excellent wife. For someone.

'I am worth winning,' Gwen said, smiling at Miss Pike. 'And I would never wish you to forget that, Miss Pike.'

'I could not agree more,' came Percy's voice. 'Well said, Gwen.'

Chapter Nineteen

The shock and surprise on Gwen's face was palpable, and Percy regretted for a moment that he had allowed his tongue to be so unguarded.

If only he had thought—had stopped himself from speaking so quickly. If only he had pulled Gwen aside after her conversation—or rather, altercation—with Miss Pike. He could have taken her into a quiet corner, gained a moment to remember his words, and had the pleasure of her presence alone.

But it was too late. The astonishment on both ladies' faces was a picture of surprise that anyone had overheard their rather stern words, and Percy's stomach twisted.

He had not expected Miss Pike to be a potential audience to his declarations…had intended to make them private, not public.

But as his pulse sounded a hasty drum beat in his ears, Percy found he was starting to care less and less about the way people looked at him. As long as Gwen looked at him. Her startled eyes were wide, her pupils fixed on his, and Percy's heart soared to see the connection there. However faint. However much it had almost been destroyed.

A glimmer of hope fractured his heart.

Yes, Gwen was a fine match. Far more than she could possibly understand, and far more than he had understood until yesterday.

Percy was not going to make the same mistake again. He had lost her twice. He was never going to lose her again. Not if he had anything to do with it.

'Gwen...' he said, rather weakly.

It was not what he had intended to say. During the unendingly long ride Percy had prepared a speech so impressive, so wonderful, Gwen would have no choice but to accept him. To believe him. To love him. To understand that his heart had been bruised, but so had hers. And, while he had been dishonest, foolish, idiotic to the extreme, she had done nothing but defend herself against a man who, Percy had to accept, was not what he had thought.

It had not consisted of the single word 'Gwen'.

Miss Pike's eyes were flickering between them. 'I—I... I don't... Y-Your Grace!'

Percy smiled awkwardly. How long would it take him to truly become accustomed to hearing 'Your Grace' instead of Devereux? A lifetime, perhaps.

If he was fortunate, a lifetime with Gwen.

The orangery was starting to chill as he stood there in the doorway to the garden, so Percy stepped inside and closed the door behind him.

There was another doorway, open into the main house, and just beyond it appeared the faces of Miss Sylvia Bryant and Miss Marilla Newell, not to mention every other wallflower in the place. They were all listening carefully.

'My word...' said Sylvia, not attempting to keep her voice down.

Gwen whirled around and coloured. 'Sylvia!'

'Sorry, Gwen,' said Sylvia, with absolutely no hint of

actual remorse on her face. 'We wanted to hear what the Pike—what Miss Pike had to say.'

'Sylvia!'

'Sorry, Miss Pike,' came the uncontrite words.

'Gwen,' said Percy again, wishing beyond anything to be alone with her. This was not exactly the reunion he had expected.

'Ah,' said Rilla with a knowing smile. 'Your duke's back.'

Gwen coloured, her cheeks flushed pink, but she said nothing.

Percy grinned.

So he was her duke, was he?

Well, if fortune was with him, by the time he finished this conversation with Gwen he would be.

Though it could all go so wrong, even now.

Percy clenched his jaw. He must make it work. He was not sure how he would be able to go through life without her.

'Good,' said Rilla with apparent relish. 'Is he here to make an honest woman of you?'

'Rilla!'

Percy took a hesitant half-step back, almost against his will.

Now, that was unexpected.

Gwen had told the wallflowers, then, precisely what they had shared together—*well, hopefully not precisely.*

It was a disconcerting thought.

Making sure not to catch anyone's eye at all, Percy swallowed, and discovered to his surprise that he did not care.

Let them know.

Let the world know.

He had nothing to hide except the fact that he had been such a fool. Before knowing that Gwen had been in any way mixed up with James's death, Percy had been foolish enough to permit his mother to sow seeds of doubt in

Gwen's heart—seeds which should never been permitted to take root.

But he was here to change that. He needed her. More than Society and reason should dictate.

And, seeing her here, Percy knew just how deeply he cared.

Gwen did not belong in the Wallflower Academy, being berated by Miss Pike for being true to her own heart. She was no wallflower—not really. She had been forced to be here…forced into silence for an accident that had not been her fault…

Percy's stomach clenched. A dark deed had been committed that night, but it had not been by Gwen's hand.

'Gwen…' he said softly.

As though she had been waiting for his very breath, Gwen turned to him, eyes wide and brimming with tears, though he could not tell whether it was because he was here or because he had stayed away.

Oh, to think he had risked not having Gwen in his life. It was intolerable. He would regret these few days he had been without her for the rest of his life.

'Percy…' Gwen whispered, a single tear trickling down her cheek.

Without a word, without invitation, Percy stepped forward and brushed away that tear, cupping her cheek and lifting her chin.

Oh, when she looked at him… He could have melted right there and then.

There was something about the woman he loved… something more important than he was, than the promise he had made.

His life was only complete with her. His body craved hers, yes, but it was his heart, his very soul, that demanded she be his. He could not be without her—would not permit anyone to separate them.

There was only one person who could make him miserable now, and that was Gwen herself.

If she was still resolutely against him...

Gwen was stammering. 'B-But you cannot be here—Wh-What are you doing here?'

He glanced around them. Miss Pike looked triumphant, as though she had somehow managed to orchestrate the entire thing, Sylvia was gawping, mouth open, and Rilla had inched closer, in the clear hope of hearing more.

They could not stay here.

There were things he had to say to Gwen Knox, Percy thought darkly. *Things not for the hearing of the general public.*

'Come on,' he said, offering his hand with a twist of a smile.

Without hesitation Gwen took it, and Percy's heart soared.

She would not be so trusting, would she, he thought wildly as he pulled her out of the orangery and into the garden, *if she had entirely decided against him?*

After several minutes of striding through the freezing garden, with Percy feeling Gwen's hand in his but refusing the instinct to look at her, knowing he would do nothing but kiss her if he succumbed to that temptation, he finally found somewhere he was certain they could speak without being overheard.

Though he would not put it past Sylvia or a few of the other wallflowers to creep out into the garden and attempt to overhear them, Percy thought with a wry smile.

He could hardly blame them.

'Gwen,' he said quietly.

Gwen pulled her hand away as they stopped in the rose garden. Most of the roses were over now; only the rose

Gwen had admired so much the last time they'd been there still had a flower remaining.

'Percy,' she said, just as quietly. 'I mean, Your Grace.'

Percy waved it aside. 'Oh, Gwen, do you not think we are far beyond that?'

A rueful smile crept across Gwen's face as she stared at the lawn. 'I... I thought we were. But then we went further still, and seemed to circle back to civility. And now...'

'Now?' Percy had tried not to speak too eagerly, but he had not succeeded.

Gwen swallowed. 'Now...'

After waiting for a moment Percy became certain she was unable to speak, so took matters into his own hands. It had been by his brother that Gwen had been so injured in the first place, forced to bear the burden of a murderous misunderstanding, and he and his mother had merely compounded the injury.

It was time for him to make amends.

'I am sorry.'

Gwen looked up, her sparkling eyes meeting his. 'Why on earth would you say that? After what I have done—'

'You have done nothing,' interrupted Percy, taking a step towards her, but halting as Gwen took a step back.

She was not ready—not yet.

'Gwen, I assumed the worst in you when you told me of your...your difficulty with my brother. I was wrong. I knew you. I should have known better.'

Gwen appeared overpowered by emotion. A mere nod of her head seemed all she could manage, and Percy knew why. She still believed herself a murderess...someone who had taken a life. And that could no longer continue.

No matter how complicated his emotions towards James were—and he would undoubtedly spend the rest of his life unpicking them—Gwen should not have to live with un-necessary guilt.

Not if he could do anything about it.

Percy swallowed hard before he tried to speak. It was still painful. One did not lose a brother in mysterious cir-cumstances, and then discover one's beloved was mixed up in the sordid detail, without taking time to heal.

'Your mother would not wish you to be here.'

Percy almost laughed at Gwen's words, and saw surprise in her eyes as he said, 'It was actually my mother's idea for me to ride out here at once. But do not mistake me. I would have been here by luncheon regardless of her advice.'

Because he couldn't hide from the truth for ever. No matter his rose-tinted memories, Percy knew Gwen's words had rung true. It had not been easy to accept his brother had not been as he believed. But now, although it had taken time, the path that lay ahead of him was clear.

It went to Gwen.

'But—but I do not understand,' said Gwen, a crease across her forehead. 'Percy, you should not be here!'

'I could not stay away!'

The words echoed around the garden. Percy had not intended to speak so loudly, so vigorously, but it was too late. He simply had to speak. Had to show her what he felt.

'Gwen, do you think I could live life without you?'

Percy stepped forward and this time Gwen did not step away.

'Life without you…painful and lonely…with the great-est absence of my heart dragging me down to misery? You think I could live like that?'

'But I am no good for you!' Gwen's voice was taut with emotion, pain etched across her face. 'No good for you at all! Do you not think marrying your brother's murderess would be a mistake? My mother has made it perfectly plain—'

Percy took a shuddering breath and tried to collect his wits. She was in pain, and so was he, but together could they be healed. He was sure of it.

The question was, how could he convince her?

Percy turned away, desperately trying to think, and then turned back to the woman he loved. 'I assumed the worst of you, and that was wrong.'

'I am rather good at assuming the worst of myself,' admitted Gwen with a dry laugh. 'But...oh, Percy...do you think I would permit you to bind yourself to me? In every possible way, I am the very last person you should be considering as a wife!'

'No!' said Percy, stepping towards her, panic filling his heart. He would not let her escape him again—he had to be with her. 'No, Gwen, you don't understand—'

'I think you are the one who does not understand!' Gwen said, her voice sharp. 'You say you wish to spend your life with me, but I would bring shame upon you, upon your family, even if we...even if you offered me...'

Percy saw her hesitancy, knew it would be painful for her to speak the word which had rested on his heart for so long. 'Marriage?'

A flush darkened her cheeks as a cool wind rushed by. 'You said it—not me.'

'I know I said it,' said Percy with a smile. 'Do you think the word has not been nestled in my heart since the first moment I kissed you?'

Gwen's flush deepened, and it was enough to give Percy hope.

She has not walked away.

She had not cut him off, told him icily that it was impossible and left. She was still here. Gwen was still here, wanting him, wanting this to work.

He would make it work.

Percy stepped forward, only about a foot from her, and Gwen did not retreat. 'You…you apologised to me once, and I told you that if I ever gave you a reason to apologise, you would need to mean it.'

Gwen laughed—a coarse laugh with as much joy within it as pain. 'At the Wallflower Academy dinner. I remember.'

'Since that moment you have never given me cause to hear an apology from your lips,' said Percy seriously, his gaze affixed to hers. 'Even…even for my brother.'

A look of agonising pain flashed across Gwen's face and she made to move, but Percy was too quick this time. He grabbed her hands, keeping her close, desperate to make her see.

'Let me go!'

'You were not the cause of James's death,' Percy said quietly.

Gwen ceased her struggling, though tears had once again pierced her eyes. 'You don't know that. You did not even know I was there. It was my family's inn—'

'It appears there are quite a few things about my brother I did not know,' Percy said bitterly.

To think he had revered the man…a blackguard who had attempted to force himself upon unsuspecting young ladies.

If James had been any other man Percy would have wanted him shot. Perhaps it was a good thing he had never known.

'My mother told me… Well, she told me quite a bit about my brother of which I was previously unaware,' Percy revealed, hating that he had to sully his own brother's name, but knowing it was vital for Gwen to hear this. 'You were defending yourself, and it was by sheer chance that James hit his head on a rock. Chance, Gwen. You did not want him dead, and it was chance that killed him, *not you.*'

He spoke the final two words with feeling, seeing relief yet disbelief on Gwen's face.

She had never known.

Of course she hadn't, Percy thought bitterly.

A young woman fighting off a titled gentleman in the dark, a struggle, a fall, cries of murder, and she would have been bundled off, away from it all, to the Wallflower Academy, without any explanation.

She was due that explanation now.

'It…it was not my fault?' Gwen whispered.

Percy shook his head. No words were necessary now. He could see that the truth was starting to wipe away some of the pain, the confusion. Gwen's shoulders slackened, all the strength of her hands disappeared and she stood there, as if in shock, as though it had just happened.

'My mother…' Gwen swallowed. 'My mother said I had killed him. That I was a murderess—no one would ever want me.'

Repressing the desire to call the wrath of the heavens down upon Gwen's mother, Percy pulled her close into his welcoming arms.

'Just because your mother thought you least likely to win a man's heart,' he said gently, 'it does not mean you have not done so. Gwen, you are someone who is worthy of love. Worthy of protection. Worthy of a life without scandal.'

Gwen laughed, wiping her eyes. 'I am not so sure…' Then her eyes widened, as though she was surprised at something. 'Did—did you say your mother sent you here? But you would come regardless?'

Percy nodded. Joy was starting to creep into his heart—his bruised and rather battered heart. But it was still whole, and still hers, nonetheless.

He knew what he had to do. It was a surprise it had taken him this long.

Still holding Gwen's hands, Percy lowered himself onto one knee.

'Percy...' said Gwen warningly, an eyebrow raised. 'What are you doing?'

Percy grinned. Everything was going to be perfect. They were even in a rose garden—albeit one that had died away for the winter. He could not have wished for a better moment to propose matrimony to the woman he wanted so much.

'I may have been the one to knock you down when we first met,' Percy said seriously, looking up into Gwen's wondrous face, 'but I am the one who has been bowled over again and again by—by your beauty and your brilliance... Oh, Gwen. All I want is for you to be my wife.'

For a heart-stopping moment, one which Percy certainly did not enjoy, he was not entirely sure what Gwen was going to say. She looked hesitant, passionate emotions flickering across her face, as if each of them was attempting to overwhelm her.

Then she was on her own knees—Gwen, his Gwen—in his arms, her lips on his own, and she was kissing him, clinging to him as though she would never let go.

'Yes,' Gwen murmured, her kisses intertwined with her words. 'Yes, Percy. I will marry you. Yes, with all my heart.'

Percy's arms wrapped around her, pulling her closer.

Least likely to win a duke—that was what she had said. Well, she'd won him, and his heart—though, in truth, he rather thought he was the true victor.

Epilogue

The sunlight that flickered through the large bay window could not be real.

She must be dreaming—must have been dreaming for a long time. Weeks, in fact.

For it could not be her wedding day.

Could it?

The day of her wedding to Percy Devereux, Duke of Knaresby.

A slow smile spread across Gwen's face as she examined her reflection carefully in the tall, full-length looking glass Miss Pike had deigned to have moved into her bedchamber just the day before.

A rather startled and disbelieving woman looked back. She had Gwen's eyes, Gwen's dark hair… Gwen's face, in fact. But it could not be her.

She had never seen herself wearing a gown so elegant. It was of a periwinkle-blue satin, with scalloped edging around the hem, and little embroidered forget-me-nots within the bodice. It was a gown she could never have dreamed of purchasing in all her life.

A tutting sound came from behind her, and Gwen turned with a smile. 'Well?'

Sylvia sighed. 'It is a beautiful gown.'

Gwen glowed. Why shouldn't she, on this day when she was allowed to be the happiest person in the world?

Today she would become Percy's wife. After wanting him so much, and fearing that such a want was wrong… after waiting weeks and weeks, for ever…the day was finally here.

Her wedding day.

'The embroidery is delicately done,' said Rilla quietly. She was holding a matching ribbon in her hand, rubbing her fingers against it slowly. 'I do not believe I have ever felt such small stitching.'

'And the Dowager Duchess purchased it for you herself?' Sylvia said, in amazement.

'Lady Devereux,' corrected Gwen quickly. 'Yes. She said it was both something new and blue.'

Her stomach twisted at those words. She had not yet spoken with her future mother-in-law—at least, not properly. Not alone. She had always been accompanied by Miss Pike, by Percy, or by any number of the wallflowers who had agreed to protect her.

But she could not put it off for ever. After such a generous gift, along with the purchase of gowns for her bridesmaids, Gwen knew she could not ignore Lady Devereux for ever.

Even if she might wish to.

'I never thought this day would come,' Gwen admitted shyly, looking back to the looking glass and marvelling at the transformation one single gown had made. 'But it has.'

And after today she would never need to worry about being apart from Percy. They would be spending the rest of their lives with each other.

'I must thank you,' came Rilla's voice from behind her, 'for including us in your day.'

Gwen's heart contracted painfully. There was no bitterness in her friend's words...no envy. Rilla did not blame her for having found happiness—no more than she blamed anyone for having found joy in the arms of another. But it still hurt her. Gwen could see it in the way Rilla was quieter today than she could ever remember. See it in the way she held herself, shoulders slumped, her usually questing fingers slow and unmoving in her lap.

'I am the one who is grateful to you—and to you, Sylvia,' said Gwen with a bright smile, hoping Rilla would hear it in her words. 'I could not have hoped for two more excellent bridesmaids to steady my nerves in the past few weeks.'

Sylvia grinned as she stepped across the room, a plethora of hairpins in her hands. 'Well, I could not agree more—though it's a shame no other wallflower wished to see the spectacle. Stay still!'

Sylvia was attempting to pin Rilla's hair, one pin now in her mouth, but Rilla twisted away.

'Careful, I may end up scalping you!'

'It doesn't matter,' said Rilla with a sigh. 'No one will be looking at me. They'll be looking at Gwen—quite as they should.'

Gwen swallowed.

She was not going to let this conversation overwhelm her.

'They will look at all three of us.'

'I am just glad of the excuse for a new gown,' said Sylvia with a laugh, pins spilling out of her mouth. 'Blast— sorry, Rilla!'

Rilla shrugged as the hairpins fell to the floor. 'And I am grateful too, even in all my dourness. After all, this might be the closest I get to being a bride myself.'

'Nonsense!' Gwen spoke automatically, hating the defeated tone in Rilla's voice, but there was not much she could say to dissuade her.

After all, she might be right. No gentleman who had ever attended one of Miss Pike's invitations had ever shown a mite of interest in Rilla, despite her beauty and witty conversation. They could not see past her blindness—a sad irony.

Sylvia was chuckling as she helped Rilla put on a pair of earbobs. 'You know, sometimes I think this place is packed to the rafters with rebels, not wallflowers.'

Gwen giggled, sitting on the edge of her bed as she watched her. 'What on earth do you mean?'

'Well, look at us,' said Sylvia, straightening and placing her hands on her hips. 'Me, least likely to actually be a wallflower... Rilla, most likely to become Prime Minister, given half the chance—'

'I still haven't ruled it out,' said Rilla with a wicked laugh.

'And you, managing to bag yourself a duke!' Sylvia finished with a laugh.

The three of them giggled—until a voice cut through their merriment.

'Yes,' said a woman's cold voice. 'Yes, she has.'

Gwen turned in horror, knowing even before her gaze reached the doorway precisely who it would be.

There was something about that family, she told herself miserably, *that made them excellent at standing in doorways and overhearing conversations not intended for them to overhear.*

Lady Devereux was standing there, her arms folded.

Sylvia's laughter stopped abruptly, but Rilla's chuckles continued on for a few heart-stopping moments. Gwen wished she could tell her to be quiet, but her mouth seemed to have frozen and she was unable to say a thing.

Oh, this was it.

Never before had she heard of a wedding being cancelled merely an hour before it was supposed to take place, but she had done it now!

She had offended her future mother-in-law, right before her eyes.

'We…we are not laughing any more,' said Rilla, her joy subsiding. 'Why?'

'Because,' said Gwen in a strangled voice, 'Lady Devereux is here.'

There was a moment of silence, then Rilla broke it. 'Ah.'

'We will wait for you downstairs,' said Sylvia hurriedly, rising even as Gwen turned around to beseech her with her eyes to stay—not to abandon her to her fate. 'Come on, Rilla.'

Rilla rose without a word, and Gwen knew that if she was not to be abandoned by them both she would have to speak.

'I am sure Lady Devereux can have nothing to say to me you cannot hear,' Gwen said desperately, looking at Sylvia with wide eyes.

'I would not be so sure,' said Lady Devereux in clipped tones as Sylvia and Rilla passed her.

Gwen swallowed as the door shut behind her two friends, leaving her alone with her future mother-in-law who had once described her as a flower unremarkable compared to a rose.

It would not be a pleasant meeting, but then, it had had to come. She could not avoid her future mother-in-law for ever. Perhaps it was better to have it out now, here, on her own terms. She was in her own bedchamber, at least.

Still, somehow Gwen wished it had been after the wedding, not before. There was a strange sense of foreboding in her stomach telling her that if she was not careful there would not be a wedding at all.

Oh, if only they had not been laughing about her 'bagging' Percy!

'Miss Knox,' said Lady Devereux in clipped tones.

Gwen smiled weakly. All she had to do was get through this conversation without embarrassing herself. How difficult could it be, really?

Lady Devereux stared at her without smiling. 'A pleasant day.'

Gwen waited, sure the older woman would say something else, but no more words seemed forthcoming.

It was down to her, then, to provide the rest of the conversation. Easier said than done.

'Yes. Very pleasant.'

Very pleasant? Were they talking about the weather?

Gwen had laughed at Miss Pike once when she had tried to teach them about small talk, had considered it ridiculous that resorting to talking about the weather would be a reasonable response in a conversation with someone in Society. But now she could see just how desperately those topics of conversation might be needed in discomforting situations.

Speak. She needed to speak—needed to say something… anything! This was her chance, Gwen knew, to say something to her before the wedding and without an audience.

It was not as though they were going to have any other mother in attendance, after all. Gwen could still remember the sickening sensation that had settled in her lungs as she had read the letter from her mother that had come in response to hers about her impending marriage.

She was to marry Percy Devereux, Duke of Knaresby. Gwen had foolishly believed her mother would be happy—

would be pleased that her daughter had managed to find such a wonderful match.

She should not have been so naïve.

What had that paragraph said?

I think it absolutely disgraceful that a daughter of mine should have decided not only to marry above her station, but above the rank of her own mother's husband. You can forget any hopes of us hosting your wedding reception, let Miss Pike do so if you are so ready to take her advice. How dare you show me up? How dare you?

Gwen had burnt the letter. There was no point keeping anything that dripped such hatred.

Lady Devereux cleared her throat. 'So. You are marrying my son.'

Gwen nodded, and felt a little spark of the boldness she had always been told to force down rising within her. 'Yes. And I am glad to be. And grateful.'

Was that too sycophantic? Gwen could hardly tell. But she knew it was important that Percy's mother knew just how much she loved her son—how grateful she was to have him.

After such confusion, after discovering a tangled past which neither of them had known about until it was too late, Gwen was certainly grateful that they had managed to make their way here, to happiness.

Happiness that, Lady Devereux permitting, would last for ever.

'You are grateful?' Lady Devereux raised an eyebrow. 'I am afraid I do not approve.'

Tension bubbled in Gwen's stomach, bitter bile threatening to rise up her throat, but she managed to swallow it. 'Really?'

'Yes, really,' said Lady Devereux calmly. 'I do not know why you are so grateful. 'Tis my son whom I believe is the lucky one.'

It took Gwen a few moments to realise she had not misheard the woman. Percy the lucky one? Percy, fortunate to be marrying her?

There was some mistake, surely. Perhaps Percy had informed his mother that Gwen had a large dowry, or a connection to an impressive family—which she certainly did not. It made no sense! Why, after such harsh words only a month ago, was Lady Devereux so taken with her now?

But despite Gwen's silence a slow smile had crept over Lady Devereux's face. 'I did not raise him to be a duke, you know. My brother-in-law was married, had two sons… Even when they died it never crossed my mind that Percy would inherit the title. In a way, I think that has made him a better man.'

Gwen swallowed, forced herself to speak. 'I would agree, my lady.'

'And now he can continue to be a better man by marrying someone who is not interested in his title, but in him. In Percy. The man,' said Lady Devereux with a small twinkle in her eye. 'You have endeared yourself to me, Miss Knox, for that. You have won his heart. That wins my loyalty.'

It was all Gwen could do not to sink weakly to her knees onto the floor. Only now did she recognise the tension in her bones for what it was: fear. Fear that Lady Devereux, Percy's mother, the only other important woman in Percy's life, would reject her—as she so nearly had done at that terrible afternoon tea.

'And I believe I owe you an apology.'

Gwen blinked.

Had those words truly come from Lady Devereux's mouth?

The older woman looked uncomfortable, her hands twisting. 'I... I should not have spoken to you so that day, nor the other wallflowers. It was wrong of me. I beg your forgiveness.'

If anyone else had said those words Gwen would have been hard pressed to believe them. No one apologised to a wallflower without significant cause, and Lady Devereux certainly had not been put under pressure by anyone.

Save perhaps Percy, Gwen thought hastily. But even then she could not imagine Lady Devereux would be easily swayed by her son.

But there was a strange look on the woman's face...one that Gwen could not understand.

Regret?

Fear, perhaps?

Lady Devereux walked towards the large bay window, looking out onto the garden. Her eyes were misted, and there was a strange smile on her face.

'I never liked these curtains,' she said quietly. 'But I liked the window. I liked feeling as though I was close to nature...as though, if I wished to, I could escape and disappear out into the wilderness and not return.'

Gwen stared.

No. It could not be—

'I was surprised when Miss Markham sold the place to Miss Pike,' said Lady Devereux with a sigh. 'I had hoped it would close... But there it is.'

She turned to face Gwen, who spluttered, far more rudely than she had intended, 'Y-You were a wallflower here? You cannot have been!'

Lady Devereux raised an eyebrow. 'Why? Do you think

you are the only woman placed here because she is far more trouble than she's worth?'

Gwen laughed, hardly able to believe what she was hearing. It was wild…it was nonsensical…it was…

Believable.

What was it Sylvia had said? Those words she herself had thought numerous times after coming to the Wallflower Academy?

'You know, sometimes I think this place is packed to the rafters with rebels, not wallflowers.'

Gwen swallowed. 'I… I do not know what to say.'

Lady Devereux took a deep breath. 'Quite right too. You'll have plenty of time to think about it later—and then, Your Grace, I hope we will get to know each other better.'

It took a moment for Gwen to realise what Lady Devereux meant, and this time she really did reach out for the side of her bed to sit down upon.

'Your Grace…' she whispered.

Her future mother-in-law chuckled. 'You'll be the Duchess of Knaresby in just under an hour, so you had better get accustomed to it. Here.'

Lady Devereux stepped across the room and pulled from her reticule a box covered in blue velvet. She placed it in Gwen's hands.

'Open it,' she whispered.

Gwen did as she was bade, her head spinning.

Inside the jewellery box was a sapphire tiara.

'You already have your something new and blue,' said Lady Devereux softly. 'I thought you would appreciate something old and borrowed. Blue as well, I suppose. The Devereux sapphires.'

Gwen stared in wonder at the beautiful tiara. It was more fabulous than anything she had ever seen—and only now did her stomach squirm as she wondered, with a jolt, just how many other jewels might be waiting for her in her new life.

Her new married life…as a Devereux.

'Th-Thank you.'

'Oh, you don't need to thank me,' said Lady Devereux with a crisp smile. 'I never had a daughter, and it's high time I spoiled someone. Now… Haven't we got a wedding to go to?'

The day sped by so quickly Gwen could hardly remember it.

A rush of colour, of laughter, of joy. Solemn music and solemn vows, and then smiles all around her.

She saw Miss Pike seated in the front row on her side of the aisle, with a rapturous look at having married off one of her wallflowers so well.

There was a squeeze of her hand. Gwen looked down to see Percy's hand had taken hers, and he smiled as he squeezed it again.

'Ready?' he whispered.

Gwen took a deep breath and nodded. And as they swept down the aisle hand in hand, husband and wife, she could not understand how her heart could withstand such joy, such eager happiness.

She had everything she wanted.

Almost.

'Percy,' Gwen said suddenly, halting in her steps as soon as they'd stepped outside the church. 'We have forgotten something.'

Percy's beaming face was transformed into one full of panic. 'We have?'

Gwen leaned forward and kissed him delicately on the side of the mouth. 'We have forgotten to make any plans for our honeymoon!'

'Oh, you can leave that to me,' he said with a laugh. 'I have some ideas…'

Gwen was not given a chance to ask what they were—his lips had already captured hers, his hands were tight on her waist, and Gwen lost herself to his kiss, to the tantalising, tingling sensation Percy always sparked in her.

'Well, really!'

Gwen and Percy broke apart with wry smiles as Miss Pike's words reached them.

'You have done that before,' Gwen said in a smiling whisper.

Percy grinned as their wedding guests poured out of the church. 'Yes, and I intend to do it again—and again—with increasing frequency.'

'Your Ladyship!' Miss Pike was bustling past them straight to Lady Devereux, with a respectful yet eager look on her face. 'Now you are in a way indebted to the Wallflower Academy. You have your daughter-in-law, and what a fine woman she is. I wonder whether you could see yourself…?'

Percy groaned, and Gwen could not help but laugh. 'It appears your mother is about to be roped into improving the Wallflower Academy! Or at the very least, heaven help us, hosting more afternoon teas…'

Percy sighed and pulled her closer. Gwen's heart was beating so quickly she was certain the whole congregation could hear it. 'Well, perhaps you and she can do an exchange. You can come and live with me, and we can send Mother to the Wallflower Academy.'

He laughed at his jest, but Gwen merely smiled. It was clear Lady Devereux's son had no idea that she herself had once been a wallflower. Fascinating…the secrets one kept from one's family.

'And now, my Duchess?' said Percy with a grin. 'What shall we do now?'

Gwen took a deep breath and felt all the tension and stress and worry—all the things she had believed would hold her back from happiness—fall away.

'Be happy,' she said simply. 'For the rest of our lives.'

'Miss Pike, what an outrage!'

'And try to keep your mother happy,' said Gwen hastily, with a laugh as Percy groaned.

Lady Devereux was staring at Miss Pike in horror.

'Come on. We had better go back to the Academy. The wedding reception will begin soon, and I do not believe it safe to leave Miss Pike and your mother together.'

Percy shook his head with a smile. 'I love you, Gwen—and you have won my affections so utterly I am afraid I am quite in your power.'

Gwen's heart almost burst with joy.

'Good. Just as you should be.'

* * * * *

Least Likely to Win a Duke
*is Emily E K Murdoch's debut
for Harlequin Historical!
Look out for the next book in her
The Wallflower Academy miniseries,
coming soon!*

HISTORICAL

Your romantic escape to the past.

Available Next Month

Duke For The Penniless Widow Christine Merrill
Spinster With A Scandalous Past Sadie King

....

Miss Georgina's Marriage Dilemma Eva Shepherd
Wedded To His Enemy Debutante Samantha Hastings

4 brand new stories each month

HISTORICAL

Your romantic escape to the past.

MILLS & BOON

Keep reading for an excerpt of
MARRYING HER VIKING ENEMY
by Harper St. George — find this story
in the *Her Untamed Warrior* anthology.

Prologue

'Traitors will be punished.' Rolfe's words rang out over the gathered crowd, punctuated by the roar of the newly set fire at his back.

A black cloud of smoke rose high in the air, filling the village of Banford with its acrid scent as tongues of flame licked hungrily at the hut's thatched roof. It was engulfed like kindling, half-burned to the ground by the time a blaze flickered to life on a second one. Tightening his hold on his stallion's reins to be ready should one of the Saxon warriors dare to attempt to fight him, Rolfe ignored the sharp ache in his shoulder from yesterday's battle. He refused to show weakness before these people, especially when he had to make certain that his words were heard.

'We found one of your neighbours among the Scots we battled yesterday. Durwin was there as a friend to them, giving information to our enemy, and he raised his axe to us in battle.' Durwin had been a simple farm worker with no sword to his name. He'd had no cause to meet with the Scots. No cause save the wounded pride that many of the Saxons seemed to share when it came to the Danes. On his cue, his men cut Durwin's blanket-wrapped body down from a horse and laid him respectfully on the ground.

Rolfe and his men had come directly from that confrontation to this village on Alvey lands where the traitor lived. Cnut, Rolfe's man in charge of the Saxon village, had quickly led them to Durwin's house. Thank the gods that it had been empty. Rolfe didn't relish the task of making women and children homeless.

'But what of his brother Osric?' An old woman's voice rose from the people who had come from their homes to watch. They all stood huddled together, a few with blankets over their shoulders to guard against the snow that had started to fall. The flakes hissed when they touched the flames that engulfed the second hut. 'Was he there, too?'

Cnut stepped forward. 'They've been suspected of fraternising with the Scots for months. Osric hasn't been seen in days. Can anyone vouch for his whereabouts?'

Of course no one could. Rolfe knew in his gut that Osric was fraternising with the Scots. Everyone in the village knew it, but no one would give up that information. It was why Rolfe had given the order to burn both of their houses. It was the only way to send the harsh but necessary message that traitors would not be tolerated.

'You are people of Alvey.' It was a simple fact that should need no reminder. 'You were born here and your loyalty should lie with your lord and lady.'

A few in the crowd nodded along with his words, but

many only stared at him. Pockets of rebellion had broken out since his Jarl, Vidar, had married their Saxon lady, Gwendolyn. Rolfe was hopeful that the melding of their people would continue, but it was inevitable to face some resistance. Their only choice was to catch it early. It was particularly disconcerting in this case because the village of Banford was the closest to the Scots who lived just north of their border. A rebellion here could have devastating consequences should they join with the Scottish army, which was why it was particularly important that he squash any seeds of uprising now. 'Lord Vidar and Lady Gwendolyn will not tolerate traitors. Anyone known to be giving information to the Scots will have their belongings seized and risk execution.'

A grumble of unease ran through the gathered crowd, prompting his dog, who had been lying beside the horse, to get to his feet, his ears forward. 'Easy, Wyborn.' Rolfe kept his voice low and the mongrel settled while still keeping alert to the possibility of danger.

'Consider that we Danes have not butchered your people. We have not taken your land from you. Will the Scots, who have haunted you for generations, be so fair? Will the Scots allow your women to choose their own mates? Will the Scots extend silver to the families who marry their warriors?'

He paused to look over their faces, hoping that his words rang true for them. The people murmured, but not one of them stepped forward or offered comment. This brooding rebellion was merely misplaced pride. If sense prevailed, they would come to understand that.

For real peace to be fostered and to thrive, they would have to accept that the Danes were here to stay.

'Your lord and lady have offered you all of these things. We have come to live in peace and to unite our people. The Scots will not offer you that. They will befriend you, only to enslave you.'

Rolfe gave a final nod and swung his horse around to walk to the edge of the village. Cnut and Wyborn walked beside him. 'Are any other men missing besides Osric?'

'None from the village.' Cnut nodded in the direction of the fields and the farmhouse set with several outbuildings on the outskirts of the village. 'I couldn't say about the farm. Since I've been here Godric keeps most of his people to himself, but I will question him.'

The wheat field was fallow now with the arrival of winter and, though most of the trees were bare, a hill hindered a clear view of the house. Godric was known to dislike the Danes, but so far had done nothing that would cross the line to outright treason. However, Rolfe had been gone from Alvey all summer—first visiting Jarl Eirik to the south and then Haken up north where he'd come across Durwin meeting with the Scots—and things might have changed. He'd need to speak with Vidar before doing anything in that quarter.

'Thank you, Cnut. Send word if Osric returns or you have more information.'

'Aye, immediately.'

Rolfe set his heels to his horse and led the way from the village, some of his men falling in line behind him. The rest of his army had been left to return home in the longships, while he detoured to Banford. Wyborn ran out front as if he sensed they were going home. The wound from the spear Rolfe had taken to his shoulder the day before ached with every jolt of the horse. It would take over a day of hard riding to make it home to Alvey. He'd been gone for months and was ready to be home. He only hoped this show of treachery wasn't a sign of things to come.

NEW SERIES COMING!

RELEASING JANUARY

Special EDITION

Believe in love.
Overcome obstacles.
Find happiness.

For fans of Virgin River, Sweet Magnolias or Grace & Frankie you'll love this new series line. Stories with strong romantic tropes and hooks told in a modern and complex way.

In-store and online 17 January 2024.

MILLS & BOON

Want to know more about your favourite series or discover a new one?

Experience the variety of romance that Mills & Boon has to offer at our website:

millsandboon.com.au

Shop all of our categories and discover the one that's right for you.

MODERN

DESIRE

MEDICAL

INTRIGUE

ROMANTIC SUSPENSE

WESTERN

HISTORICAL

FOREVER
EBOOK ONLY

HEART
EBOOK ONLY

f @millsandboonaustralia 🐦 📷 @millsandboonaus